PRAISE FOR

"A RICH, INTRICATE FANTASY AND AN EXCEPTIONAL
DEBUT. P. M. FREESTONE IS AN AUTHOR TO WATCH"
Amie Kaufman, New York Times *bestselling
co-author of* Aurora Rising.

"UNLIKE ANYTHING I'VE EVER READ BEFORE. A
SWEEPING AND SENSUOUS DEBUT"
Samantha Shannon, New York Times *and* Sunday Times
bestselling author of The Bone Season *and* The Priory of the
Orange Tree.

"P.M. FREESTONE DELIGHTS WITH A NOVEL
JAM-PACKED WITH INTRIGUE AND A WELL-CRAFTED
PROTAGONIST... A LUSH DEBUT THAT, MUCH LIKE
A GOOD PERFUME, LINGERS WITH THE READERS
FOR DAYS"
Diva Magazine (Book of the Month)

SHADOWSCENT

CROWN
OF
SMOKE

SHADOWSCENT

CROWN OF SMOKE

P.M. FREESTONE

SCHOLASTIC

Scholastic Children's Books
An imprint of Scholastic Ltd
Euston House, 24 Eversholt Street, London, NW1 1DB, UK
Registered office: Westfield Road, Southam, Warwickshire, CV47 0RA
SCHOLASTIC and associated logos are trademarks and/or
registered trademarks of Scholastic Inc.

First published in the UK by Scholastic Ltd, 2020

ISBN 978 1407 19506 3

A CIP catalogue record for this book
is available from the British Library.

Printed by CPI Group (UK) Ltd, Croydon, CR0 4YY
Papers used by Scholastic Children's Books are made
from wood grown in sustainable forests.

1 3 5 7 9 10 8 6 4 2

www.scholastic.co.uk

For Dida: my first hero.

*And for Serena, who helped me find
my way through the smoke.*

CHAPTER 1

LUZ

Protect the two prizes, all others are expendable.

The message had arrived in Aphorai City, tucked into the protective lining of a shipment case that had once carried desert rose oil. How terribly apt. Almost on the nose, really. I've long known the Magister is a cool operator, but even I raised an eyebrow.

Alas, retrospection won't get me very far out here.

The edge of the Empire is for doers, not thinkers. Takers, not speculators. Local dreamsmoke fabricators go head-to-head with the Rangers, mercenary gangs battle for what's left over, and everyone else ekes out a living in the cracks between. And here I am, smuggling a weakened prince, an upstart of a girl, and their two burly companions through the fray on the way to the Sanctuary.

Ah, the vicissitudes of dedicated service to the Order.

At the border, a town of tents has been woven out of the worst threads of the Empire's desire for control, combined with the lawlessness of the lands beyond. The most brutal of the supposedly peacekeeping Rangers and the most nefarious of the allegedly scrupulous trade regulators have drifted here over the preceding turns like dust gathers behind the back door of an otherwise fine establishment.

"Where's the Aphorain army?" the girl asks, her voice smarting as if the lack of provincial representation is a personal slight.

She's drawn her horse level with my camel. Hers is a stylish beast, I'll give her that. Dark and sleek and, by the way it turned its nose up to the inferior chaff at the last trader camp we passed, discerning, too. An equine after my own heart. For now. Only the Primordial knows how it will fare as we get closer to our destination.

The girl had a question, didn't she?

"I suspect they've been redeployed," I offer.

Thanks be to Asmudtag that Daddy Dearest didn't insist on coming along for the ride. It's a rare man who knows his limits. I'd venture that's why the Magister was drawn to him all those turns ago. He knew his place. He was never going to snuff out her flame. Nor shine brighter. And he *is* rather handsome. If you're into the grizzled veteran type.

Oh, it's going to be a long ride if I cannot still my mind.

Or quiet the girl's incessant chatter.

"What are they building?"

Dozens of labourers toil under the command of vicious foremen, their deeply tanned backs bending and sweating in the morning heat. Almost half their number have the mark of felons – metal plugs in place of noses. The others sentenced for lesser crimes, then. Or working off debts.

I watch them struggle, schooling my expression to neutral. "A wall."

On the camel I purchased for him at the Aphorai City stockyards, Nisai, First Prince of Aramtesh, removes the diaphanous veil of the lapis-blue gown I disguised him in, and runs a silk sleeve across his brow, his eyes narrowed to a squint against the glare and grit. "For what town? I've not noticed this settlement on the imperial map updates."

I smirk inwardly. *Settlement.* That level of reflexive diplomacy could never let you doubt this boy grew up in a palace. Such a polite term for a ragged bunch of tents and slightly sturdier marquees of heavy felt.

"My sources say the Regent gave the order while you were indisposed, my Prince. I believe the decree made special mention of the need to … how was it put? Ah, yes. The 'need to protect imperial resources and lives from outside incursion' and something about 'restoring Aramtesh to greatness'. Or was it … leadership through 'strength and stability'? There's always something new being squawked by the imperial criers."

His brow furrows. "But the Seson Territories are on the other side. My role as heir names me caretaker of those lands."

Caretaker? An empty title. For moons, the Rangers have been doing nothing out here to help the refugees from the unending conflicts beyond the border, deep in the territories where the borderlanders always seem to be at war about one thing: lack.

Lack of resources. Lack of law. Lack of hope.

Many of those fleeing were skilled and could offer value in Aphorai City, more value than moving rocks from one place to the next. Unfortunately for them, province standard practice seems to have been superseded by imperial orders.

I cluck my tongue and my camel ambles on. "I'll make sure to not be present when you have that discussion with your dear brother. Now, please, my Prince, re-cover your face."

The Losian former Ranger, now acting as the Prince's Shield, moves closer, bringing with her the scent of leather and the coconut oil that keeps her battle braids sleek. She extends an arm sculpted with muscle to help his imperial highness with his veil.

He bats away her hand. "I can do it myself."

"It's crooked, my Pr—"

"It may be the first time I've worn a dress, but I'm not incompetent," he huffs.

"And may I compliment you on how well you wear it." It's the Aphorain guard – the one who veritably bathes in amber. "The colour suits you."

It could be my imagination, but the Prince's dark brown eyes suggest a smile behind his correctly adjusted disguise.

Among the ragtag bunch of traders who cluster around the makeshift settlement like flies on a carcass – and smell about as pretty – I find one who will sell me a troupe of stocky Hagmiri mountain ponies in exchange for our camels and a heavy pouch of silver coin. It's a blatant gouge, but unfortunately necessary for my present mission.

We make our way towards what will soon be a gateway in the foundations of Regent Iddo Kaidon's wall. The sun glares down, like it's chasing us out of the Empire. I bribe the Ranger on the gate more heavily than usual in an effort to stave off pursuit of another kind. "I trust that adequately compensates your discretion?"

He stares blankly ahead. "For what? Can't recall seeing anything worth reporting."

Splendid.

"Ponies?" the girl enquires when we've barely led the animals out of earshot.

I look to her horse. "I thought you'd approve, petal."

She looks out to where the first peaks rise from the haze-smudged horizon. "Surely you're not taking us into the mountains?"

I just tap my nose.

We ride on, out into a landscape that's more dust than desert. I've never enjoyed this part. The filth finds its way into every crease.

At least there's precious silence.

"A while since you've been this way?" the girl starts up again as if I provoked her with my thoughts.

I don't reply.

Her brow wrinkles at my lack of acknowledgement. How exhausting it must be to take everything as a personal insult.

"Or maybe," she draws the word out, clearly thinking she's about to follow it with something clever, "you've never actually been where we're going. That's it, isn't it? You have no idea if we're on the right path. If there even *is* a right path."

If she thinks that's going to provoke, she's not as sharp as I thought. I beam a beatific smile upon her. "You'll just have to wait and see, won't you?"

She fixes her fierce eyes even tighter on me. "You're enjoying this, aren't you? Getting a thrill out of sniffing your own mysteries, is that it? You're as bad as Sephine."

I suppress a flinch at hearing the name of the woman I served for turns and instead blink at the girl mildly, letting silence do the work. Silence undoes most people when wielded correctly. I've already learned it sends this one writhing in her own skin.

"I mean, as mysterious as Sephine … or at least as mysterious as…" The girl must realize she's stumbled into uncouth territory. She looks away, and I think that's going to be that. But then her whisper is brought back to me on the wind. "Who even *are* you?"

"Unless you'd like to discuss the ontological intricacies of the existentialist philosophy of the Great Bloom, petal, you'll have to be more specific in your line of questioning."

"For a start, are you really Luz, or Zakkurus?"

I study her, but for once her eyes are innocent of spite, and her tone had been matter of fact. It's a genuine question, not a taunt. "Has it never crossed your mind that I could be both? I'm Luz when I'm Luz. As the Chief Perfumer of Aphorai, it was helpful for me to differentiate by using my family name."

"But Zakkurus is … he's a …" She has the decency to blush.

I give a slow shrug. "You want to know the words to refer to me with. While many read Zakkurus as he, for me, the closest would be they. She, they – I'm comfortable with fluidity. And in the eyes of divine Asmudtag, both are simply part of the all."

She ponders my words, then nods. As if that is that.

Which is a good thing, given the road ahead.

North, we journey.

Ever north.

By the second day after we'd crossed the border, the terrain begins to slope upward. I wouldn't normally ascend into the foothills this early in the journey; swifter passage is to follow the dust plains until the mountains spread further west, forcing one to climb or retreat. Such a direct route is minimal risk when I travel alone or with only a single charge – tracks are easily obscured, finding cover is less challenging. A group this size is something else entirely.

My instructions mentioned nothing of speed, so it's best we take the more difficult path where there's not another soul to lay eyes on.

The Order will simply have to be patient.

I'm hardly surprised we haven't come across anyone else. Nobody who didn't know our destination would have any reason to venture this way. None of the borderlanders come here, there's little to no resources. With no borderlanders, and so far from the edge of the Empire, there's nothing for a Ranger, either.

Potentially there are valued metals beneath the ground – it's striated with bands of sickly green and wan grey. Extraction would be a major operation, however. No caravan guard would be in their right mind unless they demanded triple the wages they'd warrant within the Empire. It's simply not worth setting up a supply chain this way, praise the Primordial.

We climb slopes that are bald of vegetation. Even the resilient camelthorn bush that thrives without moisture or care in Aphorai declines to sink its roots here. The lack of flora means dust puffs from the earth with each step of the ponies; choking clouds billow around us every time the wind deigns to make itself known. When we strike camp, the faces of my charges are streaked with green-grey mud made of grime and sweat, while it would not be an understatement to say we all verge on the malodourous.

It's high sun the following day when we reach a ridge. My nose twitches. Another scent beyond our pungent selves has begun to thread through the otherwise monochrome landscape.

It's time.

I hold up my hand, calling a halt.

As if on reflex, the big Aphorain guard holds out a water-skin to the girl. She waves it away.

"Drink," he says.

She sighs and puts the spout to her lips.

I retrieve several cloths from my saddlebag. "Fold these over thrice, then tie them over your face and mouth. Ensure the ties are secure, and the fit is snug."

Rather predictably, the girl plants her hands on her hips. "Or what?"

"Or you can discover for yourself what I'm attempting to protect you from. Your prerogative, petal."

I pass the cloths out. The Losian Shield glowers at the square of fabric but does as I say. Splendid. She may be recalcitrant. But she's not stupid.

When they've all got their masks in place, I fix my own and lead them up over the ridge.

I'd usually bind any cargo I bring this way, but the Magister will want more than their safe delivery to the Sanctuary. She'll want that commodity even more precious than dahkai: information. Finesse over force it is.

I pass the Prince a pair of thick leather cuffs, linked by chain. "My Prince, please affix these."

The Losian steps between us. "Not going to happen."

8

I allow myself a melodramatic sigh. "Sorry, Pik, is it?" I know full well it's not.

"Kip," she grates.

"To *me*, Kip. I want him to use them to bind *me*. Unless you'd like to tie me up instead?" I give her a long, slow wink.

She returns it with a flat stare. "Ask nicely."

I hold her gaze. Those near-black eyes of hers really are rather lovely.

Behind her, the Prince coughs politely.

Flashing a smile at the Losian, I peer around her bulk and hold out a small scroll. "If I start to act strangely towards you, my Prince, you must show me this. I must read it in full and respond appropriately to any manner of question you ask of me before you remove the cuffs. If I still fail to convince you of my lucidity, you must have me knocked out. Otherwise I'll be a danger to you."

He blinks his big brown eyes. "Sorry?"

"The next valley is the only accessible pass towards our destination for hundreds of miles. It's burgeoning with sultis vines. You'll know the leaf is chewed by those who wish to forget, yes? Breathing their flowers or the fumes from their sap is even more potent. Too much, and it meddles more seriously with one's faculties. Given I'm, shall we say, *suspicious* of others at the best of times, should something untoward happen and the valley overwhelms me to the point where I'm not entirely myself, I'd not want to do anything regretful. When we're above the cloud line, it will be safe to remove them."

The Prince holds out a hand. Is that a tremble I see? Just the slightest? Excellent. He needs to keep his wits about him. A touch of doubt wards off complacency.

I grace him with another smile, this one reassuring. "I would never cause *you* harm, my Prince – short-term memory is the first to succumb to sultis, and you've been known to me for more of my turns than not. Alas, I cannot say the same for what I would do to any of these others. Even if my motto has always been to give every soul one chance."

The Losian harrumphs, spits in the dirt.

"Filthy habit," I snap.

She folds her arms across her chest. "That my chance gone, then?"

She doesn't move, but there's something in her eyes that alerts me. Failed Ranger or otherwise, the Losian can handle herself, and she's ready to. I expect there's enough up my sleeve to deal with her if it becomes an issue, but perhaps not without breaking a sweat. And I do so despise sweating.

We're hardly a half mile into the valley, the vines draping from the rock walls, spidering in tangled tendrils across the ground, when the girl begins coughing behind the fabric over her face. She reaches up to her mask.

"Leave it." My voice carries until the echoes are swallowed by the creeping vegetation.

Her gaze flicks to the Aphorain palace guard. "Bar? Where are we? Who are these people?"

By the grace of the Primordial, I knew she was sensitive. But this soon? And this acute? She truly *is* her mother's daughter. Alas, she already doesn't recognize anyone but him.

She jerks on her horse's reins – such an uncharacteristic move – and angles the mare's head back the way we came, riding in a wary circle that crushes more of the sultis, milky sap splattering across hoofs.

"Rakel." The Aphorain guard's voice is muffled through his own mask. "Wait."

"Not until you tell me what's going on here." The next thing she's sliding from her horse, tearing the cloth from her face. She starts to back away, eyes wild, like she might turn and bolt in the next breath.

"Boy." The word lashes out despite the cloth over my face. "Now's the time to earn your keep. Be a hero and fetch your friend, would you?"

The girl takes another step back. Three more. "You're not seriously going to take orders from a stranger, are you?"

The guard looks between me and the girl, his usually handsome – albeit still puppylike – face betraying his uncertainty. He swallows audibly. "Is that entirely necessary?"

I could *die* of tedium. "It's not star-charting, boy. Simply pick her up and tie her to her horse."

Now he holds up his hands. "I'm not. . . It can't be me... You don't understand. We have history."

"I understand more than you know."

But all the great lump does is stand there, dopey as a sleepy toddler.

Then the Losian steps past him. In a few long strides she reaches the girl, lifts her from her feet and swings her over her shoulder as unceremoniously as a sack of barley.

A lady who gets the job done. Commendable.

"Hey!" the girl squawks. "Get your stinking paws off me!"

"Here." I hold up a vial of lilac-coloured liquid. "I'll throw it to you."

11

The Losian snatches it out of the air with her free hand and eyes the Aphorain guard. "You too gutless to hold the horse, too?"

The mare is skittish, forcing him to jog to catch her bridle in hand. The horse fights him, pawing the ground beneath her, only sending up more and more pungent sultis sap. "Calm, girl, this is for her own good."

I'd think that beast had more brain than any of them, as she settles enough for the Losian to swing the girl over the saddle.

"Open the vial and wave it under her nose for a few breaths."

She does as instructed. Swift. Proficient. I'm beginning to like this one, despite her rough edges.

"Keep going," I urge. "It will kick in soon."

As expected, a dreamy look washes over the girl's features.

I allow myself a satisfied smirk. Didn't even have to uncuff myself.

With the girl subdued, the Losian recaps the vial. She looks askance out over the sultis vines. "What would happen if you got lost in here?"

"You'd wander until your body could wander no more. As many have done."

"And then?"

"You've seen what's beneath. Rock and nothing much else. How do you think the vines get the nutrients they need for survival?"

It's the first time I've seen her formidable frame shudder.

❋

I recognize sorrow when I see it.

The return of the girl's memories seems particularly cruel. As is the usual way, she recalled things in sequence, oldest to newest. At the outset, she looked suspicious of all of us but the Aphorain. Then she relaxed towards the Prince. Then she began to talk animatedly of the Prince's Shield, asking where he was, why he wasn't with us.

They all look stricken. I figure I may as well be the person to tell her the truth. She was never going to feel endeared towards me. This won't render that any different. And it would be harsher to leave her chattering obliviously away about the Shield until the realization crept up on her.

"He's dead," I say. No point in framing it differently. Even the finest perfumer cannot make rancid ingredients into a soothing balm. "He died at the palace."

She squints at me, in that same way she's always done, as she tries to work out who I am and whether I can be trusted. "I don't believe you."

Come sunset, the girl crumples forward in her saddle and gives a bone-chilling wail.

Now she's remembered.

And for all I can tell, it's the blow that finally breaks her.

She rides silently in the middle of our group. Through unspoken agreement the others have positioned themselves around her, as if she were going try to bolt again at any moment. I almost tell them not to bother – anyone can see that her fire has been extinguished. But if their care helps us make good time, then so be it.

The amber-drenched Aphorain rides beside her. He had draped a blanket around her shoulders when the cool of the foothills turned to the chill of the mountains. Every now and then he draws his mount in close and reaches out to straighten it.

She doesn't seem to notice.

Or care.

The moons both rise early, lighting the way, so we ride through the early part of the night. The weather isn't kind, the clear sky brings a frigid chill and the wind forfends conversation. Which is good. I need to think. Whatever the Order is going to have me do once the Prince is delivered to safety, I must be ready. One step ahead. Always at least one step ahead. That was Sephine's failing. She was too focused on the now, while other players manoeuvred around her.

Just shy of midnight, we make camp in a depression between the rocky tors. The Losian sets about scraping a fire together, well-shielded in the ground lest the seemingly deserted mountains have eyes. The Aphorain helps me with the horses – the girl usually would, but she hasn't moved an inch since dismounting. The Prince must be positively famished – for once he dishes out the trail rations of dried fruit and meat and roasted nuts rather than waiting to be served.

We eat in silence, before each clearing enough of the pebbles away to hopefully get some kind of sleep. The girl wraps herself in her blanket and lies down, facing away from the fire. The others tried to talk to her, but they can't reach her, not in grief like that.

My words least of all could offer comfort, so I watch and wait for each of them to find their sleeping rolls. They've stopped asking questions of me each night, about where we're going and how long it will take, too cold and bone-tired for curiosity.

When the fire needs more fuel, I take up a stick of mourning incense along with the last of the peat bricks from my pack. We're going to have to make it to our destination tomorrow, or it's going to be a freezing night beyond.

Only the Losian stirs when I rearrange the glowing embers to achieve the slowest burn. She opens one eye, but doesn't otherwise move.

Nobody else sees me lay the mourning incense beside the girl's sleeping face.

CHAPTER 2

RAKEL

It's the ache in my back that wakes me.

I must have been hunched tight in a ball all night. I remember drifting in and out of sleep, feet numb with cold, the scent of cypress and … something else. I could have sworn it was marjoram, used for the second stage of mourning – the time to cherish memories of those who've gone to the sky.

I open my eyes. I wasn't imagining it. A fine stick of grief incense lies not far from my nose. The expensive kind. Made with a high ratio of fragrance to powder.

I'm not stupid. I know it's a signal to keep going. To begin to move forward. *Memories are blades and loss keeps them sharp*, Ash said to me once. Losing someone you love is hard enough, losing them twice is a special kind of cruelty. After the sultis incident, there's a part of me that wants to stay here, waiting for the cold to numb me for ever. Maybe someone has noticed.

Barden and Kip are preparing the ponies for another day of trekking higher and higher into these Rot-forsaken mountains. Beyond the activity, Nisai sits at the edge of camp, burning incense in prayer. It takes a while for the scent to reach me; the colder it gets, the less I can rely on my nose. Ah. There it is. The same as the stick in my hand. Sweet of him to think of me even in his own grief.

I can see why Ash was loyal to him. So, loyal is what I'll be, too. If this Sanctuary that Luz speaks of lives up to its name, then I know Ash would want me to put one foot after the other until we made it there. Until the Prince is safe.

Through, he'd say, taking my hand. *The best way out is through*.

We mount up and strike out for another day of misery. Above us, the snow line beckons. I've never been this close to snow before. Even when I was with Ash in the Hagmiri mountains, so suffocating with their thick-canopied vegetation compared to the bare rock that now surrounds us, we didn't climb this high.

The rock formations up here are so different to the Aphorain landscape. We're surrounded by grey stone in vertical peaks that claw at the sky. They're all angles and shards, so different to the sandstone of the lowlands where the weather scours off every sharp edge. The temple in Aphorai City used to be the tallest peak in my world. These make it seem an anthill.

I should be excited. Curious. Not just for the Sanctuary. But for a much deeper mystery.

My mother.

The few hours we spent at home in my village before setting out on this journey were supposed to have been joyful. Instead it felt as if a groundshake heaved the desert beneath my feet. I should be glad she's alive. Should be relieved. The weight I've always carried on my shoulders, that my life was at the cost of another's, has lifted. But it's been replaced by a gaping hollow. The feeling of being unwanted. Abandoned.

I let you live in the shadow of a lie, Father attempted to explain. *For that I will always be sorry. I wanted to keep you safe. I wanted you to have your own life. When she told me she was leaving once you were born, and that where she was going she couldn't take us, was forbidden to take you. . .*

I'd reeled at that. *She didn't* have *to leave? She wasn't forced?*

He'd looked hopeless, like he was trying to find an impossible balance between blame and forgiveness. *Yaita felt compelled to leave. I don't know all of her reasons, but I know that she needed above all else to dedicate herself to a higher cause. The Scent Keeper let it be known that she had died of birthing fever, and that at Sephine's mercy your mother would retain the honour of a priestess and be sent to the sky. I was sure I was the only one outside the temple who knew the body they burned on the funeral pyre was not your mother. Knowledge, I was told, that would see me – and you – endangered if it came to light.*

In the here and now, rain mixed with ice begins to sting my face. I can barely see two horse lengths in front of me.

The numbness seeps back in with the cold.

We've been walking for ever, I've been running for ever, and for what? More secrets. More lies. The answers I would have moons ago been so keen to find at the end of this journey no longer seem so important. Everything seems dull. Grey. Futile.

I'm putting one foot in front of the other. I'm keeping going. But that doesn't mean I'm all right.

Barden rides close. He's good at watching me like a hawk, but too clunky about it for me to not notice. It should be a comfort, having my friend here. But I can't seem to feel anything. Just like this landscape – rock, snow and no signs of life – I'm empty.

The cold days and colder nights we've been through blend into one frozen hell. The only change today is, as we move higher, the snow becomes more and more compacted. We're soon forced to dismount to cross entire stretches of ice, our feet threatening to slide out from under us at each step, the usually sure-footed ponies scrabbling for purchase.

I have no idea how long we've been walking, climbing, trudging higher when Luz holds up a hand, halting us.

We're a mere few paces from the edge of a cliff. The wind whips the hem of my robe, snakes bitter fingers through my short-cropped hair. I don't try to stop it.

Luz stands on the brink like it's no matter, peering down to where the stone drops off into a ravine that makes the canyons near my village seem mere wrinkles in cloth. The bottom disappears in blue-tinged mist. I can't for stink nor stench see beyond it, even though the blurriness in my vision since healing Nisai seems to have begun to subside. Or maybe I'm just learning to live with it.

Ahead, the path all but vanishes. There's only a thin ledge, barely the width of one of the mounts Luz purchased back at the border. It's never been clearer why she chose mountain ponies.

Now, she sweeps her gaze over us. "Single file only, my lovelies. Lead the animals. And if you don't like heights, hide it. The beasts will respond to your fear more than they'll fear the height itself."

Perhaps the truest words I've heard from those lips. I stroke Lil's neck. "We'll be fine, won't we, girl?"

My mare remains still. Ready. Warm and alive. More than I can say for myself.

"Lostras, you lead?"

Kip nods. She doesn't even balk at the familiarity. She was the first to get used to the nickname Luz assigned her.

"Next our Prince, then Lord Amber."

Barden scowls. Others are still not used to their nicknames.

"Then you and Midnight, petal."

I don't bother correcting her on Lil's real name.

"And I'll bring up the rear."

I huff derisively, my breath clouding for a moment only to be snatched by the wind. "So you can let one of us find out where the most dangerous ground is?"

"So it's easiest for me to double back and fetch our Prince's mount. I'll be the only one who must cross thrice."

Oh.

"But good to see you getting some of that bite back. I've missed being surrounded with vinegar fumes." The last is said with one of her infuriating winks.

We form a line, the others leading their mountain ponies, me leading Lil.

Kip begins, taking it slowly but surely. Nisai follows, testing the ice with the heel of each of his crutches before letting them bear his weight. I wonder if it would have been better for someone to carry him. Then again, would *I* want someone else to have control of my fate like that?

Near the halfway point, his crutch slips.

I suck in a breath through my teeth.

Then Barden is there, one strong arm steadying Nisai, the other holding his nervous pony back at a safe distance. The Prince gathers himself and focuses again on the path.

Then it's my turn.

The ledge looked narrow from a distance. Up close, it feels even tighter. It's barely wide enough for us, Lil's flanks scraping the rock face when it leans close. I look back and notice the stirrup on her other side hangs over thin air.

"Eyes to the front, petal!" Luz calls.

And for once, I agree wholeheartedly with her.

I keep moving, one foot after the other.

Near the point where Nisai almost slipped, something unexpected reaches my nose. I'm sure I'd have smelled it earlier if it weren't for how the cold distorts the world.

There. A beast, like an oversized lion without a feathered mane, prowls the opposite side of the ravine. Its coat is pure white, hiding it almost completely against the snow, except where blood stains its muzzle. Guess it recently fed. Hope that means it's not looking for another meal anytime soon.

"Calm," I murmur to Lil without looking back, hoping she doesn't notice it. We take another step.

Then Lil snorts, stamping at the ledge, sending splinters of ice tinkling down into the ravine.

"It can't get to you," I tell her.

But it's a predator, and she's a prey animal, and there's death in the air. I can't be stuck out here with her losing her head. She'd never willingly hurt me, but instinct is powerful.

I look to Barden. He's made it across. Back on solid ground, the Prince is breathing relieved plumes of mist.

The way is clear. I take another step and flatten myself against a shallow depression in the rock face. "Go!" I command my horse.

She hesitates, then skitters past.

I glance back to Luz. Her pony gives a nervous huff but seems otherwise fine. And when I look back to where the big cat had been there's now nothing but a flurry of snow.

With how much I trust my eyes these days, I'd think I had been seeing things if Lil hadn't have spooked.

"Keep moving," Luz orders. "It's probably on its way back to its den, but I've no inclination to test that theory."

I breathe in deep, exhale and take another step. I'm moving so slowly and carefully that I feel as much as hear it when the ice cracks. I try to shift my weight, but I'm sliding. I twist, only for my foot to skid out from under me. Then I'm coming down on my front, grazing my chin as the breath whooshes from my lungs.

The realization comes to me, sudden and shocking: my legs are dangling over the edge of the cliff.

"Rakel!"

Barden's voice. It comes from the other side of the pass and echoes around the peaks. Too far to lend a hand.

I cast about. There's nothing to grab to haul myself up, and I'm sliding, slowly, on the freeze-slick rock. Sliding towards the end.

Somewhere in my numb mind, I wonder if that would be so bad. We must be close to the Sanctuary now. Nisai's safe on the other side of the pass.

Here, the fall looks so long, it would be almost like flying. And then it would be over.

No more cold. No more emptiness.

No more endless roads.

No grief.

Just nothing.

Then, long fingers wrap around my wrist, blue eyes boring into me. "Don't even think about it, petal."

With strength that belies her lithe frame, Luz lifts me back to the ledge. "My orders are to deliver you to our destination. I'd rather you not be a sack of frozen sludge scraped from the bottom of a ravine when I do. Now. Anything broken?"

Bruises will no doubt be blossoming across my ribs from the fall, and my shoulder aches from being pulled back from the brink. I bit my tongue when I hit the ice — copper oozes in my mouth — and my grazed chin burns in the freezing air. "Couple of scratches, that's all."

"Lovely. Now let us put this precarious moment behind us, no?"

I stare blankly in reply.

"After you," she insists, pointing the way ahead.

On the other side, Kip gives me a nod.

Nisai regards me with gentle eyes. "Are you well?"

Barden barrels past and envelopes me in a hug. "Stars, Rakel. Almost thought I'd lost you there."

I manage something resembling a smile.

So did I.

❋

It's late in the day when we crest a ridge.

Luz lets out a self-satisfied sigh. "Splendid tidings, my tattered travellers. It's all downhill from here."

I peer ahead. The ground slopes down, sure enough, but there's nothing else to remark. Everything beneath us is shrouded in thick grey cloud.

We set out towards the mist, the air growing damper with every step, like the tiniest of raindrops have been suspended mid-fall. Then the fog is clearing or, more to the point, we're clearing it.

We've been leading our mounts since the pass. Now Barden stops his so abruptly I almost walk into his pony's rump.

I squint, but all I can see is jagged rock, ice, snow and smoke-grey sky. "What is it, Bar?"

"There." He bends his knees until he's at my level, pointing almost directly ahead. "Down below. A valley." Awe laces his voice.

And then I see it. Far below, so distant my eyes can no longer make out the details.

A thin smudge of green.

Life.

For the first time since the sultis valley, I feel something akin to curiosity. It's not exactly wonder, but it could be its lesser cousin.

The way down is the steepest trail I've ever walked, even though we switch back and forth across the slope. The first thing that changes is the wind. It's been our constant companion since we made it higher than the foothills, howling and tearing at us. Now, on the leeward side of the last ridge, it falls quiet.

Next, the ice begins to melt. It drips from the rock like I'm back in the caves of Trel, where Ash and I found Azered's bones. Where he first showed me the vulnerability I'd had no idea he masked. When trust started to unfurl between us.

I take the two sticks of incense from the pocket of my robe. Cypress. The first stage of mourning. Marjoram, the second. Once the others have passed me along the trail, I gently lay the cypress on a ledge beneath weeping icicles.

An offering, I suppose. May the mountain remember Ash as I do.

Moss is the first sign of life. Then small heathers. We pass cliffs sheeted with runoff, more and more gathering until it's forming tiny waterfalls in the crevices. It's almost musical, a chorus of liquid voices. I raise the marjoram to my nose and inhale, letting myself remember Ash's voice. The way he sang at the camp in Edurshai, deep tones – warm as sandalwood and dark as smoke – soaring into the night.

Soon, shrubs start to appear, roots gnarled as they burrow their way into the thin soil accumulated in the cracked rock. Further still, grass dots the track. The chill recedes from the air and I begin to smell things again: the earth beneath Lil's hooves, the shy sweetness of a clump of tiny pink wildflowers I've never seen the likes of before.

Flowers. The only time I've heard talk of the mountains beyond the Seson Territories is in tales. And those speak of a dead place. Barren. Endless. As if it's not even real, just somewhere that exists in myth. At the edge of memory. I've never had any reason to doubt them until now.

I push back the hood of my cloak and bend to touch the petals.

Luz appears at my side. It's unnerving, the way she can move silently like that.

"This…" I point to the flower. "How is this possible?"

"The elevation is so drastically different from the surrounding mountains that it allows for clement temperatures. And you've already seen the main source of water – there's a steady supply of melt even in the dry season. Why wouldn't it be possible?"

"The stories I've heard of these mountains. . . They say nothing of this."

"Splendid! I and my colleagues take that as the highest of compliments." Her gaze traces the ridge above us.

Was that movement? There. The glint of metal. A weapon? Armour?

"Let me guess: you're not going to tell me anything about that, are you?"

"I could spin you a fine yarn, petal. I have bard blood in me. But the Magister has reserved the right to brief you. And the Magister gets what the Magister wants."

The Magister. The Order. The Sanctuary. So many ridiculous names. I wonder what my mother thinks of all this. When Father spoke of her, he said she was pragmatic. It was something that first drew him to her. Is this nonsense something she got used to over time? Or did she come to enjoy the secrets and games?

We resume our trek and I begin to make out more details of what I presume is our destination. Carved from the grey granite of the mountains is a huge circular structure like a wheel laid flat. But before I can make out any more details of the inner part of the stone ring, we've descended lower than the line of sight. All I know is it covers a ground area bigger than all other buildings I've seen in my life, Aphorain, Ekasyan or anything in between. It makes even the imperial palace and temple complex seem small.

Nisai is so wide-eyed that I feel like I'm getting a glimpse into how he would have looked turns ago. A boy awed by a grand sight. I never thought I'd live to see something grand enough to wow a Prince.

We eventually find ourselves looking up at a blank wall that otherwise must be three, four, maybe even five storeys high.

"Halt," calls a voice, presumably a guard's, from a small opening in the wall.

Luz sighs. "We're not really going to have to go through this whole performance, are we?"

The guard, a fierce-looking woman with a square jaw, large brow and hair as grey as the surrounding rock, leans out and glowers down at us.

"Fine, fine," Luz says. "Greetings, Stoneleaf. I seek entrance to the Sanctuary of the Primordial Divine on a mission sanctioned by Snowthorn."

The guard nods, seemingly satisfied. "Wait where you are. An escort party will be assembled."

"I can handle this myself. Just open the gates."

"Rules are rules, Sandbloom."

I snort laughter despite myself. As if "Snowthorn" and "Stoneleaf" didn't sound ridiculous enough. "Sandbloom?"

"An unfortunate ceremonial throwback." Luz grimaces. "Just makes everyone sound like they've had smoke blown up their butt."

Luz flashes me a smirk. I find myself returning it. That's a first.

A grinding noise begins somewhere inside the rock. Then a vertical line appears in the stone. The line becomes a gap and soon two great slabs are rolling back into the walls like sliding gates.

When they stop, Nisai steps forward, running a hand over the now-flush surface. "What a fascinating mechanism."

"Impressive, no?" Luz asks airily, as if merely showing us a new rug.

The woman called Stoneleaf appears, and with her, several more guards form up around us. They're all women, unlike the few who served in the Aphorain army, or the presence of Kip in the Rangers. They look formidable. Lean. Skin weathered by the mountain weather. Shoulders seeming all the broader for the grey-and-white fur mantles draped across their shoulders.

We're led inside the stone structure to a walled yard. There, more guards move to take our mounts. I hesitate. It's not like I'm prepared to hand Lil over to just anyone.

"She'll be well cared for," Luz says.

"She'd better be," I glower, then stand on tiptoes and give Lil's bridle a light tug at the same time. She leans her head down, so that I can speak in her ear. "If you smell anything off, I give you permission to bite. Just reserve kicking until it's absolutely necessary."

She bumps me with her nose.

"Good girl."

We're led down a long hall dimly lit with some sort of greenish fire that transports my mind back to the Library of the Lost. We emerge into a huge circular chamber, the floor dropping away in stepped terraces towards the centre.

Opposite the door, the wall is dominated by a giant statue just like the one at the Library. A human-ish figure, seated on a massive but simple throne. Its carved features give nothing about its identity away. Smooth scalp and face, slender limbs, one hand palm up, the other palm down. Barefoot at the base.

Asmudtag.

It's hard to work out what the place is meant to be. Some kind of temple? A huge prayer room? A stage for troupes of players?

On a platform below the statue, several figures wait. Again, all women. Their robes are all made from the same greenish weave – with some minor variations in design. But there's nothing else alike about them. Tall, short, heavy, waif-thin. Some as old as the Chroniclers, and others appearing ageless, like Sephine.

Is one of them my mother? Would I recognize her if it was?

Luz takes the steps two at a time. When she comes face-to-face with those waiting, she dips a courtly bow.

Nobody moves.

Nisai catches my eye, concern etched in his features. I hesitate, then wave him on as if I'm simply making way for him on protocol.

He takes the hint, and mounts the stairs, Kip beside him. Barden and I follow.

"Your Imperial Highness," Luz says in a voice that takes me back to the perfume trials in Aphorai, the way Zakkurus held the crowd enthralled. "First Prince Nisai, heir of Aramtesh, may I introduce you to the currently elected officers of the Order of Asmudtag. Our Procurator, Administrator and Preceptor."

"Their what?" I mutter, mostly to myself.

"Official names for people who get things done, sign off that things got done, and teach people how to get things done." Nisai's lips barely move as he whispers back to us.

"And," Luz continues, "the current Magister of the Order."

"The person who speaks of what *should* get done," Nisai murmurs.

I'm surprised that it's the youngest-appearing woman who steps forward and bows. As she straightens, I take in her features. My hand goes to my locket. The rest of me freezes, feet locked to the floor.

"Welcome, our Prince." She speaks loud enough that it's obviously not just Nisai's ears she's intending to reach. Guess her and Luz are ingredients from the same perfume.

"On behalf of the elected officers of the Order, may I extend this exceptional invitation to the Sanctuary."

Exceptional? Don't suppose they get many visitors all the way out here. Or maybe it has something to do with the fact that Barden and Nisai are the only men we've seen since arriving.

"In the name of the divine Primordial," she continues, "we pledge to keep you safe from those who organized the attack on your person, whoever their identity may be revealed to be, so that when the time is right you may return to take up your inheritance and maintain balance in the Empire. Please let my people know of anything you require for the comfort of you and your companions."

Nisai inclines his head, a gesture I guess is equal to an elegant bow when it's coming from a prince. "Your hospitality is most appreciated. May I have the honour of your name?"

"Here, I am known simply as Snowthorn. But before that, I was called Yaita."

The square-jawed guard who first greeted us at the Sanctuary entrance clears her throat pointedly.

"I will not lie to my own kin, Stoneleaf," Yaita says.

The guard – if that's truly what she is – doesn't hide her disapproval.

Yaita looks to me and steps forward, a smile of overwhelming warmth now on her face.

I don't return it.

I had tried to imagine what it would be like at the end of this road. But I wasn't prepared for this, like looking at an older version of my reflection in the oasis pool of home. Dark hair hanging in loose waves past her shoulders in the same way mine did before it was shaved. Eyes the same amber hue as mine, too widely spaced to be considered by many to be pretty. Striking. That's what she is.

From when I was a small child, I would lie awake at night and imagine I was talking to my mother. She was always a hazy presence in my imagination, a kind of benevolent glow of a figure. I'd tell her everything, my fears, shames, hopes, dreams. I told her when I first managed to leap a dry stream bed on Lil's back without tumbling from the saddle. I told her when I'd first noticed Barden sprouting a beard, and even though he'd shaved it just as quickly, I'd noticed he'd started looking at me differently – a look that I didn't realize at the time would mean that one day he'd hope for something more from me than I could give to him. I told her when I first realized Father had the Rot and how terrified I was of what that meant for him, and, selfishly, for me.

The woman who stands before me heard none of those things whispered into the night. She may be unsettlingly familiar because of the portrait I've worn around my neck since I was a child telling secrets to the dark. She may have once wanted a family. She may have borne me, given me life.

She may be all of these things. But she's also something else.

A stranger.

"Daughter," she says, voice thick.

I'd never quite believed I would be here. And now that I am, I have no words.

She steps forward, bringing with her the scent of desert rose and smoky incense. Gently, she takes both of my hands in hers.

I snatch them back.

Her brow creases, then smooths again. "This must be a confusing, challenging experience, and I imagine you are exhausted. Your animals will be stabled and cared for. You will each have quarters; the Primordial knows that these days we have the space, though it wasn't always so."

The last sets the other Order members to murmuring. I catch a "by Their grace" among the other words.

"Our menu will be limited compared to what you're used to, my Prince, though I think you'll find our cook does an admirable job of balancing taste with sustenance."

Among the green-robed attendants, a rosy-cheeked woman, thin as a river reed, stands a little taller, chin a little higher.

"Please, rest. We shall meet on the morrow. Sandbloom will show you all you need between now and then."

Luz dips the same elegant bow and begins to descend the stairs. After a moment's hesitation, Nisai follows, Kip at his heels. Barden gives me a look that's part question, part commiseration.

"Wait!" I can't believe this. "That's it? Greeted and dismissed, just like that?"

The Magister gives a single, slow nod. "Until the morrow." She smiles again before making her way down the other side of the platform, towards a door opposite the one we entered through.

Luz retakes the stairs three at a time. Her fingers wrap around my arm.

I don't move.

She bends so that her lips are close to my ear. "Those legs of yours better remember how to walk, petal, unless you want me to sedate you and have your guard friend carry you out of here."

"You wouldn't dare."

But if I've learned anything about Luz, she would.

I let her lead me from the chamber.

Out in the hall, she lets go of my arm. "That went surprisingly well."

"Not from where I'm standing."

"I beg to differ, petal. You mother took a risk. A calculated one, but a risk all the same. It was just as likely they'd call an immediate Conclave. Days of debate just to decide if you could even stay. Judging from what we just saw, though, I expect once the officers have met, they will grant you run of the grounds." Her tone is now chatty, as if nothing was amiss. "Apart from a few select areas."

I sniff the air. "Smell that?"

She raises an eyebrow.

"Just caught a distinct whiff of oh-so-surprised."

The eyebrow drops back down. "Lovely to see you're back to your sweet self. Though yes, as you're a guest here, it's natural you won't have free rein. At least for now. In the meantime," she says, her voice rising so the others can hear, "there's a training ground for those of you who would like to keep your physical skills honed." Behind me, Barden and Kip murmur to each other.

"For keeping a sharp mind," Luz continues, "there is an archive. Not as impressive as the Imperial Library, but I'm

33

sure you'll discover some interesting texts that you'll not find in any other collections."

Nisai had been keeping his expression mild but his eyes light up at the mention of archives. I remember how Ash wished the Prince could have seen the Library of the Lost with us, how much he loves books and scrolls.

We're each given a room along a corridor that's curved just enough to seem like it's never-ending. When I'm shown through a thick stone door that somehow moves smoothly on a kind of hinge mechanism, I expect darkness and cool, even chill, air. But there's a window of faceted glass splaying the sun's last rays into splotches of rainbow across the wall and floor, the room almost as big as the entire house I grew up in. The air is mild, rich with the scent of clary sage candles, and when I reach out a hand, the smooth stone feels warm.

"Pleasant, no?" Luz gestures to the light. "The orientation of the complex encompasses the path of the sun and the shadows thrown by the surrounding mountains as the starwheel turns. Now that there are so few of us, we move quarters seasonally. The cold doesn't have time to penetrate during the night, while the cooling that does occur during the hours of darkness ensures the heat cannot become stifling during the day. We draw lots each time – one quarter a single room cell, the next a suite. It prevents any … unbecoming squabbles."

"Everything in balance," I murmur.

"For now," Luz agrees. "I'll leave you to get acquainted with the minutiae. You can find my quarters down the hall."

"Keeping a close eye on us, then?"

"As the Magister said, you're welcome to stay as long as you like. And I recommend you take up that invitation until we are satisfied that you're safe to return."

"We're prisoners, then."

"Of course not. But I imagine Yaita will be quite disappointed should you decide to vacate prior to meeting with her."

"I don't give a sack of camel scat what she—"

"And if you do choose to leave, we'll require you to chew enough sultis that you never knew you were here, even before you pass through the valley. I'm not one to gamble."

Even if I wanted out of here, I never want to go through those realizations again.

She shrugs and presses a square of stone that recedes into the wall. The door swings closed as she leaves, shutting with a soft click.

I cross to the polished granite basin in one corner, alongside a deep bath. Thick bars of soap sit in a woven basket. I bring one to my nose. Lime and basil. Unusual combination.

The bed is covered with a blanket decorated with an embroidered six-petalled flower. Dahkai. Just like the carvings in doors and stone back in Aphorai City – though this one is inside a circle. When I sit, the mattress yields kindly beneath my weight. I give the pillow an experimental prod. Feathers. Laced with chamomile and lavender to aid sleep. Seems the Order of Asmudtag enjoys its creature comforts.

There'll be time enough for washing and rest. But first, I want to see what the others have made of all this. I tentatively press the mechanism I'd seen Luz use on the stone door. It slides open.

Out in the hall, Kip is guarding the next door down.

"How is he?" I enquire of Nisai.

She folds her arms. "Are you tired after all that travel?"

"Exhausted."

"Then imagine how he feels."

She's right. I've been so preoccupied with my own grief that I've not been checking in on Nisai as much as I should have. It's clear the poison continues to have lingering effects, even if he does seem to grow stronger by the day.

"You know where Barden is?"

She waves down the hall.

I start in that direction.

Light spills from a doorway. But it's not Barden's. It's Luz's. She's standing over a large desk piled with scrolls. She gestures for me to enter, sinks into the chair behind the desk and takes up a scroll from the pile, waving it under her nose.

"Pass me the molshir essence, would you, petal? Top shelf, third jar from the left."

I retrieve the jar, knowing the right one from the purple-red hue extracted from the plant's leaves.

Luz dips a brush in and washes a thin film over the scroll. As if by magic, words begin to appear behind the others, these ones pale and glowing rather than of dark ink.

"How'd you do that?"

"My informants are thin on the ground, but they all honour our system. We only ever write surface-level messages that are completely innocuous if intercepted. The real message is hidden beneath. But if you use the wrong reagent, you'll destroy it."

"How did you know this one needed molshir?"

She taps her nose. "The code is in the scent. Whatever perfume used on the scroll has a matching reagent. And the codes are updated regularly."

She studies the scroll but gives nothing away as to what it reveals.

I crane my neck, blushing when I realize she's noticed.

"You want to see, petal?" She rises from her desk and hands it to me.

I take the scroll and pretend to read. Luz leans against the desk, long legs crossed at the ankles, as she watches me.

The letters on the parchment are a mess. Reading is a big-enough challenge at the best of times, let alone with two messages running into each other. But I'm not about to let Luz in on that. Everyone here seems to act all high and mighty, as if their scat doesn't stink. And Luz is just as annoying as ever, like sand in your clothes – once it's there, it's almost impossible to get rid of every last irritating grain.

So while I'd love to know what's in that message, I'm not going to give her the satisfaction.

Finally, I manage to make out a few words.

Ekasya.

Shield.

Dungeon.

Dead.

Each word is a blow. Just because you know something is true, doesn't mean it doesn't hurt to be reminded of it.

"Satisfied, petal?"

I hand back the scroll, swallowing hard. Luz stands and crosses to the fireplace, lights the parchment with a candle and tosses it into the grate. Leaning on the hearth, she watches as the message goes up in pungent smoke, expression unreadable.

When there's nothing but ashes, she returns to leaning on the desk and pops something into her mouth, taking a long moment to roll it over her tongue. The exhale is practised, elegant, and curls towards me as if it had been sent on an errand. Clove. "You can't read, can you? I thought as much back when you signed your contract before the perfume trials."

"As if I can't," I sputter.

"Don't consider changing trades – you're a terrible liar. Being able to read, on the other hand, is useful no matter one's vocation. Reading can take you wherever you wish to be. It's one of your many shortcomings that we'll have to remedy, long term." She looks back to the fire, the flames reflected in her dark blue eyes. "Though it's probably for the best, on this occasion."

"What's that supposed to mean?"

She stands and brushes invisible dust from her robe. The movement reveals she's still wearing her travelling clothes beneath. I would have thought she'd be the first to want to wash away the stench of the trail.

She runs her hand along the shelves, retrieving a jar and a series of vials she slips into a leather holder, rolling it up and tying it securely. Both get stowed in the pack beside the door. "Feel free to take a look around. Use anything you need while I'm away."

As if it's a reflex, my gaze flicks to the shelves. There must be hundreds of ingredients here. Many of them I've never heard of. "Away? Where are you going?"

I turn back towards the desk.

But Luz is already gone.

CHAPTER 3

ASH

"I must survive," I murmur to the sweltering, sticky stone of the cell wall. "I must survive."

It's a refrain I've repeated countless times over countless hours until the words themselves almost become devoid of meaning. Perhaps all it is now is the very sound of them, the feel of them whispering from my mouth and into the hot, fetid air of the dungeon, that tethers me to this life. Without them, my mind may have lost itself.

I thought I'd known pain. The heartache and fear of my father seeing me as a curse. The anguish of watching my mother wither and fade before my young eyes. The deep, gnawing hunger that only comes from being a child alone in the streets for moons on end with barely a morsel of food passing your lips. Old pain. Buried pain. The blades of memory dulled with the passage of time.

There has been newer pain, too. The devastation of seeing Nisai on the verge of death – a harm I should have protected him from. The anguish of knowing I'd led Rakel to what could have been her end. I can still see the guard

39

who seized her in the throne room and the red, red blood trailing from where his knife pressed against her throat.

After that, only agony. The pain when I was no longer *me*.

Now I know I've never had a notion of true pain.

None at all.

How many moons have I been here? Two? Three? Four? Long enough to grow a full beard, long enough for it to mat with filth.

During that time, I've been scraped, sliced, my veins drained of vial upon vial of blood. Heated metal instruments seared red welts in their wake. My arms were stretched on a rack until they dislocated from my shoulders, only for one of Zostar's black-robed Guild of Physician assistants to count the heartbeats it took for my joints to click back into place with a sickening pop.

And Zostar himself? He satisfies himself with excising sections of my tattoos with the smallest and sharpest of scalpels, the neat segments of inked skin and flesh quivering in specimen jars as he bears them, smiling, to wherever he's conducting the rest of his macabre research.

Through it all, my body heals. Even if the middle toe they removed down to the knuckle didn't grow back as they hypothesized, the wound took mere days to knit over the bone until it was once again embedded beneath flesh and smooth skin.

More than once I've wished it wasn't so, that instead of healing I'd succumb to festering or blood loss and slip from the mortal realm.

Because next came the long nights when I realized through a searing fog that Zostar must have ordered them to stop putting Linod's elixir in my water. Nights I spent sweating and shaking, emptying my stomach on to the floor because I couldn't make it to the slop bucket, retching and convulsing as my body was wracked with cramps long after there was nothing left to expel. Then, I shamed myself with the amount of times I wished I would die, wishing the curse that courses through my veins to make me whole again would this time fail.

But even during the worst of it, there would be distant glimmers.

Amber eyes that challenge with fierce tenacity or question with tender fragility. A smile that spreads warmth through my chest. The scent of desert rose.

I'd remember why I must persevere.

Rakel is out there somewhere, far above this labyrinthine dungeon. She's in the light. But for how long? She has no idea who was truly behind Nisai's poisoning. Who hunted us across the Empire. Who hunts her still.

In the worst of the most-recent sessions, when my captors flood a sealed-up room with a rancid-smelling smoke until I'm choking, hands curled into claws that want to tear open my own throat for the chance at some air, the only thing that keeps me from succumbing is my thoughts of the two people I most care for in this world.

Where are they? Are they together? I imagine them taking refuge somewhere safe; Rakel's determination to set things aright will burn like a fever. Nisai will stay her hand until he's confident of a plan. He'll be thinking of the big picture, of what's at stake, that the threat could have come from so many places within the capital or beyond. That he must be certain before his next move.

Would it have yet crossed his mind that his biggest enemy is the man appointed physician to his father? The man who has long been closest to the ailing Emperor, if Kaddash has not yet finally succumbed to the Affliction. The man who paved the way for Iddo to take up the Regency, and who undoubtedly plans to strike Nisai down again.

"I must survive," I repeat to the wall. "I must find a way out of here."

"Ash?" The timid enquiry comes from the next cell.

I'm too exhausted to move, but for a small, sad smile on my lips. Until I found myself in the dungeons beneath Ekasya, I never would have thought I'd be relieved to know the walls have ears.

"Ash, I've got to tell you something. It's important." Del's almost-adolescent voice warbles and breaks on the last.

I haul myself to my feet, rolling the stiffness from my neck, and cross to the opposite wall. There's a crack in the mortar near the rear corner of the cell, down at shoulder height if I sit with my back to the hot, clammy wall, the black Ekasyan stone as heated as it gets in the sun up on the surface far above. It's just enough space to hear through.

"I'm here," I murmur into the gap.

"Thank the Twins." Del's Hagmiri accent is pronounced enough to be evident even in whispers, betraying the fact he only left the mountains recently. The boy had visited the capital with his elder brother and neither of them, apparently, were prepared for the press of Ekasya's market. They'd been separated, and Del found himself lost in the warren of back alleys off the main spokes of the city's boulevards, where he ran into two large men who had snatched and bound him and thrown him on the back of a cart. The only thing he'd noticed was they each had a tattoo of a black sun on the inside of their wrist.

The Brotherhood of the Blazing Sun.

It would be cruel to tell him so, but the coincidence of Blazers finding him so soon after his arrival in the city seems … off. I'd wager his brother had always intended to trade more than the cedar oil they'd spent weeks lugging on their backs down from the Alet Range.

And if that's the case, may mother Esiku's wrath fall upon the poor boy's excuse for a family. Nobody that young should be down here.

"What is it?"

"Lark heard something."

Larkai, the girl from the Ekasyan slums in the next cell over from Del. Younger again. Couldn't be more than eight turns, the poor wretch. Her cell shares some sort of vent with Del's, letting through hushed voices along with the steaming air escaping from the mineral springs that provide hot water to the palace far above. One way or another, with whispers between cells and across barred hallways, the prisoners have linked a chain of communication.

At last count, there are twenty-eight of us in this wing of the warren-like tunnels. Most are from the capital's slums, but a few, including Del, hail from further afield. I'm the eldest by a half dozen turns. For the first time in my wretched existence, I find myself a default leader, the younger ones looking to me for guidance, no matter how much I wish it weren't so. At first, I'd wondered if Del was perhaps a spy of Zostar's. A ruse of innocence to keep close watch on me. But there's no reason to keep so many of them for such a purpose, and my heart believes there's truth in the boy's earnestness.

I tilt my face towards the wall. "Out with it, then."

"She heard two of the Testers talking."

The Testers. The name the kids have given to the physicians working with Zostar. Or *for* Zostar – the longer I'm down here, the more I witness and hear, the more that seems to be the way of things. But whether Zostar is working for someone else, I have no idea. Perhaps he is working only for his own ends.

Truth be told, that terrifies me.

Something scrapes on the other side of the stone as Del shifts his weight. "They're starting another round soon. One said they're getting closer to answers. The other said he would prepare the Room."

An involuntary shudder wracks me. It's clear they're trying to discover whatever it is that makes me heal quickly. The Room is the place I've come to associate with sessions where I'm exposed to various smokes and steams, some of them pleasant, some of them downright noxious, like the aftermath of explosive powder. Though I've learned even the sweet-scented ones can carry a punch. I can't last too many more sessions in there. Even if my body does, my mind was on such shaky ground after the last round…

"Ash?"

"I'm here."

"There's something else. They said they were including the young ones this time."

How cruel for Del to have to think of himself as no longer young, before he's even grown fuzz on his chin. But nobody could be young after spending any amount of time down here. Sometimes that makes me feel as old as the Emperor. Yet other times I feel barely more than a child myself.

What is Zostar intending for us? The children have nothing in common other than each of them was unwanted, or wandered where they shouldn't have.

Wandering where one shouldn't. That turns my thoughts to the day I met Nisai. When we were set upon by … Blazers.

"Del? Has anything unnerving ever happened to you? I mean before you came to Ekasya. Perhaps when you were younger? You might have blacked out and woke up to find you'd … done things."

"What kind of things?"

"Have you ever *hurt* anyone?"

There's a pause on the other side of the wall.

"Once," the boy whispers. "A boy in my village took my fishing pole. Said he'd throw me into the river and catch me like a lossol eel."

"And what happened?"

"He was bigger than me. Faster. I didn't know what to do. He cast the hook into my hair and it caught on my ear. Burned like the five hells combined as he dragged me towards the water. It was rushing that day. Mad and frothing white. So, I pushed him. He landed on a rock. I felt good about it at the time. But then he limped for days. I felt terrible."

I suppress the urge to laugh in relief, instead rolling my neck to ease muscles that had ratcheted tight. "You were only trying to defend yourself."

"Not what my parents said. They said I'd done something evil. Said I was cursed."

The tension returns and my heart clenches with it. "Cursed?" I reach for the prayer braid that's no longer wrapped around my arm.

"Aye. Because I came into the world on the unholy days." He swallows the end of the last word, almost as if he was stifling a sob. "I was born in the Days of Doskai."

45

Footsteps begin down the corridor. They'll be coming for me first; they always come for me first. On the occasions they do take Del or Lark, it's only to question them. But just because they haven't harmed them physically yet, it doesn't mean the voice in my mind doesn't speak the truth: *When they run out of patience with me, they'll start their experiments on the younger ones.*

The gods may have truly turned their backs to me, but if I don't get Del and Lark and the others out of here, who knows what they'll be put through.

The footsteps come closer. Four pairs. They never send less than four guards, despite my shackles. And every one of them seems on edge now that Linod's Elixir no longer numbs me, their furtive glances and white knuckles giving them away.

I don't blame them.

"Ash?" Del has been silent since his confession, but he must have heard the approaching guards.

"Try to get some rest. I'll be back before you know it. We're going to find a way out of here, I promise."

The door slams shut behind me.

This is *not* the Room.

Whereas the Room is not much bigger than my cell, this place is huge, larger than thirty or forty cells combined. It's floors above – I was half shoved, half dragged up flight after flight of stone steps. This far back up the interior of Ekasya Mountain, I wouldn't be surprised if this space covers half an entire level. What was its original purpose? A storeroom for the imperial complex? An armoury?

It's dimly lit like the floors beneath, but even I can smell that the candles in their iron sconces anchored around the walls and supporting pillars aren't tallow like the rest of this place. They're something incongruously cleaner. Wax. More than a little upmarket for a prisoner.

Everything wavers in the flickering light. Or perhaps that's just my fatigue. But I could swear on merciful Azered's way-finding that there are figures watching from behind the barred openings in the walls.

And then I get a waft of it. Perfume. I have no idea of its constituent parts, but whatever it is, it smells expensive, and none of Zostar's Physicians, or the man himself, seem to ever smell of anything but antiseptic pine. What could anyone of the means and predilections to wear luxury fragrances be doing down here?

Certainly, they couldn't be in their right mind.

Across the floor, on the other side of the vast chamber, a door opens. Three men saunter in, wearing armour without any provincial affiliation, nor imperial sigil from the palace. The only sign of who they are, of where their loyalties lie, is the sun branded on their black boiled leather.

There's no longer even the pretense of hiding the alliance between the Physicians and the Blazers. Cold dread claws its way up my spine – what has enabled such audacity?

Two of the men are bigger than me. Lumbering brutes of half again my weight, thick as Trelian bulls with solid muscle. Running into one of them would be like running into a wall.

Brute Number One has a dark beard that birds could nest in. The other could be his blond cousin, a rug of chest hair sprouting like straw from his leather vest.

The third man is about the same size as me. And I'd

47

wager he's just as swift on his feet by the way he steps lightly, lean legs and defined calves speak of agility and a capacity for a standing leap. He's the one I'll have to look out for.

The last thing I want to do is fight. Not here. Not now. Not with the fight that is coming later when I make good on my promise to get Del and the others to safety. And from there, whatever I have to fight through to get to Rakel and Nisai.

The blond Blazer throws me a wooden sword.

I let it clatter on to the stone. I can take a beating. I'll return to my cell sore but satisfied and soon to heal.

He grins, as if this is merely a game and he holds all the key pieces. "You don't fight, we'll bring one of the kids in here to do it for you."

I don't doubt it.

I take a deep breath, then let out a long, controlled exhale and move to pick up the training weapon. Soft pine against their metal. Zostar may not care for these men, but he does care about resources. It would seem he's not a man to tolerate unnecessary waste by starting me on equal footing.

As soon as I've retrieved the sword, the two big Blazers head straight towards me. I'll wager they'll strike at the same time. But already the smaller of the trio has circled wide. The quick one. No doubt he'll come in from the flank when I'm distracted.

It won't be enough.

I vowed to survive and survive I will.

Out beyond the light of the wall sconces, more shadowy figures gather behind the bars. Sweet mother Esiku, how many of them are there? Some watch in silence, some snigger to each other. If this many are here, surely this operation – whatever it is – must not be entirely a secret. Perhaps it's not even an open secret. I search among them for who might have worn perfume, but then my blond opponent hefts his axe.

The blade glints in the low light, the back of it finished in a cruel hook. He takes the first swing, and I dodge, but he recovers quicker than I'd like. Did I underestimate him? Or have I underestimated how much a diet of thin gruel has slowed my own reactions?

His dark-haired friend slashes with his sword and I only bring up my wooden version just in time. It shatters, splitting along the grain, making the bones of my wrist feel like they're fracturing along the same lines.

The weapon is now half its original length. But I don't care – it's also sharper. I twist low, getting under my foe's guard, and slam the splintered sword up through the soft flesh under his chin. He topples like an oversized sack of barley.

His blond friend's smirk vanishes.

We circle each other. He now knows the game is not in his favour, and the new uncertainty in his steps suggests he thought it always would be. He comes at me, axe whistling through the air in great arcs. I'm forced to retreat, weaving wide of each deadly swing.

I've lost sight of the third Blazer, the small one, but I can hear him. He's moving on quiet feet, breathing near-silent breaths behind me.

A much louder noise rings out from the edge of the arena. The scrape of one of the heavy doors opening. Followed by the muffled cries of someone gagged. The scuff of boots on stone. The kind of steps, unlike those of

49

my fleet-footed opponent, that are doing nothing to hide their presence.

I dodge another axe blow and feint to the side, drawing the brute to overreach and unbalance himself. It affords me enough time to put several paces between us, enough time to swing around and take in the new arrivals.

I'd been prepared for three, four, perhaps five more Blazers.

There's only two.

And, Esiku have mercy, a girl.

Her alabaster-pale face is partially concealed by a gag, green eyes wide with fear above the tightly wound fabric. Her hair is greasy and hangs in ropes like river weed. It could have been mistaken for brown in its filthy state, but there's enough auburn beneath to show through.

No. Surely it couldn't be. But she holds herself straight, with the same willowy grace of someone I knew from the Imperial Library, where she spent days up ladders balancing stacks of books. A grace that always made Esarik, usually as chatty as a Losian parakeet, forget all his words.

"Ami?"

By the looks of her, she's been here a while. She's much skinnier than when I last saw her moons ago. Her tunic, smeared with muck, hangs from her frame, collarbones prominent at the neckline.

She tries saying something, but the gag muffles the words.

The guard on her right yanks her arm.

For all I know, she's the last of my friends in the capital. But why capture her? Why bring her in here for me to see?

I force myself to relax my stance. Maybe she's just a decoy. A distraction while they rush me.

But they don't come for me.

Instead, two hold Ami's arms wide. The third traces his blade from her midsection up to her throat, drawing a bead of blood from her neck in cruel imitation of Rakel that fateful day in the throne room. He waves the dagger suggestively in the air, a lascivious grin across his stupid face.

I know it as well as I know the dawn.

He's going to kill her.

Unless I kill him first.

And that's when the other guards rush me.

I duck under the first. Slam the second into one of the stone pillars, grimly satisfied at the crunch of his nose breaking before he slumps to the floor, out cold. The remains of my wooden sword catch Ami's captor in his brow. It was a glancing blow, but it's enough to split his scalp, opening the way for blood to pour into his eye.

"Behind me! Now!"

I grab her hand and she stumbles forward, staggers, and crumples to the arena floor.

Azered's breath, she's fainted.

The door opens again.

More Blazers. Two. Four.

For each one I cut down, another takes his place. I can't protect her. I can't. There's too many.

Is that a palace uniform among them? What is a palace guard doing here? After the throne room, when the shadow part of me tore free and killed so many, I can't kill another imperial servant. I won't. This must be a mistake.

But he's advancing with the Blazers.

He must be working with Zostar. *How could you?* I want to yell. *You're fighting on the side of torturers.* Not just *my*

51

torturers. Del's, Lark's. The others'. They're on the side of hurting innocent children.

As I parry another blow, the itching starts. The burning along the lines of ink beneath my skin. That feeling of unfurling. Of imminent separation.

No.

Let them have what they want, says another voice. *Let them know true pain.*

CHAPTER 4

RAKEL

I can't find sleep.

Even after what should have been the most relaxing bath. This bed is so stinkin' soft, and the pillows are even worse. In the moons I've spent mostly on the road, and a lot of that sleeping outdoors, I would have given anything for a bit of comfort. Now all this pampering means I can't get a blink.

At least that's what I tell myself. Easier to blame the furniture than the fear of what sleep will bring – grey eyes I'll never see again, the safe feeling of a familiar presence keeping watch over our camp, a first and final kiss stolen through dungeon bars.

Dreams only wake me in tears. It's easier to lose myself in the storm raging through my waking mind, swirling around a single thought.

Seventeen turns.

Seventeen turns of me thinking I'd been the cause of my own mother's death. And when I finally meet her, this stranger, this so-called Magister, says she'll explain it all "on the morrow"? And then the only person we had who resembled a guide just ups and leaves without the barest whiff of warning?

My stomach rumbles. I hadn't been able to eat before bed. I was too rattled. But now that it's quiet, and I'm not getting much rest anyway, a midnight snack wouldn't go astray. The Magister did, after all, say the cook was happy to provide.

With a sigh, I throw off the bedcovers.

I take one look at the pile of crumpled travelling clothes in the corner and decide against it. Instead, I pull on one of the clean robes from the chest at the foot of my bed. I catch sight of myself in the mirror. I haven't owned anything green before. It's ill-fitting, with too-long sleeves and a hem that skims the floor rather than where it should be at my ankles. But even I have to admit the colour suits me.

Just as it suits the Magister.

Ugh. It's almost enough to put me off the thought of food again. Almost.

Out in the hall, I hesitate. I have no idea where the kitchens even are. Though whether I go left or right, I'm guessing the curving hall will eventually lead me there.

Left it is.

It's eerily quiet as I pass door after door. I'm about to turn back, thinking I've bet on the wrong route to the kitchens, when my nose tells me I had it right.

I freeze, breath hitched.

The warm, homey scent of baking bread wafts towards me. It means something different to me than it used to and I don't want to take it in. It's Ash's favourite smell. He told me how he used to steal away to the kitchens in the early morning with Nisai, when they were both young. How the cooks would fuss over them, giving them the slices from the best of the loaves fresh out of the oven. How it made him feel like he finally had a home.

Lack of air makes me start to feel woozy. Still, I resist breathing. I consider fleeing back to my room. Better an empty stomach than steeping in the pain of memory, surely.

But I'm not going to be able to avoid smelling bread for the rest of my turns. Sooner or later, I'll have to learn to live with it.

I close my eyes and force myself to take a deep, slow breath before continuing along the corridor.

The aroma leads me down a narrow flight of stairs and through a small door. Seems servants still get the out-of-the-way entrances here. When I press it open, warm air envelops me like a hug, and the cook I run into beams so brightly I think she may hug me, too.

I stiffen, and she gives a knowing nod, stepping away to take down a glazed ceramic plate. On it goes a huge triangle of finger-thick bread with herb-strewn goat's cheese. My mouth waters.

"Thank you," I manage as she points me over to a table in the corner. It's gently lit by the coals and their reflections bouncing off a score of copper cooking pots hanging from racks suspended from the roof.

A half dozen Order members sit at the near end. I don't recognize their faces from when we arrived, but they're wearing the same green robes everyone seems to wear here.

"I disagree, Payuz," one woman says, voice strident. "Tenet Sixteen refers to the purity of the soul required for a ceremony to successfully channel the will of Asmudtag."

The woman called Payuz shakes her head. "You're always jumping to something esoteric. Tenet Sixteen is simply a reminder from the ancients to make sure you wash your hands before you start. Otherwise you risk contaminating the ingredients."

Their companions are divided into those who laugh and those who *tsk* indignantly in response.

I look beyond them, towards the fire where another figure sits, head bent over their plate in thought, or prayer. They're keeping their own peace. I'm in no mood to talk, so I decide they're the better bet.

Not wanting to sit too close to the stranger, I choose the stone bench nearest to the fire. Happily, the flames have banished any chill from the slab.

"I used to take that very seat when I first arrived."

Great. Guess everyone in this place is up for a chat. I stare down at my food, hoping she'll get the message that I'm the exception to the rule.

"Though I think the last drop of heat-loving blood fled my veins turns ago – too warm in Aphorai for me these days."

She slides her plate halfway down the table and into the light.

Of all the stinking—

"Couldn't sleep?" the Magister asks. "I requested you be afforded the best of our chambers."

"That's part of the problem."

She studies my face, then nods. "The beds. It took me some time to get used to the softness, too."

It's like she can see into my mind. Irritated, I take a bite of my bread and chew deliberately slowly. The cheese is delicious, the aromatic dill the perfect pairing. I refuse to let good cheese be ruined.

"The bed's fine," I lie. "It's the lavender in the pillows. I'm not into lavender."

"Oh?"

I think back to the smelling salts after Luz – who I had then known only as Zakkurus, Aphorai's Chief Perfumer – had drugged me. "Long story."

"Perhaps you may one day tell it to me."

"Maybe. If you tell me where Luz has gone."

"Sandbloom is on Order business."

"Let me guess, you can't tell me as I'm not a member of the Order."

She glances to where the others are locked in their heated debate. "I'm afraid so."

I want to press her. Does she know about the scroll Luz received? Or about Ash's death? But she reminds me too much of Sephine, who I could never get answers from. For now, the urge to protect myself, to not start something that could see me dissolve into helpless tears, wins out.

The silence stretches between us, but it doesn't seem to rattle her. Finally, she places her hands on the table and leans closer, taking another furtive glance towards the others. "If you wish to speak *privately*, my chambers are further down the hall. I don't tend to sleep in the early hours of the morning."

"Feeling guilty about something?"

She doesn't so much as blink. "I find it's when I do my best work. I gave up everything to be here. My family. My home. I do everything I can to honour that sacrifice."

Ah, there it is. She's a martyr. The noble one. Who lost

so much. Poor her. "You walked away from a daughter who needed you."

"To help so many more in need. You think you're more important than the throngs who suffer from the Affliction? More important than your father's life?"

Oh, that's too much. "What do *you* know of Father? You left him! Did you know he was sick when you left?"

My voice had been rising with each word, so that by the time I'm finished, the others have stopped talking, their curious eyes turned to us. The Magister makes a show of gathering her plate and spoon while giving the other Order members a mild "nothing to see here" smile.

"Of course not," she hisses when they've gone back to their conversation.

I shift in my seat. "Then when he did get sick. You must have heard. Why didn't you help?" The last is said in a softer voice than I'd intended. It sounds like a child's pleading, and I want to slap myself for it.

"This is the best place I could have been to help. Looking for a cure. My new salve, the one Hab – your father – has now, is an incredible advance even if it's not the permanent remedy we need. And in my absence, Sephine watched over you. She did whatever was necessary, I'm sure. She was never one to shirk a duty."

"She didn't care a whiff about Father! And it wasn't her duty, it was *yours*. When you have a child, you look after them."

"I did what I could from afar. Surely my letters helped you understand."

"Letters? I don't know what you're talking about."

She frowns. "I wrote to you every moon."

"And every single one of them just happened to get lost on the way from your secret mountain lair?" Under the table, my hands clench into fists. "Maybe you're out of touch, but lying to people hasn't become acceptable since you left the real world behind."

She flinches and looks away. I've managed to find a way through her armour. She stares into the flames, silent. It's a silence heavy with meaning. If only I knew what that meaning was.

Finally, she rises from the table. "If you would like to know more about my work, the cook can show you to my chambers."

I keep my eyes on my plate until she leaves.

The last mouthful of bread and cheese is hard to swallow. I sit for some time afterwards, watching the fire die down as slowly as the flames of my anger.

When the cook comes to add another brick of fuel – I'd think it peat or charcoal if it wasn't for the unfamiliar sweet notes in the smoke – I ask for directions.

I have to know.

In the Magister's chambers, sheaves of parchment are spread across a desk, and several elaborate distillation apparatuses are lined up along the wall – tripods and blown glass spheres, vials and burnished copper tubes. I cough. Whatever it is that she's got steaming away in the corner, it's enough to sting my throat and make my eyes water.

No wonder she leans beside an open window, chewing on the end of a stylus as she reads a scroll. She somehow looks younger in the pose. I don't even know how old she was when she gave birth to me – but back then she couldn't have seen many more turns than I have now.

Unless she's the same as Sephine – ageless.

When she notices me, she holds up a hand. "I wasn't sure if you were coming so I commenced another experiment. You don't want to breathe too many of these fumes. Let's walk, shall we?"

"Sure." Suits me. I'd not exactly relished the idea of sitting face-to-face with her.

She strides ahead, guiding me through the main corridor and up a spiral staircase carved from the stone structure itself. It's windowless, and I lose track of how many circles we wind upwards, thankful for the way my legs have toughened up over the past moons.

When we emerge outside, the sight sends my skin prickling.

I had imagined the complex was big. But this is something else. The curving corridor indeed goes around in a complete loop – we only saw one part of the structure upon our approach. Now, we're looking out over what I can only think of as a great, circular valley completely enclosed by the stone complex. A continuous balcony, wider than three of Father's house joined together and edged by a low stone wall, forms a rim around the top, like the lip of a vast oil jar. The other side is so distant it fades into a blur, either from the lack of braziers on that edge, or because I still can't see long stretches as I used to.

Terraced plantations slope gently down to a centre point far below. The gardens remind me of the Eraz's estate in their layout, though unlike in Aphorai, the terraces go down and down and down to where they disappear from view. I recognize some of the plants – saffron crocuses, yolketh shrubs with their fleshy leaves full of the bitterest juice, a line of purrath trees, their sweet blossom perfuming the night air. Many of the other plants are unknown to me.

The Magister moves to the edge of the balcony and sits on the wall itself.

I keep a pace or two back. "What exactly is this place?"

"The Sanctuary serves many functions. It has been a stronghold for centuries for those who dedicate their lives to Asmudtag. A place where in hostile times we can retreat, watch and wait."

"Sephine spoke of Asmudtag. I thought the temple … wasn't into that kind of thing."

"The temple itself indeed favours the Younger Gods. But the Scent Keepers retain the link to what came before. Asmudtag was the first deity, self-willed into existence. Like the Divine Primordial themself, the Order is dedicated to balance in all things. And we have always worked towards that end. I will continue to do so until the day I go to the sky. It is to this work I sacrificed so much. As did you." She bows her head at the last.

"Sacrificed?" I scoff. "You mean *lost*. Or are you forgetting I didn't really have a choice in the matter?"

Somehow, she maintains that still-water calm. "I wanted to show you this to try to help you understand. These gardens are the very reason I came here in the first place. Noticed how it's particularly clement? Some believe the entire Sanctuary is imbued with the will of Asmudtag. Others would argue it's the specific combinations of weather, altitude and the thermal springs at the base of the valley. Regardless, the conditions of the Sanctuary allow us to grow flora from a vast array of climates."

I push my hands into the sleeves of my robe. *Mild*, she

says. Pff.

"We have a specimen of every plant from the Empire. Some even from the warring lands beyond the Midlosh Sea. Since the Shadow Wars, the Sanctuary has, in essence, been the home of scentlore. Most recently it has been crucial to continuing my own – and Sephine's – research into finding a cure for the Rot. I'm getting closer; my treatments are lasting longer and longer. I know from Luz's reports you've seen the evidence for yourself. But we're not there yet. If you stayed, I would hope you would become a part of that work. You have talent."

"Talent inherited from you?"

"Perhaps. Aptitude tends to run in the female line. But it is unpredictable. Generations can be skipped. Whether you inherited it from me or not, you have more than proved yourself. Surviving the elixir of the Scent Keepers is testament to that. Your success in healing the Prince also speaks to a natural ability."

I begin to pace, needing to move my body while my thoughts catch up with themselves. Though the drop into the gardens isn't huge, I keep away from the edge. Even the slow descent into the circle of darkness unnerves me, and after the sultis, I'm not about to start messing with any plants I don't recognize. "Why didn't you just bring me here in the first place if you really cared?"

"Those who join the Sanctuary are expected to forfeit their old lives," she says, running a hand over the balcony wall as if reassuring herself that she's seated on something solid. "There was little I could do to help from this far away. What I could do, I did. Sandbloom saw to your freedom when Sephine perished, did she not? And I had faith in you."

My folded arms tighten over my chest. "You were testing me."

"Shrewd. That is good. But on this occasion, it wasn't the only reason. The best way to get you out of immediate danger was to get you out of Aphorai City. All the information our people have assembled on the eldest imperial son over the turns speaks of a single-minded pursuit of justice. Which is to say, Iddo Kaidon's own personal interpretation of justice. It's hard to comprehend he and his brother come from the same line."

"You really do care for Nisai's safety, then."

She nods vigorously. "He's the hope for the future. Thoughtful. Humane. Willing to listen to opposing views. When he ascends the throne, if he has the right people around him, he stands a chance of ushering in an age of tolerance and learning we haven't seen in the centuries since the Great Bloom. We need him. Desperately. Otherwise things are only getting worse."

She flows to her feet. "Please. Walk with me. There's something else you must see."

I follow her around the top terrace, the curve so gentle you could almost think you're walking in a straight line. The more I see of this place, the stranger it feels. A kind of ancientness that makes my lifetime seem but a whiff on the wind.

Finally, we come to a door two segments over, flanked by a pair of guards. One moves to open the door ahead of the Magister. They exchange a solemn nod, but neither speak as we pass. Hardly reassuring.

Inside, there's a small chamber lit by those eerie green

wall sconces. The Magister waits until the outer door closes, then turns her attention to me. "You may want to brace yourself," she advises as she pushes open the inner door.

A cloud of warm air greets us, just like it did earlier in the kitchens. But this place carries with it a reek that doubles me over into a gag. I'd know that smell anywhere.

Rot.

The stench is so thick it's as if it's coating the very walls. A mix of anger and disgust courses through me. The only time I've smelled anything remotely like it was in the dungeons beneath Ekasya Mountain when I was trying to find Ash – so many of the prisoners there seemed to be Rot sufferers. I never thought I'd come across something like that again.

The Magister grimaces. That she's not enjoying this either is small comfort.

We walk along the halls. They're near identical to the ones where me and the others have been assigned sleeping quarters, the stone doors shut. About half a dozen along, the Magister stops and presses the mechanism.

"Hello?" she all but whispers around the opening.

"Come in," a weak voice calls.

She opens the door and gestures for me to follow. Inside, the stench of decaying flesh subsides a little, though it's still an underlying taint in the room.

The room is sparsely furnished. On the bed, a middle-aged woman lies propped on her side. The hip that faces the ceiling is heavily bandaged. Despite the air being slightly clearer in here, I've got no doubt about what lies beneath the dressings.

The Magister performs a strange gesture, palms together, thumbs under her chin, first fingers to her nose. Maybe it is a prayer. Maybe it's a gesture of respect or apology. "Please forgive the intrusion."

"You're always welcome, Yaita."

"Taimez, may I present my daughter, Rakel."

The woman beams. "And so she is! No doubt, given those eyes." She looks me up and down. "Your mother talks of you often, you know. Proud as peppercorns, she is. Wouldn't hear the end of it if I was the only one here."

I muster the closest thing to a smile I can give through gritted teeth. What does the Magister even know of me? Guess it's easier for her to blow smoke about how proud she is to strangers than it is to do the right thing. But I don't want to be rude to this woman. Though she's cheery, she must be in awful pain.

"Has there been any change?" the Magister asks her.

"Still holding."

"But no closer to scabbing over?"

Taimez looks almost apologetic, as if she were the one speaking to a patient about their recovery. "Afraid not."

"Stay strong," the Magister says, taking Taimez's hand and squeezing gently. "I'm refining the formula in a new direction. This could be the one."

"If the Primordial wills it." She gives a half-shrug with her free shoulder.

"She is all," the Magister intones.

"She is all," the woman returns.

"We'll let you rest," the Magister says, and leads me from the room, closing the door quietly behind her.

"You're testing your concoctions on her?" I can barely

contain my outrage. "What if it was the wrong thing? It could make it even worse."

"The Affliction is a death sentence. We're doing everything we can to help, which is more than I can say for anywhere else in the Empire now Sephine's gone." She gestures up and down the hallway. "We provide them with hope, and in the absence of a cure so far, we give them as much comfort as we can."

"Hope?" I blurt, thinking of the guards we passed at the main door to this wing. "They need to be locked up to have hope? I won't be a part of that, if that's what you're asking me."

"They are free to roam the grounds during the day," she says as we pass back through the main door with no obstruction from the guards.

I take a gulp of clean air, feeling a little ashamed at the sheer relief of being free of the smell of impending death.

"They agree to a curfew at night to ensure they're getting adequate rest to aid their convalescence. Pain can addle the best of minds, so we must also take precautions that they don't attempt to leave once they're here."

"They may as well be prisoners."

"No. Ask them yourself if you wish. They are pilgrims who have sought the healing power of Divine Asmudtag, selected by the Order for their devotion. They give us the opportunity to know when we're getting closer to a cure, and we do everything we can to extend their lives. Their gift to us could save your father and so many others.

"I've dedicated my life to trying to cure this plague," she continues. "The manner in which I did so is something for which I shall need to atone. I am truly, deeply sorry for the pain it caused you. However, I will not apologize for working towards ending the suffering for so many."

I can't argue with her logic. But my heart is raw at the thought of those poor patients beyond the guarded doors.

"So indeed" – her voice is cool now, like she's distancing herself again – "immerse yourself in past wrongs, nurture whatever ill will you bear me for the way I failed to nurture you. But know this: when you are ready to turn your face towards the future, to focus on what is yet to come and to be a part of making that, I would have you at my side. By the grace of the Primordial, you have proven yourself more than proficient – you are an innovator. And that is what we need. A new twist on the old recipes. I fear we've fallen stale here, repeating the same incremental experiments. We need a new approach. You'll be provided with your own supplies, your own apparatus."

My own apparatus? Access to *these* gardens? In other circumstances, it would be a dream come true. I want to believe that there's a role for me to play here. That I could help find a cure. Not just for Father, but for all those who suffer from the Rot. But there's still a missing ingredient in this perfume she's wafting around me.

"There are plenty of people with the Rot in Aphorai. Sephine did her experiments there. Why couldn't you?"

She nods, no longer distant, but smiling. Like she's pleased with me again. It ignites something inside me, the unexpectedly warm glow of her approval. I shake my head to clear it.

"I had to come here because of the key ingredient. Sephine had her position, and Sandbloom's as Chief Perfumer, to siphon as much for her experiments without causing attention. I was making my own progress, but there wasn't enough for both of us. I had to make a choice. A terrible, difficult choice, to come to the one other place where there was a supply."

She points. "There, don't you see?"

As she's talked, she's kept walking slowly, a seemingly aimless stroll around the huge circular terrace above the gardens. Now it's clear she had a destination in mind.

I follow her arm, squinting down at the rows and rows of plants now directly below us. My eyes still aren't what they used to be before healing Nisai, so I'd missed it until it was highlighted. But now my attention is drawn, I see. Distinct foliage I haven't laid eyes on since that fateful night in Aphorai. The night Nisai was poisoned. The night all of this started.

Dahkai.

The darkest bloom. The most precious commodity in Aramtesh. A plant that has only ever been successfully cultivated in Aphorai City. The bulk of it shipped to the capital as the most expensive perfume in the Empire.

"We're running out of time," the Magister says. "My topical salve helps, but it's only a temporary solution – a reprieve from the symptoms. Our research indicates that a true, lasting cure will rely on the most finite resource in Aramtesh."

Finite is right. There won't be another Flower Moon for a generation.

"If we don't manage to create that cure with our remaining stores of dahkai, the disease will continue to spread. If we take too long to find the correct formula and there are too many patients to cure with the amount we currently have, the disease will have won. For ever."

The weight of her words bears down on me. She's talking about a point of no return. Where we couldn't help even if a cure was found. There simply wouldn't be enough of it.

"The question, my daughter, is this: will you stay and help me?"

CHAPTER 5

LUZ

All things in their due and proper order: first, I need information.

Aphorai City greets me like an old friend. If an old friend were harbouring a barely concealed grudge.

I'd made far better time travelling back solo, and entered the gates in nondescript trader garb – travel-stained linen smock and loose-fitting trousers. I augmented the outfit with a cartload of woven Edurshain baskets I'd bought from another trader on the approach to town, and for good measure added the legitimacy of actually paying the required tax. The product sold swiftly in the markets, especially as I could afford to not haggle more than the minimal amount necessary to maintain appearances while I caught up on local gossip. If I'd offloaded the goods too cheap, someone would ask questions.

After that, I visit an inn near the Eleventh Gate, where I've kept a room on retainer for the past two turns. I'm greeted by the innkeeper's daughter. She gives me a saucy wink followed by a hopeful smile.

"Business first, my lovely."

She somewhat sulkily shows me to my room.

When I emerge on to the plaza in the next sector over, I'm no longer a trader: I'm the Chief Perfumer of Aphorai, en route to inspect one of my premium workshops. Today's business is necessary, but since Sephine's death I feel off balance performing the expectations of the position. It's only the barest hint of insecurity, but it chafes until my mood is raw.

Naturally, I abstain from revealing my discomfort upon arriving at my destination. I take pains to greet the various workers, flipping a coin to the powder rats – incense grinders are the lowest paid of all the roles – and two or three coins to those among them I know have young children to feed. It's as likely the silver will end up lining the pockets of a dreamsmoke den owner than a fruit seller's, but that's not my choice to make.

Finally, I reach my office. The solitude is a welcome, if temporary relief. I roll the antique river-reed blinds over the windows that look on to the inner courtyard. Sometimes the semblance of privacy is almost as good as the real thing. As long as one stays cognizant of the difference.

No matter the duration for which I'm detained elsewhere, my servants ensure a plain taper is always burning. Now, I use it to light a flame under an oil steamer, tapping several drops of lemon balm essence into the receptacle. I wash the dust of the street from my hands with violet water then remove the silver circlet holding back my hair and shake it out, combing my fingers through before setting it back in place.

My desk is piled high with parchment. I've been gone longer than usual – I don't venture to the Sanctuary often; it's not the sort of place one goes on a whim. When I am required to make an appearance, I can usually make the trip swifter than the last one when I was … encumbered. Still, whatever orders, would-be supplier tenders and regulator reports that are in that stack can wait.

First thing's first.

I write and seal a small scroll and hand it to the errand boy who stands outside the room. "Take this to Lady Sireth. The new samples she requested are available for inspection at her earliest convenience."

The lad scampers off, and I settle down to the tedious side of the Chief Perfumer of Aphorai's role – administration.

It's several hours and a tray of sweetmeats later that a strident voice rings out over the din of the workshop.

"How many times do I have to tell your employer, I will not be summoned like some *ordinary* consumer. New products shall be delivered to be assessed at *my* leisure." The tone is haughty, cold, the word "ordinary" dragged out long enough that a whole sentence could have been spoken in its place.

Sireth.

Daughter to Malmud, Eraz of Aphorai Province.

Perfume aficionado.

And desperate to become the Aphorain representative on the Council of Five when Prince Nisai finally assumes the throne. And he will, if I have anything to do with it.

I don't trust Sireth. She's far too ambitious to be trusted. But she's smart enough to be useful. Very useful. A kind of knock-off version of someone else I know. Someone for whom I have the utmost respect.

Me.

Sireth and the Chief Perfumer have an understanding that goes back more than a turn now. On the surface, it's all business. Sireth gets to indulge her predilections for the latest and best of all of Aphorai's fragrances, and the cover to venture out from under her father's nose and into the city on "shopping" expeditions whenever she desires.

I, on the other hand, get gossip from the capital – the fashions and fads of the Ekasyans I might otherwise miss when "out of town" – filtered through the Aphorain courtiers, ambassadors, visiting merchant elite. I've been relying on civilian informants, and so had Sephine, since the Emperor refused to appoint another Scent Keeper. It's not perfect. But what truly is, in the clandestine information game?

Sireth enters the room, shrugs off her crimson silk cloak and lets it fall to the floor like a pool of blood. She unceremoniously sweeps a ledger and several scrolls off the divan. The ledger thuds hollowly on the ancient floor tiles, and the scrolls roll away in several directions.

My fingers twitch at the mess. Disorder walks hand-in-hand with danger in my line of work. But I keep my expression bland as Sireth flops down in place of the trappings of bureaucracy.

She looks to an upper corner of the room, as if she's addressing the point at which the limewashed walls meet the reed-woven ceiling. Her nose wrinkles. "Is that lemon balm?"

"Indeed."

"Feeling a little nervy?"

"It's not for my benefit. You were rather ... *shrill* out there."

73

She huffs and dangles a hand languidly over the back of the divan. The other twirls a necklace of winking rubies around bejeweled fingers. "You seem to keep forgetting I'm not one of your employees. One of these days I won't accept your thinly veiled summons. Then where will you be?"

I lean back in my chair and cross my ankles on my desk. "You couldn't stay away if you tried."

This old game. Sireth relishes the performance, and gets petulant if I don't oblige. I've long suspected her true delight derives from how bored it makes me to go through the same asinine motions.

"Any day I could refuse."

"And forego an excuse to escape Daddy Dearest's estate?"

She drops the pretense. "More like any excuse to get out from beneath the slimy gaze of that letch Radreth." It's warm in my office, but she shudders as if cold water had spilled between her shoulders.

"The Ekasyan ambassador is still on the estate? I thought Malmud would have cleared the decks after the … diplomatic incident." It's the understatement of the turn, perhaps the century, referring to the poisoning of one prince and the lockdown of the province capital by another as a mere "incident".

She waves that away. "He's keeping the perfume in the bottle for now at least. Our easterly neighbours are getting tetchy. Seems they're even less impressed with the Second Prince's so-called Regency than we are. But to sever all ties with the capital … that will mean more than a diplomatic incident."

Indeed.

Los Province lies to the east. They've never really trusted the Empire. I suppose I'd also nurse a certain slightedness if half of my territory had been consumed and cursed in the Shadow Wars. The Wastes of Los stretch from the Aphorain border in the west of the province all the way to the Trelian border in the south, robbing the Losians of most of their arable land aside from the thin strip along the coast.

Of all the pre-Imperial kingdoms, Los was by far the strongest. And proudest. It paid the price for both of those traits, though never truly relinquished either. Which is why, given the excuse, it might be the first to shake off the yoke of imperial rule. Founding Accord or no Founding Accord.

"And Ekasya?" I enquire.

She gives me a doe-eyed gaze. "It's approximately four days' ride and then half again on a barge if the weather holds and you have the funds to acquire a decent rowing cr—"

"Sireth," my voice is flat.

She pouts. "You're no fun today. But yes, there has been some interesting news. A rumour, really. But even rumours have a price in times like these." She sits up, reaches an arm tinkling with bracelets to the bundles of test incense on the edge of my desk, and gives one a derisive sniff.

It's a cheap shot, and I don't reward it. "Yesterday or tomorrow, the fee is the same."

She shrugs and lazes back on the divan again. "Seems there's some sort of gambling ring that's sprung up among the courtiers in the capital. I mean, I can't blame them, the Emperor never holds court any more, let alone stages any of his legendary parties – what it would have been to have seen those, don't you think? Anyway, the nobles are bored. Apparently, a few of them have joined in on some racket where they're pitting prisoners against each other in the

75

catacombs beneath Ekasya Mountain. Making wagers on the potential victors."

Prisoner against prisoner? Would such a disgrace truly spring from the minds of the idle rich? Or did they have particular inspiration?

Sireth waves a hand. "It could be flights of fancy. But how am I to know? I'm never getting to the capital at this rate."

"I wouldn't lament that, the heir isn't your type, anyway."

"He *is* a little short, I'll grant you that. But that half-smile of his can be quite disarming."

"You know you're not *his* type either."

"Because I'm his second cousin?"

"Because you're a girl."

"He puts all his ingredients in one perfume?" Her eyes widen in mock innocence. Then they're just as quickly narrowing. "I've been thinking about that, actually. I certainly have no problem with an arrangement that suits us both. Even if I'm appointed to the Council, it's such a temporary position in the grand scheme of things. It could be quite convenient if our families stayed closely linked but we didn't have to—"

"And don't even think about whether you could have a son and get him adopted. You know the line of inheritance can't go to the same province twice in sequence."

"Well…" She goes back to twining her necklace between her fingers. "That older brother of his could be an alternative. He's deliciousness personified."

"Rigid and uptight, too, if his handling of the situation here was anything to go by. And now he's at least in part responsible for the single biggest political upheaval we've witnessed since before the Great Bloom. Is there any connection between him and this gambling ring?"

"I don't know."

I swing my feet down from the desk and sit forward, businesslike.

"Truly," she insists. "I only get snippets, remember? Gossip. Though there is something else you might like."

I raise an eyebrow.

"Rumour has it, one of the prisoners they have fighting is my cousin's old Shield."

"Impossible. All reports said they executed the poor wretch."

She shrugs languidly.

I keep my features impassive. I'm not about to let Sireth know this is the most important piece of information she's given me in the entire duration I've known her. She may think it only a rumour. For me it's of greater value. Corroboration.

"What about your father, what does he make of all of this?"

"He raged and blustered when he found out Nisai was no longer in the capital. Then aunt Shari sent word that he had been healed, and that calmed Father down a little. Still, he'd just as like to go marching to Ekasya demanding answers about the so-called Regency. My cousin is the first hope in over a century for an Aphorain Emperor, and Father wants him on the throne. But with the dahkai plantation gone, the province is poorer than ever. Hardly the time to fund a war."

"You sure he'll sit tight?" I take a long, slow, calming breath.

Lemon balm. It *was* a good choice.

"Aunt Shari will calm him down. She's sent word she's coming home. The Regent has 'temporarily relieved the Council of Five of their duty', whatever that's supposed to mean. I never knew their jobs included vacation time."

A chill goes through me. It means Iddo Kaidon has the audacity – either from arrogance or ignorance – to go against the Founding Accord. Once the Accord is broken, the Empire will begin to crumble. The northern provinces have been on edge for turns, watching for a slight from the capital, waiting for a reason to revolt.

There's only one sure outcome of the Empire fracturing.

War.

If we go down that road, thousands will die. And the Order will have failed in their mission to maintain balance. To preserve peace. *I* would have failed.

I do *not* take failure lightly.

"Hello?" Sireth waves a manicured hand in my line of sight. "You haven't sniffed one too many of your own concoctions, have you?"

I give myself an inward shake. Good informants are hard to find. Sireth has thus far been true, and I've no reason to think she's turned sour with the latest events. I'd trust her dirt as much as the next. But I need to know more. There's no room for speculation. Only certainty.

I rise from my desk.

The action sends a clear message. This meeting is over.

"Don't forget your samples," I remind her as she retrieves her cloak. "I'm sure you'll find they've been packed with the usual care."

And the usual coin in the lining.

She scowls, but it doesn't stop her lightly placing a farewell kiss on my cheek as she passes.

I don't blame Sireth for not having the full story. That doesn't mean I'm any less irritated. I *loathe* going to the capital. That foreboding black-stone monstrosity where half the court thinks bathing once a week and spraying themselves down with perfume the rest of the time is good hygiene.

It seems, however, there's nothing else for it.

If the Shield is alive, I have a duty to the Order to find him.

I cross to the window and throw open the shutters. The temple dominates the Aphorain skyline. The great five-sided stepped pyramid, crumbling at the edges, casts its shadow over the sectors beyond, including the neighbourhoods a Chief Perfumer would never be seen in but which only a few turns ago I frequented. Out there awaits myriad back alleys, the rows of shacks bordering the tanning yards, and most of all the colonies of Afflicted that are growing like one of their ulcerous wounds, the disease seeming more virulent with each passing turn.

There's only one thing more important than the primary tenet – balance is all – of those who follow Asmudtag: *Mercy until maturity.*

The very tenet I've lived by since swearing allegiance to the Order. Find as many children in Aphorai City who were of the right age and didn't go through the naming ceremony at birth. Find them before the Blazers can find them. Bring them to the Scent Keeper. Because it was only Sephine who could salvage them, take away their corruption, lock it away within herself. Ever since the Shadow Wars, magic shouldn't have been in the world.

But "shouldn't" is a pale defence against "is".

The dark magic *is* there, lurking in some and not others. There's always been the superstition. Children who came into this world during the Days of Doskai, the brief time every six turns when there's an occultation in the night sky – Doskai's moon blocking Kaismap's moon from view – all shadows thrown by the Lost God's gaze. I'd watched some of the infants born on those nights, and there was no way to tell which would have it in them and which wouldn't. Sephine had her theories. Most of them revolving around the scent of death. Those who drew their first breath from another human's end. They were the ones who fell under the shadowed god's influence, latent instruments of a war he wished to revisit upon the world. Even if it weren't causation, it was correlation. We found more of them living in poverty than among those who could afford a naming ceremony. More whose first scent would be of ulcerated flesh. The Affliction that promised death.

A theory, Sephine said.

A likely truth, I thought.

But there was one thing that Sephine was adamant about. Magic, light or dark, cannot be destroyed. Only transferred. Absorbed. Until the night she channelled too much.

Mercy until maturity.

How many young ones did I take to Sephine? How many did she treat, giving them sultis and letting them go before they knew anything other than they'd got lost in the back alleys of what was to them a labyrinthine city? They'd return to their families, no longer any more of a danger to them than the next person. No longer fighting themselves.

But now it's not Sephine's words reverberating between my ears, it's my uncle's, who trained me in a much different life skill. *Trust your nose if you want to survive*, he said, right before they finally carried him off for operating the longest-running unregulated dreamsmoke den in Aphorai City.

If I've heard anything of the Prince's Shield, he's beyond the point of saving. That smoke has long gone to the sky. It's tragic, really. The Magister's girl obviously feels genuine care for him. The grief she displayed on the journey to the Sanctuary, the look in her eyes when she recognized the mention of him in the scroll I let her view.

It seems … distasteful. A waste, even.

I almost hope he's not alive.

Because then I won't have to be the one to kill him.

Dawn finds me well rested.

It's a skill; the more intense the situation facing me, the better I'm able to sleep. There's little logic in tossing and turning through the night when you need to be able to rely on your faculties at dawn.

Admittedly, I had help. I'd venture the innkeeper's daughter has a spring in her step this morning, too.

I present myself at the Eraz's estate, ostensibly to find out if our province governor has any last requests before I journey to the capital as his emissary. I'm greeted by a chamberlain, though "intercepted" is perhaps a more accurate term. The man's new, and walks with pole-straight carriage, his nose in the air, slightly wrinkled as if he's stood in something putrid.

When I request an audience with the Eraz, the chamberlain informs me with unconcealed satisfaction that it's far too early for Malmud to grace us with his presence. According to the officious sniffling, even the

Chief Perfumer will have to take their place in line with the others who have already petitioned for an audience today.

I feign disappointment and survey the room, letting my expression sink into increasing pensiveness with each appellant my gaze falls upon. "Alas," I begin, "I was simply after an individual of high enough station to sign off on this shipping notice."

"Shipping notice?"

"Our regular incense consignment destined for the capital. I'd hate it to be late with things … as they have been. One wouldn't want to contribute further ill to relations with the capital. But I'll be sure to let the Eraz know you followed protocol when I finally get to speak with him, you needn't worry."

He beckons me to hand over the manifesto, the movement so jerky it's as if he's attempting one-handed applause.

I comply.

He gives it but a cursory glance and a sniff. "I'll not have my master weighed down with simple logistics." He produces a cylinder seal from his sleeve.

I produce an ink pot with a flourish.

And, by the Primordial's grace, it is done.

If our esteemed Eraz did rise early, I'd have to convince him to give his Chief Perfumer orders to present himself at the Ekasyan court on his behalf. Instead, the new chamberlain will be explaining why Malmud's best barge has been commandeered for a trip he hasn't authorized. An impertinence on my behalf. But if I have to go to the capital, at least I'll be doing it in style. One can only hope everything else about this journey goes as closely to plan.

Outside the estate, my litter awaits. I nod to the bearers as I recline on the cushions. "Eighth gate, lovelies."

They'll take me as far as the south trader camp outside the walls. From there, I've organized an escort fitting for the province Chief Perfumer's overland trek to the river.

There's a commotion before the gate. Throngs have amassed where it would normally be a bustling-but-orderly thoroughfare. I shift my weight, seeking a better view. Camels are piled high with a variety of goods: open-weave sacks of dried rock figs, stacks of tanned animal hides, racks of mismatched vials and jars – run-of-the-mill essential oils and salves – clinking slightly every time the animal bearing it switches its tail against the flies.

Men in white robes with a thin purple trim at the hem wave each beast on, jotting down notes with a charcoal stylus.

Imperial tax collectors.

"Filthy thieves," an Aphorain accent calls.

One of the officials looks up from his notes and down his nose. "These contributions are required for the new imperial army, built by the Regent for the protection of all Aramtesh."

The crowd ignores that, instead starting up a chant: "Thief. Thief. Thief!"

I feel their anger. They've watched their taxes go to enrich the capital when their arable land is nothing on what it was when the tax rates were set, especially after the Great Groundshake moved the river several turns ago. Now the tithe they pay is in motley supplies. The last vestiges before even the previously wealthy can no longer feed themselves. They will watch their children starve. I've had my fair share of malodourous information, though I'm sure the imminent death of one's offspring must be a truly terrible prospect.

And for what? A new martial force? Even if they are not formally educated, these people aren't stupid. They know this does not bode well for their futures.

The chanting crowd closes in around the Emperor's men.

Mobs burn like a krilmair oil fire. Once ignited, there's no hope of controlling the flames.

Whilst I have every sympathy for my fellow Aphorains, I have more important scents to trail. I'm also not particularly enamoured with the idea of witnessing an imperial tax collector torn limb from limb.

I lean over to speak in the lead litter-bearer's ear. "Try the tenth gate. Swiftly, now."

CHAPTER 6

RAKEL

For the best part of a moon, I've walked a loop around the Sanctuary in the early hours, checking that Lil has feed and fresh-raked sand to roll in, giving her a lunge around the stable yard so she doesn't go stir-crazy. Today, as usual, I return via the outer wall so I can watch the sunrise over the grey and white of the mountains, the rose pinks of dawn making the ice-covered peaks blush.

As the air warms, I catch the faint scent of smoke from the kitchen fires, the impossible mix of blooms drifting from the Sanctuary's plantations.

Smoke and flowers. A turn ago, I'd never have thought that combination could make me feel so far from home.

I pace, wondering the same things over again. How we'll find out who put Esarik up to triggering the Prince's poison. When we'll have a breakthrough with the cure for the Rot so we can cure Nisai's father and mine, stop the spread through the Empire, and go back to some semblance of our normal lives.

If there even is a normal after what we've lost.

Who we've lost.

As the sun rises, I light a stick of grief incense. This is my routine now. Letting tendrils of smoke drift with my thoughts of what could have been. The one time of day I don't try to stop myself thinking of Ash.

The Sanctuary begins to wake. The light coaxes the purrath tree blossoms open, and fat fuzzy bees appear to seek the sticky pollen. No wonder there are so many hives dotted around the terraces.

A figure emerges from the door to the halls of living quarters. Nisai has taken to retrieving a handful of scrolls from the archive and studying them on the balcony ringing the Sanctuary. He waves away the green-robed Order member trailing after him. I've heard the Prince rant several times about the "shambolic state" of the archives. I guess he's not loving being babysat by people he thinks can't even keep scrolls in the right order.

It's probably a good thing the archives are a mess. Being out in the fresh air can't hurt Nisai's long-term recovery from the poison and the moons he spent indoors, unmoving.

Remembering the poisoning brings up more thoughts of Ash. Of his sacrifice. It wrenches at me, but I try to remember that it wasn't for nothing. The last of the incense smoke curls into the air. I send another prayer to Azered with it, that if our souls do linger after our bodies are gone, that Ash is at peace knowing Nisai is safe.

It still feels strange, praying after not having done so since childhood, like a new pair of boots that is taking for ever to wear in.

For what do I know of the gods? Until Ash transformed in the throne room of the palace in Ekasya, and then when I saw the darkness first swirl around Nisai when I gave him the true cure for the poison, I hadn't believed in magic, let alone any supernatural sky friends. Because if I let myself believe in something like that, I also had to believe they'd turned their backs on me. And then I'd have to ask why. It was never a question I wanted to waste time on. Never a question I truly wanted answered.

I huff an audible breath and start down the stone steps.

With the Prince in clear sight, Barden and Kip pass the time sparring further around the balcony. Sometimes they'll fight with weapons, but more often than not Kip teaches him *lo daiyish*, the barehanded combat of the Los Provincial Army. Barden's a quick study, but he's still only able to pin the tall Losian once every tenth bout or so. And even then I wonder if she's letting him get the upper hand.

Not today.

Barden lunges, but Kip ducks under him. Quick as a sniff, she's twisted behind and has him face down on the flagstones, his arm pulled so far up behind him he grunts in pain.

"Yield," he manages. "I yield."

Kip stands, shaking her head in apparent disgust. "Riker's rod, how many times do I have to say it? Brute force lands you in more trouble than it dodges. A rigid posture is a vulnerable posture. Easier to break." She extends an arm corded with wiry strength and helps him up. "Think about trees. Those with supple branches survive the storm."

Barden waves his arms around in a terrible imitation of a rock fig blowing in the wind. "Stay bendy. Got it."

Kip shakes her head again, though this time it's accompanied with a low, throaty chuckle. Seems Barden's charm can even get through her defences.

They square off for another round and I approach Nisai. We exchange a formal nod – bowing never got past the awkward stage for me, and Nisai didn't remark on it when I stopped trying. I plop down on the last of the steps next to him.

He gives me one of his lopsided smiles. "Come for the show?"

"To see you, actually." I gesture to his crutches. "Any better?"

"I still can't bear my own weight for long stretches without them, if that's what you're asking."

Hmm. I would have thought he'd be getting more strength back in his legs by now if he was ever going to use them unaided again. But surviving an ancient magical poison like blackvein is no ordinary injury. It's not like it can be compared to a sprain or a break.

"I'm experiencing fewer cramps in the night, which is a blessing at least."

Experiencing. Trust Nisai to soften his own suffering for those around him. I've heard the stifled moans of pain drifting down the hall in the quiet of the dark hours.

"Let me know if you need any more slumber tea. The more sleep you get, the quicker you'll mend."

"I'm beginning to wonder if I've done all the healing I ever will."

He pinches his nose between thumb and forefinger.

"Still getting the headaches?"

"It's not so much the discomfort that plagues me." He lifts his other hand from the scroll and it slowly curls back in on itself. "It's just … hard to concentrate. Things aren't taking root in my mind as easily as before. If you had told me a turn ago I'd have the chance to study even *one* of the ancient scrolls in the Order's collection, I'd have been ecstatic, ready to bridge as many gaps in our knowledge of the Shadow Wars as possible, and of the subsequent centuries until the Empire's founding. But now, the only gaps seem to be in my memory. I read something, and it's gone the next day. Not even the faintest scent left behind."

He looks directly at me then, and his dark eyes shine with barely contained sorrow. "Sometimes I think my mind is even making things up. It thinks I read a scroll one day, and the next, it's vanished from the shelves. Like it didn't exist."

"Maybe someone just moved it? It's not like they're great at keeping house."

"Perhaps. But that doesn't explain how the scrolls I know I did read…" He twirls his fingers in the air in the gesture for smoke. "Gone."

"Try not to be so hard on yourself. Time can be a great healer." I get to my feet. "Though I'd better get to work before you-know-who sends someone looking for me."

✳

The Magister was true to her word.

For the first time, I have something I've coveted for as long as I can remember – a full, imperial-standard apparatus. It takes up a third of the bench that runs along one of the walls in the Sanctuary laboratories. All the benches run beneath windows looking out on to the terraced gardens at the heart of the complex. Partly for inspiration, but more importantly so any dangerous experiments can be ventilated at short notice.

The Magister has been setting me small tasks each day, their difficulty steadily increasing until she's satisfied I won't waste a single sniff of the most precious of all our supplies: dahkai. It feels like she's running me through my paces in the same way Father checks the fitness of a horse he's training. Maybe such a methodical bent was common ground for them.

"What do you know of scentlore?" she asked at the beginning. "How much did Sephine teach you?"

I shrugged, trying not to be distracted by one of the other Order members who had a flask of purple liquid at such a rapid boil it looked in danger of overflowing. "Essence of nothing mixed with an alembic of thin air. I wasn't in her service long. She tended to keep my hands full of vessels needing to be scrubbed, and her laboratory locked."

The Magister closed her eyes and sucked a breath between her teeth. Seems there's a whole lot of frustration bubbling under the surface when it comes to her and Sephine. Or maybe it's just barely contained impatience – the sense of urgency among her and the handful of other Order members I've seen her converse with over research notes and vials is as pungent as eucalyptus oil.

"Perhaps best we start with principles, then." She gave a flask full of blue-green liquid a swirl. "Scentlore, in its overarching, collective form, is a mix of empirical botany and a little alchemy, which is made possible from the remnants of magic that the gods left behind when they departed the mortal realm. That's the most logical place to start."

"The gods?" About as far as you can get from logic, if you ask me.

"Yes. Tell me what you know of them."

The blood felt like it was draining from my face. If this was a test, I was going to fail it. Memories of the perfume trials back in Aphorai City flashed through my mind. I couldn't afford for this to go that way. I still don't know how much of her heart the Magister left behind when she left Father and me. But I know my own heart. I've spent turns wishing it might be possible to cure Father, and here was my chance.

The Magister watched me closely. "Be honest. I simply need to be aware of what knowledge you lack."

I breathed a little easier at the reassurance. "I know that Asmudtag was the first. The Primordial. That according to what the temple teaches, Asmudtag had six children, though they always count the twins Zir and Tro as one, so five, really."

She raised enquiring eyebrows.

"And there's also the Lost God, but that isn't in the temple teachings."

"I asked what you know, not which beliefs you've heard that the temple sanctions. What else?" she asked, placing the flask of blue-green liquid into a shallow pot of water and lighting a flame beneath.

"That … centuries and centuries ago, the Younger Gods are supposed to have walked the land among mortals. Now the temple prescribes a set of specific scents to supposedly reach their home in the sky if you want your prayers to be heard."

She nodded approval. "Sacred scents are indeed crucial to prayers. Not only to capture the attention of the gods, but to sustain them."

"Sustain? Are you saying prayers are like food?"

"A somewhat abstract analogy, but yes."

Until these past few moons, I didn't even believe the gods existed, so I just thought the different values on prayer scents was a way for the temple to squeeze more zigs out of believers. Rich people always thought they had the upper hand with the divine realm, at least that's the way they act.

At the thought, a chill passed through me. What if the rich really did have some sort of extra advantage when they sent their prayers to the sky? What if wearing dahkai perfume really does offer more than luck and makes doors open to a better future foreseen by Kaismap? If you're literally helping keep a god alive, what kind of favours would your magic sky friend do for you?

If it's true, that would explain so much.

"And your knowledge of sacred scents?" she asked.

I gave myself an inward shake. "Zir and Tro are all about the waterways and, ah, new life."

The blood returned to my cheeks in a blush. "Sex" is for sure not the kind of topic anyone wants to talk to their elders about in detail. Especially a parent.

"They favour waterlilies and the kigtai blossom that grows beside mountain streams," I continued. "But then they're also into violets and calamus, too. Guess twins get double the choices. And Esiku is the goddess of growth." She's also the mother goddess, but that's not something I wanted to put between me and the Magister right then. "She's into trees, apparently. Likes her sandalwood and cedar." My voice hitched on the last word, so I hurry on. "Amber, too. The resin sort."

Cedar only make me think of Ash. How I used the essence to clear my mind, to keep me grounded, until I used it to oil his armour the night I watched over him after treating his wounds from the lion hunt. After that, he took to using it himself. Now I'll always associate it with his loss. I've not thrown my personal supply out, but I don't breathe it in public any more. Tears still follow.

"Riker is into fresh things. Mint. Orange. Bergamot. They say the god of youth always lives in the now. And Azered is timeless. Labdanum. Thyme. Associated with the soul's journey from this life to the next." Truth be told, I never used to think about having a soul, let alone needing to have it guided to the sky. Surely you'd just go "up" until you arrive at your destination. Unless you're destined for one of the hells, of course.

"Very good. And Kaismap?"

"God of foresight. Dahkai is reserved for the most important prayers, but most people have to settle for purrath blossom as a substitute."

She nodded. "Indeed. And though that is the crux of the temple's programme for the everyday person, here, we operate outside of that paradigm."

"Like the Scent Keepers."

"The Scent Keepers are elected from within our ranks. They play a pivotal role in our efforts to maintain balance across the Empire, mitigating between the temple and the sources of secular power – the Emperor together with each province's Eraz. When the Younger Gods left the world, it was indeed part of a sacred covenant to ensure we never saw destruction again on the scale of the Shadow Wars. At the same time, Asmudtag granted the Scent Keepers a boon of their own."

She used a pair of long, patina-stained tongs to remove the flask from the heat and hold it up to the candlelight. The liquid had turned from bright blue-green to almost black. A sickly-sweet aroma of too-ripe fruit wafted towards me. I knew that smell. I used it to heal Nisai of the last of the poison.

"That's…"

"The elixir of the Scent Keepers. It allows a limited kind of alchemy. Channelling the will of Asmudtag to move or absorb or alter a particular substance or energy, but never to destroy it. The first Asmudtagians, earnest to ensure peace across the Empire, sought a way to see into the future to avoid another devastating war. They believed the answer was in dahkai, that the flower would hold a remnant of the god Kaismap's foresight. But when the Order used the Asmudtagian elixir to try to harness the plant's properties, the will of Asmudtag sought balance. Instead of gaining scrying powers, it granted the ability to see the future in another way."

I thought back to Sephine, the only Scent Keeper I'd seen before arriving at the Sanctuary. And during that time, she never seemed to age. Back at the Library of the Lost, the Chronicler had spoken about this. "It made them long lived."

"Very good. Unfortunately, it also had another consequence. One that would balance out the turns of life the users of the elixir would now have. It would take lives from others. It's how Sephine and I came to be convinced dahkai was key to our research."

"I don't see the connection?" But my stomach began to feel more and more unsettled. I swallow, tasting acid.

"We believe it was the Order's folly, its hubris, that brought the Affliction into being. Asmudtag is balance. Asmudtag is all, light *and* dark. Without the consequence, the covenant of the Younger Gods would have been broken."

"You mean… The Order *created* the Rot?"

"Yes," she said simply.

I leaned over the bench and opened the window, desperate for some fresh air. Out on the balcony overlooking the inner core of the Sanctuary, two patients from the next sector were sat at a carved stone table, a shnik-shnik board between them. They were talking, smiling as they moved the pieces around, and yet one cradled a bandaged arm, the other stretched out a footless leg in the sun. All because this so-called Order wanted to play games with the gods.

"You paint yourself as all holy and high, the answer to the prayers of the poor and weak, and you created something that is killing thousands of people. You're … you're the worst of them."

"It didn't kill thousands to start with." Her tone was patronizing, like explaining something as obvious as scat stinking. Then she sighed and rubbed the spot between her eyebrows. "The Affliction is a result of an inadvertent failing of the Order, yes. But it wasn't me personally who brought the contagion into being. I was not alive then. I was not the catalyst. I have, however, dedicated my life towards a solution. You know this better than anyone. You know what we gave up to be here."

We. She thinks of her and me as *we* now. Could I ever believe that's true? Maybe a small part of me already does, however much the rest of me screams denial.

"I tell you this because you'll begin working with dahkai soon. It would be a futile waste of your abilities for you not to have all of the information. Very few who aren't ordained have been entrusted with this knowledge in the past. Very few indeed. But I trust you."

I suddenly felt the weight of the conversation. It was heavy, but the heft was somehow gratifying. Like lugging a full harvest of citrus fruit, knowing that with careful treatment and handling, it could lead to some of the finest essential oil.

"I'd ask you to keep this knowledge to yourself, my daughter."

I narrowed my eyes. "You're ashamed."

"I am, in that I'm part of something that had such a damning mark on history. That's not why I make this request of you. I ask because circumstances are incredibly precarious at this juncture. All the reports I've had of the Prince have only enhanced my respect for him. He is the leader on which we pit our hope for a better tomorrow."

"Then what's the problem?"

"The Prince is also human. It's his humanity that is one of his greatest strengths. But it can also be a weakness in relation to one aspect of his life."

I finally caught a whiff of her meaning. Nisai's father was struck down with the Rot just as my father had been. He could just afford better care from the start, from the finest Physicians. "The Emperor."

"Indeed."

"Nisai's a student of ancient history. Wouldn't he already know about this?"

"The secret is closely guarded. And has never been committed to ink."

"But surely if it was *centuries* ago—"

"You found the facts confronting, did you not? As for the Prince, even the most reasonable person in the world would struggle with the knowledge that the very people he has sought safety with are the reason he needs safety in the first place. If his father had never become Afflicted, he'd have had a very different life. And even if he is able to accept that we are not our ancestors, we are not even our parents" – she gave me a rueful smile at that – "I would not want to do anything to impede his recovery. This revelation would only cause him stress and confusion."

Uncertainty roiled in my guts. Nisai would want to know about this. Just as I would want to know. I'd like to think it wouldn't change anything about what we're doing here. But there are so many moving pieces. Every day seems to uncover a new secret, and if there's anything I've learned since the perfume trials in Aphorai City, it's that I'm only ever getting the barest whiff of what's going on behind the scenes.

Sometimes the only way to truly know which way smoke will blow is to light the incense. Only once you do, there's no taking it back. I've had my fill of secrets, but I've also had my fair share of trouble from opening my mouth before I've realized what I'm talking my way into.

"I'll do as you ask," I told her.

At least for now.

✳

I stare at the vial in my hand.

Unlike the bejewelled or finely cut crystal I've seen before, this one is plain. Utilitarian. It's hard to believe it contains the same substance. But it doesn't make it any less precious.

Dahkai.

I once thought I might rise through the ranks in the Eraz's perfumery back in Aphorai to the point where my work would involve the so-called darkest bloom. It's no longer just a perfume for rich people or those who believe in the gods and want to send a special prayer to Kaismap, thinking they'll see the future. Now it's the key to so many people's lives. To Father's life. I never imagined I'd be here, doing experiments that might stand a chance of curing the Rot.

My hands shake as I work out the tiny stopper. I pause, willing my breathing to evenness. There's no room for clumsy mistakes here. This work is far more precise and fiddly than anything I've ever tried before. It requires a deft touch.

I take a hollow copper tube, thin as a newly sprouted reed, from the rack and thread it into the vial just until it touches the surface of the liquid. Clamping my thumb over the other end traps a single drop. I transfer it carefully to the repository of the distillation apparatus and close off the pipes. It will mix with the other carefully measured ingredients as they steam. Now it's simply a waiting game while the flame heats the vessel.

And at the end … something to test.

"Any progress?"

I startle at the Magister's voice behind me. The copper tube drops to the floor with an almost musical series of hollow notes. My cheeks burn. The last thing I want her to think me is bumbling – unworthy of working with such a rare ingredient.

As her footsteps approach, I retrieve the tube and place it in the pile of used ones to be cleansed. Then I make a show of taking down the latest steps in the journal I've been provided. My daily lessons with Nisai mean I'm slowly getting the habit of making the ink form letters, even if my notes are still more shopping list than explanation, sometimes with little sketches in place of the words I don't yet know.

"May I?" She asks, gesturing to the notebook.

I step aside.

"Mmhmm," she utters as she reads.

I hope it's a noise of approval.

"Ah."

There it is. The snag.

She straightens. "I'm afraid we've already tried introducing a fixative with each distillation. It didn't have a noticeable effect compared with omitting it."

"You mean it's wasted?" I look meaningfully at the still where the steam from the formula I'd painstakingly prepared is beginning to condense and drip into the receiving flask.

She smiles, but it's a brittle kind of smile. "It was good thinking. I can see why you'd pursue it."

A strange concoction of guilt and frustration simmers at my core, rising like the steam that is now useless. Can't she just get angry? It'd be easier to deal with anger than … disappointment.

She passes my notebook back along the bench. "The ingredients may be lost. But it's an important lesson for the future – we should make sure to discuss the approach you're going to take before committing supplies to it. After all, it wouldn't be efficient for me to expect you to scour my notes at this stage."

I feel my face flushing again. *At this stage.* A polite way of saying, "You've got talent, but your skills aren't yet up to snuff … and while you're at it, learn to read *properly*."

"Perhaps for now, you should stick to making salve. We need to ensure there's enough to keep the Affliction from progressing further in the resident patients. It's an important task – it will free me up to push forward with the more experimental work."

The message is clear – if we were in a perfumery, I'd be demoted to being a powder rat, grinding ingredients for incense and nothing more.

She gives me another smile, this one more encouraging, and heads for the door.

I return to the bench, removing the flame from the distillation apparatus to begin the cooling process. Being ordered back to making salves almost feels like being sent back to my village.

I swallow down the sting of it. The quicker I can make the current standard treatment, the quicker I can rejoin the work towards a cure, and the quicker I can get it to Father.

The cure would give Nisai choices, too. If the Emperor was healed, he could resume the throne. Sort out what's going on in the capital with the Regent and whatnot. The Hidden Prince might not have to remain hidden any longer.

I take down a clean measuring flask from the rack.

Lives and empires turn on what happens in this very lab.

There's no time for pride.

CHAPTER 7

ASH

When the sleep is as deep as death's embrace, it's a long, clawing journey to consciousness.

I find myself lying on my back, the stone warm and clammy beneath me. Judging by the way I feel, the latest fight in the underground arena wasn't a dream. Someone or some*ones* – I expect a couple of Zostar's brutes not involved in the show – must have dragged me back to my cell. I test each limb gingerly. Nothing is broken, no wounds beyond the superficial. Bruises, scrapes, aching muscles.

I need a plan. Del, Lark and the others are relying on me. I have to help them escape just as much as I have to warn Rakel and Nisai. And Ami is here, too. If she lived. I've tried to keep track of how much time has passed since I saw her, but I can't be certain. Nothing in the darkness is certain.

How in Kaismap's far-seeing name am I going to get us all out of here?

Not sprawled on my back, *that's* at least for certain. I groan and sit up.

"Del," I murmur through the wall.

"Ash? You're awake! Thank the Blessed Twins." He's whispering, but the fervency in his words rings clear. I imagine he is making the sign of Zir and Tro on each shoulder. He may have been left for dead by his family down here, but his Hagmiri heritage has not left him. Once again I feel a pang of sadness. He doesn't deserve this. None of them deserve this.

"Are you whole, Ash?"

A harsh, low laugh escapes my lips. Whole. What a foreign concept. "I'm well enough," I tell the boy. "How long has it been since they returned me?"

"Five bowls of sludge and a change of the stench bucket."

Sludge. Wooden trays splattered with a ladle of thin barley porridge. A dry husk of Ekasyan bread if we're lucky. I never thought it would become something I despise. But if Del has seen what passes for a meal in here five times, it's been days since the arena. Only Kaismap knows the atrocities Zostar and his lackeys have committed since.

"Did they take you? Do anything to you?"

"No. Some of the others, though."

"Larkai?"

"She's here. They didn't take any of the young ones. Just those about my age. A couple didn't make it back. But the whispers said an Edurshain girl on the next corridor made a blade from her spoon and put down two of them when they tried to take her. Two grown men, Ash, can you believe it? I've never met anyone from Edurshai before. Are they a warrior people?"

Other than the ambassador to the Imperial court, I'd never met any Edurshain before Rakel and I travelled into their lands. I involuntarily rub my arm, where a dart pierced the skin as a parting gift from the young tuldah herder without whom we couldn't have saved Nisai.

"What's the girl's name?"

There's a scrabble in the next cell and a whisper I don't catch as Del confers over at the opposite cell wall. Then he's back at the gap in the mortar. "Mish. Her name's Mish."

Mish?

"Lark speaks of her like she's her new hero," Del continues, a little awe creeping into his words. "I get it, too, especially after she managed to find out on the whisper trail where your friend is being kept."

Edurshai is so sparsely populated that it wouldn't be a flight of fancy for it to be the Elelsmish who helped our search for the ingredients for Nisai's cure.

And if it is her…

I shake my head. Oh, Mish. I really should have tried to persuade her to stay with her people, even though she did seem like she was already on the outside. *Off to seek her fortune,* she said. Is this gods-forsaken place where she ended up? I add her to my mental list of those held here. In their freedom, I'll perhaps find some small measure of atonement.

"What about me?" I ask. "While I was out? No other tests?"

"A few came and bled you. I couldn't catch everything they said, but they think your blood is … different to ours. Magic or something."

I run my hand over my wrists. My fingertips find the scabs of several tiny incisions, some new, some almost fully healed.

"Magic belongs with our—"

"Shadows," Del finishes grimly.

The scuff of sandalled feet approach my cell. I shift to sit cross-legged and face the bars running along the front. Just in time.

"Please record that after four days since the incident, the subject has regained consciousness."

The owner of the imperious voice paces slowly in front of the bars, hands interlaced behind his back, his plain black robe dragging through the filth of the dungeon floor.

Zostar.

On the other side of the hall, as if he's determined to keep the furthest he possibly can from me, a younger physician scrawls notes on a hand slate. Next to him sits a small cage containing a bright orange bird, its head tucked under its wing, asleep.

"Please also note that the subject appears disorientated, perhaps suffering from mild delusions, evidenced by talking to himself."

"I was praying." The last thing I want is for this fiend to realize I've a way to communicate with Del and the others.

"Indulge me. What does a Child of Doskai pray for, if not to master the gift from his god?"

I taste bile. *"Magic belongs with our shadows. Behind us."*

"I've never truly fathomed why so many cling to that platitude, as if it offers protection. Weak minds, perhaps." He produces his white kerchief and mops sweat from his brow, the heat of the dungeons no place for his head-to-toe rough-spun wool. "The only safety in this world," he continues, "is derived from knowledge of how to defend one's position. Magic brings strength. We're on the verge of realizing your full potential. I personally will be overseeing the next phase. Others in your position would be grateful."

"The only thing I'd be gratified by is your end."

"You're sounding as myopic as my former colleagues," he says, clucking his tongue as if talking to a child. "I expect now they see the heights I've ascended, they're regretting not valuing my work. I wouldn't have asked for much once I'd made my breakthrough," he mutters. Though now he's speaking into the air in front of him, as if addressing someone who isn't even here.

The hair on the backs of my arms rises.

"An invited lecture," he continues with his invisible conversant. "In the grand university hall. A soiree hosted by the rector. Perhaps a building named in my honour." He shakes his head, then heaves a melodramatic sigh. "Indeed! Hardly indulgent when the magnitude of setting us once again on the path to progress is taken into account."

He pivots and starts back towards the bars, eyes agleam in the torchlight. "You could be a part of a brave new future. You are a beneficiary of Doskai's divine generosity. He would not have his Children wait for some imagined afterlife in the heavens. He would make you divine here in the mortal realm. Impervious to injury. Resistant to disease. Free of fear. And I am not too proud to admit it would be far superior to have you as a willing participant in my research."

It's you, Ash. The final ingredient is you. I believe you're the key.

Rakel was right about whatever was needed to heal Nisai. Now it seems Zostar thinks I'm the key to something far more terrible.

"And if I was to participate willingly?"

He perks up at that, stepping closer still.

Just a little more. I only need reach your throat, old man.

"Assist me to unlock the same potential in others that you've demonstrated, and I will see that your librarian friend remains unharmed. Assist me well enough, and she may even go free. Who knows, perhaps I might feel so obliged that I would make a case to the Regent for your own release, should you agree to serve our cause.

"But you must decide soon. My research progresses, and should I discover what I need without your help, the offer shall be withdrawn. After all, you've never been an ideal specimen. And the new regime has no tolerance for recalcitrants."

Rakel's words echo in my memories. *Honour can go broil in shit and sulphur.* When she thought I would sacrifice myself for Nisai's honour, she'd snapped. Any kind of alliance with Black Robes is anathema to everything I stand for. But in the dungeons, honour won't bring me any closer to finding a way out of here.

Teeth clenched, I nod.

Zostar's gaze fixes on seemingly nothing again. Coming back to himself, he gestures to his assistant. "Please note that the subject has turned a corner in his relations with the programme. He will resume testing willingly."

Another black-robed figure sprints down the dungeon hall, skidding to a halt, breathless. "My lord." He addresses Zostar, even though the physician never carried a noble title before. "We're under attack! In the next branch. Smells of blackpowder. Everyone choking." The young man is bent over, hands on his thighs, each sentence barely making it out between wheezes.

"Attack?" Zostar clucks his tongue. "Don't be so foolish. It will simply be a buildup of fumes from the hot springs. Close off that wing and open the vent shaft."

"But my lord, if you don't—"

"Pass the order. Close off the wing. There will be much greater casualties if we do not."

I've known physicians to cut off a hand or foot to try to save a patient. I can't decide if Zostar's order is humane or heinous. Perhaps both.

"No, my lord—"

"No? *No?*" With strength that uncannily belies his age, Zostar grabs the messenger by the throat and slams him against the wall. "Perhaps you'd like to join them? That can be arranged."

The younger man sinks to the floor. If his eyes were wide before, now they're round with terror. "Please, my lord." He points to the cage at the third physician's feet. The bright-feathered bird is now on its side, legs stiff and straight. Still.

"Move," Zostar barks. "Now." He launches into a shuffling run, the messenger scrambling after him. The receding slaps of sandalled feet against the rough-hewn rock are almost farcical.

The younger physician's expression shifts to disbelief as he watches them go.

"Hadn't you better run along after *Lord* Zostar?"

He slumps aginst the bars of my cell. "They're dying in there. Asphyxiating." His tone is strangely distant. "Our work was meant to help people. So they could be like you. No Affliction. No succumbing to a festering wound."

He's in shock, but this is not the moment or place I want to engage in a philosophical conversation.

"I wanted to help people," he repeats. "That's why I wanted to be a physician. And now…" He gazes up the hall and then back to me with the haunted look of a person who has just realized what they've become.

I seize the opportunity, my hand darting out through the bars and closing around his wrist. "You can help them now. Give me your keys."

He shakes his head. "I can't. Lord Zostar, he'll—"

I yank his arm into my cell. He stumbles against the bars. Off balance, he struggles, but it's the pitiful flailing of the weakest animal in the herd. I can feel my strength returning, coursing darkly through my veins as one hand keeps him pinned in place and the other reaches for the ring of keys hanging at his rope belt.

I drop my prize on my cell floor and reach up with the other hand, cracking the physician's head against the bars.

He slides to the dungeon floor. He'll have a headache when he wakes.

If he ever does.

Perhaps a past version of myself would have felt pity.

I am no longer that person.

❋

I break out Del first, then Mish.

The pale-faced girl regards me solemnly, her silver-blonde hair shining in the torchlight despite the filth. "Greetings, Ashradinoran. It is so very good to see you, but we should make haste."

She's not wrong.

I curse when I find Lark isn't in her cell. Zostar's men must have taken her for tests, which means she could be on another floor entirely. I dearly hope it wasn't the one with the choking fumes.

While I scout ahead, Del works on freeing as many others along the way as he can, until there's a half score following me along the dark stone tunnel. Next, we set out to locate Ami.

I lose count of corridors we hurry through, but only after I lose count of the cells we pass. There must be dozens, possibly even hundreds. How many of them are here only to serve Zostar's whims? It tears at my heart that I won't be able to free each and every one.

When we find Ami, she gives me a quick, fierce hug. I press my fingers to my lips and she nods, falling in with Del and the rest.

Several times I peer around a corner just in time to retreat into a doorway as one of Zostar's black-robed figures rush by. The noxious fumes the young physician reported have the Blazers and the physicians scurrying like ants in a kicked nest.

We make it to a set of stairs. A pair of guards man the entrance to the next level up. I clench my jaw in frustration. We can't double back. We still haven't found Lark, but going lower just takes us further from freedom, and closer to the fumes taking down Zostar's men. I motion for the others to wait.

Then I gather myself, coiling my strength before rushing up the last stairs and into the hall.

The first guard's nose crunches under the heel of my hand before he's so much as blinked. The second moves for his weapon but doesn't unsheathe it before a blow to the stomach knocks the wind out of him and an elbow to the temple sends him slumping to the floor.

This level is more neatly hewn from the rock and better lit. It's also almost eerily quiet. But what's most disturbing is the group of courtiers who pass by when I return to fetch the others, chatting animatedly on the way to the underground arena.

How many of us are being pitted to fight? Even the youngest ones?

When the courtiers are gone, we keep moving.

Ahead, there's a muttered curse and a rhythmic clank. I press up against the wall and ease my head around the corner. Two Blazers stand behind an iron grate, one working a lever that winches it open. The grates were installed as a series of defenses in case Ekasya Mountain was ever invaded from the slopes below. To my knowledge, it never has been.

The barest of breezes brushes by my cheek. That corridor must lead to the outside.

Then the pair are coming through and straight towards the junction where we wait.

Which branch will they take? Straight. Or around the corner. It's a half and half chance and everything rests on their choice. All I can think is that it would make sense for them to continue straight on – I've no idea what is up there but the lights are spaced more regularly that way, and we've passed nothing but empty cells for the past few turns. I mouth a prayer that I'm right. Though who knows if any of the gods would ever again listen to the likes of me. If they ever did.

"Back," I whisper. We retreat three, four paces down the tunnel branch.

The footsteps come nearer.

Then they're past us, their voices retreating. I dare to move my head out enough to see the way they went, just in time to see their backs disappear around the next junction. I allow myself a slow, controlled exhale.

"This way." I motion for the others to follow.

We round the corner and pad closer to the gate.

"You there!"

Two more Blazers, silent until now, step out of the gloom.

"Stay here," I tell the others.

Stooping my shoulders, I affect a limp and slope towards the men, hands out in front of me, like I used to when I was very young and found myself on the streets of the slums.

The men exchange confused glances. The last thing they expect is a would-be escapee approaching them in supplication.

Their hesitation opens the crucial moment for me to lash out for the one on the right's throat, sending him staggering back, fingers scrabbling at his neck like he could claw back his breath. The knife that was in his belt is now in my hand.

A heartbeat later, the pair we evaded earlier come pounding towards us.

And in the close quarters, everything turns to chaos.

Mish and Del have retreated towards the cover of the offshoot corridor, herding the other children back with them. Smart. Ami is edging towards the gateway, no doubt feeling the pull of potential freedom.

"Keep behind me," I bark at her, but it's too late. There's a Blazer between me and her now.

I tackle the second last of them, my shoulder slamming into his abdomen. I'm rewarded with a pained grunt. The world tilts, and we go down in a tangle.

Something gives way beneath me and for a heartbeat I think I've broken one of his bones. Then the gate begins to lower, one ratchet-notch at a time. *Azered's breath*. He must have landed on the mechanism.

The gate lurches down another peg.

Clank.

My palm is slick with sweat. I tighten my grip on the knife and rear back enough to find space for the blade between the Blazer's ribs. One teeth-gritted thrust and the point finds his heart. He stiffens. A gurgling cough sprays blood across my cheek. Then he slumps for the last time.

Clank.

Ami is on the other side of the gate, backing away from the last Blazer. I lurch under the descending iron bars and with a sweeping kick knock his feet out from under him. I aim a knee at this throat, seeking to crush his windpipe.

He rolls free and on to his haunches, springing at me. The crash of his full weight sends me staggering. We drop to the floor, wrestling, all fury and survival instinct.

Hands find my temples. If he gets a good grip, those arms are strong enough to snap my neck. Instead of trying to twist free, I counter with a blow of my forehead to his nose. He grunts and flings his weight to the side, so that we're both grappling to gain the dominant position.

Clank.

He wins. He's on top, hands at my throat. I claw at his face, thumbs seeking vulnerable eye sockets. It's enough for me to throw him off balance and regain the upper position. We're under the gate now, so that I'm trying to keep my opponent pinned while avoiding the iron spikes.

He gets a knee up, winding me, and I collapse to the other side just as the grate slips on the last of its winch and comes crashing down with sound that's half booming clang, half sickening crunch. The Blazer lies pinned to the floor, twitching. Blood oozes from his perforated torso and the corner of his mouth. An iron spike meets the stone floor a mere inch from my face.

I get to my knees, sides still heaving with effort. Even if nobody heard my struggle with the Blazers, this latest noise is loud enough to alert half the dungeon.

We won't be alone for long.

Ami has her hand clapped over her mouth, her eyes wide. She may have read about brutal battles for turns in the Imperial Library, but none of that has prepared her for the stink of fear, sweat and blood, the finality of seeing another being's life depart them. Thank the gods she fainted in the arena.

But I can't afford her losing her faculties. Not now. I edge towards her, holding out my hands like I'm approaching a skittish animal. "It's over. Breathe. Take a deep breath in, count to five as you let it go."

She gulps air, but manages to let it go more slowly with each breath.

"Better?"

She gives me a tight little nod and hugs her arms around herself.

I turn back to the grate. Relief washes through me as Del and Mish creep back out into the light. They're unharmed.

But they're now on the wrong side of the grate. I wrap hands bruised from the fight around the lower bars, brace my weight, and heave.

"Give me an assist with this?" Del and Mish take up mirrored position on the other side of the grate and we try again. Even with the three of us, it doesn't budge.

"There." Ami points to a lever on the other side of the grate. "That mechanism will open it."

Del grabs the iron handle and gives it a tug. Just like the grate, it doesn't budge.

"Move over, I'll help you." Mish bends down, wrapping her hands above his. But still, nothing. Del falls back, breathing heavily from the effort. "It's jammed."

"Try again. Bend your knees. Lift with your legs, not your arms."

The pair do as I say. Del looking to Mish. "On three?"

She gives a tight, determined nod.

He counts down and they lift again, groaning with the strain. Nothing. Not an inch.

The mechanism must have become jammed in the fall. I pace back and forth across the corridor. If only I could reach the lever through the bars. Perhaps it's just not yielding to two young bodies weakened from moons in the darkness with nothing but gruel. Or maybe if we had something to tie around it to get leverage. A rope made of our smocks? The tattered fabric would never hold up under that strain. Or would it?

Mish rises to her feet. "I came to seek my fortune. Alas, it is not what I imagined. In the tales that will one day be told of the dark happenings here, my name shall be on the side of light. That is my fortune now."

I'd think she was being overwrought if I didn't know flowery speech was part of her upbringing. "Mish, I'm sorry."

"Don't be. Heroes are forged in the flames of adversity. This is my fire."

"I'll help her," Del says. "We'll find Lark, too. You should go. We'll cover for you."

He's so earnest. After only whispered conversations through a cell wall, he's willing to sacrifice himself to save another.

Not on my watch.

"I won't leave without you. Either of you. And the others. I promised we'd all get out, and we will."

Mish shakes her head in the gloom, her hands wrapped around the bars of the grate. "The younger ones need someone to take care of them. Del and I will stay. But if you go, you can do something about this. You truly believe the First Prince is alive? Seek him out. All the tales I ever heard of him said he had a true heart. Go. Go now. Find him. Then return for us."

Footsteps, heavy and purposeful, echo from somewhere in a distant corridor.

I wish there was something else I could do. But if I stay, I know I'll never get another chance to escape.

Men's shouts echo through the tunnels, angry and alarmed.

"I'll get you out of here," I vow, voice thick.

"I believe you. Only not this night." Mish gives me a solemn nod and then turns back down the tunnel.

Del thumps his hand to his chest in a salute that's all earnestness and no training and follows after her.

My heart aches as I watch them leave. So brave and selfless. They shouldn't need to be those things. Not now. Not ever.

I grab Ami by the arm and we take off in the opposite direction, running as fast and as quietly as we can. My ribs burn where the scars are split. Ami's struggling, her breath coming in ragged gasps, hand clutched at her side. She's not used to this kind of exertion, especially not with what she must have been through these past moons.

I've got to keep her moving.

"We're going to make it," I reassure her. "We just need to keep up the pace. One foot after the other. Count your breaths, try to control them. Breathe with the opposite stride each time."

Echoes of angry shouts reach us from back in the direction we came. They've discovered the bodies. I desperately hope fleet-footed Riker watches over Del and Mish so that they make it back to their cells unnoticed. Otherwise they'll be punished for something they never deserved. And this time it will be my fault for leading them to more horror.

But here and now, all I can do is one thing. The thing Rakel would say to me if she were here.

Through. The only way out is through.

CHAPTER 8

LUZ

My entourage is halted at the great cedar gates of Ekasya.

Halted *and* searched. This is unprecedented.

"Do you not have the smokiest idea who I am? Or were you hired to play the buffoon?" My voice is imperious, intended to carry to as many ears as possible. The more who know the Chief Perfumer of Aphorai Province has arrived, the better. If I'm going to get to the essence of what's going on in the city, I don't want them feeling surprised. I want them to think they're ready for me. At times like this, it's much more useful for your target to think they have the upper hand.

"All those entering Ekasya must pass the checkpoint."

"Since when?"

"Since the Regent ordered it."

I eye the man. He wears the sleeveless chainmail of the city guard, but something seems off. He's a fraction too cocky. And while he's large, it's not the endurance-lean physique of a Ranger.

Time to do away with dignity. I climb off the litter that has borne me from the docks to the capital's entrance,

117

lurching to the side as I feign twisting my ankle. As if desperate not to tumble to the flagstones, I flail for the guard's arm. It's enough of a distraction to edge the padded undershirt he wears beneath his mail further up his wrist.

There. Only partially revealed but unmistakable. A black sun.

"Why, you're a formidable one, aren't you?" I squeeze his meaty forearm in apparent appreciation, though it's everything to hide my revulsion.

He pulls free of my touch, but not before a greasy smugness slides into his expression.

As the guards make a show of inspecting my entourage and our paraphernalia, I watch them with the same feigned appreciation.

This is worse than I anticipated.

A member of the Brotherhood of the Blazing Sun allowed into Ekasya's guard? Like the Rangers, the capital's guard are supposed to be a neutral force, protecting the city and the imperial family and administration but not furthering any other agenda. Known members of any radical group, whether secular separatists or fringe sects like the Blazers have until now been refused admittance to service.

How many of them have been allowed to join the ranks? More pertinently, who is doing the allowing? The Regent himself? Or someone within his employ?

I need answers.

Naturally, I know where to find them.

The unfortunate business at the gate was official business.

Tonight has nothing to do with the Chief Perfumer of Aphorai.

The alley is as nondescript as any other, dominated by a pile of ancient refuse that passers-by could be forgiven for concluding had simply accumulated over the turns. But that would be to do Sneryis's people a disservice. One of the many reasons the majority of Ekasya's citizens remain blissfully unaware of this place is this tower of ephemera – artfully arranged, maintained and scented – to be equal parts nondescript and uninviting.

At the end of the alley is an arch in the stone wall, with several steps leading down to what appears to be a servant's entrance. In all actuality, it *is* a servant's entrance.

I, however, am not here to serve.

I bypass the door and take the off-puttingly damp and musty sunken path to its seeming dead-end, pressing my hand *just so* on one of the stones.

A section of the wall gives way on silent hinges and I step through the opening into the antechamber. It's a nondescript room, bare of furnishings except for a multi-tiered shelf of jars and vials on one side and a welcome counter on another.

Opposite is a second, unmarked door.

No line this evening. Splendid. I have all respect for orderliness, but I will never develop an enthusiasm for queuing.

The girl lounging at the reception counter wears raven-dark silk and a glaze of boredom, lips painted blood red against pale skin. "You're too late."

"Greetings to you, too, Tillis."

"I have nothing else to say to you, Luz."

"Are you vexed with me?" I lean on the counter, flashing her my baby blues with a curl-lipped smirk. "Come now, tell me why you're so very vexed with me. Is it because I never write? Or because I left in such a hurry that morni—"

"I don't care enough about you to pay attention to anything you do," she lies. "You're simply too late. Nobody could make an addition tonight."

Ah, I see. The price of entry at Sneryis's is standard. Anyone who could afford to frequent a relatively upscale establishment could cover the fee. But only a few could pass the entrance requirements – add a new ingredient to the base note Sneryis has chosen as a room scent for the night and have it pass muster. If it doesn't, your name goes on the blacklist for a turn. In the information game, a turn is a very long time indeed.

And Sneryis has … fluctuating tastes. Nevertheless, it's imperative I gain entrance, no matter how complex the evening's fragrance has already become.

I motion to Tillis, and she waves a vial under my nose.

A single sniff reveals tonight's offering is incredibly detailed. A dozen flowers play harmonies with several fruits, while no less than six layers of woods join the chorus. Beneath that, restrained but still evident, hum several rich, smoky resins. Even I'm hard pressed to single out the exact number.

This is not the challenge I expected.

"You think I couldn't handle this?" I press a hand to my heart. "You wound me, Tillis."

She passes me the vial with a sarcastic smile and a "be my guest" gesture.

In honesty, there truly isn't much room left. Though perhaps I shouldn't be surprised; with the city in upheaval, it's no wonder that the black market, not least of all the information brokers, are doing a roaring trade.

I examine the shelves. Many bottles of single ingredients remain, but if Tillis says I'm too late, I'm guessing Sneryis has already had his fill of florals and balsams and turned some would-be clientele away. The only chance I'll not meet the same fate is to identify a surprising note. One that doesn't tip the entire scent symphony over into raucous clanging.

Everything in the concoction so far is somewhat warm. I could risk muddying it with another layer, or disrupt it entirely with something unexpected.

My fingers dance down the shelves of bottles

Lavender? No, too astringent.

Camphor? By the Primordial, no. I turn back to Tillis, gesturing to the jar. "Does anyone in their right mind ever try this?"

"You'd be surprised," she drawls.

Ah. Here we go.

Mint.

I take the bottle back to the counter.

Her expression reflects her scathing opinion of my choice. "You know the risk here, yes?"

I stare flatly at her.

"I have to ask. Ry gets haughty if I don't. Rules are rules and all that. How many?"

She means drops. "Three," I tell her. Let's walk on the wild side.

In they go. Almost clear. Innocuous. But with cool, crisp bite. A tinkle of icicles. She swirls the vial then disappears through the door I hope to pass through.

It's a tedious wait. I lean against the wall, ankles crossed, and pop a clove pastille into my mouth.

When it's melted away, I start on another.

And a third.

One would think Tillis is stretching this out as a small revenge. Before now, I'd have ventured she was above such pettiness.

Finally, she reappears and gestures to the door with a scowl of petulant defeat. "Ry has such a soft spot for you."

I give her my most beatific smile. "He's not alone."

Stepping into the inner sanctum, I blink slowly, letting my eyes get used to the darkness. One can never really know what to expect – Sneryis keeps the colour scheme a surprise, a non-linear rotation through the rainbow. It's not cheap to achieve, either. Glorified powder rats he keeps on retainer have to constantly feed the braziers various powders to change the tint of their flames. Tonight, the shadows of some of the sharpest, deftest operators in the Empire are cast against a glow of imperial purple.

Is Senryis feeling patriotic? And if so, to which of the Kaidon brothers?

Or is it more of a turned-up nose to the political upheaval of late – imperial heirs can go missing, the Founding Accord can be broken, and yet still Sneryis has an establishment full of select clientele. Just the way he likes it.

I scan the bar. The wall behind is lined with clay jugs and glazed bottles in various hues. Silver cups for those with a predilection for the drinking game of Aphorai – Death in Paradise – and carved crystal domes with handles for those who seek the smoke-scented white spirit of Hagmir.

I take my seat at the polished black stone bench. "River Gold, if you please."

The barkeep is discreet enough to not voice the question in her eyes.

"It has pleasing floral notes. And I find hops refreshing."

"No judgment. Just don't get many orders for beer."

My drink arrives in a bronze tankard beaded with condensation. Sneryis ships ice down from the Alet Range and the beverage is delectably cold. I take a swallow, closing my eyes to fully savour the sensation of cool, bitter liquid trailing down my throat.

A tall figure takes the seat beside me. He stares straight ahead, rubbing the carefully curated lines of stubble along his jaw, so perfect they could have been painted on his skin. "Thought you'd never make it."

"I'll admit Doubt had her naughty way with me for a moment, too."

He tilts his head, aquiline nose angled to the ceiling, eyes closed, impossibly long lashes curled against his cheek. Almost imperceptibly, his nostrils flare. "What did you manage to add to that concoction?"

"Mint."

"Ha! Let nobody call you anything if not audacious."

I give him a slow wink. "So, why did you go quiet on me?"

"Have you had your head up a select orifice since you arrived?"

"Fair." I've always liked Darzul. He's one of the good ones. He'll be keeping himself as far removed from the current ruling regime as possible without walking away from the capital.

"First thing's first. Whatever you want this time, it will cost you."

At least he *was* one of the good ones. "You jest."

"It's not for me. It's to help people get out of here before it's too late. Ekasya isn't going to get any more liveable if the regent keeps walking this road. Whether it's lack of money, food shortages, or getting on the wrong side of the heavies holding the city at their mercy … lives are going to be lost. These are people who've helped me for turns. They've helped *you* for turns. I'm not going to roll over without doing the same."

"Exactly how much is this going to cost me?"

"How much have you got? Bribing the guards isn't going to get any cheaper the longer this plays out."

I sigh. "Fine. What's mine is yours. Everything but what I'll require to get out of the city again. Agreed?"

He gives me a solemn nod.

"Now, I need your assistance locating someone."

CHAPTER 9

ASH

Ami and I emerge into the Ekasyan sun, pain shooting through eyes that haven't seen more than torchlight in what feels like half a lifetime. Above us, the imperial complex looms, emanating a foreboding that makes me feel like I've reverted to childhood. My home is once again alien to me.

I look back, but the only thing following us is my guilt at not leading Zostar's younger captives to safety. I send a prayer for mother Esiku to watch over them until the day I can return. May that day come soon.

Below, the city itself looks different. Perhaps the change is in my imagination, perhaps it's me who's changed. It takes until we thread our way through the first of the laneways to realize what it is that's gnawing at me – it's quiet. As if people are staying off the streets, keeping indoors.

It's unnerving. Not least of all because it's the first time I've faced the city, or even simply anywhere outdoors, without Linod's Elixir coursing through my veins to calm me. Even so, my hands are steady. I feel stronger than I ever have, which doesn't make sense given the gruel and inactivity of the dungeons.

There's no time to contemplate, though. We pass by a plaza, and Ami angles towards the first gathered group of people we've come across. I'd prevent her from doing so, but don't want to create a scene. Thankfully, she hovers at the fringes as the small crowd listens to the herald give the day's announcements.

There's an assurance more grain will be coming to the city before the next moon.

A reminder there's a curfew in place – the first I've ever heard of one in the capital.

And a notice of a reward.

"The Hidden Prince becomes Missing Prince! The Regent will pay dearly for any information leading to the return of his most beloved brother."

Nisai. If Iddo doesn't know where he is, then there's hope.

As the gathering dissipates, Ami plucks at her stained smock, nose wrinkled. Out here in the light, I finally see how much we've been marked by the grime of our incarceration. The lines of my hands have dirt embedded in them. It's caked under my nails. And now that we're in the open, away from the overwhelming humid dankness under the mountain, I can tell I don't exactly give off the perfume of roses.

"We have to get cleaned up," I tell Ami. "We might be able to pass for beggars, but if a patrol finds us, they're likely to throw us straight back into the dungeons even if they don't identify us."

"I know a place," she says, and starts walking.

"Wait," I hiss. "Where? Tell me. We're in this together."

"Esarik's."

Something nudges at the corner of my memory. Something terrible. Esarik was there. The day in the throne room, when we failed to cure Nisai and I …

Ami shakes her head, her eyes stern. "You don't get to look at me like that. Even by aristocratic standards it wasn't improper. I *married* him."

"It's not that. It's about Esarik. I…" I choke on the words.

"I know he's gone," she says curtly. "They used that knowledge to torture me. They wondered why I stayed loyal to a Prince who couldn't keep even his friends safe."

I bow my head.

Because I have the creeping suspicion that it wasn't Nisai to blame.

✳

Before I was a fugitive, I would never have imagined it could take the best part of a day to traverse the capital. Ami and I slink along back lanes, only edging out to the spokes of Ekasya's main thoroughfares when unavoidable. At those points, we keep our heads down and walk deliberately, but not so quickly to suggest we're fleeing.

More imperial guards patrol than I remember, while fewer ordinary citizens crowd the streets with their gossip or wares. It could be a foreign city – one in the military states over the ocean we've only ever heard traveller tales from at the imperial court, too distant for regular trade or diplomatic relations.

Eventually, we reach one of the few half-respectable neighbourhoods outside the walls; the houses and shops are the last to be made of stone, many of them built up against the wall itself as if clinging to a notion they are part of Ekasya proper by proximity.

At the gate of a complex of half a dozen dwellings, Ami bends to feel under the lip of a waist-high urn containing a lilac shrub. It's almost finished flowering, so that the last few sprays of blossom are browning and ready to drop. I remember how she used to bring the first blooms of the season into the Early Imperial section of the palace library. Was this the very plant they were from?

Something scrapes and a spider drops out on to Ami's wrist. She clamps her other hand over her mouth, stifling a shriek as she shakes the hairy creature off. She bends to look under the rim before continuing her search. Then she gives a little *hmph* of satisfaction. In her hand is a key.

We enter a courtyard bathed in the golden light of early evening. It's quiet, the noise of the city seeming more distant than it actually is, the only sound from inside the complex a singing Trelian lark perched on one of the clay-tiled roofs. More potted lilacs dot the paving stones.

The scent seems from another life.

A life that's gone to the sky.

"I don't know if they know about this place," she murmurs. "We should be careful."

I follow Ami up a narrow flight of stairs to an intricately engraved door. The key she retrieved from the planter turns smoothly in the lock.

I don't know what I expected, but it wasn't this.

It looks like a single-room garret, a fireplace on one wall and an alcove with a tap and copper trough for ablutions on the other. Perhaps the modest dwelling was well furnished, but now it's in shambles. The bed has been wrenched away from the corner and left at an angle. Drawers from a cherrywood sideboard have been emptied and upended. Books bound in expensive aurochs leather sprawl every which way, broken at the spine or fallen from toppled stacks. Scrolls are half unrolled, some torn or crumpled, an undeniable boot print emblazoned across one.

"Seems they got here first." Ami looks at the wreckage with sad eyes, then steps forward to right the nearest chair. It wobbles on three legs as she rubs her hand over the back. "Esarik would be devastated."

"I thought he lived near…"

"His father bought him a manse on the main imperial boulevard further up the Mountain, but this is where he comes when he wants – *wanted* – to think. Be himself. I'd thought nobody knew about it but me. When Zostar's men first took me, I used to imagine escaping and coming here to wait for him."

I don't reply. Instead, I ease one of the drawers back into its frame, feeling the urge to put the room to rights, as if such a pathetically small gesture could help assuage my guilt at my friend's downfall. How am I going to broach it with Ami? And if what I suspect is true, what does Nisai think of it? He's never truly admitted to himself what my curse is. He's always seen it as more protective than destructive. Would this make him finally understand?

"Here, let me find you something to wear." Ami picks through a pile of scattered fabric and holds out an outfit that looks distinctively Esarik – dark trousers and a simple but elegant long-line tunic in fine charcoal-coloured weave. At least the colour is appropriate.

"Are you sure? I don't want to…" It seems I'm no longer capable of finishing a sentence. But what can I say?

She hands me the clothes. "He'd want his things put to good use."

I accept them with stiff formality, and nod towards the taps in the alcove. "I'll give you a few moments to yourself. But make them swift. Whoever turned this place over may return."

I draw the door shut behind me and lean against the wall, forcing myself to breathe deep and even as I survey the lilac-studded courtyard. Further down the slope, a woman hums as she pegs out laundered bedsheets on a terrace between terracotta-tiled roofs. Other than the relative quiet we witnessed in the city's main thoroughfares, everything seems as it should be.

Ami sticks her head out the door. "Your turn."

She's run fresh water into the tub and left a bar of soap beside it. More lilacs. I smile sadly. No wonder Esarik adored them. The thought only makes me think of his end. Of Ami's loss.

My chest tightens as fragments of memory flash through my mind. The throne room. The shadows moving. Blood. Everywhere, blood.

My friend's among it all.

The lilacs suddenly smell sickly. Laced with guilt. My jaw clamps tight against a dry retch.

I wash as quickly as I can, douse myself with a bucket over my head, then towel off with the white linen Ami left hanging over a hook. The freshness should be an incredible luxury after feeling like I've been marinating in my own filth for moons. It probably would be, if I didn't have to face the clothes. Esarik was almost as tall as me, but the Trelian was slim. I tentatively pull the tunic over my torso, not wanting to split a finely stitched seam as it strains across my shoulders.

Then I let the bathwater out, pausing to watch the residue of the dungeons drain from the basin. If only I could wash away the whole experience just as easily.

The sound of knocking brings me back to myself. Ami must have taken my silence as a sign I had finished up, though she still opens the door gingerly.

I avoid her gaze, instead bending to pick up a tripod that was toppled beneath a window, where a star-glass had apparently been set up. Better to focus on the problem before us. "Do you have a plan from here? Your family?"

Ami didn't talk much of her family, but I remember she was one of three, her father a modest carpenter, her mother a much-in-demand seamstress. The latter's designs popular enough among the merchant class and minor aristocracy to have paid for Ami's apprenticeship to the Head Curator at the palace library.

She shakes her head. "I don't come from the sort of family who would appreciate me bringing this kind of trouble to their door. And even if I did, I don't see how they could possibly help. I have to move on to another library. If I'd done so sooner, Es ... he could have come with me. Got away from his father. And the Guild of Physicians. I didn't know who was worse back then, Zostar or Lord Mur."

I scowl. "I'd say it's become very clear. Now, though, we should try to make contact with the Council of Five."

"Did you not see, in the arena?" She runs her fingertips down the wooden frame of the alcove, where a door may have once been. "They were *courtiers*. How do we even know there weren't Council members among them?"

My mind conjures an image of Nisai's mother, Shari. The woman who allowed me to enter the palace as a boy, and to sponsor the training that would lead to me becoming her son's Shield. "They would never be involved with something as heinous."

Her hand keeps moving down the doorframe, then pauses. "You can't be certain how deep this goes. I would never have suspected the Head Curator, either. But then he began frequenting certain pre-Imperial collections, locking himself away with clay tablet fragments from the Shadow Wars and esoteric scrolls that so-called alchemists produced in the century following. Visits from Zostar and his colleagues became regular, and they became more and more impatient with each appearance."

There's a click as a section of the doorframe slots inwards then protrudes just far enough to grasp. Ami gives a little sniff of satisfaction and slides it out like a vertical drawer. It contains a number of compartments, some with tightly wound scrolls, others with coin purses.

Other than Ami, only Kaismap must have known Esarik had such foresight.

Or was it paranoia?

No. He would have told me if he was in some kind of trouble. Or at least told Nisai. Wouldn't he?

I shake my head. "If I could get to Councillor Shari, she'd help us. I know she would."

Ami tosses me one of the coin purses. "Even if you're correct, how do you propose to get past everyone else to find her?"

She stuffs the other purses and scrolls into a satchel that reminds me of Rakel's. Eagerness and frustration war with each other at the thought – for all I know, Rakel could be in the next courtyard, or at the other end of the Empire.

As for Ami's question, I don't have an answer. There is no way back into the imperial complex. Daring the trek up Ekasya Mountain to the wealthier sectors of the city would be an incredible risk. I still don't know how closely Iddo's entwined with all of this, but I don't for a heartbeat think he would welcome me with open arms.

Ami crosses the room and begins to rummage in the contents of a cupboard, now piled on the floor. "We'll think better if we eat."

There's some ancient bread as flat and hard as a roof tile. But there's also a clay jar of fine olive oil, and another sealed vessel that reveals some olives, their black skins wrinkled and coated with herbs. After the slop of the dungeons, it's a veritable feast. Yet my stomach remains unsettled, and I have to force myself to face the food.

I snap off a piece of bread, dip it in the oil, and begin to chew mechanically. The tripod I'd righted beneath the window catches my attention. With the bread in one hand, I cast about for the star-glass that would have sat in the frame. Esarik had taught me half the constellations I know, but I never knew before now where he sat and observed them from.

There. Beneath a tattered scroll. And the lens is still intact. I return the cylinder to the tripod and stoop so my eye is level, sweeping the focus across the rooftops.

Back up the mountain's slope, a patrol of city guards marches between the buildings. It's only a heartbeat before they've disappeared from sight again but … is that a Ranger leading them? They've never before had any role in keeping the peace inside the walls of the capital.

Has Iddo ordered the Rangers to implement a lockdown of the palace complex? And if he's been able to do that, what of the Council of Five? Zostar had said they had control of the temple – that Nisai had recovered and that's where he was holed up.

I train the glass up to the gloss black stone of the imperial complex. The terraces of the temple are fuzzy.

"Adjust the focus," Ami says from behind me. "Twist the front section until you have clarity."

I do as she says. The building becomes clear. Dread lances through me. There are guards patrolling as expected. But every one of them is a Ranger.

I pass the star-glass to Ami.

Her lips become a thin line as she gauges my meaning.

"I can't believe the Council would let Iddo's Rangers take control. Nisai would have never allowed it." I begin pacing. "If Iddo's put a reward on Nisai's return, I'd wager Nisai is well clear of the city. But is Rakel with him? If he made it out after she healed him, I have to believe she escaped, too."

"Who's Rakel?"

"She's from Aphorai. When I met her, she was working for the Aphorain Scent Keeper." I figure "work" is an innocent glossing of details. "She was there the night Nisai was poisoned, and the Scent Keeper died. At first I thought one of them was responsible, or both, but it turns out first impressions truly can be deceiving. She was the one who saved him, in the end."

"She sounds … impressive."

I find myself genuinely smiling for the first time in moons. "That's one word to describe her."

Ami begins pacing the room, rolling up scrolls and re-shelving books as she goes. "I think Aphorai's our best bet. It's Nisai's ancestral Province, for one."

"It's a long way to go on a hunch."

"We can't stay here. And what is the likelihood your girlfriend has returned home, too?"

"She's not my—"

"Remember how many turns I've known you, Ashradinoran. There's only one other person I've ever heard you speak like that about, and he's missing as well. If this Rakel did all those things you say, then she's the kind of person I'd like on our side."

I nod. "I need to know she's all right. And even if Nisai's not with her, she might know where he is."

"And there's an Aphorain library I'd like to consult, too."

"Oh?"

She waves the air as if fanning away anything of consequence. "Just a regional branch I'm interested in."

Memories of the Library of the Lost, hidden deep within a maze of canyons in the Aphorain desert, come flooding back. "You're a ... Chronicler?"

"An apprentice *curator*, you mean."

"No, a Chronicler. Like those at the Library of the Lost."

"I'm not sure what you're referring to other than a legend that's—"

I fold my arms. "I've been there, Ami. Rakel and I sought help from the Chroniclers when we were looking for the cure for Nisai."

Her evasiveness melts into curiosity. "Truly? You've seen it?"

"Briefly. Before Rangers caught up with us."

"Rangers?" Her features pinch in worry. "At the Library?"

"We left in too much of a hurry to confirm, but they were in the vicinity."

"I'm not a Chronicler. Perhaps with twenty or thirty more turns of service, I would have been tapped on the shoulder. I did want to be one. I *do* want to be one. I care about knowledge and its preservation. Deeply. But if Rangers have found the Library of the Lost, and now they're working with Zostar…" She trails off, her eyes darting to her packed bag on the floor between us.

"What is it?"

"I have to get to the Library of the Lost. I have to warn them."

"All right," I concede. It's a long shot, but it's all we've got. "Only, I can't leave yet. I made a promise to the others. Del. Mish. Lark. I can't go without finding a way out for them, too."

"You and what army, Ash?"

I want to slam my fist against the wall, but instead rest my forehead on the cool stone. Guilt. Frustration. Fear. Whatever I'm feeling, emotion isn't going to help us. The only solution is to stay constant. Stay in control.

Ami gathers her bag. "Let's see what else we can salvage, then be ready to move."

It's a sound plan. I'm not surprised. Ami's always had a smart head on her shoulders. It's what Esarik always claimed, with one of his secret smiles: it was what he most adored about her.

And here I am, in his treasured hideaway, wearing his clothes, about to leave with the girl he married in defiance of his father. My mind finally forces the image in front of me, the one I'd do anything not to see. The wounds in Esarik's torso. Deep gouges through flesh and viscera. Grievous injuries. Damage that said he was never getting up again, even if I wasn't … present enough … to determine the moment of death.

Harm inflicted by the beast.

Inflicted by *me*.

I draw back from the window.

"Ami," I begin, voice grave. "Before we go any further, I have to tell you something."

"Oh?"

"This won't be easy to hear…" I mentally cast about, searching for the right way to broach my confession.

She squints in the slanted rays of evening, studying my face. "It was real, wasn't it? In the arena, when Zostar's men attacked us … the shadows. I fainted, and came to … I thought they … moved. I wasn't just imagining it, was I?"

I wince, but don't reply.

Slow horror creeps into her expression. "*You're* what Zostar was searching for, aren't you?"

I steel myself. No going back now. "I'm cursed, yes."

She gnaws on a cuticle. A nervous gesture I've never seen her do before. "This … power. How does it work?"

"I don't know," is all I can say, hopeless.

"It could take over at any time? You could… Would it kill me without you knowing?"

"Not exactly. I tend to get a particular feeling when it's going to…" I reach for the words to explain something I've always done my best to avoid examining too closely. "When it's going to happen. I just… I can't control it after it releases. It's only happened three times. Once when I was a boy. Days ago when you were there. And, in the throne room when … when…"

"When what?"

137

I hang my head. "When Esarik died."

"Wh-what do you mean?"

"I … the shadow killed him. Please believe that I didn't intend for that to happen. If I could have stopped it, I would have… My curse, it…"

She takes one, two steps back, her hands coming up in front of her. "You should leave."

"Ami, I'm sorry, I never meant for—"

"Get out!"

Voices reverberate around the courtyard below. Men's voices. I rush to the door. Black jerkins. Red sun. Blazers.

"We have to get out of here."

She's still got that horrified look on her face, mixed with anger.

"I can get us clear. Please. Let me help you. Then we can talk about this properly. But we have to go now."

She shakes her head.

Heavy footsteps begin to climb the external stairs.

I press a finger to my lips, signalling silence. I left the children behind. I won't leave Ami, whatever she now thinks of me.

I grab her hand and drag her from the garret.

❊

We run headlong through the slums, as if my life has come full circle.

It's familiar and yet alien territory in the gloom of dusk. So much has changed, the lean-to stores have different rudimentary signs, and the shacks have been altered or rebuilt from the city's detritus so that the lanes carve new thoroughfares. The layout may have changed, but they're still the alleys I used to zigzag through as a child, running with a group of older boys. They wanted riches, thrills, and the euphoria they'd only ever find in dreamsmoke.

I just wanted to survive.

Ami's breath comes ragged behind me. She slipped my grip as soon as we escaped the courtyard ahead of the Blazers, flicking her fingers as if something foul clung to her. At least she's following. Back at Esarik's garret, I feared she would let herself be caught rather than follow her husband's murderer. The awful truth is I couldn't have blamed her if she had.

Perhaps she *should* run in a different direction. Perhaps she's better off without me.

We round a corner into a blind alley and skid to a stop. Ami's hands go to her knees, as she gasps for air. She can't keep this up much longer.

I point to a pile of refuse up ahead. "We'll take the roofs for a bit. Here. I'll help you up."

Ami balks for a heartbeat, then looks behind us. There's nobody there, but there soon will be. We climb on to the pile and she hitches her foot into my interlocked hands. I boost her over the lip of the roof and hoist myself up after.

A strange melancholy pangs in my chest. It would be full dark by now if both moons weren't cresting the horizon. It's the only time the slums resemble anything close to beauty, a sprawl of makeshift dwellings and broken dreams cast in silver. I wonder how many loved ones of Zostar's Ekasyan captives lie awake out there, not knowing if they'll ever see their child or sibling again.

I have to find a way to get those kids home.

To do that, I have to find Nisai and Rakel.

Ami looks out across the patchwork of reed-and-daub roofs uncertainly.

"Keep near to the edges," I instruct. "About where the walls are. We don't want to crash through."

We set out, skirting crumbling chimneys and leaping precarious gaps, my heart in my throat each time Ami's footsteps falter.

I feel the heat and smell the metallic steam before I catch sight of the first forge – the smith working through the night. My parents' workshop was not far from here. We'll pass it soon.

I signal to Ami and help lower her to the lane below. She puts space between us as soon as her feet find solid ground, backing away and clutching her bag in front of her like a shield. I drop down after her, maintaining my distance.

The sign for my father's shop is no longer hanging over the door. It's propped against the boarded-up storefront, rusted. Is he too old now to work? Or did some injury befall him?

I don't have the time – or the inclination – to find out. What would I even say if I faced him? *You were right, father. I'm cursed. An abomination. You should have thrown away the key when you locked me in the cellar.*

I give myself an inward shake. There's no time for this. Even if it seems like we've evaded pursuit for now, Zostar's Blazers won't give up. If they're anything like the ones who found Nisai and me when we were young, they'll know the slums like the backs of their hands. Slums that I've been a stranger to for ten turns.

We keep moving through this disconcerting mix of familiar and foreign, landmarks of old mixed with new layers, all of it barnacles clinging to the side of Ekasya

Mountain between the mudflats of the river and the city walls.

The one thing that hasn't changed is the way to the water.

There's no light other than the moons; nobody wastes candles or coals on these streets. At a time like this the darkness is welcome, because I'm about to do something I haven't done since last living in these parts – steal.

The banks of the great river are a motley mix of sheds and makeshift moorings, driftwood driven into the silty shores. Weed-festooned ropes hold dinghies at bay. I inspect each of them, looking for the shine of water in the moonslight that indicates they're leaking.

The first one is a death trap. The second not much better.

Panic tries to sink its claws, but I shove it back down.

The third has a slow leak.

The fourth looks sound but is moored with an intricate security knot.

Fifth vessel lucky, I gesture to Ami.

"You expect me to get in that? With *you*?"

"Consider the odds that our Blazer friends will treat you more kindly. You're a scholar. Make an evidence-based decision."

Behind us, Ekasya Mountain looms out of the plain, like the entire city is glaring down, judging, condemning. I look towards the east, where in a few hours dawn will streak the sky. I need to be far from the capital by then, need to be on my way to finding the people I love, and return to fulfil my promise to Zostar's captives.

I unhook the sodden rope from its peg.

Ami doesn't move.

It would be easier to leave her here. Cast off, and not look back. But I owe it to Esarik to see her to safety. Safely to the Library, if that's what she wants.

I gesture to the tiny boat. "You're free to hate me. Free to strike out on your own later. But please, for now, let me get you out of here."

CHAPTER 10

RAKEL

My eyes sting from too much smoke and steam and too little sleep. I resist the urge to rub them, knowing the traces of various experimental ingredients on my leather work gloves would make it like setting my face on fire.

It's late, the entire compound quiet. Even the Magister has sought her bed, though I know she'll rise again hours before dawn – her best research hours.

Mine are now, with nobody watching over my shoulder. I wouldn't be able to make any progress towards the cure both my and Nisai's father need if I were fumbling with nerves.

There's a polite knock at the door, a clearing of a throat.

Think of the Prince and he appears.

Kip and Barden file in behind him.

Unusual. I straighten from where I'd been leaning over the bench, painstakingly measuring out doses of the Magister's salve – the temporary solution to the Rot. After giving the Prince the nod that has become our customary greeting, I stretch my arms above my head, fingers interlaced. I'm rewarded with a satisfying series of pops.

Nisai winces at the sound of my cracking knuckles. "Can I talk to you?"

"Must be important if it's kept you from your bed." It's more a comment to Barden – he'd never pass up the chance for a bit of shut-eye, whereas Nisai has been burning many a candle in the Order's archives. Then again, I've often seen Barden there with him of late.

Kip closes the door behind them. Then she bolts it.

"Is that needed? Nobody comes in here other than the researchers."

She gives a single, grim nod.

A flask of diluted dahkai simmers over the oil burner in the background and unease begins to bubble in me to match.

Nisai props his crutches against the bench and gestures to one of the stools. "May I?"

I wave him on. "Sniff yourself senseless."

Stenches, Rakel. After his headaches, his concerns about memory, after the poison that caused them, you say something like *that*? To a *Prince*?

"I'd feel more comfortable if you would also sit." He looks to Barden, who gives him a firm nod and places a leather-bound notebook in front of the Prince.

It's not his usual journal.

"All right." I say, carefully stripping off my gloves and setting them on the bench. "Out with it."

The Prince takes a deep breath, seeming to steady himself. "There's something about the Affliction that you should know."

Ah. I knew this would come to light eventually. When the Magister had asked me not to share the origins of the Rot with Nisai, I'd been dubious. It felt like a betrayal, however small. But now, seeing his furrowed brow and dark eyes grave, I can see exactly why she made that request.

"Go on," I say.

"There's a way to combat the Rot."

A relieved laugh escapes my lips.

Nisai and Barden exchange a worried glance.

"I know," I tell them. "When you were poisoned, they gave my father medicine to halt the progression while Ash and I were trying to find the antidote. Figured it's the same stuff that's been keeping your father alive." I gesture to the measures of topical salve I'd been working on.

"I'm not talking about a treatment." Nisai places his hand gently over mine. I can't recall him ever volunteering physical contact. The touch itself isn't unpleasant. It's how unusual it is that makes it worrying. "Rakel, I think there's already a *cure*."

I shake my head. "Impossible. Nobody else could have enough dahkai."

"Nobody else has, as far as I can tell. I found this," he says, handing me the book.

Now that I'm looking at it up close, I can see it's not too dissimilar from the Magister's research notes. Though it's more yellowed and scuffed than that, and it has that almost-sweet vanilla and leather aroma I've come to associate with older documents. It must be from turns ago.

I flick through the pages. I can't read everything, but it's fairly clear these are indeed research notes.

"It's just some old experiments."

"Whose experiments?"

"The Magister's, I expect. Looks like her writing. It'd make sense. She was working on the cure with Sephine for turns before she left for the Sanctuary." The part of me that's a daughter may not be able to forgive that, but the healer in me can come to terms with it. Maybe even admire it.

"I understood as much. But look closer." Nisai pushes his crutches aside and hoists himself so that he's sitting on the bench next to the book, legs dangling. It makes him slightly taller than me. I wonder if that was on purpose, some sort of throwback to court politics where he thought he deserved the higher ground.

Irritation pricks my temper. "You know I can't read every word yet."

"No, examine the *page*. Closely. Try to see *past* the letters."

I scowl at him, half ready to demand he just tell me what's on his mind. That I'm not in the mood for games. Especially not over a matter like this. But a tickle of curiosity has me now, and I turn my attention back to the open page. There's the ink of the Magister's notes. Some hand-drawn diagrams. Near the corner, there's a small hole in the parchment that's been carefully stitched together with neat thread.

Nisai points. "Look, see here?"

I squint at the page. Behind the inked words, there's a pattern of tiny marks, no bigger than a pinhead. "The dots?"

"Those are the hair follicles from the animal whose skin this was made from. Anything else?"

I squint. There *is* something. It's faded, like embroidered cloth left too long in the sun. "Are those … letters?"

"I knew you'd see it." He gives a satisfied nod, then looks to Barden. "Would you pass me that candle?"

Barden complies without hesitation.

The Prince lifts the page and holds the flame at a safe distance directly behind it. The faded writing becomes slightly easier to see. Faint. Almost the same colour as the parchment itself. It's hard for me to make out, but it looks like a similar pattern to the actual notes.

"There are various documents within the Imperial Library where the original ink has been scraped away, or various reagents have been applied to cleanse it. Parchment isn't cheap, nor is book-binding."

Reagent. I've heard that word somewhere else. Luz. When she received the tiny scrolls carried by bird. The scent on the message indicated which reagent she should use to reveal the true message beneath the surface writing.

"So, these letters came before the dark ones?"

"Indeed. This book appears to have always been used for the same purpose. Laboratory notes. Except the ones behind these? They're different. They indicate the formula was successful. Rakel, they speak of a cure."

I exhale, letting the breath puff out my cheeks as it leaves. "It must be a mistake."

"Perhaps. Or perhaps there is more to it than that? Is there anything you've heard while working with the others? What about your mother, has she spoke of anything like this? It's important. It isn't just for the sake of our father's as individuals. It's also the Emperor's life at stake."

I lean back, gripping the bench. "Mistakes happen all the time. You think you've created something and then it doesn't stick. Doesn't stay in the form you want. At worst, it's devastating. At best, it's embarrassing. I've already made that mistake myself since we've been here. It's no wonder the Magister scrubbed it from the notes."

If I'm honest, I might have done the same in her place. Nobody likes to be wrong. And in her position, she wouldn't want to lose the confidence of those around her over a mistake like that.

"Rakel," Barden begins, using that tone he does when he thinks I haven't been listening. "If there's any sliver of doubt in your mind…"

Part of me wants to argue. But if the Prince truly believes it, if he truly thinks there might be a way to cure his father, then I have to know. Because that also means there could be a way to cure my father.

"When?" I ask.

"This afternoon," Nisai says. "We would have come to you straight away, but I wanted to check and recheck. I wanted to be sure."

"No, when was this earlier version written?"

"If we go by the date, around seventeen turns ago."

Seventeen turns. Not long after the Magister must have first arrived here. Or … not long before she left Aphorai City.

I gesture towards the notebook. "Can I take this?"

Nisai doesn't protest.

"I'll see you both later."

"Where are you going?"

"Where do you think?"

The Prince pinches the bridge of his nose between thumb and forefinger. "Tread carefully, Rakel. It may be best we keep this to ourselves until we can figure out what it means."

In the sixth hell I'll keep it to myself. Enough secrets. If there's anything in this, I want to know. And now. I blow out the flame beneath the flask I was heating when they arrived, tuck the leather-bound book under my arm and move towards the door.

"Rakel?" Nisai calls. "Rakel!"

Then another voice. Barden's. "Let her go."

Seems he's learned his lesson.

✳

I slam my fist on the door to the Magister's quarters.

After what seems for ever but is probably a matter of moments, she opens it, one of the Sanctuary's green robes pulled hastily around her. "Did I oversleep?"

I don't reply, just shoulder my way into the room and drop the notebook on the bed. "Tell me about this."

She opens the cover, takes in the first few pages of contents. "If you want to discuss these experiments, best we do it in the lab. Give me a few moments to dress."

Oh no, I'm not falling for that. If there's anything in this, I'm not giving her time to think up an excuse. "Judging from its contents, I think you'd rather discuss this in private."

She frowns and scoops up the notebook. Crossing to the window, she perches on the viewing seat. It commands a view of the entire inner circle of the Sanctuary, the gardens glowing in the greenish light I've still not quite grown accustomed to. She pats the space beside her.

"I'll stand."

With a shrug, she opens the book.

"I've marked the spot."

"How many times have I requested you not fold the corners of..." She goes quiet as her eyes trace the page.

"Well?"

Her hand goes to her mouth.

So it *is* something of significance.

"Don't even think about lying to me. Because I'll test it. Don't think I won't. I'll go down to the patient's sector and wrap myself in used bandages and give myself the scents-be-damned Rot if that's what I need to do."

"Let me explain."

Her voice is quiet but with those words, I know. The realization knocks the wind out of me. It's suddenly close in here, like the air has been sucked from the room.

"You already had it," I manage. "You already had it and you didn't tell me. You didn't tell Father. You could have cured him! How long did you know? Could you have saved his leg?"

She surges to her feet. "This isn't about your father!"

"Then what is it about? Why am I wasting time trying to find what has already been found?"

"The balance has been tipped! Until we work out a way to cure the Affliction with less dahkai, we cannot cure everyone. And we *must* cure everyone or the cycle will just repeat itself. We'll be trying to put out an inferno with a cup of water. I'm trying to keep you safe, don't you see?"

I shake my head. "But Nisai's father. The Emperor. We could potentially stop a *war* with this."

"And then what, my wise daughter? The Emperor is Zostar's puppet. He has been for turns."

"How can you know that?"

"Who do you think counselled Kaddash against appointing another Scent Keeper in the capital?"

Everything I know about court politics has been gained since I got caught up in all of this, but even I can see she's got a point.

"If we release a cure made with such an expensive and rare resource as dahkai, only the enfranchised will ever be able to access it. The nobility. There will be no trickle-down to the poor. We must make it accessible to *all* from the start if we're going to stop the disease. And that means we must be able to fabricate enough of it. I found a cure, yes. But it used too much dahkai. We need a better formula for this to work. The Order voted long ago, the cure would only be released when there was enough for all."

I snatch up the notebook. "You might be able to turn your back on Father, but I cannot. I'm taking this. I'm curing him."

"They won't let you leave with that book any more than they'll let you leave with the dahkai you'd need."

"They?"

"The Order."

The bitterness in my mouth is hard to swallow. "And those poor people you're testing on?"

"They would have no better prospects anywhere else."

There's a sudden, cold directness to her voice and expression. Something that reminds me of Sephine. Something I learned would be futile to rail against.

"I understand," I say. Though understand doesn't mean I have to like one whiff of it. Or agree. "I'll show myself out."

❋

What in the sixth hell is—

The bell at my door jangles again, my sleep-addled brain jangling with it.

I never meant to doze off, but before I even open my eyes, I can tell by the lack of clary sage infusing the air in my room that my candle has long gone out. When I do open them, it's to pitch black. Must be somewhere between moons-set and sun-up.

I peel my cheek from the parchment and gently straighten my neck. The muscles cramp and I try to stretch them, realizing I must have fallen asleep at my desk. Before me sits the notebook with the Magister's cure. An actual cure for the Rot. Known for all this time.

Ugh. There goes the bell again. Someone's really putting it through its paces.

Yawning, I shamble to the door.

There's no one there.

I stick my head out into the hall. Two chambers along, Kip argues with the practical woman from the kitchen my first night here – Payuz, the Administrator's assistant – as to whether the Prince can be woken. Barden emerges from the next door, blinking like a canyon owl.

Payuz has the decency to look apologetic. "The Magister has requested your presence in the main chamber."

I knuckle the sleep from an eye and call to her: "The Magister couldn't wait until a more human hour?"

"There is to be a Conclave."

"A which cave?"

"A *Conclave*. An official administrative meeting of all ordained members of the Order, only ever assembled to discuss and vote on matters of substantive doctrine."

Administrative meeting? Substantive doctrine? I wave my hand and turn back towards my bed. "I'm not an ordained member of the Order. My vote's for more sleep." And time to figure out what to do about this situation, or at very least get a chance to speak with Nisai about it. I shouldn't have kept anything from him from the start.

"The Magister asked me to inform you a message has arrived. It's from Sandbloom. It shall form the basis of the discussion."

Now I'm fully awake.

Apparently Kip is convinced Nisai needs to know, too, as she opens the door to the Prince's chambers and disappears inside.

I duck back into my room and shove on my boots. Closing the door behind me, I pace the hall, wishing I could rake my hair into a braid – it's long enough now to smooth down with water or balm, but I know after half a night's sleep at my desk, it will be sticking out every which way.

When Nisai emerges, he's plucking at his robe, clearly irritated. "I'm the First Prince. I can't go to a formal meeting like this," he huffs.

"Like what?" I ask.

"Rumpled! Mussed! Dishevelled. I haven't been sent clean and pressed attire this moon. Now I've had to don this robe ... *twice*. I can still ... *smell myself on it*." He huffs a lock of thick, dark hair from his eyes.

I look to Kip.

She folds her arms across her chest. "I'm a guard, not a laundress."

Nisai gapes at her.

"Impersonating a river cod isn't going to change that, my Prince."

I stifle a snort. There are very few ways to get up Nisai's nose. Seems expecting him to do his own chores is one of them. Another time, I might have joined Kip in teasing him about it. Right now, there's more important scents in the air.

Payuz politely clears her throat.

We all fall in behind the older woman, even the Prince, as she leads the way to the main chamber.

I wish I could tell Nisai about the conversation I had with the Magister about the cure, but I have no idea who this Payuz is, and who else might overhear. *They won't let you leave with it*, the Magister had said. I decide to hold my tongue. See what unfolds.

When we finally emerge into the chamber, the sight stops me in my tracks. The ceiling gleams with that glasslike blue-black stone, the constellations of the star wheel studded with silver just like the Library of the Lost's main chamber. Below, the floor has been carved into level upon level of terraces until, at the very bottom, there's a floor and a round table of the same blue-black stone with a huge firepit in the centre. When we were on the road, Ash had described the Council of Five chambers, and how similar the round meeting table there was to the Library's. Guess there was some kind of historical fashion for this kind of stuff.

The terraces are already scattered with green-robed residents of the Sanctuary. I wonder how many are left to join us. Gathered here like this, their number is far fewer than I expected. The place is barely half full.

Payuz leads us to a mid-level terrace. Kip takes up station on the row behind Nisai. Barden and I sit either side. Once settled, Barden pulls a stretch of fabric from his kit bag. A needle and thread look tiny in his hands as he repairs what looks like a frayed seam in a Sanctuary robe. I smirk despite myself. Kip may refuse to be Nisai's laundress, but Barden's happy enough as his makeshift tailor. I shouldn't be surprised, Barden's always done anything to get ahead.

If he ever had a fragrance named after him it'd be called Amber Ambition.

The Magister appears, along with the other so-called office bearers of the Order. My stomach flip-flops at the sight of her in her formal role. This is what she spent my lifetime working her way towards. It hurts, but, deep down, there's a spark of admiration. She set out to do something. And that is what she did.

Unlike my own churning emotions, the Magister's features could be carved from stone with all she gives away. What it must be like to be so … controlled.

Like Ash, comes my first thought.

Until he wasn't, follows the traitorous but true second.

When the Magister reaches the table, she holds her arms wide. "My thanks and the thanks of my fellow office bearers to the Conclave for assembling so promptly. Trust that I would not have disturbed you at such an hour were it not warranted. This night, we have received information that could alter the course of all our futures. I ask you to make a decision that could reverberate through the turns, after even our long lives have come to an end."

The room is silent, though several members exchange glances.

"I ask you to listen to all of the evidence presented," the Magister continues, "and equally to heed the Divine Primordial's voice in your heart. At the conclusion, we shall take a vote. It will be anonymous, so you might have your say without fear of reproach."

A murmur of approval ripples through the crowd.

"Without prevarication then, let us now turn to the content of Sandbloom's report from the imperial capital."

The Order member behind me sucks in a breath. Others furrow their brows or shift uncomfortably.

"What stink's got up their noses?" I whisper to Nisai.

He leans close. "My father refused to appoint another Scent Keeper after the last went to the sky. I expect it had … knock-on effects."

"The report," the Magister continues, "contains three matters of great import to relay. Firstly, the Emperor is dead."

Now it's Nisai's turn to jerk to attention.

A murmur ripples through the assembled Order members. It's hard to tell whether they're pleased or annoyed. Perhaps some of each.

Nisai's still rigid, but his face has gone the kind of blank that only a potent mix of shock and sorrow brings. Just because the Rot was killing his father for turns, doesn't mean he was ready for it. Time and again I've imagined the same thing happening to Father, and yet I know I still wouldn't be ready. I hesitate for a moment, then gently, briefly lay my fingers on Nisai's forearm.

The Magister waits until the murmuring in the terraces has died down. "Second, the usurper Regent has broken the Founding Accord and deposed the Council of Five. While the southern province representatives remain, the Aphorain and Losian Councillors and trade ambassadors have departed the capital, and the unity of the Empire is now gravely at risk."

I exchange a look with Kip. The Losian is stone-faced, but the tightened cords in her neck betray her agitation.

"Third, civil war is not the greatest threat to maintaining balance across the Empire and beyond. Sandbloom has reason to believe the Brotherhood of the Blazing Sun have made progress towards unlocking the secrets of the

Children of Doskai. And what's more, a fully matured individual is now roaming free."

Silence falls, so sudden and heavy you could hear a petal drop.

It makes my heart sound like thunder in my ears.

"My colleagues, this could be the first herald of the next Shadow Wars."

I leap to my feet. "What's his name?"

Several irritated faces turn my way. Guess you're not supposed to interrupt the almighty Magister. I don't care.

She looks apologetically at Nisai. "The report speaks of the former Prince's Shield."

I stagger back, my legs colliding with the terrace so that I thump on to the stone rather than sit. It's as if the room has tilted. What was level is now askew.

He's alive.

Ash is alive.

A soft hand takes mine. Nisai. He looks straight ahead, but I have no doubt what the gesture means. I'd never spoken about any specifics of the bond Ash and I formed on the road, but I always felt Nisai knew our grief was shared on a level that words would struggle to describe.

"Perhaps," the Magister begins, "the Conclave would see fit to have the Shield brought to the Sanctuary. Where if needed, he can be … managed."

Managed? What does that even mean? Whatever it is, the Order doesn't like it. Murmurs of irritation have erupted around the terraces.

An elderly Order member climbs to her feet. Payuz moves to help her, and my mind goes to the day we arrived. The Administrator. "You say this is Sandbloom's missive?"

"Indeed."

"Then I trust Sandbloom's capacity to locate and deal with the problem. This spawn of the Lost God won't be left to roam long."

Spawn? I'm starting to feel as fond of this woman as I am of the reek of back-alley latrines.

The Magister clasps her hands in front of her. "If what is truly happening in the capital is an attempt to understand the old magic, to harness it for ill use, it seems foolish for us to throw away our only chance at understanding it ourselves."

"We understand all too well," sputters an outraged voice from somewhere in the seats behind me. "He is an abomination. 'Mercy until maturity' is the code all of us must live by when it comes to the Children of Doskai. If you don't recognize the dangers they entail, perhaps you're no longer fit for your office."

"Agreed!" Another voice.

This time a shout. "He must be destroyed!"

The Conclave descends into a sea of squabbling.

I rise to my feet, steadier now that the shock has been replaced with determination. "I would speak for Ash!"

All heads turn towards me. It's what I needed, but I suddenly feel like I'm pinned down by their stares. I take a deep breath, and push through. "Any violence he has ever committed has been to protect Nisai. Or me. I saw it, in the capital. It's only when the lives of those he cares for are in danger that … that the shadow takes over."

"You're drawing this conclusion from a single incident?" the second woman to interrupt the Magister earlier now scoffs.

"There's another one I can vouch for," Nisai says, standing with the help of one wooden crutch. "A long time ago, but I bore witness. And nothing has made me doubt ever since."

"With all due respect to the First Prince, he is but young. He does not grasp the gravity of the situation. One of the Lost God's children roaming free is anathema to the delicate balance of our peace."

I exchange a glance with Nisai, then Barden. When I look back to the Prince, he makes the barest movement with his hand. Guess he wants to see this play out.

"Curing the Affliction must be our highest priority," the old woman continues. "Cases are at an all-time high. The contagion is rampant. The next Days of Doskai are imminent. If they come about again without a cure, then so many children born during those days will draw their first breath from the stench of death. Within a generation, the Brotherhood will have their wish – an army for Doskai, enough to force the masses into the Lost God's worship, opening the door for his return. Then we are all lost."

An army? Of those like Ash? Do they actually believe that's possible?

The Magister spreads her hands low at her sides, making a tamping down motion. "That is true, my colleagues. But if we don't do something now, we might not even have until the next occultation of the moons," the Magister urges.

Stink on a stick. They truly *do* believe it.

"Magister, your sudden change of view surprises me, We must focus on the larger, longer-term ramifications, not the immediate and the individual. The Shield is but one aberration. He should be dealt with as any other Child of Doskai we missed in the past. I see no reason to act any differently."

"I admit I used to be convinced that the only way to prevail was to take a long-term view. To measure life not by turns but by generations. Epochs, even." Her eyes single me out in the crowd. "But I have learned through recent moons that there is a false choice between the individual and the bigger picture. They are one and the same."

The rumbling in the terraces suggests they don't agree, and another green-robed Order member rises to her feet.

"The Procurator," Nisai murmurs. "That's two out of four of their elected officers. If this is anything like the Council—"

"Magister, you of all people know our resources are finite!" the Procurator all but shouts. "What you suggest is the height of irresponsibility! Our lands are on the brink of seismic upheaval, and the steady hand of measured leadership is what will be required to allow us to continue to serve our dedication to the Primordial's will – it takes patience and perseverance to maintain balance in these troubled times."

The Magister's palms slap down on the glass-like table, the sound reverberating around the partially empty terraces. "Patience and perseverance is what I've given for the past seventeen turns! I gave up my life to serve. And my…" She looks to me. "My family."

"Why, Magister." The Administrator steeples her fingers. "This seems uncharacteristically animated of you."

There's a murmur of approval from the onlookers.

The Procurator whispers something in the Administrator's ear. The latter nods, and whispers something in turn to the woman next to her. The third woman stands.

"The Preceptor," Nisai breathes.

"I suggest that an additional vote should be added to the ballot for this meeting."

"And what might that be?" The Magister all but sneers.

"Whether as an Order, we need to elect a new Magister. One who can keep her eye on the true stakes. I call for a vote of no confidence. You're too close to everything, you're no longer fit to fulfil your position."

"Please. I simply want us to scrutinize the problem, to make sure we're considering every angle against the full body of information available. When so many lives are at risk, when the very balance that holds the Empire together teeters on a precipice, I fail to see how that is no longer 'fulfilling my position'?"

Another of the Order members rises to their feet. "I second the motion of the Preceptor."

A rumble passes through the terraces, but nobody else stands or objects.

"Then," the Preceptor says, dusting off her hands, "may I simply remind the Conclave that a vote of no confidence is a matter of conscience, and thus a conscience vote we will today make. Administrator, please prepare the ballots. We shall resume session in an hour for the results."

As sure as smoke rises, each member of the Order gets to their feet and files out after the other office bearers. All except the Magister. She crosses to where we all sit.

"I have seen enough of these moments to know how this will go," she says, bending down so her voice doesn't carry in the now-empty chamber. "They've lost their humanity. When one's life is expected to extend well beyond a century – you develop a different view of time and of the world. I thought I could stomach that attitude for the sake of the greater good. I no longer feel I can. We should leave. Now."

"Huh," I scoff. "Why now?"

Nisai glances at me, questioning.

"It's true," I say. "You were right. They had the cure all this time."

He looks as if he's weighing that up. What it must be to be able to keep your feelings from showing on your face. I know if my father could have been cured and had died, I'd be absolutely fuming.

"There would," Nisai begins, "seem to be a sort of coincidence here – at the point your authority is being challenged, you turn away. Forgive my bluntness, Magister, but how can we trust you?"

"Only you can answer that, my Prince. I suspect the Order will want to keep you here, to ensure your safety until the situation has been fully assessed and debated. But I can get you free of this place and to your mother so that you can find a way to divert the impending political disaster. There are some guards loyal to me. They would see you safely to your family in Aphorai City."

"And what about Ash?" I raise my eyebrows at her pointedly. If she doesn't come out with it, I'm not going anywhere.

She swallows. "It's possible we're already too late."

I shake my head. "I'm not giving up on him. You want to make up for seventeen turns of neglect, you help me find him."

The challenge hangs in the air between us.

Finally, she lowers her chin in assent. "We only have a small window of opportunity. Once they've voted, it becomes as good as law among the Order. They may try to prevent us leaving as it is, but if the Conclave sanctions it,

162

everyone here is obliged to bar the way. Prepare to depart. And quickly."

CHAPTER 11

ASH

Ami refused to be drawn into discussion as I rowed us down the river. She spoke only when absolutely necessary, and then in as few words as possible. It was probably for the best. With only one waterskin between us, we're both quickly parched, and even though I'm the one sweating I don't take my full share.

The river's current did some of the work to carry us towards the Aphorain border, but it slowed to a crawl when the waterway widened, and at other times threatened to beach us on the banks. I attempted to focus on the task at hand, inwardly praying to Riker for strength, though my energy didn't seem to wane. Night or day, I braced mentally and physically, but the muscles in my back and shoulders only protested in a slow, satisfying burn. It's something that didn't escape Ami's notice – her furtive glances a mix of suspicion and disbelief.

We leave the river in the company of a trader caravan, striking out across the scrubland and dried-up canals that used to service Aphorai's farms before the Great Groundshake of 614 shifted the course of the river. Ami uses some of Esarik's silver to hitch herself a ride on one of the pack camels – striking the bargain is the most she's spoken in days.

I take the opportunity to do some trading of my own with the guards, piecing together a practical set of leathers. Perhaps if Ami doesn't have to see me in Esarik's clothes, it will blunt the edge of being in my company. Regardless, I'm relieved to be shedding the fine tailoring and wrapping a linen scarf around my head. Though my hair's grown in enough to cover most of the inked parts of my scalp, and my beard masks much of my face, I can only hope the tails of fabric that drape down over my neck and shoulders are enough to obscure the remainder.

On the third day, the great walls of Aphorai City loom up before us. The plan is that we'll only enter long enough to pick up supplies.

In the market, it's noticeably subdued compared to when I was last here. More Rangers patrol the streets with the provincial guard, and hawkers stay behind their stalls rather than spilling over into the plaza, no longer brazenly announcing that their wares are the finest in all Aramtesh.

My neck prickles with the feeling of being surveilled. Whether it's paranoia or instinct, I make the necessary purchases as swiftly as possible. Dried rock figs that I used to think I would be happy to never lay eyes on again. Some coarse barley bread. I avoid the desiccated strips of horse meat, purchasing smoked sandsquab instead.

Ami blanches.

"Don't like game?"

"I don't eat any flesh on principle. Or anything from an animal."

I regard her quizzically. "But you work in a vocation built on parchment. Does that bother you?"

"I don't dine on books and scrolls," she huffs.

I shrug. We all have our ways.

Regardless of Ami's principles, the stallholder has an open and honest demeanour about him – so I enquire where I can get a map. I'm not about to venture off the main trails in the Aphorain desert without knowing where I'm going. Doing that once was enough, and back then, I had Rakel. Even if she would rush into trouble, she'd always find a way out of it. Though I secretly came to admire that, it's not my preferred way of being.

The baker points us to a map stall, where we find intricately illuminated works that take Ami's breath away. It's a relief to see her focusing on something else, however fleeting, while I almost feel like it's an insult to ask the cartographer for the cheapest, simplest chart they have. But who knows when we'll next find funds.

When I've handed over coins from Esarik's purse, Ami clears her throat.

"We're looking for a friend," she says, fidgeting with the collar of her smock. "You'd know him if you saw him."

The map seller raises curious brows. "Oh?"

Ami opens her mouth to speak but I beat her to it. "They live outside the city. Hence the map," I smile. "It'll be great to see them again. And this will help. Thank you."

I take Ami by the arm and physically steer her away from the store. She shakes my grip, anger sparking in her eyes. "Don't touch me. Don't you *dare* touch me. Ever."

"Then don't start drawing attention to us," I grind through my teeth as we rejoin the crowds of shoppers.

"We need information! This many miles from the capit—"

"And we'll get it," I say as calmly as possible while shooting her a warning look. "I know you don't trust me, but surely you can understand that fueling marketplace gossip is the last thing we need to do right now."

I take her silence as assent. Or at least acceptance.

My next stop is at the barracks at the edge of the Eraz's estate. If anyone knows where Rakel's village would be, it'll be those who knew her father. But I'm not about to go asking for either of them directly. Once, I thought Aphorai so provincial that barely any influence from the capital reached its borders. That smoke's long gone to the sky. Perhaps there's nowhere in the Empire that's truly safe for me.

Or for Nisai.

Or, with Zostar's knowledge of her, perhaps there's nowhere even for Rakel.

The scene at the barracks is comparatively relaxed. There's not a Ranger in sight. Several archers practise their aim on reed-woven targets, a girl younger but nearly as tall as me clearly the best of them. A pair of men, stripped to the waist in the heat, spar with blunted spears while their comrades look on, cheering and hollering when a particularly good strike lands. Beside the door, a thick-bodied guard in Aphorain livery sits with his back against the mud-rendered wall, oiling a studded leather kilt.

"Wondering if you could help me," I begin, letting my accent revert to the melody of the slums, not the measured tones of the imperial court.

He squints up into the glare. "Who's to say, stranger."

"Looking to make a trek. Thought someone around the barracks would be in the know about where I'd find a reliable mount. Been through the auction pens." I punctuate my words by hawking and spitting in the dust, however abhorrent I find the action. "Pack animals for the most part. Know where I can do better? Horse, even?"

He frowns as if he thinks I've been out in the sun too long. "A horse?"

"Aye. Speed suits me."

With a shrug, he sets aside the kilt and disappears into the barracks.

Ami clasps her arms around her, as if she's somehow feeling cold amid the heat. "I really think if we just…"

She trails off as another soldier emerges from the barracks.

The newcomer's face is deeply tanned, a jagged scar on her forehead standing out all the more for the sun she's seen. "Help you, traveller? Traz said you're after a horse?"

I incline my head. "Aye."

"Ha!" She's clearly amused, though it seems good-natured. "Never heard the Mulreth Saga then?"

I remember asking the same of Rakel on the night we fled Aphorai. "I'm not planning on riding it into battle with camel cavalry. Strength and speed is all I'm after. And I prefer their gait."

She waves a hand. "No judgment here. Though afraid your options are limited. And you'll pay through the nose for it." She eyes me up and down, does the same to Ami.

I shrug and reach for my purse. "I'm prepared to invest."

"Keep your coin." She waves my hand away. "But are you prepared to go out of your way?"

"For the best I am."

"Then you'll want to head out of town. Commander—" She shakes her head. "Old habits die hard. *Hab* Ana is the man you'd want to see. Surly old bloke, but he'll see you right."

Hope flares in my chest. I'd never asked Rakel her father's name, but how many former Commanders could there be who breed rare horses? It has to be him.

I produce my map and a stick of charcoal. "Mark it for me?"

"Sure. And tell old man Ana I sent you. Lozanak's the name. Don't know if it'll count for much in a haggle, but we go back some ways."

I manage to stop myself from saluting her. "My thanks."

"And traveller?"

"Aye?"

"Don't look now, but I think you've got a tail. Done something to get the attention of the Rangers, have you?" Her hand rests casually on the hilt of her sword. By the look of her, I don't doubt she can well wield it.

I glance to Ami; her eyes have taken on a wild cast, too much white showing. There's no way to bluff through this. A wager on province loyalty, then. "I'm not in their good graces of late. A man for the First Prince, I am. Only rightful heir."

"Calm," she says. "*They're* not in the good graces of any self-respecting Aphorain these days. You hotfoot it to the gate, none of us will stand in your way. Though it is about time we stepped up the patrols for the evening." She waves over the guard called Traz and sets out towards the two Rangers.

Movement flickers in my peripheral vision. Another pair of men seated at a nearby kormak stall make a pretense of playing shnik-shnik, but I haven't heard the cup rattle with game pieces for too long.

"We need to go," I murmur to Ami, trying not to keep from too obviously mouthing the words. "Now."

For once, she thankfully doesn't object.

We set off in the opposite direction to the Aphorain guards, heading for the main boulevard back to the market. Our best chance is to lose the Rangers in a crowd.

The two shnik-shnik players have abandoned their game and done a remarkable job of closing the distance between us. Definitely Rangers.

I quicken my stride, voicing apologies as I jostle through the press of bodies. Back in the market square, I change direction sharply, checking over my shoulder that I've not lost Ami in the process. She follows nimbly.

When I turn back, I'm nose-to-nose with a live sandsquab seller. I toss the boy a silver coin and unlatch the cage, sending the birds fluffing and clucking into the crowd. Curses and cries of surprise erupt behind us and we duck lower, doubling back to a tight lane off the plaza.

Once out of line of sight, we break into a run until we're one, two, three turns closer to the nearest city gate. We pause, trying to catch our breath. My ears strain for the sound of pursuit. Nothing.

And then we're back into a main thoroughfare leading out of the city. I chance another look behind. Four Rangers argue with twice as many Aphorain guards. The locals aren't budging. I'm not about to stick around to see how long they can hold out.

We slip through the gate.

It's a tense walk to the trader camp outside Aphorai City's walls, but the guard seems to have spoke true.

Esarik's emergency coin stretches to an old nag of a camel for Ami to ride. Walking beside the beast, it's an effort not to constantly check over my shoulder.

Clear of the city, my thoughts soon turn to what we'll do once our supplies run out. Beg? Hire myself out as a mercenary? Sooner or later I'll be recognized and…

I shift my focus to the heat of the day, grounding myself in the here and now. It's as hot as the five hells combined, but I don't mind. After moons cooped up in a cell, being able to use my body still feels a welcome freedom.

The route to the oasis is near deserted. When we were travelling together, Rakel used to lament how her village was "on the road to nowhere". I thought she was at least in part speaking figuratively, but it seems it wasn't an exaggeration. We eventually pass one man and his young son with a trio of camels loaded with trade packs, but see no other signs of human life.

At camp that evening, we hear nothing but the occasional insect. It's a still night, and though there's a chill to the desert air without the sun, it's not unpleasant. I take first watch. The last time I was out here, Rakel and I travelled by the stars. I'd forgotten how incandescent they were. What I would do for a prayer braid and the holy oils for each of the gods. If ever they would heed a prayer, surely it would be under a sky such as this.

Merciful Azered. Guide me back to her?

I let Ami sleep until a few hours before dawn. We travel in the cool of the morning, take refuge at highsun until the late afternoon. It's dusk when we come in sight of the mud houses surrounding an oasis pool like a herd of livestock gathering around the shore to drink. There's the rock fig trees that Rakel used to speak about, and the huge boulder, bigger than any of the dwellings, at one edge of the water. At first glance I think its dotted with paint until I realize the splotches are pale-shelled tortoises soaking up the last warmth.

"How do we know which house is hers?" Ami drags her sleeve across her brow.

"I know there was rosemary growing at the door."

"That won't be sufficient to narrow it down here. What other details did she give you?"

Her studious approach reminds me once again of Esarik, of how they would have been together if they had full lives stretching out before them. Now we all bear the burden of unrealized possibility. Because of me.

I scan each of the dwellings. They may be of simple mud brick, but they're well kept, an aspect of most Aphorain architecture I failed to notice last time I visited the province. Most have clay urns spilling over with herbs at their front stoops, some have roses climbing over the doors.

"There." I point to where a broad-shouldered man lunges a horse, a huge grey with swirled markings like clouds or smoke, in a circular corral. One hand holds a lead rope in a relaxed grip, the other a switch he's lightly bouncing behind the horse's rump with the cadence of its hoofbeats. There's a crutch underneath his arm and his leg is bandaged at the knee but he carries himself upright. A soldier's bearing.

Rakel's father. Surely.

I nod to Ami and set out across the dust.

The man doesn't indicate he's noticed our approach, instead finishing up with the horse, and pouring grain into the animal's feed trough. He disappears between the house and the mudbrick stable.

Ami and I continue to the front door of plain and solid wood. I give it a polite rap with my knuckles.

Nothing.

I try again.

Still nothing.

"Hello," I call.

There's no answer. Where could he have gone?

I try knocking again, this time with the heel of my hand. I'm rewarded with a hollow thud and not much else.

"See if it's open," Ami suggests from behind me.

"I'm not about to play thief."

"You seemed quite comfortable rowing off with someone's boat."

"This is different," I snap, instantly regretting it. I close my eyes and exhale. I can't let my irritation get the better of me, or I'll just be fulfilling Ami's expectations and driving the wedge further.

I try the door handle.

It opens.

"Hello?" I push the door open a little further. Nothing. I take one step, and then another over the stoop.

A flurry in the shadows. The door slams behind me. I'm pinned against the wall, a wooden bar – is that a crutch? – against my throat, and the point of a knife hovering mere inches from my eyes.

"Can I help you, traveller?" The thickly accented Aphorain voice is politeness laced with menace.

"I hope so, sir."

The knife point dips a fraction at the honorific, then steadies.

"You have a daughter?" I enquire. "Rakel?"

He smiles a smile that would almost be convincing if I couldn't see his eyes. "Think you've got the wrong house. I live alone. Unless you count the gelding, and a couple of colts."

I don't blame him for lying. I could be anyone. A Ranger. A mercenary looking for a bounty on the girl who "poisoned" the Prince in case it's still on offer. But I'm sure this is Rakel's father. She has his chin, his high forehead. And I'm now witnessing close up how she knows how to hold a knife. While I'm fairly confident I could get out of this situation alive – even in this close space it couldn't be too hard to unbalance him – I'm not sure I could do it without losing an eye.

"My apologies," I begin, trying not to go cross-eyed at the blade. "I should have introduced myself. My name is Ashradinoran. I served in First Prince Nisai's household."

"And I'm the Eraz of Aphorai. I suggest you be on your way, son."

I'm going to have to prove myself. Swiftly.

"Your daughter has a black horse named Lil that you gave her on her twelfth turn day."

The tip of the knife wavers in front of my nose.

I plough on. "She wears a silver locket etched in stars, holding a portrait of her mother, who died not long after her birth – she thinks it's her fault. When she was young, she used to get overwhelmed by the mix of scents in the marketplace, so you would carry her out of there on your shoulders."

Now it's his expression that wavers.

My words come thick and fast. "She has a temper fit for royalty, and a tenacity I've never seen the likes of before or since. In the name of that refusal to give up, she once stole something from you in order to try to help you – your cylinder seal. And she has a birthmark on her upper thigh, a pale patch about the size of an imperial standard coin."

The knifepoint presses back against my throat. I press back against the wall.

Who in his right mind tells a girl's father that he knows she has a birthmark on a part of her she never shows in public?

"I, ah, I meant nothing untoward, sir. Please. Let me show you I am who I say. May I remove my head covering?"

He doesn't forbid me, so I move my hand slowly, carefully, aware of every pulse of blood in my veins. Finally, I push back my headwrap and the desert cloak from my shoulders, revealing my tattoos.

The knife lowers in time with a whistle through his teeth. Just the way Rakel does when she's stunned or impressed. Sweet mother Esiku, even his mannerisms remind me of her.

I replace the wrap. "You look like you've seen a shade, sir."

"They said you were dead. They *believe* you're dead."

"They?"

"Everyone. Your Prince. *Her.*"

"She was here?"

The door handle opens. He raises his knife again. "Ah, Hab, is it?" Ami peeks around the frame. "My name is Ami, I work – *used* to work – in the imperial Library. For what it might be worth to you, Ash is who he says he is."

I give her a grateful smile. She doesn't owe me any assistance.

Hab inclines his head. "You'd better come inside."

He leaves his crutch by the door, moving about the house with an ease of someone who knows every angle and the distance between every wall, nimbly leveraging the sideboard and table as balancing aids.

"I have some kormak, if you take it?"

"Would I ever," Ami says, sinking on to a rug-covered bench. "I haven't felt truly awake in an age."

I shake my head. I've not had kormak for turns, and I don't intend to start again any time soon. Especially since I haven't had Linod's in weeks, and I'm not yet sure of the consequences of Zostar's tests. The last thing I need is a stimulant upsetting my equilibrium. "No, thank you. Some water, though, would be appreciated."

While he fetches the drinks, I take the chance to look around the room. There's no overt signs that this man was a soldier, though there are subtler clues, if you know where to look. It's tidy to a regimented degree. A linen cloth covers the table, the sharp creases of neat folding still running across the weave. The floor has been swept so meticulously you could probably come to no harm eating your meal off it. Ornamentation is minimal, and each utilitarian item is neatly stowed on a shelf or hook, the incense burners polished to a shine. A place for everything and everything in its place.

And through the doorway into a darkened room, the gleam of a bronze Province Army officer's sword mounted on the wall.

"I'm afraid it's not hot," Rakel's father apologizes as he returns with a mug for Ami. "I only light the fire once a day when it's just me here."

"Kormak is kormak is kormak." Ami smiles, and takes a gulp, sighing with pleasure.

When we're all seated, I cut straight to the point. "Sir, you said they thought I was dead. Please, tell me what you know?"

He smiles wryly. "*Know* wouldn't be a truthful word for this moment. The only thing I'm sure of is there are much bigger forces at play than I'm privy to, lad."

I nod gravely. "Bigger than all of us."

"Your Prince and my daughter, they came by here, true. Both were shaken up. I felt for your Prince – I know what it's like to adjust to walking aids, and he was tired."

"Walking aids? He's…"

My chest aches. The poison. I don't know why I assumed it would have no lasting effect, and yet I'd pictured Nisai to have gone back to exactly as I'd last seen him before that night the dahkai plantation burned.

I regard Rakel's father from the bench opposite. I can't help but let my eyes stray to his bandaged leg. What would it be to lose a limb? Rakel said he had lied about his condition, back when it had just started. Would I have done the same? Trying to cover up a dark secret, a secret that could hurt others?

Time has already told. I'd have done exactly the same thing.

Hab looks down into his cup, turning it one way, then back the other, as if he's working towards a decision. "They were taken somewhere safe. I trust that. But I was not given any further details. For their protection, you see."

He looks me straight in the eye, with that soldier-to-soldier manner.

And knowing he speaks the truth makes it all the more frustrating.

I'm tempted to close my fist around the glazed cup of water, crushing it to shards. If they bit into my palm, all the better. The cleansing fire of pain and anger would be welcome.

Instead, I set the cup down with exaggerated gentleness.

"I understand. At the barracks, I told them I was seeking a horse breeder."

"Under the guise of looking to buy a mount? Can you even ride, lad?"

I lift my chin. "Rakel taught me." Truth be told, I was wary of the beast to the point of fear before that. But no need to mention that.

He grimaces, almost as if he's hurt.

"You have concerns?"

"Only in that now, if we want your ruse to hold, I'll have to gift you a horse."

I scratch my beard.

"And would a razor be stretching the friendship?"

I promised Ami I'd take her to the Library of the Lost.

I'm a man of my word. Though I don't believe I'll ever be able to atone for Esarik's death, it's the least I can do. We'll be quick, and I'll return to Rakel's father's – it's the likeliest place for now that I'll hear any news. And if none is forthcoming, it's as good a place as any to figure out a plan. I may not be able to show my face in Ekasya, but there must be another way to keep my promise to Mish and Del and the other captives beneath the Mountain.

If I thought the trail to Rakel's village was rarely trodden, the several days' ride to the Library – this time not a desperate night flight – is deserted. There's no footprint, not human nor animal. It could be another world. A dead world.

When Ami and I finally locate the edge of the vast ravine system, I scramble up the scree to reach the closest apex. Over to the west, the gorge carves a familiar pattern, each branch laid out in the distinctive shape that was outlined by the stars on Rakel's locket. I'd considered that image so intently it feels like it's seared into my memory.

"Would you go first?" Ami asks. "I'm not good with heights."

"Of course." It's the first time she's asked something of me since we fled Ekasya. I daren't hope it's a first step on the path to forgiveness, but it's better than open hostility.

We pick our way carefully down the slope, managing the first part without too much incident. Ami's complexion takes on a green-white cast, her lips pressed in a thin line, but otherwise she seems to be able to function. Until we approach a particularly tight switchback where the semblance of a path has crumbled away. It's not a huge gap, I could cover it with a jump, but for Ami it would be the leap of a lifetime.

She shakes her head. "There must be another way."

Frustration flares in me. It threatens to darken into anger before I rein it in with considerable effort. Not for the first time, I long for the detached calm bestowed by a dose of Linod's elixir. I scan the canyon walls. We're around a third of the way down, perhaps moving closer to half. There might be other paths further along the gorge, but none within sight.

We backtrack to the top of the gorge. Hours later, we find another route to descend. Hours more, we find ourselves down where we needed to be in the first place.

On the canyon floor, it's cool and hushed. I let Ami take a brief respite then try to retrace the steps Rakel and I took moons ago. But I only end up at a dead-end, the way blocked with drifts of sand half as high as the rock walls that hem us in.

I look to Ami. "We have to leave our mounts."

She eyes the sand drift, then tilts her chin to where the cliffs meet the sky. "I'd rather take my chance with that than those heights again."

Wading through the sand is hard labour. In some places we sink to our knees, others the sand rises even further. The cliffs above us shudder, and suddenly the sand seems like it's alive, shifting and ebbing like it's attempting to consume us. Ami grabs for my hand, and we steady each other. We hurry on, sweat beading both our brows. It was only one of Aphorai's frequent tremors, but the last thing I want is to be caught here in a full-blown groundshake.

Persistence pays, and we finally find the outer concealed entrance to the Library's seemingly dead-end canyon. The rubble and debris that could be easily assumed to be from the rare floods after torrential rain ends up marooned in a tangled mess, masking what lays behind.

Ami looks on, a dawning sense of wonder lighting her features. "How did you find this the first time?"

"We had a map. Of sorts. From the Aphorain Scent Keeper. Seems that woman had been playing a longer game than any of us realized. Her and who knows who else."

"Scent Keeper?" Ami scoffs. "They've been perpetuating reckless methods since the Empire was founded."

"How do you figure that?"

"They directed *you* here, didn't they?"

I study her for a long moment. I'd wager she speaks the truth. Yet it feels as if she's also hiding something. I'm sure of that as much as I'm sure the moons wax and wane. And who is to blame for that? She's lost the heart of any reason to trust me.

We thread single file through the narrow gap in the rock to the enclosed canyon behind. There's a lone boulder near the centre – the one I shifted to counterbalance Rakel's weight when she rushed for the entrance. Ami, in contrast, waits behind. Perhaps she's unsure, or perhaps she's still just keeping her wary distance from me.

"There's a trick to this," I explain. "You have to navigate across the correct stones or…" I gesture to the bleached white skulls at the base of the canyon walls. "Your Chronicler friends don't welcome visitors."

"The preservation of knowledge must take precedence."

"Over human life? So it's ignoble to eat animals, but it's fine to kill people to keep some dusty scrolls a secret?"

"Preserving knowledge may yet save many more lives than the would-be looters who might find this place."

I snort.

"What?"

"The last time I was here, all but two of those who worked here refused to help us. To save the First Prince of the Empire. To stop a potential civil war. Preserving knowledge is one thing. But what use is knowledge if it's kept only in the hands of the select few?"

She doesn't seem to have an answer for that.

I force myself to focus on the task at hand. Too much has happened since I was last here to remember the pattern along the flagstones. So I retrieve another rock from the debris and roll it in front of me, waiting each time to make sure the paving doesn't depress into the ground, on high alert for the sound of the mechanism being tripped.

My strategy serves me well. Soon enough, we're about a third of the way across. I mutter a prayer of thanks to merciful Azered and push the rock out on to the next flagstone. Still fine.

We're not yet to the place where Rakel got caught last time, when I heave the boulder in front of me. It teeters for a moment, then topples down on to the crack between two flagstones. There's a sound like a huge bowstring snapping. Only through reflex do I manage to drop behind the rock as several spears clash into it.

Heart thundering, I look behind.

Ami was not so lucky.

She stands, so rigid that for several terrible heartbeats I think she must have been hit and I just can't see the spear protruding. Then blood begins to ooze from a small graze across her forehead. It drips down over her eye. She makes no move to wipe it away, instead staring straight ahead to the seemingly unremarkable cliff where the weapons originated.

I slowly rise to my feet. "Are you all right?"

She blinks, as if only now realizing there's blood in her eye, and teeters on her feet.

"Here." I gesture to the boulder. "Sit."

I remove the linen wrap from my head and offer it to her. "It could be cleaner, but it's all I have. I'm so sorry."

She stares at it for a long moment, then takes it, and staunches the blood.

I hold up my hand. "How many fingers do you see?"

"Three."

Good. It must have been the most glancing of blows. Mother Esiku watches over her.

"Scalp wounds always look worse than they are."

"Truly?"

I try for what I hope is a reassuring expression. "Though it's probably best if you get this examined when we get inside. Unless you want to start a new sect of warrior-librarians. Then you should leave it – I'd wager the scar would buy you a good dose of credibility."

It's not a very good joke, but she manages a weak laugh.

"Are you able to walk?"

"I … I think so?"

At the concealed tunnel entrance, I light the candle lantern I'd picked up in Aphorai City. It barely illuminates the next step. The tunnel curves down and down and down in a seemingly endless spiral. I'm almost surprised after setting off the spear trap that nobody has come to greet us or head us off from our destination. When Rakel and I visited, it was clear the Library had set an effective watch – they knew when Rangers pursuing us had even entered the next canyon.

Where are they now?

Down, we walk, descending into the depths of the earth. I listen out for the first sign of the delvers, the Chroniclers responsible for carving out new chambers as the collections expand. But the only sounds are our footsteps and breathing, the rustle of our clothes.

Then I smell it.

"Is that smoke?" Ami sniffs the air.

"Char," I surmise. "Let's be cautious."

By the time we reach the main chamber, the odour of a fire's aftermath is undeniable. Last time I was here, the vast circular hall was lit up with a blue-green phosphorescence. Now, less than a quarter of the sconces emit their eerie light, and even that seems to be waning. The great statue of Asmudtag looms on the far wall, barely discernible from the soot and shadows. Even the carved stone walls are charred in places, where heaps of scrolls were piled against them and set alight, the only thing remaining the odd metal cylinder. A flash of mother-of-pearl catches the torchlight. The Kaidon phoenix – the imperial family's crest. I attempt not to read it as a sign of ill portent.

Further in, it appears a bonfire had been set around the Archivist's desk. Frames of some of the chairs and carved catalogue drawers have been reduced to their metal skeletons.

"Hello?" I call. "Anyone here?"

Ami runs forward and I let her go. I can only guess at the devastation she feels, at the way this would have torn at Nisai's heart if he had known of this place, only to learn of its destruction.

When I catch up to her, she's on her knees at the edge of the Archivist's platform, scrabbling in the ashes. She looks up at my approach. Tears trail between the dark smudges on her cheeks.

"Who could do this?" Her voice is plaintive.

"The more pertinent question would be – who *would* do this? And are they still near?"

She flings a fistful of ash to the ground. "I should have realized. Whenever the Head Curator wasn't around, it would be me that Zostar would seek out. I thought he was just one of those people who prided himself on being one of the intellectual elite, a physician flaunting his knowledge of history and other disciplines, like he wished he lived in the Great Bloom."

I know the type she means. The ones at any court gathering who would always be talking the loudest about the facts and anecdotes they "just happened to pick up around the place".

"We should see if anyone is still here." She rises to her feet and attempts to dust her hands of the char. "If any of the Chroniclers are left, they may need our help."

I follow as she heads towards one of the myriad doors leading from the main chamber, hoping for her sake we don't find any bodies.

In the first few rooms, my hopes are borne out. We don't find any charred corpses. We don't find anyone at all.

Ami continues leading me through the chambers. As we pass through the shelves she shines the burning torch up and down. "If they left," she muses, thumbing away soot to take note of the engraved number. "If they got out…"

"Perhaps they did. Before this happened. They seemed to have a sound sentry system when I was last here."

When we reach a particular rack, she starts furiously sifting through the char – the only parts remaining of many of the scrolls the insignia on the ends of the cylinders.

"They're not here," she mutters to herself as she rubs one clean. "None of them are here."

"What's not here?"

"We have to keep looking. You know the Kaidon insignia?"

I nod. A mother-of-pearl phoenix inlaid in black Ekasyan stone. Like the ones I'd seen nearer to the entrance.

"We're looking for the early Imperial equivalent. A silver phoenix inlaid in blue-black stone that's translucent like glass. It only comes from Ekasya Mountain. Let's spread out. If you find any scrolls intact in the surrounding racks, let me know. I need to check their numbers."

But even when our hands are blackened with ash, we find nothing.

Ami wipes the sweat from her brow, leaving a dark smudge across the makeshift bandage around her brow. We're really going to need to see to that soon.

"All the numbers immediately before and after are here. They must have been taken."

"Rangers? Or the Chroniclers?"

"For our sake, and for theirs, I hope it's the latter. Back in Ekasya, Zostar was studying the turns around the founding of the Empire for a reason. They're the earliest records made after the Shadow Wars. They're extremely rare and fragmented, but they're our only sources that come close to telling us about the shadow warriors. The armies of Doskai."

I shake my head. "What he did to me … those children…"

"I think he's trying to create another shadow army. And now he just might have the knowledge to do it."

CHAPTER 12

LUZ

Vexed, is what I am. Truly vexed.

The Shield is alive. He made it to Aphorai City and out into the desert beyond. And all the while he's somehow managed to stay ahead of me. It eventuates he's also more cunning than I expected, covering his tracks so even I was second-guessing whether I'd lost them between the city and the sands.

When I sent the girl on her quest, I told her I'd look after her father. Curing him would have used less dahkai in the long run, but that would be breaking protocol, so I kept my word, ensuring his supply of the most advanced version of the Magister's stand-in salve. Sometimes I even personally delivered it, when it suited. It's no small thing to know your actions are buying a man another moon or ten. Before the salve began to fail in some patients, I would have ventured he could once again start measuring his future in turns.

Still, the old man doesn't know that, and I've built up a decent rapport with Hab. It's good tradecraft – the more friends one has, the less one finds oneself in need of using less palatable methods than polite conversation to glean information.

Hab assured me they left to come here. Yet the positively delightful thought occurs to me – perhaps he was sorely mistaken, and a rollicking about-face will be required to pick up the trail. I truly could be perched here on the edge of the canyon's maw, getting the kind of tan I loathe … for nothing.

Oh, the tedium.

No, there we go: distant voices.

I could investigate more closely, but that wouldn't be prudent: only a fool would corner a rabid animal. So I stay at the top of the canyon. It's the best vantage point. The risk is that they catch wind of me being here fast enough to elude me in a chase. That risk is acceptable, and, I'd venture by the fact they've tethered their mounts well clear, unlikely to manifest.

A bead of sweat trickles behind my ear and I wipe it away. Aphorai born and bred I may be, but the desert has always felt … distasteful. Nothing good can come of one's body odour reaching absolute concentration.

I chose the wrong profession. Give me fountains and shade like the next civilized person.

Below me is the entrance of what was formerly the Library, the reek of old ashes persisting. Though I suspect I know full well who has been behind the destruction, it's been an act of immense restraint not investigating. When exactly it happened, the extent of the damage, is something the Order will need to ascertain. I wonder why we heard nothing. Were the stubborn old Chroniclers too proud to send a bird? Always so fusty and puffed-up with their own self-importance, and refusing to offer aid or seek it.

But that doesn't mean I'd want to see them succumb to the flames.

Movement catches my eye. Finally. Down on the canyon floor, a figure with burnished copper hair emerges from the Library's tunnel. A second figure follows, walking like a warrior. Tattoos trail from under close-cropped black hair. All the way out here, he probably figures it's safe to have not bothered to cover his head. His mistake.

It's him, no speculating about it.

Wonderful.

Only one thing left to accomplish.

I heft the small jar in my palm. A precise blend of mandragora, sultis and poppy powder. The first is enough to sedate without paralyzing, the second makes even the most stubborn forget where they were and what they were seeking to achieve, and the third makes it seem like both those states of being are the loveliest to inhabit. The poppy isn't strictly necessary, but I've always felt there's a certain etiquette about these things.

All I need do is toss it into the canyon and, on impact, it will explode. Within a few breaths anyone down there will be willing to follow me to the end of the earth, at least until they give in to an irresistible drowsiness.

From there, it will only take a flick of a wrist.

Mercy until maturity.

I should do it. Here and now. Before they see me.

Something stays my hand. Tenets must be obeyed, but nowhere in the Order's rulebook does it say you can't do a little information gathering first. I'm ever loath to leave an unturned stone. Even if the secrets beneath are like young scorpions – you can never tell how much venom they'll inject into the situation.

Instead of tossing the jar, I toe a shard of sandstone, sending it skittering over the edge as if I am but a clumsy sniffling out on their first adventure. Best to announce my presence so neither of them get any bold ideas.

They look up and I give them an exaggerated shrug of apology followed by my friendliest wave. I even summon a smile that conveys a reassuring openness that I find about as attractive as oversweetened lover's perfume on an earnest young hopeful.

The Shield shifts, an almost imperceptible change at this distance, but anyone who has ever done serious close-quarters fighting in their time would be at pains to notice.

Better diffuse any tension as soon as possible.

"Greetings, fellow travellers!" I call down as chirpily as one can when shouting. "I mean no harm."

Copperlocks clutches something to her chest. A souvenir? You can take the librarian out of the library…

"Who're you?" The Shield's baritone rumbles around the cliffs. His accent speaks of the slums, not court. Clever boy.

"Your name is Ashradinoran, yes?

"Ain't never heard that name before."

"Come now, might we dispense with this bluster? I have information for you. Not to mention water and food – looks like you're running light on both. There's a tidy little cave not far from here that I'm sure you'll find most interesting. Follow the east branch of the canyon and you should find it easily enough."

"And if we choose not to see this cave?"

"Entirely your prerogative, my wayward travellers. If I don't see you there by the time the second moon rises …"

I'll hunt you down.

"… I'll assume you're not interested in reuniting with your Prince."

Instead of starting up the canyon as suggested, he nudges Copperlocks forward until she disappears under the shade of the cliff. His Shield instincts have taken over, no doubt intending to prevent them from becoming easy arrow targets.

I sigh. "I'll have it known, I would have preferred to do this the civil way."

I toss the jar into the ravine.

✳

I lead their mounts to the cave, my human charges trailing us as docile as tuldah foals following an Edurshain herder's song.

Then they sleep. Like the dead.

I'm not perturbed. Rather, it gives me time to clear out the long-desiccated remnants of the previous resident: a black-feathered lion. Too slow or injured to hunt larger game, I'd venture it retreated here to subsist on sandsquab and canyon squirrel until it found its final rest. At dusk, I build a fire at the cave's entrance in case one of the beast's descendants decides it's time for them to follow in their ancestor's footsteps.

There's a boulder nearby, and I settle on to it, gazing up at the slice of stars above the canyon, my thoughts drifting as they are wont to do to the foibles of the Younger Gods. How disappointed Asmudtag must be in their children, to have been no better than the mortals they once walked among. Though if it weren't for…

I pop a clove pastille into my mouth, concentrating on the spiced sweetness to prevent mention of the Lost God passing my lips.

Copperlocks is the first to wake, regaining her senses with a delicate little mewl.

I return to the cave, stretch my arms wide, hands circling in a courtly flourish. "Welcome to my humble abode."

"You live here?" She blinks up at me, pupils large and dark this far from the fire, then turns the same incredulous expression down to where her hands are tied at the wrists. Bound, but with linen padding between the rope and her skin.

I'm no barbarian.

"Come now, do they not have figures of speech where you hail from?"

She may be as naïve as she is pretty, but there's a sharp intellect there as well, taking in her surrounds like she's reading whole scrolls into every detail. I'd venture she thinks first, acts second.

I wonder if that ever gets her into trouble.

Just as I might be getting myself into trouble for delaying the inevitable. Particularly now that the Shield is stirring. He groans, stretching his neck and twisting his spine one way and then the other before slumping back against the cave wall, though he's still shifting in a way that lets me know he's testing his bindings.

Naturally, they're tighter than the ones I fitted on Copperlocks.

"Who are you?" He demands again, grey eyes narrow.

I've long found that delaying an answer gives one an air of calm superiority. And if even a sliver of the gossip that's emanated from the capital about him is true, an air of calm is of the highest value in this interaction.

"Here." I hold out my waterskin, much fuller than the one tied to the Shield's sorry excuse for a pack – like he's bundled everything he owns into a ragged bedsheet – and gesture to Copperlocks.

She hesitates.

"Worried about poison?" I ask, tone arch, then take a pointed sip.

"You can't blame me, can you?" She leans forward and I gently tip the waterskin against her lips, letting her take several gulps.

It was true, there's nothing adulterated about the water. But the waterskin itself? Smeared with a paste made from suggos powder and nai balm, the latter to mask the smell. While she's drinking, she's breathing my best truth serum, which I've methodically, increment by increment, inured myself against over the turns. Painstaking work, but utterly worth the inconvenience.

I crouch in front of the Shield, proffering the water skin.

He shakes his head.

No matter, the proximity should be close enough for him to inhale sufficient amounts.

"Who are you," he grates again.

If only I had a coin for every time I'd been asked that question. "Frankly, I'm more interested in you."

The tendons in his neck leap up, and he clenches his fists, like he's visibly restraining himself. I'd posit the desert heat is flaring his temper. After all, even I'm struggling to keep my nose powdered out here. But knowing what he is, this isn't just the swelter of Aphorai. Even when he stayed in the Eraz's palace before the Prince was poisoned, my reports said he was throwing back the highest dose of Linod's this side of stopping his heart. But now…

It's true. He's far gone.

A pang of melancholy briefly aches in my chest. If he was born in Aphorai, perhaps Sephine would have saved him. Now, ending things will be a mercy in itself.

Just as soon as I have my information.

"What happened in the capital?"

The question takes him off guard. He scowls and looks away.

"You'd better find that tongue of yours if you want to see your Prince again." The lie falls easily from my lips, even if I don't care for the taste of it.

He looks as if he'd love nothing more than to lunge for me and wrap his hands around my throat.

"You can't win this one with your fists, Shield. Tell me what happened in the capital, and I'll take you to your Prince. He's safe. As is Rakel. Now, speak."

The truth serum would have already loosened the lips of all but the most restrained. A thought of grudging admiration courses through my mind. Perhaps he does have more control than I've given him credit for. But resisting a truth serum is one thing. Resisting the call of the Lost God when your very blood runs with it is another matter entirely.

"I'll not say a word until I see the Prince."

My sigh is the epitome of boredom.

All I need do is uncap the setting on my ring. One prick from finely wrought silver, a tiny break in the skin, and the poison will begin to work its way through his veins. Paralysis would soon set in. And then it will be but a flick of the wrist for a blade to bleed the life from him. If he has nothing to say, it's simply a matter of making sure he never speaks again. Right here and now.

Elegant in its simplicity. Clean. Neat. As I like it. And keeping to the tenet I vowed to uphold.

Mercy until maturity.

Though do I truly believe that is the best course of action here?

There is no easy path to certainty. Not with the confluence of power in the capital. Not when we still don't have a deliverable cure for the Affliction, to bring the provinces and their people to our side. There are simply too many variables. Too much unanswered. So many players in this game have changed, so many new threats on the field. It's not even clear if we're playing on the same game board any more.

But to doubt the Order is to doubt Asmudtag, is it not? I must trust in the ways that have ensured we were able to maintain balance since the Shadow Wars. Otherwise I'm but a mercenary.

My thumbnail finds the ring's cap and flicks it open.

If he won't speak, there's naught much for it.

One little nick, that's all it will take.

CHAPTER 13

ASH

"Stand down, Sandbloom. And release them."

I don't recognize the woman's voice or the style of green robe she wears as she steps into the light. I do recognize that she may have just prevented me from being heavily sedated. Or, more likely, dispatched. Nobody wears a ring like that without purpose.

The operative – after turns at court I'd like to think I know a covert agent when I see one – produces a small blade that cuts through my bindings like a hot knife through soft cheese.

I flex my fingers, then climb to my feet, one hand steadying myself on the cave wall. For a heartbeat, I think I see an additional shadow flickering in the campfire's glow. Whatever was in that powder bomb, it was potent.

Then the operative retreats several steps, revealing a second figure beside the woman. I blink and shake my head, trying to clear the last remnants of fog. Oh, far-seeing Kaismap, do my eyes deceive me?

It's the last sight I expected.

Rakel runs straight at me, flinging her arms around my neck and burying her face in my shoulder. In the circle of my arms, I feel her body being wracked with silent sobs. Stunned, I can only lean against the rock and hold her to me, resting my chin on the top of her head. The scent of desert rose seems to bring me back to myself for the first time in moons.

It's her. It's truly her.

The operative leads Ami and the other newcomer – a woman – from the cave. That one has a strange code of conduct, though I'm not about to complain about the breathing space she's created for us.

Rakel draws back a little, amber eyes rimmed red, tears glistening as they run down her cheeks. "I never thought I'd see you again," she whispers, as if to say it out loud would risk it coming true.

"I wondered the same thing every day," I return quietly, so it's only us who can hear.

"And then when I heard you were alive, and they said you were… They said Luz was going to… I thought I'd lost you all over again." She hides her face in me once more.

"The thought of reaching you kept me alive." The last is murmured into her hair. It's so much shorter since I last saw her, and it tickles at my nose in the most welcome irritation.

I want to ask so many questions – what has she been through, how has she been holding up … did she know where I was? But I start at the start.

"Do you know these people? Are you safe?"

"Safe enough."

"And Nisai?"

"He'll be back in Aphorai City by now. His mother left Ekasya, so he's gone to her and his uncle."

More tension drains from my shoulders.

"How did you find me?"

"I had help…" She trails off, glancing back to the cave mouth. "It's a long story. But not one for here."

She's right. There's so much to say, so many gaps to fill, but this hardly seems the place for those long discussions.

She takes my hand, her fingers warm in mind, and leads me out on to the canyon floor.

Just beyond the mouth of the cave, the operative sets about lighting a campfire. I'd have said it too much of a risk, but once the flames begin to feed on the bone-dry deadwood, it burns smokelessly. And if anyone is close enough to see the light, they're already upon us.

Ami's sitting on a smooth shelf of rock, chatting animatedly to the green-robed woman. Did her parents never tell her it isn't wise to be so open with strangers?

When she sees us, she stands, dusting off hands that were until recently bound. "You're Rakel?"

"Who's asking?"

The palace library curator holds up her hands, signaling peace. "I'm Ami. Ash has told me a lot about you."

Rakel's eyes widen. "Esarik's Ami?"

She nods.

"I'm sorry. I can imagine what you've been through." She looks to me at the last. "It must be hard to know he's gone. Even harder given the why of it."

I tense. Ami and I are at an uneasy truce. The last thing either of us need is to reopen this wound. "Ah, can we perhaps—"

"Don't worry," Rakel interrupts. "The Prince knows she had nothing to do with his betrayal."

Ami reels as if the final word had slapped her. "What are you talking about?"

I'm confused, too. Betrayal? Esarik had been true to Nisai until the last. He helped discover what had poisoned Nisai and decipher the clues to the antidote formula. He even risked his father's wrath to return to the capital in an attempt to source the true amber we needed.

"You didn't know?" Rakel asks, genuinely surprised. "Esarik set the fire in Aphorai. Sent the dahkai plantation up in flames, triggered the poison that Nisai had been primed for."

I stiffen. This is what Zostar spoke of in the dungeons. The assassination attempt was his strategy, but he hadn't completed the final stage of poisoning himself.

Rakel gives Ami a pained look. "I mean, he had his reasons. You were being held hostage."

"By Zostar," I say. "That's who blackmailed Esarik?"

"I don't know. But reasons don't undo treason. And they don't undo the deaths he caused."

"You're lying," Ami says flatly. "Esarik wouldn't hurt anyone."

I cringe inwardly. Rakel is not going to be able to let that go.

"Why would I lie?" she asks, voice rising. "After what I've been through? After what we've all been through?"

"You have no evidence."

"Oh, but we do. In the throne room, before he died, he gave me a letter. It explained everything. Yes, he'd been blackmailed, but he did it."

"No, my Esarik would never—"

Rakel jabs a finger into the air. "*Your* Esarik wrote the letter in some sort of secret language he'd made up with the Prince when they were young. What do you make of that?"

Ami's face blanches paler than the boughs of sunbleached wood. She takes a step back, stumbling over rock. Then she turns, fleeing into the night.

I move to start after her. Even if I'm the last person she'd want comfort from, who knows what's waiting out there in the dark.

"At ease, Shield." It's the operative. "I'll see to her. You eat."

Rakel lets her hands drop from where they'd been balled at her hips. "I didn't mean to drive her away. But … it's just…"

"I know," is all I say.

"I do feel for her. What's she's lost." She shakes her head, all fire gone now. "This is not what I pictured when I let myself dream of finding you."

We've all lost something since this started.

And among it all, perhaps we've lost the possibility of happy reunions.

❋

Rakel and I eat our meal at the edge of the circle of firelight.

She explains that the mysterious operative is Luz, who is also somehow the Chief Perfumer of Aphorai. But the biggest surprise is the woman who stayed the operative's hand. The so-called Magister in the Order of Asmudtag. Who also happens to be Rakel's mother.

It's a lot to take in, even after the events in Ekasya and since Ami and I escaped.

Luz soon returns with a stone-faced and red-eyed Ami, who sits on the opposite side of the fire. After the awful revelations about Esarik, I don't blame her for needing some space. My mind wrestles with my guilt so that I can barely concentrate on the food – trail rations. I focus instead on the feeling of Rakel sitting beside me, not close enough to touch, but close enough that I can feel the warmth of her. A warmth I'd dreamed of for moons.

How can two such conflicting emotions exist in the same moment?

"You're a loquacious bunch," Luz drawls.

Nobody replies.

"There's going to need to be a conversation eventually, you well realize, no?"

She's met with nothing but conspicuous chewing.

"Capital. How about a tale to start the incense burning, then? Get you in the storytelling mood? What's a campfire meal without an epic or two, anyway?"

Nobody objects.

She rises to pace before the fire. The flames leap and fall, casting shadows over her face and the walls of the cave behind her. She draws herself up to full height, so that her stage is a patch of starlit sky above.

"Hearken, and let us weave the tales of the heroes and the cowardly, the noble and the corrupt. Ours is a story of the ilk of fine perfumes, composed of disparate chords blended in harmony. Let us begin, then, with the base notes of our tale: the clash of the small kings, who each believed they commanded half the world, and in the dark parts of their mortal souls burned to conquer the other."

Where before the silence was uncomfortable, it's transformed into something different – a curious hush. This one's a born storyteller, like the bards that frequented social gatherings in the imperial court – a handful of words and your heart is in their fist.

"Which of the Younger Gods, whom among Asmudtag the Primordial's children, made the kings quarrel?" She spreads her arms wide and turns in a circle, taking in all of her audience. "Was it the twins of the waterways, Zir and Tro? Kaismap the all-seeing? Mother Esiku? Azered, merciful mistress of death? Or even youthful Riker?"

The storyteller's question hangs in the air for several pointed heartbeats, until she sweeps an arm back towards the fire. "Nay, it was Doskai, the last of Asmudtag's progeny to spring from the sacred mountain, who ignited the feud. For Doskai felt slighted when he compared his domain with those of his siblings. By night, he held sway over the near moon, but the stars were not his to command. By day, he imbued the shadows, but the sun dictated their potency. His resentment simmered over the centuries, until it had built into a sense of entitlement that took offence even at happenstance. Thus, Doskai challenged his parent, demanding dominion over more of the world."

"Asmudtag regarded their wayward son and sighed. 'Look to balance,' said they, 'and you shall find peace.' But Doskai instead went to the mortal King of Hagmir and whispered from his shadow: 'Bring war to your neighbour, and I will grant you riches beyond your dreams.' He went to the King of Trel, and threaded moonlight through his sleep: 'Take war to your neighbour, and I will grant you power beyond your dreams.' Thus he visited each and every small king until the forces of the realm of men met on the golden plains of Los, all believing one was more entitled to rule than the next.

"Now Doskai truly believed he was most deserving of all the Younger Gods, that his right to reign supreme was his destiny if he could but seize it. His gaze roamed the soon-to-be battleground, settling on the few who had prostrated at his shrines. And lo, he broke the laws of his brethren by imbuing these loyal mortals with his divine will and cloaking them in shadows. His warriors fought as demons, with the strength of six men, storming the field like a winter torrent. As long as blood ran warm from their wounds, they harried every rank, untouchable by spear or sword.

"Darkness descended over the battlefield. Broken and rent bodies strew the plain. The dreadful perfume of sweat and blood, fear and rage, reached the noses of the other Younger Gods. They begged Asmudtag to intervene. For if all devoted worshippers perished, no longer sending prayers up to the heavens, so would the Younger Gods wither and fade into the aether. Asmudtag relented. In exchange for the Younger Gods' pledge that they would never again descend from the heavens to walk among mortals, the Elder granted their high priestess, Kaiseth, a weapon to counter Doskai's shadow army."

"For turns, the forces struggled. But, one by one, the priestess and her sisters vanquished the shadows. When it was done, Kaiseth ordered pyres to rival the Primordial's sacred mountain for the slain, with boughs of sweet wood to bear the wretched souls to the sky. And Asmudtag caused the earth to revolt, the rock rising up, the ground splinting and bleeding noxious fumes, so nought would grow over the falling place of the Children of Doskai, and all who heard tell of the Wastes of Los would know the terrible price their forebears paid."

At the last, Luz bows her head. When she raises her gaze again, it's fixed on Rakel's mother. "It was sworn that thereafter the Order would dedicate themselves to preventing power from becoming concentrated in the wrong hands. Guarding against a time when men with the will of Doskai in their hearts may once again seek to control the world. The Brotherhood of the Blazing Sun fight for the opposite. They believe that the next time a shadow army is raised will be the last time. That the forces of Doskai will triumph over all, with the followers of all the other gods either converted or eliminated. Thus, shall the Lost God return to the mortal realm."

Ami gives a nod of approval, and I find myself looking at the palace library curator, not the grieving girl. "Well told. True to the account sanctioned by the Losian historians. Likely the most accurate version that survives."

Luz bows with courtly flourish. "Now," she says, businesslike. "See how easy it is to share, my friends? It's time we pooled our knowledge of the situation. Who is in charge of this foul operation in Ekasya? The Second Prince?" The emphasis is clearly on *second*. And it's a distinct contrast to what I've heard others calling him for the past moons: Regent. "Is the Emperor's Physician working on his behalf, or is it the other way around?"

"Zostar?" Ami scowls. "He'll only be working for Prince Iddo if it serves his own ends."

"Know thine enemy," Luz says. "What can you tell

us of him?"

"Zostar was a scholar until he was expelled from his professorship at the university, suspected by the board of engaging in experimental work outside the ethical rules that have been honoured since Awulsheg II's reign. When investigated, he claimed his experiments were in service of the Empire. I believe his exact words were "a necessary discomfort to protect and evolve Aramtesh". He said he was feeding and clothing his subjects, who would not have otherwise had two coins to rub together. The implication was that he was doing them a *favour*." Her nose wrinkles at the last, as if to utter the word was to breathe in a particularly heinous stench.

"After his dismissal from the university, he disappeared, perhaps for a dozen turns. Then he resurfaced, calling for members of the medical faculty who were disillusioned with the university's 'antiquated sensibilities' to join his pursuit of 'true' innovation. He convinced a handful the first turn. They convinced a handful the next. Soon his group of disaffected surgeons had formed the Guild of Physicians, with rich donors backing them."

"Ah." Luz taps her nose. "Friends in high places."

"Including the Emperor," I agree.

"Esarik…" Ami's eyes dart to me at his name, then to Rakel, then to her hands, which she busies with picking crumbs from her trail bread. "He had his suspicions. As did I. That at the heart of all the Guild's talk of research and empirically proven methods, there was a desire for discovery no matter what the cost: dignity, pain, life. Now I know it's probably what made us a target. He needed us out of the way."

I scowl. "Esarik was right. Zostar … did terrible things to me to discover the root of my curse. And now that I'm gone, he's going to be using the others."

"Others?" Rakel asks.

"Children. Cursed, like me, and imprisoned in the dungeons."

Luz pins me in an intent stare. "How many?"

"At least a dozen. But there could be more. I tried to get them out, but I had to…" I press the heel of my hand to my forehead, scrunching my eyes closed. "I was forced to choose. I promised I'd return for them. I *will* return for them. Nisai will help me."

"Very well, then." Luz stands, dusting off her hands so that her silver ring glints in the firelight. "It's lovely to see the troupe back together, but our priority is indeed to get to the First Prince. He's as safe as he can be with his uncle in Aphorai City. But he needs to know of what's happening beneath his capital."

I let myself properly exhale. In just days, I'll be back to Nisai's side. And then he'll make it possible for me to make good on my vow to Del, Mish and the other children. It couldn't come sooner. I can only send a prayer to mother Esiku to watch over them until then.

Luz sweeps past us and begins to gather her things from the cave. "We won't be able to complete the journey in a single stretch, so we'll break it up. I know the perfect place. Quaint little oasis village. Sleepy feel. Lovely place to retire, especially for, say, someone ex-military looking to raise a daughter."

Rakel kicks the heel of her boot in the dust.

The woman called Yaita, silent until now, blanches.

"You mean…"

"Oh yes," Luz calls over her shoulder. "Hab Ana's place. Daddy Dearest loves visitors, does he not?"

I take Rakel's hand.

She looks up at me. "*This* is going to be interesting."

CHAPTER 14

RAKEL

Home has never smelled so unfamiliar.

Or so suffocating.

I'd never smelled lilac here before Ami set foot in the door. Luz's violet water, cool and delicate as a fountain in the Eraz's estate, couldn't be more out of place. And before my parents disappeared into Father's bedroom, there was a combination of scents I'd always imagined but never actually experienced – his mint soap and rosemary beard oil and Yaita's smoky desert rose perfume, still worn after so many turns away from home.

When I was young, I used to wonder what my family would be like if my mother was alive. Maybe she'd love riding as much as me and Father – we'd regularly journey to Aphorai City to pick up supplies and when the scents of the marketplace got too much they'd each take one of my hands to calm me. I imagined meals around the table in this very room: herb-laced barley stew, the three of us breathing the fragrant steam. There'd be stories and games of shnik-shnik and laughter. So much laughter.

All the times I imagined my parents together in this house, it wasn't at each other's throats. Now, their voices carry from the bedroom. Hushed tones they're failing to force down to a whisper.

"You didn't give her the letters?"

"Letters? There was only one. I sent it back to the temple a moon after you'd gone. Maybe I shouldn't have, but you have to understand how it felt to—"

"How could you do that to me?"

"To *you*?" I've never heard such frustration in Father's voice. "You left! You never said if you were coming back or not. I was heartbroken. I was trying to protect her from the same."

"That wasn't your decision to make, Hab, and you know it."

"You chose your career. I chose our daughter. Who else's decision could it have been? Yours? After *seventeen turns*?"

The last is the closest I've heard Father get to shouting since he left the Aphorain army.

The others are doing their best to politely ignore the argument, bunking down in the front room, where we should all be trying to get some sleep before we push on for Aphorai City. Luz sits staring at the floor between her boots, twisting a silver ring with an elaborate setting around her finger. Ami holds a candle and pores over what looks like a charcoal rubbing on a tattered piece of parchment.

Ash has quietly slipped outside. It's time I took an ingredient out of the same perfume.

Like the days when we were travelling together, I find him patrolling an invisible perimeter. The rest of the village is quiet.

I cross the dust of the yard. When I'm near, he spreads an arm wide and I step forward without a second thought. He folds me against him, resting his chin on my head.

He's so solid, so real.

But I've noticed there's something different about him, too. I reach up to run my fingertips gently along cheekbones that have become even sharper. His scalp is freshly shaved, revealing the inked fangs of the winged lion that I now know is much more than a tattoo. The ink seems darker, as if there existed a more shadowy colour than black. Maybe I only think there's been a change because his skin has paled from the moons he spent beneath Ekasya Mountain.

Or maybe it's something more.

"Can't sleep?" he asks, in that rich, dusky tone I feared I'd never hear again.

"My father and…" I still can't bring myself to call Yaita "mother". What does that word even mean to me?

"Parents," is all he says, like it's an explanation and his way of signalling he understands all in one. It makes me remember that Father's and Yaita's secrets aren't the worse thing parents have ever done.

Regardless, I can't go back in there.

"I'm going for a ride," I announce.

Ash stiffens almost imperceptibly. "I know this is your home, but a lot has changed. Please be cautious."

"I was hoping I'd have company."

"Oh?" He sounds genuinely curious. "Oh!"

"So?"

His chin lifts as he looks towards the house.

"I think my parents have made it pretty clear they can both look after themselves. And nothing gets past Luz."

Ash's smoke grey eyes are almost black in the moonslight. "Perhaps an hour or two wouldn't risk the world ending."

I return his grin.

Lil pretends at sleep as we approach the training yard where she's corralled with her brother. She doesn't move when I throw her saddle blanket over her broad back, but when I reach to fasten her girth strap, I realize she's puffed out her stomach.

"Not falling for that," I say, waiting for her to let the breath go so I can fix the girth at the right length. "I know you're happy to be home, but Ash and I could really use some wind in our hair. You like him, remember? And we'll make it worth your while…"

The shine of an eye peeks out from under long, black lashes.

"What about a stop at Old Man Kelruk's on the way back?"

She tosses her head and snorts out the extra air she'd been holding.

"Good choice."

We mount up and set out for the distant foothills, Ash riding behind with his arms looped around me like the first night we rode together, fleeing the Rangers across the desert. Unlike that night, Ash moves smoothly with Lil's gait from the get-go. And while we don't have all the time in the world, for now I can at least pretend we do.

Once we're away from the light of my house, the stars pierce the velvet sky. All I can smell is Lil's grassy scent, crushed camelthorn bush, and the hint of cedar that emanates from Ash before the greedy breeze snatches it for herself. Let her have it. With my heart beating a counter rhythm to Lil's hooves, Ash's warmth at my back, the desert night stretching out before us, the world is set to rights. My horse seems to sense it, too; her canter along the dune's crest feels joyful.

Eventually, though, Lil slows. I don't urge her on. We'll be there soon, the smudge of the first of Old Man Kelruk's groves appearing out of the horizon's silvered shadow.

The land slopes up to where Kelruk's limewashed house gleams in the moonslight. From this distance, it's no bigger than a thumbnail, even though it rivals the richest of Aphorai City's homes. Kelruk loves to squawk that he built the place on bedrock so that it can withstand all but the greatest of Aphorai's earthshakes. But it's what oozes from beneath that rock that's made him rich – springs that provide water for the thousands of orange trees that stretch from the edge of the desert to his hinterland stronghold.

As the dunes give way to dust and rock, the first whiff of neroli reaches me.

"Nice place." Ash's breath is warm against my ear but lures a shiver from me in its wake.

"And far enough away that nobody will ever know we're around. I used to come here when I was young." I explain over my shoulder. "This is my favourite season. Aphorain sun ripens the crop right quick, so the harvest would have come and gone. Now the next bloom has begun, and the occasional fruit that Kelruk's pickers missed is the sweetest you'll find anywhere."

"Anywhere?"

"Even in fancy-flower Ekasya."

"Is that a wager?"

"It's a promise."

We reach the treeline, and Lil weaves between the rows of trunks before I signal her to halt and slide from her back.

212

Ash does the same, landing on near-silent feet. I push Lil's reins back over her neck and tie them off to let her graze on the grass around the base of the trunks. Wouldn't be surprised if it's the only green feed growing this side of Aphorai City.

Ash holds out his hand.

Almost shy now that we're alone, I take it.

The leafy canopies tower over us as we stroll, the heady scent of orange blossom gathering us up in its embrace. An image of the last time I smelled that scent flashes through my mind – arriving at the Aphorain temple after I failed the perfume trials. But that was then. Now, I'm going to reclaim the heady perfume by making a happier memory. No matter what comes after tomorrow, I'll have this night.

We pause beneath one of the trees and I shuck my boots.

Ash tilts his head in that way that makes him seem suddenly boyish, questioning.

"Way easier to climb in bare feet." I jump for one of the lower branches and swing myself up, holding the trunk as I stand and reach on tiptoes to the shadow of an orange that evaded the harvest. The stalk comes free from the branch with a satisfying snap.

"Hey, sweet tooth," I call down to Ash. "Try this."

He snatches the orange out of the air with casual ease. By the time I've scarpered back down the trunk, he's peeled it in a single curl, the clean zing of the rind joining the orange blossom in perfect harmony.

He hands me half, and I pop a segment into my mouth. There's no words for how much I've missed this taste.

"Well?" I ask around the next segment.

He chews slowly before nodding towards the stars. "I imagine this is what the gods eat."

"Pah, if they want these, they'll have to go through me first. And Old Man Kelruk. He'd scare the stench out of them. If he caught us down here he'd…"

Ash moves slowly closer. "He'd what?"

"Whatever it is, we wouldn't like it," I say, toying with the lacing on his leather vest.

Another step, this one as his hands land lightly on my hips. "Then perhaps we should be more discreet."

I edge backward until we're under the boughs, out of the gaze of the distant manse on the hill, of the stars, of the whole world. The tree's leaves are so thick it's black as pitch but it gives me the distinct feeling that nothing bad could ever happen under here. This darkness contains no threat. It's ripe fruit and honeyed blossom and that unmistakable earthy spice I thought I'd never breathe again.

As if he could hear my thoughts, Ash's hands tighten. The next thing I know my feet have left the ground so easily I could be weightless. On reflex, my legs wrap around his waist, my arms around his neck, my body as sure as my mind that there's no place I'd rather be.

If I could see mere inches in front of my face, I'd be the taller one looking down at him. There's a delicious sort of power in this moment. Even as my pulse quickens, I don't want to rush. I run my fingertips lightly along his collarbone, let my thumb trail up his throat, trace the sharp angle of his stubbled jaw, and finally graze over his mouth.

His lips part with a soft sigh.

I lean down to meet them.

Our last kiss was anguish. This one is pure need. It's searching. Seeking with lips and tongues that still taste of sweet orange between stolen breaths.

Heat is building at every point our bodies meet. Ash's hands run from my thighs to the small of my back, pressing me closer. Even through his leathers, I can feel that he wants me as much as I want him.

Until he tears his mouth from mine with a soft moan that's as much pain as pleasure.

"Ash? What is it?"

He straightens abruptly. A soldier's stance. Formal.

I don't understand.

Then he's lifting me away and setting my feet back on the ground.

"I'm sorry. I—" He inhales sharply, like he's barely holding himself together.

I remember the caves in Trel, the almost total darkness after the blue glow of the coral died out. For me, it was a part of our narrow, hard-won victory. For Ash, it triggered a panic attack.

I reach out, take his arm gently but firmly, and lead him out from under the tree, back into the pale sheen of the night sky.

"Ash, are you all right?"

He doesn't reply. His eyes are closed, and he's taking slow, purposeful breaths.

"Do you want to sit?"

He still says nothing, but he lowers himself to the ground, shifting with a wince until he settles in his usual cross-legged pose.

At another time, I might giggle. But instead I sit, mirroring him, and take his hand. I wait until his breathing has calmed completely before I speak. "Was it the darkness? Like in the caves?"

He shakes his head, eyes downcast.

I swallow, preparing to ask the last thing I want to ask. "Was it … me?"

"Perhaps." His voice is so low and quiet that for a heartbeat I wonder if it was my fear speaking rather than him. But then he raises his face, and the shadows can't hide the pain and frustration.

It's everything I can do not to jerk my hand from his.

"It's not what you think," he says, letting out a laugh that's more self-loathing than amusement.

Not what I think? There's no room for logic when I'm fighting off terrible guesses and raw, stinging doubts.

"It's that, well…" He bites his lower lip, lets it go again. "I've … I've never…"

Am I going to have to shake the answer out of him? What in the sixth hell, Ash? You've never *what*?

Oh.

Oh, oh, oh.

I try to keep my voice even, matter-of-fact. "You've never been with a girl?"

"I've never … fully … with *anyone*. You know I loved Nisai. And yes, we stole our share of affection behind the palace curtains before I realized all that needed to be set aside if I was going fulfil my duty as Shield. But even prior to that, it never went too far. I didn't let it. I was always taking so much Linod's, I didn't want to… I didn't want to not be fully me. Fully present. In the moment." He draws back, hand going to where there used to be a prayer braid around the opposite arm. "And now … you've seen what happens when I lose control."

The shadow part of him. What happened in the throne room back in Ekasya. "I don't think this is anything like—"

"How can you know?"

He's got a point. I can't know. No matter how much I believe it would be fine, *more* than fine, that it may even be something healing for both of us, I can't say for sure.

This time, he takes my hands in his much larger ones. "I want to, Rakel. Believe me, there's not much more I've ever wanted in my life. But until I find out more about how this works, how *I* work… I need to know that if we were together, I'd be completely me. Not numbed by a drug. Not governed by a curse. I'm … I'm sorry."

I rub my thumb against his calloused palm. "I hope you know I'd never want you to do something you didn't want with body, heart *and* mind."

He smiles, almost shyly. "Thank you."

"But in the meantime, just so I'm clear – kissing. Fine, yes?"

"More than fine."

I lean forward and brush my lips feather-light against his cheek.

His smile broadens. "I think I can handle a little more than that."

I smirk. "Good things come to those who wait."

He throws up his hands in mock defeat. Then his smile turns mischievous. "You never said the same."

"Sorry?"

"You didn't say the same."

Why does it feel like I'm suddenly unable to smell the orchard for the oranges?

"I'd wager," he continues, "that means *you've* done it before."

I burst into laughter, but my cheeks burn. Thankfully moonslight doesn't show up a blush. I stand, dusting off my trousers, hopping from one foot to the next as I pull on my boots.

"It's probably time we got back."

I scan the surrounding lines of trees. My long-distance sight has been on the slow improve, but I still have to squint until I spot Lil several rows across. Ash falls into step beside me. When we reach my horse, she lifts her head and nips Ash on the shoulder.

"What did I do to deserve that?" he asks, ruffling her mane. She lets him.

"Asking ridiculous questions, probably," I retort.

On the ride home, I'm painfully aware of Ash's bulk behind me. I realize I'm sitting further forward in the saddle than is good for Lil, my heels not properly down, even though I try to tell myself nothing has really changed.

I shift my focus to pointing out as many landmarks as I can. Places I would know were there even if I couldn't see at all. My whole world until not long before Ash and I first met. When there's nothing of interest left to note, I figure I might as well get what I really need to say out of the way.

"Twice," I blurt.

"Pardon?"

"You heard me. I've done it twice. Once to get the awkward first time out of the way, and the second to check if I actually liked it."

He chuckles at that, soft and throaty. "And your verdict?"

"It was nice. But not groundshake material. Figured that was probably because it wasn't with the right person. Not that he shared the same opinion."

"Ah. Barden?"

"Uh-uh." I can't help but wonder if the space I've been keeping between us is turning cold.

"You could have told me it was none of my business, you know."

"I could've. But I've had enough of secrets. You're the last person I want to keep anything from."

The muscles in Ash's arms tighten.

I can hear my heartbeat. Slow. Waiting. Dreading what might come next.

But all he does is shift me to where I should be in the saddle, my back to his chest. He smooths my hair and kisses the nape of my neck.

I let myself exhale.

It's still a ways yet to my village.

Though I feel like I'm already home.

CHAPTER 15

LUZ

The ride back over the dunes to Aphorai City gives me time to reflect.

It was a fractious interlude, though not without its parochial charm. The girl was reunited with her father and stole an evening with her beloved Shield. Copperlocks pored over her collection of scrolls and fragments as if she were trying to read her destiny in a cup of kormak. And, judging by the din emanating through the mudbrick walls, Yaita and old man Hab had the former-lover's tiff to end all former-lover's tiffs.

It was clear upon our departure in the cool hours before dawn that there was no rekindled affection, no sign of reconciliation within that most convenient and yet often confining of arrangements: marriage. Others may have seen two hands clasped for the briefest of moments. They may have comprehended it as a poignant gesture. Perhaps a symbol of regret, an acknowledgement of the turns and love lost.

I'd ventured I was the only one to catch the glint of the

vial that Yaita pressed into her estranged husband's palm.

Until the girl slows her horse, dropping back to ride alongside my camel. "It was the cure, wasn't it?"

I sniff. "You'll have to be more specific, petal."

"What Yaita gave to my father."

"What do *you* believe it was?"

She shifts her gaze to Yaita, who rides some distance from the rest of us, her mind no doubt still back at the oasis village. Then the girl reaches down to stroke the mare's midnight neck. "What do you think, Lil? Did she do something purely decent after all this time?"

"If you truly want to know, wouldn't it be best to ask your mother rather than your horse?"

The girl shrugs. "I trust Lil more than either of you."

"I'm wounded. Deeply wounded. And to think I'd ventured you'd be grateful for my showing mercy to your Ashradinoran."

She gives me a long, considering stare. "Why *did* you do that?"

There may be a time and place in our futures for an explanation, but this is most certainly not it. I return her frank appraisal. "Never question my motives, petal."

"Pah."

She nudges the beast's flank with her heel and rejoins the Shield. He'd been the most relaxed I'd seen him earlier in the ride, but the closer we get to our destination, the more rigid he becomes. Copperlocks, on the other hand, rides absently, sketching in a notebook. One lurch from her camel and she'll topple into the sand. I suppose that's her prerogative.

As the great walls of the Aphorai City appear above the

dunes, something else demands my attention. Movement – along the ridge of one of the emperor dunes that leads towards the city. I've used it enough times to observe comings and goings to know it's a decent vantage point.

It's too far to know whether they're friend or foe, so prudence demands acting as if it's the latter.

I draw my mount level with the others. "Let us pick up the pace a little, shall we?"

Copperlocks' head snaps up. "What is it?" she asks, a nervous wobble in her voice.

"Rangers always scout in pairs." The Shield scans the dunes. "If that's what they are, there will be more nearby. There. The ridge opposite. And further along."

"It's almost as if they knew we were coming," the girl says.

I curse inwardly. Am I slipping? Was Old Man Ana's house being watched? Or did the Shield and Copperlocks have company before that? I'd run a perimeter around the Library and not seen another soul, did I miss something? Or did the girl and Yaita inadvertently stumble into one of their scouts without being any the wiser?

Speculation won't help. We need a solution. Other than the winged lion of Aphorai flying from the battlements, there's no way to discern what's taken place in the city since I last left. If Ekasya has turned into a foreign land, what manner of welcome will we find behind the walls before us?

I'd venture it couldn't be significantly worse than where we'll find ourselves if we're apprehended out here.

"Keep your mounts faced forward. We'll maintain that we're unawares until we're level with the first group, then we'll put on some speed."

The girl eyes the camels. "I'm not sure they'll be as fast as—"

"And if it looks like it's going wrong, you and Midnight here give your all to reach those gates and get help. We have to trust that the Prince safely returned and the balance of power inside those walls tilts in our favour. If we don't make it, our fate is in your hands."

"You trust me to do that?"

"I have no choice."

The Shield balks. "Someone else can take my horse. If anyone's left out here, it should be me."

"We don't want to draw any attention by playing musical mounts." Though by the looks of the first pair of figures getting to their feet, it's too late for that. One raises their arms in the unmistakable stance of an archer.

"*Ride*," I bark.

They don't have to be told twice.

❋

It's only by the Primordial's grace that we avoid becoming human pincushions. It wasn't through lack of effort; the arrows rained, one sticking in my mount's pack uncomfortably close to my thigh.

When we're through the gates, I'm compelled to do a *lot* of fast talking. It's not the easiest thing to accomplish while trying to catch one's breath at the sharp end of a whole patrol's spears. Eventually, the guard captain appears and we come to an understanding that he'll let us pass. Thankfully, it doesn't cost nearly as much as the same transaction had in Ekasya.

It's clear Aphorai City is preparing for a lockdown of its own. Buildings in the outer edges of the sector are being boarded up. Sacks of rocks and quivers of arrows lashed together are making their way up pulley systems to the battlements. Province Army officers work alongside the Eraz's own guard to draw water from the wells and stow it safely in barrels should the groundwater be compromised. Above it all, the sound of smith's hammers on metal rings out. Armour. Weapons. Reinforcing braces for the city's fifteen gates.

And, most importantly, not a Ranger in sight. Yet.

I look to the Shield as he self-consciously tucks the cloth covering his tattoos tighter, and consider my options. The general populace can be superstitious at the best of times. When their safety is under threat, their minds are even more volatile. Our first stop will be the Chief Perfumer's manse; my people are the very essence of discretion. From there, I can set out solo to meet with the Prince directly at his uncle's, without getting waylaid by a jittery crowd looking for something to exorcise their fear upon.

I lead the way through the streets. When we arrive at the plaza closest to our destination, two guards block the way.

"Papers, please?" For good or ill, he doesn't recognize me. Yet unlike their Ekasyan counterparts, the Aphorain guards have kept the semblance of civility.

"We're friends of the Chief Perfumer. Perhaps you'd let the appropriate valet know we've arrived?"

"No can do, I'm afraid."

With valiant restraint, I maintain a mild expression.

"Can't? Or won't?"

"Can't. For good reason, mind. Forgive me for saying, but your friend never struck me as the generous type. S'pose when it matters, it matters though. Donated all their resources – staff included – to the city's defence."

Suspicion curls like incense smoke around my thoughts as I peer past the guard into the plaza. It's abuzz with members of the Eraz's household staff. There. Among the hive. A particularly officious steward. One who no doubt gleefully seized the opportunity to exact bureaucratic revenge after being duped by the Chief Perfumer into signing away the Eraz's own barge for my trip to the capital.

It's distasteful. But it's not worth the fuss. At least for now.

The next best place to seek refuge is the temple. Given the high priestess is technically in charge until another Scent Keeper is agreed upon, she could have moved into Sephine's quarters after her death. She chose not to. She's always been a reasonable woman, but that action garnered even more of my respect. Not to mention that the best place for the Shield to be – whether the future bodes well or otherwise for him – will be under her watch.

Temple it is.

I force a smile for the guards and turn to the others. "Change of plans."

The girl opens her mouth but I stop her with a snap of my fingers. "Not now, petal. Please, not now."

The distance between the perfumery and temple has always been a mild inconvenience, but today it's positively grating. Rather than the usually orderly to and fro of business, people are behaving erratically. On edge.

At least when we reach the temple estate, the guards admit us without pretence. We're escorted through the gardens of lavender and neroli, olive and bay, and up the endless flights of stairs to the high priestess's quarters on the second tier of the temple's five-sided pyramid.

The woman herself sits at a desk, her head bare of hair or adornment, her body draped in a sleeveless tunic tucked into the crimson-feathered skirts of her office. Her face is creased by deep lines of consternation. It would seem the bunches of holy thyme suspended from the low ceiling and the vetiver and opoponax incense have not brought on the spiritual calm one would hope. The burdens of unexpected leadership, one supposes.

She waves the guards away.

"Luz." She greets me, businesslike. "And is that you, Yaita? How long has it been since you left our halls? Twelve? Thirteen turns?"

"Seventeen."

"And did you accomplish what you set out to do?"

Yaita looks as guilty as an acolyte who slept through dawn prayers. "Not entirely. Which is why I'd ask your permission to access Sephine's quarters. I'd continue my work with what remains of her resources."

The high priestess nods assent. "The Prince has been notified of your arrival. He shall join you in the archives after evening prayers." She wrinkles her nose so that the lines of consternation twist into aversion. "You've had a long journey, please refresh yourselves. Someone will be here soon to show you to some lodgings."

"Where is Nisai then?" Rakel asks. "He's not on the Eraz's Estate with his uncle?"

The high priestess gives Yaita a pointed look. "Your daughter, I presume?"

"Yes, High Priestess."

"Impertinence runs in the family, I see."

Yaita mumbles something but the high priestess is already moving on.

"And you." She jabs a bony finger at the Shield. "You're only being granted sanctuary because your Prince requested it. But you must not miss a prayer."

He nods, seemingly unperturbed. "Of course, holiness. I'm grateful for the opportunity. It's been too long since I've had the chance to visit a temple."

Satisfied, the high priestess stands and smooths down her feather skirts. It's a signal of dismissal that goes over the heads of most of the others. "Off with you, then. Clean up and proceed to your meeting. It's impudent to keep Princes waiting."

As the acolytes refresh the candles along the temple halls after evening meditation, I join the others in the archives. The Losian stands guard by the door, arms crossed, wearing her traditional scowl and battle braids. She grunts acknowledgement as I enter.

What a splendid new development. I flash her a smile in return.

His Imperial Highness, the First Prince and Emperor-elect, sits at the head of the table. Though his journey was shorter than ours, it appears it has taken its toll – he looks more than a little haggard. The big, amber-drenched

Aphorain sits close beside the Prince, as if he has no concept of courtly protocol. Though given his time spent in the palace, I'd venture he is entirely aware of his infraction.

In contrast, the Shield seems out of sorts. A lingering look passed between him and the Prince when he entered, but that was the extent of it. Now it's as if Ashradinoran doesn't know his place. He's trying to appear relaxed, but he can't sit or lean or stand for more than a few moments before prowling to another side of the room. Every so often he glances sideways at the Aphorain guard.

Amber, to his credit, ignores him.

"Your highness," I greet the Prince, honouring him with the most elaborate of bows. "Lovely to see the troupe back together."

He inclines his head.

Copperlocks has already half buried herself in scrolls. I pull up a chair across the table from her and turn it around, straddling the seat so I can lean folded arms on the time-polished back.

The Prince rests interlaced hands on the table. "My mother arrived back in Aphorai a few days before us. She has confirmed that my brother disbanded the Council of Five."

"Treason," the Shield scowls.

"I'm loath to put it so bluntly, but, technically, yes. My brother is in breach of the Founding Accord. He is also amassing an army back in the capital. My mother and uncle are united in their response."

"My Prince, with all due respect," I say, "marching to the capital is not the answer here. I've seen the forces camped at the base of Ekasya Mountain. Even a moon ago they were far more than Aphorai alone could muster. And from what I found in the capital, their numbers are likely to have swelled with more mercenaries since."

"Which is why we're not preparing to march. We're preparing for a siege."

CHAPTER 16

ASH

Anyone using their eyes or ears would have already worked it out – Aphorai City will soon come under attack. But hearing it out loud still causes a hush in the room. I try to catch Nisai's eye again, to read his thoughts from his expression, but he's using that measured-movement gaze he employs when he wants everyone in the vicinity to feel included in the conversation.

Everyone except me. Before all of this started, it would be a completely normal state of affairs for me not to be actively involved in a relatively public occasion. But after everything, the realization stings.

"How long do we have, my Prince?" Luz enquires.

"Scout reports suggest days. A quarter moon at most. The walls have never been breached, so we remain convinced this is the best place to make a stand. The imperial treasury won't last for ever – a protracted siege will see loss of mercenaries in the attacking force. Even so, we must know exactly what we're dealing with." Nisai leans forward, addressing me directly at last. "Ash, when you were back in Ekasya…"

It should be like the sun has finally decided to shine upon me, but now I'm the one who looks away. This is not something I want to get into here, in front of relative strangers, without having the proper chance to sit down with Nisai. And truthfully, it's not something I ever want to burden him with. He'll take it on, bear it as his own. Judging by the looks of him, and the circumstances we find ourselves in, he's got enough on his plate. Nothing good can come of me labouring over the sordid details. "I was in the dungeons. Imprisoned by your father's physician, of all people. And he has others. Much younger than me. We need to find a way to free them."

"Zostar? Zostar Alak?"

I nod stiffly.

"But how could he have control over the penitentiary without..." Nisai's features work as he processes the information, quickly moving through the implications to draw the logical conclusions. "When you were incarcerated, did you witness anything that *proves* my brother is in league with Zostar? Is this a knowing partnership he's entered, or is it calculated opportunism on Zostar's part?"

"Zostar heavily implied he had your brother's ear. How much credence you give the rantings of a reprobate is up to you."

"Even reprobates can speak the truth," Luz observes.

The muscles in my jaw ratchet tighter – what matters is freeing Mish, Del and the others, not the precise level of blame we should assign Iddo. "I don't know exactly where Iddo stands in this. What I do know is that Zostar is chasing something. And he thinks I'm key."

"It does seem you were a fixation," Nisai agrees.

231

Seems? *I was tortured*, I want to roar. But I bite down on the inside of my cheek until the taste of metal fills my mouth.

"What we need to know," he continues, "is what does understanding your power, the remnants of Doskai's magic, actually achieve for Zostar? What would he actually do with that knowledge?"

"The Lost God was into tearing things apart," a voice rumbles from behind me. Kip. "My province lives with the consequences of the Shadow Wars to this very day. The Wastes are a godless place. And we'll be like chaff under a scythe if he actually manages to create and control a new shadow army. Figuring out how the Lost God's children work and how to control them is a logical first step."

I flinch involuntarily at "one of his children". *You're no child of mine*, my father used to say, as if I was more curse than boy. It makes me think again of Del and the others beneath Ekasya. Either stolen from their families or maligned by them. Now, they're relying on me.

Luz twists at one of her silver rings. "Bring back the warriors, bring back the Wars."

Kip gives her a tight nod.

Nisai's brow furrows. "I always knew Zostar was ambitious. But nobody rises from obscurity – or from disgrace – to become personal physician to the Emperor without cunning and intelligence. I simply can't comprehend how any thinking person could wish to plunge us back into slaughter and chaos. Wanting power is one thing, but that implies there would be something or someone left to wield that power over."

I close my eyes, inhale slowly through my nose, gathering myself to give a reply that sounds rational.

"My Prince." Luz beats me to it. "If I may. To me this bears the hallmarks of *divine* ambition. It doesn't have to be logical. Ancient scripture foretells of Doskai's struggle to seize power by being the only one among his brethren left standing with worshippers. If this Zostar's a true zealot, he doesn't need there to be an Empire to rule over when the ashes stop burning, because he thinks by then he'll have become one of the Lost God's most favoured in a new regime. Copperlocks, you're the history expert. Is that about the right of it?"

Ami's eyes are wide, but she manages a nod.

Nisai massages his temples. "Most favoured of a god? Zostar is in his twilight turns, and as head of the Guild of Physicians, he must have had a wealth of knowledge before this. Could he truly believe that?"

"I've been face to face with him," I say. "I wouldn't put it past him to think he will be made new again by his god in return for his service. Made immortal, as he seemed to be testing to see if I was."

Nisai's eyes light up. "You're immortal? I've always known you to heal quickly but … truly?"

"Of course I'm not immortal," I snap, suddenly frustrated that he's more fascinated with what I am than what I've been through to survive and make it back to him.

He reels as if I'd struck him, and I immediately regret the sting in my words. What is wrong with me? None of this is Nisai's fault. He didn't ask to be poisoned. Didn't ask to have to flee the only home he knows because it's become a nest of vipers who want him dead. He didn't even ask to be heir.

Then the Aphorain guard shifts. Barden. He squeezes Nisai's shoulder. You don't simply *touch* the First Prince of the Empire. I want to slap his hand away, or twist it behind his back until he…

I give myself an inward shake.

Luz clears her throat. "All right, Copperlocks, what do you have for us?"

Ami looks up more than a little nervously. "It might be nothing."

"Let us be the judge of that," Nisai says gently.

"We know from the histories that at the end of the Shadow Wars each of the small kings pledged never to harness the Children of Doskai for another battlefield, yes?"

"That is the accepted version of things," Luz agrees.

"But it was a full cycle, 125 turns, between then and the Founding Accord. A time of darkness and unrest. In many parts of the Empire, the crops failed. In other parts, there weren't enough able-bodied left to harvest them. A high proportion of those who had survived the conflict succumbed to starvation. There wasn't time or energy to spare on scholarship or history. People were just trying to survive."

"Almost anything we know of that time," Nisai picks up, "comes from spoken stories that weren't committed to parchment until after the Empire was founded, and some of those accounts were revised again during the Great Bloom."

"We have no accounts from anybody who actually lived to see what happened?"

"Precisely."

"Still," Ami continues, gesturing to the piles of scrolls on the table before her "even stories that have been handed down a hundred-fold usually have a kernel of truth at their core. And many of the stories talk about the provinces putting in place plans for the future. Safeguards, should they ever be caught in the same position again, neighbour declaring war on neighbour under the influence of the Lost God."

Luz props her chin in her palm. "Safeguards? Is it possible our ancestors were simply indulging a flight of fancy?"

Ami unfurls a scroll, weighing it down at the corners. She gnaws at a fingernail. "When multiple sources speak of the same thing, I suspect corroboration over coincidence. If there's anything the histories agree on, it's that the shadow warriors, the wraith forms of the Children of Doskai, were untouchable by sword or spear. Arrows passed straight through. But the accounts say there was a weapon. Something that could combat them."

I push back from the table and walk away several paces, then turn, jaw clenched. "Forgive me, my Prince." My voice is strained, formal. "But why this talk of weapons? Why not concentrate on stopping those who share my curse from being used for ill in the first place? Those children are innocent. They need our help."

"It's not that simple," Nisai says, eyes on his notebook.

"Seems straightforward to me."

Luz holds up a hand. "Let's say we can each bring ourselves to believe such a weapon exists, and that if Zostar works out how to raise a shadow army, we can be equipped to oppose him. Where might we find this weapon?"

"We'll keep working on joining the dots," Ami says as she unfurls a scroll and weighs it down in the corners. "Between Nisai's personal research over the turns, and what I've gleaned from Es—" She stops still, staring down at the scroll for one, two, three slow blinks. Then she clears her throat. "From what I've gathered, we've been able to see a pattern. Of the sources that do talk of such a weapon, they hint at them being hidden beneath the ground in undisclosed locations. Closely guarded secrets through the generations."

My posture is now entirely rigid. "And when you acquire this weapon, will I be the test case?"

The question hangs in the air. Ami shifts in her seat. Even Barden has the sense to look uncomfortable.

Rakel has been uncharacteristically quiet all this time. Now, she sits forward. "So, we've got a rogue Regent who wants to be Emperor so bad he might lay siege to his brother's home city, who has teamed up with a doctor who is trying to create a magical doom army and, what, take over the entire Empire? Because said doctor may or may not be possessed by a god who thinks everything is his for the taking? And if that's true, the only chance we have is finding some legendary weapon? Is that pretty much what you're all saying?"

She looks at each of us in turn.

Nobody disagrees.

Rocking back in her chair, she lets out a long, low whistle.

"Well then," Luz says, "my Prince, Copperlocks, may I suggest you continue narrowing down the possible locations for these ancient weapons? A little insurance never hurt anybody."

Nisai inclines his head. Ami is already back to her reading.

"Petal," she says to Rakel, who, to my surprise, doesn't balk at the name. "I expect Yaita will appreciate your help. The Affliction doesn't need curing any less because we're staring into the abyss of a siege."

"Lostras, Amber" – Luz points in turn to Kip and Barden – "you two fine specimens make friends with the temple guard officers. Put their people through their paces. You're fresh blood, and we need to know if there's any weak spots we need to address to make sure our imperial highness is safe during his stay. I don't want security to be lax with all these distractions."

"You." She jabs her finger in my direction. "Help them out. Don't make me regret bringing you along for the ride."

Or you'll finish the job you started back at the Library? I want to say. But I give her a grudging nod.

"Now if you'll excuse me, I'm overdue a meeting with a certain bureaucrat over the ill-considered commandeering of a certain perfumery."

"Am I losing my senses," I wonder aloud after Luz strides from the room, "or are we all just going to take orders from a perfumer-spy who, half a turn ago, none of us knew from a bar of soap? Why in Kaismap's far-seeing name would we do such a thing?"

Nisai folds his hands on the table and gives me one of his most sage expressions.

"Because she has the best ideas."

CHAPTER 17

RAKEL

I work with Yaita through the night in Sephine's laboratory.

Not long after dawn, I admit defeat, my eyes refusing to stay open. I'll need at least a little sleep if I'm going to be able to concentrate.

Out in the temple halls, the aromas of siege preparations wafts from each room I pass. In one, acolytes cleanse cloth bandages in vats of vinegar. The astringent steam mixes with the sweet, warm smell from the next room, where honey from the temple's many hives is being pressed from the comb, ready to seal wounds. Frankincense burns in the braziers, cleansing the air and bringing calm to the injured who will be brought here. In the final room I pass, sticks of dark and smoky labdanum incense are being laid beside stretchers, ready for offerings to Azered before the casualties are able to be taken to the roof of the temple and sent to the sky.

It's almost overwhelming, but from the tales Father and his old comrades used to swap when they thought I was asleep as a child, I know it's going to get much worse once there's also the stench of blood and fear, burning flesh and loose bowels.

Escaping on to the first-level terrace, I look out over the gardens below. The breeze brings a kinder balm – vetiver and neroli, lavender and holy thyme, all warmed under the Aphorain sun.

I scrunch my eyes to slits while they get used to the glare. There. In the next garden over, between the lines of glossy-leaved bay trees, Ash and Barden face off in a training bout of the weaponless *lo daiyish* fighting style of Kip's home province. The Losian circles the two, barking instructions and points of technique as a contingent of temple guards look on.

Good. Maybe doing something physical will help Ash feel more himself. Vent some of his frustrations in a controlled way.

The Prince looks on from a safe distance, his crutches propped against the stone bench beside him. Two firebirds tending the herbs in the next garden over have raised their heads to watch. Guess I would too, if the fact I'm having trouble tearing my eyes away is anything to go by.

Barden and Ash are of a height, and they're both stripped to the waist, but that's where the similarities end. Barden's bulkier than Ash, barrel chest and heavily muscled shoulders gleaming a deeper copper brown. Ash is harder, more honed. Sharp angles and sinew, speed and coiled strength, the dappled shade making it seem like the ink of his tattoo moves and shifts across his tawny gold skin.

Just as the thought leaves, Barden charges his opponent. Ash catches his shoulder, and they stand, arms locked, struggling against each other, neither giving ground.

"Style, boys, style!" Kip bellows. "Brute strength is not your friend here."

I suppress a grin. As if she'll ever drill that into them.

Finally, they break apart, their sides heaving from the effort, and retreat to the edge of the training ground.

I wouldn't mind staying to admire the view, but the sport isn't going to make up for how tired I am. I'm about to head to my room when something flashes in the sun.

Swords? They brought swords with them? Actual metal, not wooden ones? What in a thousand stenches are they playing at? Even blunted, the blades can do some real damage.

"You can't be serious!" I yell down at them.

But by the way Barden is giving ground – he's always been much better with spear than sword – I can see they're completely serious. The clash of swords ringing out around the compound speaks of *deadly* seriousness.

Kip throws up her arms and stalks back to stand by the Prince, making no effort to lower her voice as she curses colourfully enough to make the most seasoned soldier blush.

It's a mild morning, but the breeze is cool, and the exertion of the fight has both opponents sweating, Barden's hair plastered to his scalp.

"Feeling the strain, friend?" Ash taunts.

Barden's too focused on Ash's bladework to reply. Though he's a lightning-quick flirt, he was never any good at pressing the mental advantage in a fight.

"Lost for words, for once?" Ash taunts, pressing his attack. "Not so smart at the sharp end of a sword, eh?"

Dull though the blades may be, I cringe every time they send a deep clang echoing around the temple garden's stone walls.

"Suppose you're relying on some *other* skills these days, eh?" Ash lunges, but it's a feint.

Barden barely recovers in time.

Out the corner of my eye, something darkens like clouds passing in front of the sun. Only the sky is clear and blue. I'm imagining it. I must be. He wouldn't. He doesn't even know *how*. It's only ever happened when he or someone he loved was threatened. When he …

… *loses control.*

"Ash!" I call, but he doesn't hear me. Or he pretends not to.

I try another angle. "Barden, stop it! Surrender."

But I know Barden too well. His competitive streak is sparked. This is beyond a training bout for him. The Prince is here, watching them, and Barden's got something to prove. He won't let up until he's won. He'll give it everything to show he's the best.

Then I *feel* the shift as much as see it.

This time, it's unmistakable. It sends my mind back to Ekasya, to the throne room when Ash…

And then in the temple, when I imbibed the Scent Keeper elixir to save Nisai…

Now, the shadows around the garden – from the sculptures of gods and goddesses, the leaves in the breeze and the dark lines of tree trunks – begin to waver like they're water, the darkness ebbing and surging like smoke towards…

Ash.

He's calling them to him. Does he feel it? Is he just trying to scare Barden into surrender?

Or is he losing himself? The last time I saw that happen, it was carnage.

No, no, no.

I have to stop this. Before Ash can't bring himself back from the brink.

Before this goes too far.

I turn on my heel and sprint back towards the laboratory. Skidding through the door, I ignore Yaita's surprised look and flip open the cover of my satchel. Jars and vials rattle as I rummage through them, hands trembling. There. Grabbing the vial of green-black liquid, I leave my bag and run back the other way, barely avoiding Luz as she walks in the opposite direction along the hall.

Out on the terrace, I scramble over the balcony and into the first bay tree, shimmying down the branch and dropping to the ground. I forget to roll. Pain jars up my legs, like my bones are trying to grind my knees to dust. I grit my teeth through a wince and hurry into the gardens.

My view is partially obscured by the trees. One moment I see a flit of Ash's sword, the next it's the deep bruise already blooming on Barden's shoulder. There's no sign that they're letting up. Damn their stubbornness to every stinking one of the six hells.

I unstopper the vial of Sephine's Scent Keeper elixir. It's hard to force myself to breathe deep when I know how much it will burn, but I push through it, gasping, drawing the sickly-sweet fumes up into my nose and down into my lungs.

I can see them even more clearly now. The shadows swirl around Ash. If there were a colour darker than black, this would be it, the lines of his tattoos deepening like they're absorbing all surrounding light.

Is this what happened last time, in the throne room? Before the winged lion tore free? Before it bathed the floor in the blood of so many palace guards. And the blood of Ash himself, the pool of red spreading out from his helpless body as the shadow beast took over.

I can't let that happen here. I *won't* let it happen.

"Ash, stand down!" Nisai shouts. His face is wan. Does he see it, too?

But Ash is no longer his Shield. There's nothing about him here that says servant.

Instinct courses through me, telling me to keep my distance, to retreat. But I need to separate him and Barden. I remember how it felt with Nisai. Of drawing the shadow in the poison to me, both by force and by will. At the time it was alien. Strange, unfamiliar. Like I'd reached into another realm and was grasping at something not of this world.

This is different. I can feel Ash's presence in the shadow. Somehow, I understand that it senses me, too. That it *knows* me.

If it's anything like the poison, and if I can just get close enough, I can take some of it on. Absorb it like Sephine did. Maybe bring him to his senses.

I circle behind Ash. Barden has been pushed back to the edge of the grove. He's so focused on Ash, I can't even tell if he's noticed my approach. He feints one way, then dives the other, dropping his sword and taking up a garden rake in one smooth motion. He tests the balance as if it's a spear, his weapon of choice. The more familiar arm seems to rally him, and he pushes forward.

The shadow around Ash seethes. Something akin to smoke begins to rise from his tattoo. His lips pull back in a rictus snarl.

Barden's rake doesn't last long. It was never meant to stand up to anything but tilling soil and tidying leaves. The look of satisfaction on Ash's face as it splinters is nothing short of chilling. He advances on Barden, the claws of the winged lion on the backs of his hand beginning to drip blood.

Several of the temple guards exchange glances, as if they're wondering if they should intervene. Others look on with expressions of growing horror.

"Ashradinoran, cease and desist!" comes a shout from across the garden.

Maybe it's the desperation in the Prince's voice, maybe it's the sound of his full name, but something makes Ash hesitate.

I take my chance.

I leap in and reach for the aura of darkness emerging from Ash's shoulders. Rather than my hands passing through the smoke-like substance, they grasp it like it's solid, sinking in. At my touch, as if it were a far greater force, Ash stumbles forward.

Barden seizes the moment, swinging the butt of the broken rake around, driving it into Ash's stomach.

The shadows writhe around my hands, coiling up my wrists, my arms. It burns unbearably, white heat searing my skin until I expect to smell my flesh cooking. The darkness quivers, rippling like a desert mirage before sinking into me, soaking into every pore.

I stagger and collapse to the stone as a bone-deep ache rolls through my limbs.

Strong hands gently turn me on to my back, and Ash's face floats into view over me, his expression once again his own.

"I'm fine," I lie, gasping for breath. "Just … put your Rot-be-damned weapons down."

Off to the side, Luz has appeared in the circle of onlookers. She doesn't say a word, only twists a silver ring around and around one long finger.

Then Kip and Nisai are there, too.

The Prince signals to the temple guards. "Escort Ashradinoran to his quarters."

"My Prince?" Ash asks, his expression a painful mix of doubt and alarm.

Nisai doesn't acknowledge him. "Post a pair of guards outside his door, on my order, until otherwise advised."

CHAPTER 18

ASH

I thought I'd be able to escape from my roiling emotions by focusing on the physical.

I was wrong.

Now confined to my room after the training-session-turned-duel with Barden, and by the Prince I'd dedicated my life to protect, I cycle through more emotion than I used to feel in a turn when I still had Linod's to hand.

Humiliation. Shame. Anger. Frustration. Guilt.

I'm not even sure what happened out there. Things escalated so quickly, and then Rakel… What did she even do? And what, more importantly, did it do to her?

My thoughts are interrupted by one of the temple guards opening the door. He gestures for me to follow.

"Rakel? How is she?"

"The girl lives."

Part of the tension I'd been feeling releases. "Can I see her?"

"I'm to deliver you to the Prince."

It's not what I was expecting, but it's not an unwelcome development. I'll have my chance to explain. I'll make amends. Perhaps Nisai has even thought on my objections to the shadow weapon, that after today he realizes how important it is to prioritize rescuing Del, Mish and the others. He'll shift focus from wasting time on the search for some ancient relic to figuring out a way to help those I left behind under Ekasya Mountain, before Zostar finds a way to use them against us.

When I reach his door, it's open. Kip stands in her usual place outside, but two sets of laughter reach me in the hall.

Kip waves me into the room where I find Nisai and Barden halfway through a game of shnik-shnik, Nisai shaking the game cup in preparation for his turn. A siege is imminent, I've been confined to my cell, and meanwhile it's been all fun and frivolity? How is Nisai letting Barden influence him so?

I clear my throat.

The cup stills.

Kip grunts at Barden, motioning with fist and thumb for him to leave the room.

Barden says something quietly to Nisai before rising to his feet. I couldn't decipher what he said, but Nisai responds with a grateful smile that sets my teeth on edge. I know that smile. It's usually directed at me. Dark envy courses through me.

I've got nothing against Kip, but I can't say I'm sorry to see the back of Barden as the pair of them file out. It feels like he seeps his way into everyone's good graces, just like the amber oil he wears permeates every room he enters. He must bathe in the stuff. How he can afford to on a guard's wages is anyone's guess.

When the door shuts behind them, Nisai motions me forward. "Thank you for coming."

"No thanks needed. It's where I belong."

He doesn't respond, only looks at his hand in his lap. The silence stretches.

"It's probably best I'm candid," he says, continuing to avoid my gaze. "It will hopefully save us both from some unneeded awkwardness."

Avoid awkwardness? Feels like there's suddenly so much awkward in the room we could drown in it. It's the first time we've been alone together in the best part of a turn. It should be comfortable. A well-worn privacy. But here he is, refusing to look at me.

"Ash, please, sit." He gestures to the place where Barden had just been. Something contrary sparks in me, unknown and foreign, and I choose the chair diagonally opposite.

"Ash, I'm not going to be Emperor."

It takes several heartbeats for his words to register. Why would he say such a thing?

"Meaning no disrespect," I begin, the words falling false from my lips. He's my best friend, the person I've served for half my life, and here I am simpering like some conniving courtier. I clear my throat and begin anew. "Your father is dead. Now you're Emperor. That's how this works."

"No, I've made a decision. I'm going to renounce my claim to the throne."

I blink once, twice.

"It's my memory, Ash. It's not … what it used to be before the … before I was incapacitated. If I don't have my faculties, what will I be? Ineffectual at best." He wrings his hands as he talks.

I want to reach out to still them. But I force myself to restraint.

"At worst? Who knows what troubled waters I could lead our people into. Especially with Zostar on the scene. I've seen how he manipulated my father. I will not be a tool for destruction in the same way. My brother—"

"There's never been a Regent since Aramtesh's founding." I grip the arms of the chair, trying to steady my mind through steadying my body. "That there is one now doesn't bend the terms of the Accord, it shatters them."

"Even if I weren't doubting my faculties, my abilities, the unrest that has so quickly simmered to boiling point is a demonstration that the Accord itself may no longer be enough to hold the Empire together."

"What are you saying, Nisai?"

"I'm saying I think we need a new model. A fresh start. The kind of arrangement where voices of dissent can be heard without reproach. Perhaps, to start with, expanding the Council of Five, with each province having direct representation. But perhaps later something larger still – like the Conclave held by the Order to decide matters of import. I admit I thought them initially a rabble, but I've been talking with people."

"With who exactly?"

He ignores that. "I've begun to think rule by one person, one man … it could never truly serve an entire Empire."

If I ignore the worst part of me, the jealous part, I have to admit it's an interesting idea. Perhaps a fine dream, if it could be made to work. But now isn't the time to make such changes. We need to deal with Zostar and the resurgence of the Blazers first. I need to keep my promise to the children beneath Ekasya Mountain.

"The point is, Ash, if I'm renouncing my claim to build something better, then it only follows that your duties have been discharged."

My grip on the table tightens, the knuckles going white. "You need protection more than ever." It hasn't escaped me that the last time we were alone was in Aphorai City, when I failed in my duties as Shield.

"Nisai, I know what I let happen to you was terrible. Unforgivable, even. But you must stand up to your brother. You *must* deal with Zostar. Did you not hear anything I said? There are children being experimented upon. They're being *tortured*. You can't start creating a better world until the threats from this one are vanquished."

"War only begets war, Ash."

"Then find a better way."

He throws his hands up in frustration. "That's what I've been trying to tell you! I can't *think*! Not like I used to! I'm not retaining information, I'm not making breakthroughs, I'm running the old routes over and over in my mind, wearing grooves so deep I don't know if I'll ever escape them."

"You're First Prince." I pause, then correct myself. "You're *Emperor-elect*. It's your duty to lead us out of this. Your duty to stop the atrocities in Ekasya. Your duty to *find a better way*."

"Duty," he scoffs then tilts his face to the ceiling, laughing darkly. And with that laugh, the temperature in the room seems to change, the heat of our anger replaced with a chill. "Your precious duty. Treasured duty. More important to you than anything else." He reaches for his crutches and rises to his feet, turning his back to me. "It was more important to protect me than to love me."

The words are a fist curled around my heart. "We had no future! Once you were Emperor – you'd have to produce an heir. A wife from every province. You'd be expected to share a bed with at least one of them."

His shoulders slump. "That's duty, not love."

"And my duty *is* my love. It's bigger than desire. You once asked me what makes a good Emperor. Don't you remember? Back in Ekasya? It's you. You, Nisai. It's one of the many reasons I've always loved you. Your questioning, your desire to find the good in all, your fascination with how the world works and how it might be made a better version of itself. You *will* make a good Emperor, whatever you decide to do with that office one you hold it. But you must take it, first. And an Emperor needs a Shield."

For all he reacts, he might not have heard a single word I uttered. He's deathly still. Frozen. What I'd do to be able to see his eyes, to know what he's thinking. Is he ashamed of not claiming his birthright?

Or is he ashamed of me? What I'm capable of. The destruction. The growing darkness.

"It's—" My throat constricts around the words. "It's more, isn't it? It's my curse. It's not something that just seemed supernatural when we were boys. Now it's undeniable. And now you're intent on finding a weapon against it. You don't want me by your side any more, do you? Because of what I am."

Nisai turns so fast one of his crutches slides out from under him and for a terrible moment I think he's going to lose his balance. But then he rights himself.

"It is, isn't it?" I press on, a cruel barb in my voice I've never directed at him before. "You didn't mind when it was something amorphous, something legendary, something fascinating you could research. An answer just out of reach. But now you know, now it's real. Now it can do what I've always told you. Now I'm a not just a killer bloodsworn to you. I'm a monster."

He shakes his head.

I advance on him, closing the space between us, my voice lowered to a growl like I'm some kind of wild animal. Out of control. "You don't want to dismiss me because you're not intending to take the throne. You *fear* me."

I expect him to retreat. But he holds his ground until there's only a handspan between us.

"Emperor is a title," he says. "An office. You may not agree with me walking away from it, but it is possible. Your power, however, is an inseparable part of you. Whether I fear you or not is irrelevant. Many now see you as a threat not unlike Zostar, and because of that, you simply cannot perform the duties of Shield."

He reaches up, his hand soft against my cheek. "Know that I will always love you."

The words tear into me. They're true. But they're laced with sorrow.

Then he straightens, lifts his chin and assumes the regal expression I've come to know as the difference between the First Prince of Aramtesh and simply Nisai.

"Ashradinoran, you are dismissed."

✳

Back in my room, I don't bother lighting any candles. What do I need to see? There's nothing to read. I could write, but what would I write of, and who would I write to? And would the guards posted outside the door even permit a message to be sent from inside this room?

Perhaps this is Ekasya Mountain all over again. Exile. Isolation. Darkness. Perhaps it is all a creature like me deserves.

I find myself laughing harshly into the emptiness. The dark used to trigger my fear. Now it's familiar. Almost comforting.

I lie back on the bed, its softness almost comtemptible, and imagine taking out the guards. Fighting my way free of here. It wouldn't be too difficult. They're clearly not trained to the same level. If I timed it right, their demise might not even be noticed for some time.

What am I even *thinking*?

I shake my head. This isn't me. Those guards are doing nothing but their job. They're not the enemy here. Even if I could give them the slip without harm, what would that achieve? Nisai clearly has made his decision about me. And, given the circumstances, he's as safe here – within the walls of Aphorai City – as any place.

And after today, what is Rakel thinking? If I could speak to her, explain, what would I say? What sort of life could I offer her? Am I going to deteriorate further than this? Lose control in the mildest conflict? I could go back on Linod's Elixir. It might keep me steady enough to find some mercenary or guard work. Perhaps we could even return to Lapis Lautus – Rakel said she enjoyed the smuggler city with its cosmopolitan ways.

But Linod's is only a temporary solution. Rakel knows that better than anyone. And running away would also be breaking a promise – I said I would go back for Del and Lark and the other children under Ekasya Mountain.

There must be a way to help them to freedom. I just don't know what that way is.

If nothing else, at least it's quiet enough to think.

"Ash?"

Correction. It *was* quiet.

"Ash? The guards won't let me in, but they've stepped away so we can talk. We've only got a few minutes."

I glare into the gloom. "What are you doing down here?" Emotion roils in me, so powerful and foreign. There's anger at the intrusion warring with embarrassment that I should even need the seclusion, and, as I rise and cross to the door, pressing my hands against it, a longing to reach for her, to have her touch make me forget.

But would that be using her the same as Linod's? A crutch?

"I could ask the same question of you," she says, anger sparking in her voice.

Oh, to feel as if your rage was righteous. A pure, cleansing fire. Not polluted like my torrent of thoughts, scum and detritus swirling in the current.

"Nisai's worried about you."

He's worried about *me*? I burst into laughter. It's harsher still, guttural.

"Ash, what happened between you two?"

Now that is a genuine surprise. Nisai must not yet have informed anyone of his decision. Perhaps it's a benevolent gesture. A kind act of charity to let me control when others know of my dismissal. Or perhaps it's yet another example of Nisai refusing to face his responsibility.

But I know Rakel. She's not going to let me out of this without a fight. Perhaps I should be grateful for that.

"He dismissed me."

"From his chambers?"

"Permanently. He dismissed me from duty." The words feel like a weapon – as if they'll deal the mortal blow and make this all irredeemably real. But they can't remain unspoken. That is the coward's way. "I am no longer his Shield."

Silence from the other side of the door.

"He fears me now. He fears what I am." I force a ragged breath into my lungs. "And that's not all he fears. He says he is going to renounce his claim to the throne. That he'll defer to the Council or some kind of collective decision-making. A Conclave, he called it. But it doesn't make sense. He was always going to be a better Emperor than Kaddash."

There's a pause, then a sigh. "It's the headaches. His memory hasn't been what it was since the poisoning. He's genuinely struggling with the idea of ruling. Maybe that's a good thing. Maybe the Empire needs change."

"But he'll mend. And he has advisors to support him. And—"

"Ash, he may *not* get better. We have no way of telling. It's not like people regularly get poisoned with blackvein and we have a bunch of examples of how it turns out. And in the meantime, he doesn't trust himself. You of all people should be able to relate to that."

"What I think clearly doesn't matter any more."

"It matters to me." Her voice is quiet, timid even.

I wish I could put my arms around her, draw her close. I want to. But even if we were on the same side of the door, I'm not sure I could. My pain is a wall between us. For so many turns, my life has revolved around Nisai. Now that has been cast aside. I've got nothing in reserve to comfort someone else, however much I might wish to. Regardless of how much I might love them.

"Ash, if you could be free of your power—"

"Power? That's the word Nisai used. Why don't any of you say it for what it is? A curse."

"Your curse, then. If there was a way for you to be separated from it, permanently, would you take it?"

There's that laugh again. Full of contempt. Almost a growl. I would not believe it was coming from me if I didn't hear it from my own ears.

"Would you, Ash?"

"In a heartbeat."

"Then I think I can help." Her voice is low and even. She's serious. "What I did today, when you lost control… It's like what I did to cure Nisai of the final part of the poison. The shadow part."

I turn away, pressing my back to the door and sinking to the floor. "I don't think that's how this works."

"I believe it, Ash. Nisai did, too, remember? Part of the reason he was in Aphorai back when all this started was to find out if Sephine could help you."

Movement catches my eye. In the sliver of light spilling in from the hallway outside, Rakel's hand appears under the gap in the door. I hesitate, then lay mine over it. All of a sudden she's so much more real, the skin marked with the nicks and burns of her work, the new callouses beginning to form on her right hand where she's been learning to write.

"Ash, you did so much for me. You kept me alive, you sacrificed yourself in the throne room and … I love you. Let me help you. I've imbibed the Scent Keeper elixir and survived. For whatever rhyme or reason I've been granted the ability to channel the will of Asmudtag, as they call it. To balance things. I just need to work out how not to…"

"Not to what?"

"I guess there's a limit for anyone. When Sephine took the poison into herself to keep Nisai alive while we found the antidote, she… But surely it's only a risk, not a given."

The implication is clear. I pull my hand from hers. "You said you don't believe I'm a monster."

"I don't," she insists.

"Then stop trying to make me into one. How could you think I'd agree to that?"

The silence descends between us again, thick and heavy, the gossamer connection severed.

The shadows move slowly on the floor as Rakel gets to her feet. She pauses for several heartbeats, then her footsteps recede slowly away from the door. I want to call out to her, to thank her, to tell her we'll find another way through this. But I don't utter a word. Because every step she takes away from me is a step back towards the light.

And I belong in the darkness.

CHAPTER 19

RAKEL

After the fight, everyone fussed over me like I was a sick child.

Barden accused me of "my usual recklessness" by rushing in, though Yaita was the worst. She kept appearing wherever I went throughout the day, and at dinner, her eyes followed my every move.

It's only Luz who has been conspicuously absent. I saw the way she looked at Ash before the guards confined him to his quarters. She knows more than she's letting on. And I want answers.

Now that the others are no doubt asleep, I try to tread lightly, boot heels ringing uncomfortably loud in the empty temple hall as I approach the light coming from a room near mine. The door is ajar, barely enough to make out the figure within.

Zakkurus.

They recline on a divan near the fire, hair pulled back by a silver circle. Their robe is deepest midnight blue, the twin to the one they wore the night I first met them in Aphorai City, except the lilies are replaced with tiny silver stylized dahkai blooms. There's make-up, too. Pomegranate lip stain, and rur ink lines eyes I know are blue but are now colourless in the dim light of the fire.

It's as if the Chief Perfumer never left.

A silver cup dangles from their long fingers – Hagmiri apricot wine, judging by the sweet scent of mountain summers floating towards me.

"Did you simply want to watch, petal, or can I help you with something?"

I startle, heat flushing my cheeks. But I find my hand pushing the heavy, carved door completely open. I take a tentative step into the room. "I realized I never thanked you. For…" I gesture vaguely, as if talking about the very air itself. "What you've done for us. And out in the desert, when you didn't—"

"Do my job? With Ashradinoran?"

"Yes."

"I may still. If I'm forced to." They lock eyes with me, gaze hardened to ice. "Don't get precious, now. You're loyal to your love. I'm loyal to something bigger: a cause. And to that, my dedication is unwavering."

"You sound like Yaita."

"It's not a coincidence."

"But can you help? With Ash?"

They take a sip of wine. "No."

"You mean, you *won't* help him."

"Tell me of a person who doesn't cast a shadow and I'll know you for a liar." Another swallow from the goblet. "But for what it's worth, petal, I don't think he's evil."

"How noble of you."

They hold up a hand defensively. "Patience. I'm trying to explain. Ashradinoran was born on the Days of Doskai. His first breath was of the scent of another's end. I've seen many who carried the same curse that he now grapples with."

My irritation turns to curiosity. "That's how he became what he is? Born at the wrong place at the wrong time?"

"It's a little more complicated than that, and we don't know for absolute sure, but that's my theory."

"How do you know?"

"It's how I first came to work for Sephine. Initially I was charged with finding others like your surly friend."

"Like Zostar has been doing?"

Their jaw drops melodramatically. "Mentioned in the same breath as the rogue physician? I'm hurt, petal. Truly hurt."

"Then enlighten me."

"I was Sephine's Finder. I would go out into the city and identify any children who had shown signs of the Lost God's curse. I grew up in the neighbourhoods they were most likely to surface in – places where the stench of death was never far from breathing its fetid heat down your neck – so whenever there was an incident in Aphorai City, I was able to follow the rumour trail before things got out of hand."

"And once you'd found them?"

"I'd bring them to Sephine, who, by the Primordial's grace, would set them free of Doskai's influence."

"Channel the will of Asmudtag," I mutter. "I thought as much. Sephine. Her eyes, she … took the curse into herself. With the Scent Keeper elixir? Like the way she took as much of the poison from Nisai as she could when he first fell ill?"

Zakkurus nods approval "Always knew you were a swift one."

260

"Then… I… Is it…"

"Perhaps try to articulate a complete thought. Makes communication so much more efficient."

"Can I do that for Ash? I've survived the first imbibing. And the second. I could do it again."

"Not without great risk. Mercy *before* maturity, remember. Sephine was the most powerful Scent Keeper alive. I doubt even she would have attempted such a thing on an older subject. Not that she ever needed to, under my watch. I never missed a case. Alas, Ashradinoran was born in Ekasya, not Aphorai.

"What's more…" There's a pause as Zakkurus sips their wine. "He's been tortured. We don't comprehend the half of it, and of what I *have* heard, none of us could predict who we would become if we were forced to endure such an ordeal. Only the Primordial could anticipate what would be left of us. Would it be enough to survive the ceremony?"

I don't want to admit the truth in their words. I don't know what would be left of me either. But to admit they're true might be to admit I'm losing Ash, after having just got him back. I don't know if I could bear that. Not again.

"Ceremony?"

Now the silver cup gets tipped all the way back. "It's unfortunate that things have changed over the centuries. Even within the Order, there are clashes over nuances of scripture, debate over what is the true will of Asmudtag, how the remnants of magic in the world should be deployed. It no longer seems as simple as 'mercy until maturity'."

"But I thought you believed in everything the Order–"

"*I* endeavour not to have my judgment impaired by the latest dogmatic fashion." They run a fingertip around the rim of the cup. "You've heard the tenet *Asmudtag is all*, yes? That's because the Primordial *is* all. Imbued in every one of us, in the Younger Gods, in the land itself. Only through Asmudtag can we find balance; the Younger Gods have proven their foibles are as many and varied as our own. The Shadow Wars demonstrated what happens when equilibrium is lost. Chaos reigns. Countless lives are forfeit. There are those who would see the Empire in ashes in the name of their own victory." With a flick of the wrist, the last drops in the goblet fly into the fire. The flames reply with a hiss. "But of what value is a crown of smoke?"

They frown at that, as if their words meant something more once they'd spoken them. Then they flow to their feet and take my shoulders in their hands, expression serious. "Seek your answers among Sephine's records."

"This better not be one of your tricks."

"You wound me."

"But why help us?"

"Because you asked."

"I don't believe you."

"Come now, petal. Haven't I ever told you never to question my motives?"

I lift my chin. "I'm not scared of you." *Even if I was once.* "Tell me why you'd stick your nose out. Sparing Ash. Telling me of Sephine's work."

Zakkurus looks away, but I can tell they're looking at nothing, eyes fixed on a spot somewhere in the middle of the room. "Because it could just as easily have been me in his position."

I open my mouth to reply, the questions in my mind vying for first place. But before I can get any of them out, Zakkurus crosses to where the contents of their travel pack have been neatly lined up on a side table. There's a tinkling of glass, but with their back turned to me, I can't see what they're doing.

Then they return and slowly, deliberately, usher me from the room. On the threshold, they pause, pressing something into my palm.

The door swings closed.

I stare down at the *two* somethings in my hand.

The first vial is labelled. Sultis. It's well sealed, but I still shudder at the thought of the valley full of vines where I lost and regained my memories on the way to the Sanctuary.

The second vial has no label. But it's a dark liquid I'd now recognize anywhere.

Scent Keeper elixir.

I have to find out how it works.

Luz had organized for both Yaita and me to have access to Sephine's old quarters, but when I arrive, I find them empty as hoped. Good. I don't want to have to deal with a lecture while I look for what I need. Still, knowing Yaita, she'll only snatch a couple of hours sleep before she returns to her experiments. I'd best hurry.

I light a candle against the coming darkness. Sephine's scrolls are all kept in a fancy cabinet. There's row upon row of them, some simply rolled, others in protective cylinders of plain metal or intricate inlays, gleaming in the flame.

There's another cupboard on the far side of the room, a larger one. I'm hoping it's a wardrobe, but when I open it racks of clay tablets stare back at me. I groan. This is going to take too long.

Think, Rakel. If Sephine wrote down the method for how she relieved the Children of Doskai from their curse, would she have committed it to parchment, or clay? I would have guessed tablets would be reserved for contracts and the like, remembering the day I first met Sephine on the temple heights, when she'd bought out my indenture to Zakkurus.

I return to the scrolls.

I've got no idea where to start. But I'm not going to give up on Ash yet.

Especially not with an army soon to be at the gates, Nisai searching for a weapon against Ash's kind, and Luz caught in the crosswinds of some kind of test of faith.

I pull the nearest scroll out and unroll it. It's in Sephine's distinctive handwriting, flowing together and with extra accent markers so that even when she wrote me simple lists I had trouble deciphering them. This one's an ingredient list for the current Eraz's great-grandfather's favourite scented aftershave balm. Not for the first time, I wonder how old Sephine was when she died. The next scroll is for the current Eraz. A "hair restorative" tonic. There's a scrawled note in the margin that brings a smirk to my lips: "utter twit, bald is good enough for us, is it not good enough for him?".

I walk my fingers a little further down the shelf. A formula for women who don't wish to bear children. I hesitate for a moment, then slip it into my satchel.

It's becoming clear the scrolls are organized by subject, so I decide to take a sample from each shelf. When I pull out the next one, something slips near the back of the cabinet, rasping along the wood. I reach my arm in, fingers scrabbling for the dislodged object. Freeing it from the dim cabinet reveals it's not a single thing, but many – a stack of folded sheets of parchment, tied with a worn strip of leather.

I slip the first from the stack.

I imagined they could be anything. More recipes. Shopping lists. A diary. Who knows, maybe Sephine was even a secret poet. But it's none of those. It's not even in the same hand that all the other scrolls were written in. That doesn't mean I don't recognize the lettering.

It's Yaita's.

And each scroll begins with my name.

There's enough letters here for a turn if she was sending them every moon like she claimed. I pull out the remaining scrolls from the shelf, stacking them between the chair and the wall so they don't roll away. And there, tucked at the back of the cabinet, are more bundles of folded parchment. Maybe even seventeen of them.

My mother *had* written to me every moon. The letters just hadn't been passed on.

I go back to the first one, the one that appears to be most recent. It talks of my seventeenth turnday, and, as if I was still a child, of how tall I must be now.

When I was younger I yearned for some way to know my mother, thinking it impossible. The whole time, there were letters here. Part of me understands why Father did what he did. But another part feels robbed. I could have had this – if not an actual mother, then at least some sort of idea of who she was, that she knew of me and cared.

For that part of me, I'm tempted to go through more of the letters. See if it changes the way I feel about Yaita. Maybe it would make her seem less of a stranger.

Only a one-way conversation is no conversation at all. It's sad to feel so distant from something that was meant for me. But there are more urgent things that I need to see to. For someone who was there when I needed them most. Someone who puts those he loves first.

I put the letters back where I found them – maybe I'll get a chance to return to them one day – and unroll the next scroll.

Here. This is something to do with naming ceremonies. Now we're getting somewhere.

CHAPTER 20

ASH

"No closer." The words come from one of the guards outside the door.

I surge into a sitting position.

"Is he not allowed any visitors?" Rakel. Her voice oddly muffled compared with the guards. My heart thumps against my ribs. "That's not very humane. The Prince said he would be treated with all respect."

"Ashradinoran is observing quiet contemplation. My orders are to uphold that."

"I can be quiet. I'll be here and then gone before anyone's the wiser."

Why is she pressing them? I can't imagine she thinks that's going to make them stand down.

"I, ah… I don't think we should." Spikes of confusion punctuate the second guard's words. "We were supposed to… Can you remember our orders, captain? Why are you wearing a mask, girl?"

"Oh, just step aside, would you?" Rakel's tone is haughty, now.

The sound of the bolt sliding back precedes the door opening. For a heartbeat she hesitates on the threshold, limned in light. Then she shuts it behind her and leans heavily against it. There's the sound of cloth hitting the floor, then a sigh of relief. "For a moment there I thought I'd used the wrong dose... Ash? Where are you? It's darker than the Days of Doskai in here."

"Blasphemy," I say on reflex.

"After everything we've been through, not least of all today, you're getting preachy on me?"

I rub my hand over my shaved scalp. "I'm over here. On the bed."

She shuffles across the floor, no doubt feeling her way with her feet while her eyes adjust to the relative gloom. There's a thud as she stumbles against the low table, followed by a string of curses under her breath. I should jump up and guide her; I can see perfectly fine. But something stops me. The voice that has been telling me since I was a child that I am a curse. That I'm tainted with darkness. That I'll only bring grief to those I love.

And above all of that, there's an even starker fear: after two episodes and a near miss, and all so relatively close together, I no longer know if I can trust myself.

Even with her.

"Rakel, stop."

Her footsteps pause.

"I... I think you should stay over there."

Her faint silhouette shifts, drawing closer. "Ash, I'm not scared of you."

"An error of judgment at this point. You know what I've done. You've seen what I am. This morning, who knows what ... could have happened."

"What I know is that you won't hurt me."

"Rakel, you weren't *there*." The words come out more accusation than explanation, surprising even myself. "You don't know what they put me through. Under the Mountain, Zostar and his cronies they … experimented. A lot of the time I wasn't even conscious."

She's fumbling for the candles I didn't light earlier. "Ash, you know I had no idea you were alive, don't you? I never would have left you if I did. Do you know that?"

"Yes."

"Then you also know I won't leave you now."

I stand, holding up my hands as if they're the last line of defense. "It's different now. I'm afraid… I'm afraid I'm not who I used to be. I don't even know half of the things they did to me, their purpose, if there will be any lasting … effects. I don't know how or when I'll next lose control. This morning, with Barden, it wasn't life and death. That was … anger. Rage."

Light flares, and she's there, features illuminated in the warm flame of the candle as she uses one to light the next, setting them down on the table. She's only a couple of steps away now. The scent of desert rose drifts around me. And with it, the last of my resistance crumbles. I've lived a life sworn to protect another, but with Rakel, it was always different. And now she's here.

I step forward, closing the distance between us until she's in my arms and I'm sighing into her hair, the tension I'd held through countless prayers and hours of silence slowly draining from my muscles.

When she draws back enough to look up at me, her eyes shine with withheld tears. "Please, Ash. Let me help you."

"I won't have you risking your life for me."

"That's not your choice to make."

I'm silent.

"If the roles were reversed, you'd do the same for me."

"In a heartbeat," I respond without hesitation.

"Then treat me as an equal."

The challenge crackles in the air between us: dry tinder ready to leap into flame. *She's not your charge*, I remind myself. *You are not bloodsworn to her.* The person I'm bloodsworn to – *was* bloodsworn to – comes to mind, along with some of the last words he spoke to me. *It was more important to protect me than to love me.*

"Rakel, I'm scared. Of what I'm becoming. Of what this might do to you. To us."

"Me too," she admits. "But think of it this way – if this works, we could be helping so many more. The children beneath Ekasya Mountain, for a start."

"That was my promise. Not yours. You don't need to take that on."

She shakes her head, smiling. "Do you know how I kept going when I thought I'd lost you?"

I raise my brows in question.

"I thought of what we would say if we were facing the problem together."

"The only way out is through." I smile.

"Through it is. Tonight. Now. The sultis won't last for ever on those guards."

"Where are we going?"

"The top of the temple. But first, you're going to need to help me with some supplies."

CHAPTER 21

LUZ

Oh, my poor disgruntled head.

Even before I open my eyes, I know that first act will hurt. It's an accurate assessment. At the first crack, the candlelight lances into my brain. I turn just enough to see the nightstand. The clay jar of apricot wine had been sealed yesterday evening. Now, with the candle burned low enough to suggest we're closer to the coming dawn than the previous dusk, it lays on its side. Empty.

Memories of last night weave in and out of my thoughts, fleeting and fickle. Sitting before the hearth. Brooding. The girl lingering at the door. Me giving voice to my thoughts like a mewling amateur.

I'd shake my head in disgust. But that would just make its sorry state worse.

There's one thing I don't regret: something needs to be done about the Shield. Proof of concept, I believe the empirically minded refer to it.

There's another rap at the door. Rather insistent for this early. Unless that's not the first time they've knocked.

"What is it?" The words crash around my skull like an aurochs in an essence emporium.

"A message." A muffled voice returns.

"Leave it."

"It's not standard protocol to—"

"I said *leave it*. On the floor."

The hall goes silent.

I rise and splash water on my face, wiping away last night's make-up. That's not me today. A small pot of particularly potent smelling salts sits on the ledge next to the basin. I remove the lid and hold it under one nostril, closing off the other, and inhale. Vile stuff. Nevertheless, I repeat the exercise on the other side, then dab my wrists with sweet almond oil laced with violet.

My mind begins to ever-so-slowly clear as I don a fresh robe and open the door.

A dainty scroll teeters rather forlornly on the stone threshold. By the smell of it, the message is from further afield than I expected. I pop the seal and close the door behind me.

The note is rather frivolous. Seeming for all intents and purposes a family update between two sisters from Aphorain provincial nobility. Such-and-such has had another baby, such-and-such has been accepted into the Eraz's personal guard, such-and-such will be holidaying in the Trelian riverlands next spring.

I lift the corner to my nose.

First impressions hold true. Orris root.

I select the required reagent from the shelf, lower myself ever-so-gently into my desk chair and get to work. Soon, an entirely different message sits before me.

Frivolous is the last thing one would call this one. Darzul gets straight to the point in the first line: the Regent's forces departed Ekasya for Aphorai City earlier than we had expected.

I cover my face with my hands, allowing myself a loud, exasperated exhale. Oh, for the days when delivering the Affliction cure to the Emperor and restoring balance in the capital was a remote possibility. With our ruler's death, the last chance of averting this war has been snuffed out.

After allowing myself a moment, I keep reading. It seems the propaganda machine has been working overtime to taint the outer provinces with a treasonous stench and Zostar's forces have been growing in response.

Other reports are even more disturbing. Villagers' fear-fuelled tales of a vanguard who can work dark magic, mists of smoke or shadow rising to choke or asphyxiate anyone who stands in their way. There lies the most disconcerting news of all: from what the Shield reported, these were ordinary children. Bewildered. Homesick. Terrified. Now Zostar must have finally found a way to bend them to his will.

The pounding in my skull intensifies.

The scroll concludes its glad tidings with the notification that Darzul has now left the capital and will not be returning. Other than the Brotherhood and the Rangers left to secure the city, Ekasya is now a veritable ghost town, making it even more dangerous to be gathering intelligence than before. Those who could escape being conscripted into support services for the Regent's forces have long fled. Anyone remaining who isn't a believer is conspicuous.

The flames left the hearth sometime in the night, but there are still a few glowing embers. I could sacrifice the scroll to their dying hunger, watch it blacken and curl and join the ashes. Keep the information close and set out to deal with this myself. But it's getting too urgent for that. And too big.

Even my abilities have their limitations.

I swallow down the acidic taste at the back of my mouth. I'm unsure if it's the message or last night's over-indulgence. I reroll the scroll, slip into a pair of silk slippers and close the door behind me.

It's no surprise to find Yaita in Sephine's old laboratory. She's not yet given up on the cure, and while her daughter prefers to work by day, Yaita often toils in the final hours of night. This pre-dawn is no different.

"We have to act," I announce.

"Good morning to you, too, Luz."

I ignore that and shove the scroll on to her desk. She picks it up, almost as if it might be something encrusted with filth.

Her eyes trace the words. "We must keep a cool head."

"No more equivocating, no more contingencies."

She sets the scroll down, gently, carefully, dangerously so.

But I've started this now. Nothing shall be gained for leaving it half finished. "I don't like our chances, but we could try to deal with it ourselves."

She fixes me in an appraising stare.

"The Order is being willfully ignorant so as not to risk their own necks. Where has that got us?" I snatch up the scroll, using it to punctuate each point as if ticking off a list in the air. "An Emperor dying on the eve of a civil war, when he could have been saved. An army on the march to Aphorai City, no doubt to remove the true heir, the last troublesome piece from this Zostar's game board. The beginnings of the

Lost God's terrible legacy being resurrected. Yet still, there might be time to avert the worst. Though I daresay we've reached the point where the risk of sending me alone is untenable."

"They're children. Mercy until mat—"

"Mercy is a luxury we *cannot* afford! The stakes are getting higher, and we need to rise with them. This is no longer merely a choice between two brothers sitting on the throne. If the Order won't step in … and if you won't help me … I'd venture I could find assistance elsewhere."

Her dark eyes fix on me, shrewd and narrow.

Long moments pass.

I don't look away.

Nor does she.

Suspicion and the rapport we've developed over the turns guides her to the truth. "What have you done?"

"Simply a little preemptive preparation, should it have come to this. The Order won't help, Sephine's no longer here, and I couldn't rely on you deciding one way or the other. Who else was I meant to engage to ascertain whether any of this can be salvaged?"

She rises, moves to stand in front of me. She has to look up to meet my eyes, but the fire there makes her far more intimidating than another of the same stature.

"Luz, where is my daughter?"

CHAPTER 22

RAKEL

Until I lost the perfume trials, I never thought I'd enter a temple complex. Until I healed Nisai – when he was laid out on it in the Ekasyan temple like it was his deathbed and he was about to be sent to the sky – I never thought I'd live to see a great altar. All I knew about these places was that they were where the firebirds lit up your hard-earned prayer incense. You'd stand here, watching your money burn, hoping the scented smoke grabbed the attention of whichever magical sky friend you wanted a favour from.

It's also where naming ceremonies are conducted. At least that's what everyone told me. I never had one. Growing up, it was just Father and me, so I wasn't about to see any other big family events. And just like most others in my village, I wasn't able to afford to go as a guest: you attend the ceremony, you pay for a prayer offering. No exceptions.

Still, I know there's one thing Ash and I will be doing very differently from a naming ceremony. Tonight we'll be closing the top level of the temple off from the sky. Part of me is always going to find it hard to take the idea of gods in the sky at face value, but the last thing I want is for Doskai to catch a whiff of what we're going to be trying to do to one of his so-called "children".

No short cuts. It finally sinks in how true the talk of this place was. How ancient and grand the space is, with its five-sided walls rising thirty feet or more, the parts of the ceiling not open to the sky held up by strangely carved stone columns, like bunches of river reeds tied together. I've never seen anything like them before in Aphorai. It's almost as if the inside of the building doesn't match the outside. No matter. From what was recorded in Sephine's notes, there's no better place to generate enough smoke in an enclosed area.

Standing in the centre of the chamber, below the sky, thinking of all the things that have been prayed for from this space, all the people who believed their nearest and dearest were being sent to some kind of beautiful next life, all the babies that were loved and fortunate enough to have their lives blessed, I feel small.

Ash beckons me closer. "Look," he says, pointing to the square of night above us. "It's Esmolkrai."

"What?"

He draws me in, my back to his chest, and points over my shoulder so I can follow the line of sight. "The serpent, remember. The bright star – there – his eye, blessed by Kaismap. Perhaps it'll afford us better luck this time. It's travelled a long way since we last saw it."

"So have we," I whisper.

Ash doesn't reply, only tightens his arms for a moment. Then he drops them and steps to the side, regarding me with a smile that's at least part forced.

"Are we ready for this?" I ask, trying to return it.

"I'm not sure I'll ever be truly ready."

"Guess we should make a start then."

"Indeed."

I light the first of the five main braziers that stand at each corner of the room. It catches easily, already pre-laden with kindling and charcoal for the firebirds to greet the dawn in a couple of hours. I wonder if my mother was the one to do it.

Ash crosses to the next huge copper dish and does the same. We work our way around until they're all burning, lighting up the chamber.

Already feeling the heat emanating, I roll the sleeves of my robe to the shoulder. "We have to close the roof. I'll get this side, you take the other."

He nods agreement and we set ourselves to the long metal handles on opposite sides of the room, cranking them round. It seems little effort to Ash, but I have to throw my weight behind each turn, stretching up on tiptoes at the highest part and almost hanging my entire body from the handle to bring it back down. Guess this is how the firebirds keep in shape.

We keep turning. And turning.

Nothing happens.

Sweat begins to bead on my forehead with the mix of heat and strain.

Still, nothing.

I push worry away. I've heard stories about how this works. That deep beneath the baked clay bricks of the stepped pyramid there's a mechanical skeleton, rigged so that the roof can be opened and closed, so that the huge vents along the side of the chamber can be sealed or aired.

A deep grating sound begins, setting my teeth on edge. The next breath, the huge roof begins to close in from

278

each side, inch by inch, until the last stars of the night are blocked from view by twin stone slabs that meet each other with a dull thud. I hope it wasn't loud enough for the acolytes sleeping two tiers down to hear, and that the higher ranked priestesses are still fast asleep.

I drop my hands from the lever, panting. Red patches of skin have appeared where my fingers meet my palms, one of them raised into a blister. The firebirds who normally do this must have hands of leather. Or maybe the lever is just that stiff because it's rarely used. Maybe it hasn't been closed since Sephine went to the sky.

I turn to Ash, ready to empty the first of the five packets of powder I put together in Sephine's lab on to the brazier coals.

He doesn't say anything, just gives me a grim nod.

I dump the powder into each of the braziers, careful not to extinguish the flames just starting to take hold as embers. Then I mix the precise amount of Scent Keeper elixir with water, diluting it to the measurements in Sephine's notes. The dark liquid hisses and spits, bubbling with the sickly yellow powder until the embers are coated with the stuff.

The stench is overpowering.

Some kind of sickly sweet overripeness, like every plant that ever bloomed or fruited was mixed in a vat and left to rot in the sun.

That would have been bearable, but there's more, too. The sulphur-like powder Ash carried in a sack from the old Scent Keeper's quarters and up the hundreds of steps to the top of the temple is rotten eggs and rust, sewers and verdigris, damp caves and rain falling on hot rocks.

I swallow down the urge to gag.

Well, Asmudtag, I say inwardly in that way I've come to think of as my own version of praying. *You are all, as they say. So if you're around, I could really use some help with this next bit. Even just a whiff?*

CHAPTER 23

ASH

The smoke emanating from the braziers is some of the most noxious I've ever smelled. I have no idea how Rakel is managing to get through it. I've seen her gag at things that are barely half as objectionable.

It takes me back to the acrid, stinging vapours Zostar and his cronies used to release into the Room during the tests they conducted under Ekasya Mountain. It's not the same, but even my blunt sense of smell can determine there are commonalities. My heartbeat quickens with the recognition and my survival instincts kick in, searching for the fight.

But while the enemy is on the approach for Aphorai City, there isn't an external threat in the immediate vicinity. It's just me, Rakel, and the smoke billowing from the braziers. The doors are barred. The roof is closed.

I'm trapped, says a voice in my mind. A younger voice.

No. I'm here willingly. I want this. I want the part of me I've always been ashamed of, the part I've always feared, to be gone.

I hoist myself on to the altar, trying to keep my breath calm and even.

"If this is anything like healing Nisai," Rakel says, "or like out in the training yard, this isn't going to be over without a struggle. But if it gets too much, we can stop and open the vents. Nothing says we have to get it right first time."

She's trying to remain positive, but I know her well enough to see through it. We don't have time to try this over and again.

The more I breathe of the caustic smoke, the more hurt and frustration courses through me, red and blinding. I clamp down on it. Even if I deserve this curse, Zostar's captives do not. They're being used. And if I can lead the way to freeing them not just from the Mountain but from the very thing Zostar wants to exploit, then that's what I must do.

I breathe deeply of the acrid fumes and let just a little of it burn into anger at the injustice of it. But I don't let the rage consume me. A single flame, not a wildfire. Barely enough to wake the part of me that is always there in hibernation. The darkness that always waits. Ready.

Itching begins along my inked skin as the shadows start to shift and weave in and out of the clouds of sulphur and strange elixir vapours. The beast stirs, riling to be set free, but I keep it contained, focused, a single plume of smoke channelled through a censer.

The edge of my vision darkens. Shadows writhe across the walls of the huge chamber, plunging to the floor and darting back up to the roof where they rear and churn, as if in fury that they're closed off to the last of the night.

My skin burns, the beast fighting for release. Drops of blood begin to form along the backs of my hands, as if the tips of the tattooed claws are digging into the flesh. And just like smoke from incense, the shadow begins to rise from the ink.

Rakel approaches, her expression equal parts fascination and dread. She reaches out, holds her hands in the air above mine, in the path of the darkness. Closes her eyes. Breathes deep, tendrils of smoke curling around her face. Tendrils of shadow *reaching* from the back of my hands to her palms.

She flinches as they make contact.

My control slips, the shadow surging forth. I jerk back.

"I'm fine." She grates from between clenched teeth.

"Are you sure?"

She nods. Jaw set in determination. "I can do this."

CHAPTER 24

LUZ

I thump on the upper level door with the heel of my fist.

"Open up, petal."

I wait. Nothing.

It's no surprise. The ancient entry must be half an arm length thick. Even if I expected an attentive welcome, there's no guarantee anyone inside would have heard.

I pull the picks from my belt and set to work on the lock. It's heavy, stiff and rusted. A mechanism that hasn't been secured for turns. The most fun kind of lock to pick. If you're a masochist.

"Hurry," Yaita snaps.

"Calm, now. Locks are like people. Rushing at them doesn't get you in any faster."

As if to demonstrate the point, the left pick slips and my finger scrapes the inner edge of the keyhole, snagging enough to draw blood. I'd keep working, but my hands are going to be slick with crimson if I let it flow. I tear a strip from my sleeve and tie it around the pathetically small wound.

What a waste of a perfectly good robe.

I set back to work, straining to hear what's taking place in the chamber beyond. The door is too well sealed to see anything beneath it or between the frame and hinges. But the barest hint of sulphur and char reaches my nose through the cracks.

By the Primordial, for all I know, it's already done. The girl could open the door, swagger out, having achieved something even Sephine possibly never attempted. I wouldn't be surprised if she pulled it off. I wouldn't have led her to this if I hadn't concluded her odds were good.

Then again, she could have failed. Behind that door might already be one body, possibly two. Or there could be a dead girl at the feet of a trained fighter possessed with the Lost God's lust to conquer and subjugate everything he lays eyes upon.

And that will be on me.

CHAPTER 25

RAKEL

The darkness flowing into my hands quickens, strengthens, grows.

It was a steady stream, a trickle I could manage despite the pain, but now it's like too much water flowing down an irrigation canal, swamping over the top of a sluice gate.

Ash gasps as the tattoos up his forearms tear. Blood splatters on to the altar, droplets running races to the stone floor, others soaking into the sandstone.

Shadows coil free from his bleeding flesh and rear back like snakes before lunging for the strike. Ropes of darkness wrap around my wrists, cruel and heavy as shackles. The urge is to fight it, to draw back, to sever the bindings. To stop the acid-burn coating my skin. Find relief from the dragging exhaustion as it sinks into me.

But I can do this. I've survived the elixir before.

I have the gift.

Luz said it. Even Yaita admitted it. I will channel the will of Asmudtag, as the Order calls it. The Primordial deity stands for balance. And surely freeing Ash from his curse is an act of balance. If there is any truth in the gods, I will find it here.

An inhuman, guttural moan reverberates through the chamber.

I'd think it were Ash if it weren't so large a sound, like it's coming from a distance and nearby all at once. For a moment, I could swear the altar itself shuddered. Ash's eyes go wide, intense concentration replaced with fear.

Is he doing this? Some sort of amplified power from all the ceremonial smoke we've been breathing? Or is this him losing control?

"Ash, stay with me."

He grits his teeth but doesn't reply. I can see he's fighting, tendons standing out on his neck, muscles flexed as if he's battling to keep himself still, all the more crimson pumping from his torn arms. His war is internal and there's nothing I can do but keep going, allowing the darkness to transfer to me.

Then there's a deep shudder, the copper braziers rattling in their stands, almost like the whole temple is shivering. Is the power within Ash truly doing this? Is this what Zostar has been looking to harness?

The violent trembling begins again. And I recognize it for what it is.

Rancid reeking rankness.

Groundshake.

A big one.

The floor heaves beneath my feet.

A *huge* one.

They say this temple has stood for millennia. Through all the upheaval beneath the province. Now cracks begin to form, smaller lines fanning out from them like the veins of a leaf. One appears between my boots. First it's the width of a hair, then a reed, then a finger. I jostle to get two feet on one side, desperate not to break contact with Ash.

Somewhere beneath us, there's a horrible grinding, grating sound. The gap in the floor widens, so that I can see between layers of rough-cut stone to the twenty – or thirty-foot drop to the next chamber below. A firebird looks up through the rift, eyes terror wide, barely dodging falling debris.

Sephine's notes said nothing about what would happen if the ceremony wasn't completed. I've no intention of finding out.

"Hold on, Ash."

But the shadows are swirling with the smoke now; they're drawing to him, to me. His eyes are closed, his head rocks back, and he gives no indication he's heard.

Sherds of sandstone and mortar rain down on us, one slicing through my smock to bite into the soft part of my upper arm. I barely register the pain, too intent on what's happening overhead. The roof over the great altar is moving apart, inch by inch.

The sacred smoke of the ceremony rushes to it like a well-flued chimney, faster and faster, swirling around us and then disappearing into the sky.

The shadow that remains is everywhere. It's all over me. Stinging, burning, smothering until I'm lost in the darkness.

All is black.

CHAPTER 26

LUZ

As it turns out, my lock picking skills were not required – the Primordial saw to that.

The floor finally ceases undulating, having torn apart ancient masonry and mortar, rending a wound so deep it looks like the temple was cleaved in two. Both Yaita and I are covered in powdered detritus, blood oozing slowly from a dozen lacerations. By Asmudtag's grace, we have no major injuries.

One half of the retractable stone roof has fallen from its frame. I peer through the clouds of dust and ash still billowing in what's left of the ceremonial chamber. Trepidation courses through me at the sight – nothing else moves.

There's a scrape as the Shield emerges from the dust, dragging his left foot, the ankle at such an awkward angle I'd venture bone is broken. Still, he's cradling the girl in his arms.

"What have you done?" Yaita veritably screams at him.

"Help her," is all he says in response. "Please."

He places the girl's still form on the great altar, not far from the chasm now running through the floor. At any other time it would be sacrilege. But there's no high priestess here, and I do not share the scruples of some.

Yaita takes in the sight of her daughter's still form. A small vial of what is no doubt Asmudtagian elixir appearing from beneath the long sleeves of her robe. Ah, so Sephine had let her unofficial apprentice take certain liberties. Because I doubt the other ancients at the Sanctuary would have afforded her the revered liquid.

She lurches into a run and opens the vial, reckless in her desperation. Several dark drops fall to the floor as she leaps the great rend wreaked by the groundshake. She bends to her daughter, one hand on an unmoving shoulder, another on her stomach.

"Is she breathing?" I ask.

Yaita doesn't reply. She's inhaling deeply from the vial. Her eyes are closed, her brow creased. She's focusing her energy. I'd witnessed Sephine do this only a handful of times. The last from afar, in the dahkai plantation the night the Prince was poisoned and she tried to save him. Her last night in the mortal realm.

She places two hands to the girl's temples. The braziers leap back into flame, guttering until they're once again burning clear. If I didn't know better, I'd say I was seeing things.

By the grace of the Primordial, colour begins to return to the girl's cheeks as it drains from her mother's.

Still, she doesn't wake.

A trembling begins in Yaita's hands, her now-pallid forehead beading with sweat. The girl's chest begins to rise and fall, deep and even as with the rhythm of sleep.

Yaita sways, then topples over, her head smacking against the stone floor.

I cross to her. She's out cold. A pulse beats weakly at her throat.

As it was with Sephine, there's nothing I can do for her.

CHAPTER 27

ASH

Rakel didn't regain consciousness. Nor did her mother.

Barden didn't want to let me in to see her, but Nisai overruled him. Even so, I'm being given a strictly limited visit, chaperoned for the entire duration by Kip.

When we enter the room, Barden is sitting at Rakel's bedside, staring into space. The air is thick with sacred incense, no doubt funded by Nisai. It's a combination similar to what surrounds me when I reinfuse my prayer brand – an appeal to the strengths and mercy of each of the deities. Even Azered who guides the souls of the living to their afterlife. My throat tightens at the thought.

"What's he doing here?" the Aphorain demands.

Anguish is written all over his face, in the hunch of his shoulders, his hands flexed into fists one heartbeat and spread wide the next, like he needs something to do with them but has no idea what. Now I'm here, I suppose he's imagining the most appropriate thing would be for said fists to connect with my face.

Kip stands between us. "Barden, go check on Nisai," the Losian orders.

"I … you can't tell me what—"

She folds her arms. "Just do it."

He glares at the swept stone floor, then decides not to argue further. Hauling himself to his feet, he pointedly takes his time retying the already knotted calf straps of his standard guard-issue sandals. Then he shoves past me – shoulder and elbow tensed with all his strength by the feel of the impact – and leaves the room.

Kip takes up a seat in the corner, pulls out a whetstone and begins to sharpen one of the many knives she secretes around her person. The rasp feels like it's flaying my nerves.

"Do you have to?"

She raises her eyebrows. It's a look that says she might have been generous enough to back me being able to see Rakel, but that I best not push it if I know what's good for me.

I take the seat Barden has only recently left, doing my best to ignore the residual body heat, and gently lift Rakel's hand into both of my own. Her fingers are cool and dry and perfectly still.

"Has there been any change?"

"Nuh-uh," Kip grunts.

"Her mother? Has she come to?"

"Nuh-uh."

I don't know what to say. I've already cursed myself a hundred times over, and yet it still isn't enough. So, I simply sit, holding Rakel's hand, smoothing her hair where it has grown long enough to spike out in different directions.

My mind races through the scenes from the temple in a vicious loop. It's only when Kip's whetstone stops mid-swipe that I realize the sob I just heard was from my own lips.

"I come from military stock," she says, starting up with the whetstone again like she's using each stroke to punctuate her words.

"What's that got to do with any of this?"

"My family has had the most Province Commanders of any Losian line since the Accord," she continues. "Soldiering is in my blood. But I wasn't satisfied with that. I wanted to be a Ranger. They've always held themselves above the province forces. Their recruitment tests are tougher. I wasn't going to be looked down on by anyone, and I wasn't going to let my sister be looked down on, either."

"You have a sister?" This is the first I've ever heard her speak of family at all, let alone siblings.

"One. Younger. By a few hundred heartbeats, give or take."

It takes a moment for that to sink in. She really does hold her game pieces close to her chest. "You're a twin?"

"Whether by a breath or a turn, Tayar's still younger. She was my responsibility. And I let her down. As far as I was concerned, we were both going to become Rangers. We'd go on campaign together. Return home decorated. Make our father proud, but on our own terms. Tayar would've been content staying in Los. Just because we're twins doesn't mean we shared the same mind. But I wouldn't settle for anything less than Rangers for both of us. I dragged her out on mock missions every time I could. Sometimes going for days when we had leave from province cadet training, venturing into the edges of the Wastes. Pushing our endurance, our survival skills out where there'd be nobody to aid us."

She sets down the blade and stone, and for a heartbeat I think she's done with her tale. She stares at the ceiling for a long pause, then locks her gaze with mine.

"The last time we went out together…" She shakes her head, closing her eyes. When she looks back across the room at me, over Rakel's still form beneath the blanket, I recognize the heaviness in her expression. The familiar weight of shame.

"What happened?" I ask gently.

She goes very still, the only movement the candlelight dancing across her features. "I pushed too hard."

I can barely bring myself to ask what's on my mind. "She died?"

"No. But after that day she wasn't going to be a camp cook, let alone a soldier in the province army. And dead certain not a Ranger."

"But you became one."

"I had to. I couldn't stay at home a day longer. My presence was a taunt. I didn't want her to have to live like that. So, I left." She gestures to Rakel. "Nobody else will risk being in the same room with you. I'm here because I know what it is to hurt someone you love. Say what you have to say to her. But make it quick. You've not got all night."

"Actually, I was hoping to write something."

Kip nods slowly. "Sometimes it's easier that way." She rises from her seat and opens the door, sticking her head out. "Get us parchment and ink, would you?"

When the guard returns with the writing equipment, I find I'm at a loss for words. I never imagined willingly doing this. But I don't see any other way.

If I stay, Rakel won't be safe.

Nobody will ever be truly safe near me.

But Rakel? I know her. She'll find a way to twist this into being just a setback. And I know it's more than that. When the very earth started revolting beneath us, it was a sign. Even the gods think I should be destroyed, lest I be the Lost God's path to resurgence.

I take up the reed stylus and begin to write.

CHAPTER 28

RAKEL

I awake alone.

Someone has put me to bed, bandaged a deep cut on my upper arm, and changed me into a fresh nightgown. It's an unnerving thought, until I notice the lingering scent of violets on my blanket. It says enough about who saw to me after I collapsed – Luz.

Huh. Reunited with my long-lost mother and she doesn't even tend my wounds when I'm hurt. Can't say I'm surprised. Guess letters were Yaita's limit after all.

I sit up and the room swims. Everything in it looks soft, the edges blurred as they were after I healed Nisai, only more so. I press the heels of my hands to my temples as flashes of the ceremony return to me. Smoke. Shadow swirling, burning into me like acid. The terrible feeling of the floor heaving beneath my feet. The chasm that tore open near the great altar. The look of pain and horror on Ash's face. Devouring darkness. Everywhere black. Then nothing.

I swing my legs over the side of the bed, then wish I hadn't moved so quickly. Forcing myself to breathe deeply,

I find some steadiness. When the dizzy feeling subsides, I stand and cross the room to the silver mirror.

There's a graze on my forehead from where it must have hit the temple floor. Is that why my vision is blurred? I gently press a finger around the edge and give it an experimental sniff. The scrape isn't deep, but I'm grateful Luz still cleaned it with honeywine and sealed it with olive oil to keep it from festering.

I lean closer to my reflection. My eyes. Maybe I should have expected it, given how Sephine's were entirely dark. But it's still unnerving to see the tiny webs of blood vessels have turned black.

If this is how the ceremony left me, what about Ash?

Did it work? Is he all right?

I've got to find him. But the headache pounding through my skull, like nothing I've ever experienced, says otherwise. I lay down on the bed, intending only to rest my eyes for a few moments, only to startle awake when Kip raps on the open door. I have no idea how long I drifted.

"You're back with us," she says, a note of surprise in her usually deadpan manner. "Good."

"How's Ash?"

"Shield was here last night, checking on you."

For a moment I think she's making some obscure comment about herself, but then I remember she's never once called herself by that title, even when she was officially serving as Ash's stand-in. *A Ranger is for life.*

"He left something for you." She reaches into her leather vest, pulls out a small, folded packet and passes it to me. "Can you walk? There's a meeting. The Emperor-elect wants you there."

I tuck the packet into my satchel. I'm desperate to see what it contains. But I also know that if it's from Ash, I want to read it alone, not with Kip looming impatiently over me.

"Give me a moment," I say.

"Don't keep the Emperor-elect waiting."

"I'm not going anywhere without my boots. Not even for a Prince."

"*Emperor-elect.*"

I wave that away. "'Prince' rolls off the tongue easier."

Her flat stare ends in a shrug that says: "it's your nose you're risking".

As we start off down the hall, something crunches beneath my feet. Sherds of stone and mortar litter our path, more on the left than right. I'd thought my uneven gait was an injury or stiffness. But it's not me. The floor itself now tilts.

In the quarters the high priestess had granted Nisai, we find Barden. There's only a couple of candles lit, so he's not much more than an outline, his head bent over some documents. Strange. He was always better with his words than me – all palace guards are expected to read and write just in case – but what's caught his interest in the Prince's documents?

No doubt something that he hopes will help him climb further up the imperial ladder.

I clear my throat.

"This isn't what it looks like," Barden blurts as he jerks back, looking as sheepish as when we were kids thieving oranges from Old Man Kelruk's grove. Now, the grove makes me think of Ash.

"Where is he?" I ask.

Barden scowls. He knows I'm not talking about the Prince. "I don't know. Kip just said he'd made himself scarce after visiting you. Can't say I'm sorry." At his last words he looks painfully uncomfortable, like he's gone too far. "I mean, I'm sorry for *you*. I know you cared for him."

"Care," I snap. None of this is Barden's fault, but right now his sympathy is about as soothing as vinegar fumes.

"Sorry?"

"Present tense. I *care* for him deeply."

Barden nods, solemn, and gets to his feet, crossing the floor to meet me. He murmurs, soft enough so it's only the two of us who can hear: "Sometimes we have to let those we love find their own way."

I want to rage at him, tell him he can keep his stale-smelling advice. But I know exactly what he's talking about. Back in Aphorai, he had to let me go. To let me find my own way. Maybe if he pushed harder, I would have caved in and married him like he always said he'd wanted. Maybe I'd be living a different life now if I'd said yes. A quiet life, the wife of a guard on the Aphorain Eraz's estate. I thought I'd find that suffocating. But maybe I wouldn't have. Maybe it would have been nice. Pleasant. Safe.

I might have been wrong about what it would be like to have been Barden's wife.

What I wasn't wrong about is that I needed to decide for myself.

As does Ash. I pushed him. And look where it got us. If he needs some space to gather himself after what happened, I have to accept that.

I'm about to concede Barden's right when I catch a whiff of violets. I spin to find Zakkurus has approached on silent feet. They wear a tailored robe of night-sky blue, creating sharp angles at the shoulders before tapering in and angling out again at the waist. A row of embroidered flowers – I squint and barely make out irises – decorate hem and cuffs, the silver thread gleaming in the torchlight. A silver band holds back midnight hair, and their deep blue eyes are made up with rur ink.

For once, their expression carries no hint of mockery or amusement. "Come. The Eraz's chariot has arrived. I cannot afford not to be there when they start."

"The meeting?"

"The war council."

The only city walls unbreached during the Shadow Wars.

When I was young and still small enough for Father to carry me on his shoulders, that's what he'd say every time we entered Aphorai City. It didn't matter which gate we used or what we'd been talking about until then. He'd still stop, gaze up at the height and breadth of the defenses, the archer's slits from which more swallows than arrows had launched over the centuries, and remark in admiration: *the only city walls unbreached during the Shadow Wars.*

Now, looking down from the second highest of the temple terraces, it's undeniable that the impossible has happened. A great, gaping wound runs through Aphorai City from the stepped pyramid to the eighth gate, the one that leads most directly to the river and on to Ekasya. The gate itself is in splinters, as if some huge creature took hold of each side and tore it in two as easily as a child tears a leaf. Along the path of destruction, piles of rubble have replaced buildings, palms and rock-figs that once lined broad avenues have toppled, their roots bare to the sky.

This part of the temple, where Sephine first had me summonsed after the perfume trials, seems relatively unscathed. The palms have fared better in their planters than those in the streets below, and Sephine's garden beds are untouched. The fountain remains intact, though no water bubbles from the sculpted dahkai flower spout.

Over in the pavilion, several figures are silhouetted behind gauzy purple silk that billows in the breeze. Temple guards have formed up at a respectable distance. Zakkurus leads us past them, then motions for us to sit beside the fountain. Nisai may want us here, but even recent events haven't erased the fact that his family is one of the most powerful in the Empire. Guess it takes more than a huge groundshake to upend centuries of rules and manners.

Still, I've got a good enough view to pick out who's who. Nisai sits across from his mother, Shari. She wears a deep purple robe. A golden torque at her collarbone drips with the rubies of Aphorai and the amethyst of the imperial family. Her cousin, Malmud, Eraz of Aphorai, sits diagonally opposite, still formidable with his bull neck and shoulders and black, braided beard. A woman I don't know sits on the other side of Shari, clearly aristocratic from her fine, sky blue silk robe and the shimmering pearls pinned in an elaborate crown of gold hair.

Between light gusts of the breeze, the mix of luscious, aristocratic perfumes mingle with the amber oil of the Eraz's guard. I realize I've grown so used to being around Kip, Nisai and the others that my nose has stopped noticing their presence unless I deliberately single them out in my mind. But today, there's two conspicuous absences.

Ash.

And Yaita.

Zakkurus approaches the nobles, dipping into a graceful bow. "My condolences, your Highness. I feel the loss deeply."

Nisai gazes out over the city, then up to the partially collapsed top tier of the temple above us. No offerings will be made from there anytime soon.

"I worry for the people. They will be afraid, and fearful people will seek solace in prayer. If they cannot make their entreaties…" He looks to the Eraz. "Have you managed to assess the extent of the damage, Uncle?"

"Enough to know that Aphorai City will take turns to recover."

"As will the families who lost loved ones during the upheaval. Are they being assisted?"

"My people are already on the ground lending direct aid."

Nisai nods approval. "And the wall?"

The Eraz folds his hands over his sizeable paunch. "We might be able to build temporary defenses around the breach. But my engineers warn that overall structural integrity may have been compromised. Essentially, our fair city is wounded. It would only take a half-competent commander to finish her off. Your brother is more than that, and our scouts say we'll soon see their dust on the horizon. I'm sorry, my boy, my promise of protection to you is once again smoke on the wind."

"No, Uncle. You did everything within your power to keep me safe. Even the most secular thinker cannot deny the possibility of a link between my former Shield's reckless attempt to defy the Lost God's curse and the destruction wreaked upon our city."

303

I wince. Both at Ash's loss of position and at my role in what came next.

"I believe," Nisai continues, "this was an act of the gods."

"The Primordial, rather," Zakkurus mutters, covering the outburst by pouring cups of kormak with a showy flourish.

Shari takes a cup but doesn't drink. "I've sent word to my Losian counterpart so she knows to expect us."

Nisai frowns. "You're suggesting I leave Aphorai? My ancestral home? And go further from the capital? Mother, what happens when I run out of places to flee?"

"I'll admit Daprul hasn't always been the most forthcoming with her thoughts on the Council. But I trust her. As the last province capable of standing in defiance of your brother's so-called Regency, Los is the safest place for you now."

Malmud throws back his kormak, swallowing with a grimace. "And if we can bring the Losian army to our side, we may have some chance in standing against your brother's forces."

Zakkurus nods agreement. "Moreover, my Prince, several of the Losian Five Families are indebted to us – their appetites for our perfumes have long exceeded their fortunes. If the need eventuates, we could leverage that debt to conscript their household guards."

"Tell me you're not suggesting a full-scale war," the Prince says, looking between them.

Nobody replies.

Nisai pinches the bridge of his nose between thumb and forefinger and rises to his feet. Taking up his crutches, he paces out to the low wall overlooking the city. Barden follows, a look of genuine concern on his features as he gives the Prince's shoulder a reassuring squeeze.

They exchange a few murmured words and Nisai's back straightens. Barden may not have the wits of the likes of Ami or Esarik, but seems he knows how to get through to the Prince.

Nisai returns to the pavilion. "I'll do it. On one condition. We're not going to Lostras to recruit the army for a battle. We're going to recruit an army to show we're serious, to give us leverage to have a genuine parley. While I cannot abide Zostar and his activities, I cannot believe Iddo would drive us all into all-out war if there was any room for compromise."

"He's a good boy, really," the blonde woman pipes up. "If we could…"

Shari takes the woman's hand. "We'll do whatever we can to find a humane solution, Galen."

Is this Iddo's mother? Romantics have relished gossiping about the love story between the two Council members. Now, it seems tragic. How Galen's loyalties must be torn.

"Of course we'll work towards a compromise," the Prince continues. "But I must speak with my brother on equal terms. I have to give him a reason to listen to me; I cannot do that when he has an army at his back and I do not. So yes, Mother, I will visit Daprul and the Losian Eraz."

"Commander, not Eraz," Kip rumbles.

Zakkurus shoots her a sharp look.

"Sorry?" Nisai asks.

"Er, forgive me, Your Highness. You'll need to have the Province Army Commander onside. The Eraz can't do squat without him."

The Prince looks to his mother.

"I expect she is correct," Shari concedes. "Whenever the Council had to review any decree or make a major change,

Daprul would always consult with the Commander as well as the Eraz. Though it was naturally never remarked upon, I've always had the impression that the former's word carried more weight than the latter."

Kip shrugs. "It's the way we do things. You'll see when you get there, Your Highness. But go to the Commander before the Eraz, otherwise it will be an insult."

"I'm sure you'll not let me put a foot wrong."

Kip looks slightly ill, her gaze going to the edge of the wall. I don't know if it's because she's going to bring up her breakfast, or if she's looking for an escape route. Why isn't she happy about returning home?

"Is there something amiss?" Nisai prods.

"No, Your Highness," she says, swallowing hard.

He regards her seriously. "I'll admit there is a risk the Losians might see me as a bargaining chip to curry favour with my brother. Do you think that a likely scenario?"

"I couldn't say, But I'll do all I can to steer you true." The last is said with a thump of her fist to her chest in salute.

Malmud rises to his feet. "I'll notify my stewards. We must leave immediately if we're going to make it to the river before the enemy cuts off access." He gives Nisai a hearty embrace and heads for the stairwell.

When he's gone, Zakkurus clears their throat. "Forgive me, Your Highness, but what if you cannot talk sense into your brother? Should we not be planning for every eventuality?"

"We are. Ami and Barden will be sourcing the ancient weapon against the Children of Doskai, in case Zostar has worked out how to harness their power."

Zakkurus blinks, momentarily stunned. "You figured it out?"

Nisai smiles ruefully. "We deduced where the knowledge could be found. It seems there was more distribution of power from the time of the Founding Accord than even I knew. Another check and balance, though this one unofficial."

His mother nods. "Each member of the Council of Five inherits the location of their Province's sacred cache, passed through the generations and kept secret until the unfortunate day when it may once again be needed."

"So," Nisai continues. "We know where the Aphorain cache is. With my brother's superior army on the march, we can't afford to divert our own forces, so we'll send a scouting party to determine what is there. Barden will be my representative, and Ami will accompany them in case there's any relic or record to decipher. My mother will accompany me to Lostras, to meet with the Losian imperial wife. I would hope Daprul will see it is in all our interests to reveal the location of Losian cache. Presumably the more we have of this weapon, the better."

Zakkurus holds up a hand. "I'll take care of the logistics for your journey, my Prince. Please, go see to any preparations you wish to make before we depart forthwith."

The nobles file away, flanked by the temple guards, Kip a step behind Nisai.

Zakkurus returns to Barden and me, perching on the edge of the now-still fountain. They explain everything that happened in the temple. Yaita brought me back from the brink of death, channelling the unleashed shadow magic to herself. She's been unconscious ever since. She seems to be in a stable condition, but nobody knows if that condition will ever improve. Or if she'll ever wake.

When Zakkurus has finished talking, I look out over the city, pensive. "I never thought these walls could be brought down. And now… Just when we need them most."

The walls. Yaita. I feel awful about what happened to both, but I can't see how the groundshake was anything but a random natural event. Unfortunate, but random.

Zakkurus scans the trail of wreckage through the city, blue eyes strangely intent. "We'll one day find our salvation in Asmudtagian destruction."

"Sorry?"

"Just something Sephine used to say in the aftermath of a tremor."

"Typical Sephine riddles," I scoff.

"Possibly."

"Though one thing I did believe as a child has come true."

"Oh?"

"That I'm the likely to be the cause of my mother's death."

"Come now, a little melodramatic even for you, no? Do you truly believe that?"

I don't answer.

"Let me come at it from a different angle, then. If you'd known she might get hurt, would you still have taken the chance?"

I can't bring myself to say it. Because yes. The answer is yes. I would do anything for Ash. Something about the thought catches me off guard. It's terrifying, in a way. I never before imagined feeling such … devotion.

I remember the packet Kip gave me earlier.

I take it out and open it. Ash's prayer braid falls to the ground.

Zakkurus blinks mildly. Barden clears his throat and looks away.

Rakel—

I cannot escape the notion that our actions not only failed, but that to meddle with such forces also angered the gods – I will not be party to such destruction. By the time you read this I expect I'll have long left the city. I wish it weren't so, but this is the way I can best show my love for you – setting you free of me and my curse. I didn't want to see it, but it's clear now that I am more danger than protector to those I love. It's inevitable I will cause harm wherever I go, but from now, it will only be to those who deserve it. I've accepted there is no other way I can live my life. I hope you will one day come to understand. Until then, know the only good part of me – my love for you – remains at your side.

– Ash

The wooziness returns in a crashing wave.

A note? That's all he's left me with? After everything we've been through?

I *risked my life* for him. I thought we were a team. Guess I thought wrong. Seems being a martyr is now more important to Ash than working together on a solution. Maybe it always was, and I just didn't want to see it.

Wordless, I cross to the edge of the temple platform and sit on the edge. Down in the city, it's a hive of activity. But it's different to when we were preparing for a siege. Carts, camels, litters or on foot, people are streaming into the desert like sand in a timeglass.

I look down to the note again.

Notes. Letters. Things people send you when they think they've got more noble things to do with their life than being in yours.

Where is my life, now? At Father's? Cowering and hoping Zostar's army doesn't loot and pillage down to the very last village?

No.

I've got important things to do, too.

I turn back to Zakkurus. "What will happen to Yaita?"

They give a languid shrug.

"Take care of her? Take her to Lostras with you. I'm going with Barden and Ami. I'm going to find this weapon."

"Rather valiant of you, petal."

"I'm sick of being a game piece."

They give me a knowing smile. "Ah, you'd like to be a player."

"Stenches, no. I want the game to be over so I can go make a life for myself. The way *I* want it."

I hold Ash's note high, out over the edge of the platform. The breeze sends it rippling and flapping.

I take one last look and let it go.

CHAPTER 29

LUZ

I've heard many a tale of the Cliffs of Lostras.

It took the best part of a moon to get here, first overland back to the great Aramtesh River. We hurriedly boarded the Eraz's flotilla. With the dust cloud of the approaching army already on the horizon, I couldn't take exception with being relegated to the second finest barge. The further we floated into Los Province, the swifter the current, so that the rowers only needed to work in fits and starts. Thanks be to the Primordial, as once we skirted the Wastes of Los everyone naturally preferred to be in the sealed cabins below decks, intermittently spritzing the air with a blend of lavender and citrus in an attempt to mask the overpowering sulphurous miasma.

If malodor was the epitome of our worries, life would be splendid. Alas, one can only hope the Aphorains we left behind have found refuge. While each time I check the cabin in which Yaita convalesces, I can only wish her condition would improve as swiftly as the river flows.

At last, we cruise into the Losian capital.

Lostras is the source of tales from the dreamsmoke dens of Aphorai to the smuggler ships of Lapis Lautus. Not least of all because of where the city is perched.

One would need to have lived under a rock their whole life to have not known of the Cliffs of Lostras, the Wonder at the World's Edge. Five hundred vertical feet of sheer stone rising out of the raging ocean. For hundreds of miles either side there are no safe harbours. No craft can land, from ship to rowboat, until the cliffs lower into the only slightly more navigable eastern coast of Los Province. Even there, in comparative welcome, the shoreline bares stone teeth as jagged as a sea serpent's fangs.

Lostras straddles the last length of the Aramtesh River before the waters that flow through every province in the Empire plunge over the Cliffs in a mile-wide tidefall. It's said that the mist that billows up gives the Losian capital a climate unto its own. As the barges pull in to the wealthiest of the merchant docks, I'm rather charmed to discover the effusive descriptions do the place justice.

The plan was to disembark without pomp. But alas, even the most well-trained of the Prince's uncle's household guard can't help but gape at their surroundings. Where the bulk of the Province is a sulphurous hellscape, the neighbourhood stretching up from the river is lush and verdant. Wooden houses with roofs of palm-thatch and open, wraparound verandahs nestle in a haven of greenery and blooms. The flowers are a cacophony of colour – lilies and clusters of tiny gem-like buds that look like falling tears, hibiscus and bromeliads clinging to coconut palms, and everywhere the smell of something sweeter and more intoxicating than jasmine fills the air – frangipani.

At almost every corner we pass there's one of the leggy trees, bunches of leaves flaring out like the points of a star, pink-orange flowers blooming at their centre. Ferns with fronds as long as barge paddles line the streets and drape from the roofs providing welcome shade. Fountains bubble at major crossroads, fish with blue, purple and flame-orange scales darting through the water and occasionally leaping for a mosquito that buzzed too close to the surface.

A city like none other in Aramtesh.

Proud of it, too, judging by the straight-backed walk of the people who stride the boulevards, so much so that it takes me twice as long as the usual glance to determine servant from aristocrat. It doesn't help that they all dress similarly. Where I would have expected a clash of garish rainbow fabrics to reflect the flora, almost everyone is dressed in well-made but unadorned sleeveless robes in various shades of beige, belted at the waist. Near-identical sandals laced to the knee. The only way to tell guard from regular citizen is that their robes are augmented with scaled leather kilts in the same fashion as Aphorai. Though unlike their western neighbours, I'd venture more than a few of the civilians here have a similar level of military skill to the guards, if anything I've heard about the Losians has truth at its essence. Though for a city to forgo fortifications to this extent seems to err on the arrogant side of confidence.

Our travelling boots and caravan guard leathers aren't too out of place. And I've grudgingly slicked the parts of my skin exposed to the sun with Kip's coconut oil. I've worn countless scents to blend in over the turns since I was recruited by Sephine. But I've never felt more like a walking confection than now. I can't justifiably abstain when the

Emperor-elect has done the same. And though he rides in a litter, it's not of a quality that would be incongruous for a successful merchant.

He's playing his part. I must play mine.

The guard at the gate to the inner city is the same height as Kip, with sleek black braids and a deep gold complexion. Her comrade sports a red beard bisected on his left cheek by an even redder slash of scar tissue. He's a head taller.

"Is everyone here a giant?" I mutter.

"Only those in military service. Others are an inch shorter. Sometimes two."

It's the same deadpan tone I've come to expect from her. I can never fully decide if I'm rankled or charmed.

Kip knows how to fit in here. Little doubt about it. Even less when the guards look straight through both of us as if we're invisible.

"Let me take care of this," she says it as if it's a military command. I'm about to object when she steps forward, squaring off with the guard.

"Ranger." The redheaded guard acknowledges her badge of office grudgingly, the bronze medallion in a stylized version of the map of Aramtesh. Despite everything that's happened, she still hasn't relinquished wearing it. I'm not sure whether it is wise or dangerous to have in one's possession given the present political situation – the guard's tone was even, but it's the tight-grip that comes from discipline, not a mild temper.

"Los first," Kip salutes.

"Always Los," the guard replies, visibly relaxing.

"Step aside. We're here on imperial business."

By the Primordial's grace. I hadn't expected to dive naked into a diplomatic nightmare quite so swiftly. "Ah,

314

perhaps we should—"

"This is a local concern, stranger," the bearded guard snaps.

It's like that then. Delightful.

The curtains on the litter stir. I move closer, where they part just enough for me to get a glimpse of the Emperor-elect's silhouette. "Is something amiss?" It's the barest whisper.

"Do you trust her?" I ask. My gaze flicks to where Kip and the guards glare at each other, the silence a veritable battlefield between them.

"With my life. I would have thought that was obvious by now?"

I wonder if he's truly factored in how deep homeland loyalties can run. Have we walked into a trap, after all? Travelled all this way just to hand over a bargaining chip for Los to leverage a deal with the Regent?

Kip faces off with the guards, unflinching. No further words are spoken but, finally, the redheaded Losian gives an almost imperceptible nod.

"How did you convince them?" I ask her.

"It's not their role to be convinced. Now, keep up. There's honourable notice, and then there's giving the enemy enough time to strategize." She lengthens her already considerable strides.

"They're not our enemy, that's the point."

"We'll see," she huffs.

Once we're through the gate and out of earshot, I sniff. "Lax."

"Eh?" Kip grunts.

"They're not taking our weapons."

She chuckles at that. "When you're trained to be a

315

weapon from the time you can walk, taking away your blade isn't going to disarm you."

"Is that so?" I raise an eyebrow.

"You know where I am if you'd like to try."

"Perhaps when all this is over."

She grins. "I'll hold you to that."

As per the plan, we're to seek out the Province Commander first. We arrive at what must be the barracks. Losian architecture is most assuredly not my forte, but if it's not the barracks, we're about to find ourselves incarcerated. In my experience, armouries and prisons are usually the only buildings with barred windows.

We're led by a quartet of leather-kilted giants through a series of corridors and into a room that is open from waist height along one side. Some barracks. The view is breathtaking, I'll give them that – an uninterrupted vista across azure ocean to the distant horizon. Tree trunks angle up through the floor and out the top of the roof, forming part of the very structure itself. Orchids cling to the boughs with a tangle of silver-green roots. Birds with feathers that glow blood-red in the sunset perch along the balustrade. Firebirds. At least the supposed descendants of the mythical, man-eating version. Far less problematic as house pets.

Despite its wondrous features, the room is devoid of furniture. Not exactly a comfortable reception area.

A man enters through the opposite door. He's dressed in the same smock and kilt as everyone else, carrying himself with the same proud bearing. His black hair is streaked with silver and trimmed soldier-short. Nothing else belies his age – dark brown skin barely creased by time, limbs corded with muscle.

There's something itching at me about him. Something vaguely familiar in his high cheekbones, and the clean-shaven pointed chin.

"Sir." Kip snaps her heels together and thumps her fist to her chest.

"Los first." He returns the salute, though with far less commitment. In the Losian cultural context, this denotes Kip is of a lower rank. But not knowing either of their standings means I can't work out if it's more than simply recognizing her junior rank – an insult or mark of disdain.

"Always Los," Kip replies, though unlike with the guards, hints of a pained expression lurk behind her usual mask.

"Why have you returned, niece?"

Niece? *Niece?*

The older Losian rubs his temple. "When your father hears you are here, I will not shelter you from your shame."

What in the Primordial Divine's name have I walked into? It's so rare I'm genuinely caught off guard. I was hardly expecting such entertainment. And being ambushed by the omission of crucial information is certainly not a style of entertainment with which I'm enamoured.

"I don't plan on staying." She glances around the room. "Can the walls be trusted?"

"All eyes and ears are my own."

She gives a grunt of approval. "I work for the Emperor-elect. He's alive. He's the rightful heir. And he needs Los under his banner."

So much for pleasantries.

"Ah, Lostras?" I attempt to intervene before this gets out of hand.

317

"Not now," she snaps.

The older man shakes his head. "You chose the Empire over your own, and now you would have us do the same? Appeals from you do not fall on sympathetic ears."

"War is coming."

"To Aphorai, the last I heard. Los stands apart. We were our own kingdom once, there is no reason we cannot self-govern again."

She motions for the Emperor-elect and his mother to remove their cowls.

It's the first look of surprise on the Losian's face as he takes in their features, recognition dawning.

"This army," Nisai begins, "will not stop at Aphorai. They will continue eastward. My brother will not let Los secede from the Empire without a fight."

"And we shall deal with that if it becomes a problem. Until then, I'm not sure why you're here. You'd be better off requesting the Eraz serve you a banquet and being on your way."

Kip turns to me. "Give me the dossier."

I narrow my eyes. "I appreciate your desire to—"

"The dossier. Now. I'm not asking."

I reach into my robe and hand her the packet of parchment that I had ready for this moment. Redacted of details that are of the need-to-know variety, but with enough valuable information to make a compelling case.

"Take your time to consider these, Uncle." Kip says. "Consult with Father if you must. But read them on their own merit. Los cannot afford to be on the wrong side of this. We'll adjourn to the Eraz's estate and await your reply."

The Province Commander takes the packet. Gives his perfunctory bow.

It's shallower than when he greeted us.

Lovely. We've somehow managed to depart on more tenuous terms than when we arrived. I make a mental note never to go on a diplomatic mission with Kip again.

We're summarily escorted from the barracks. When we're clear of earshot, I round on her. "You didn't tell me your uncle is the Province Commander of the Losian Army."

She shrugs. "He's not. My father is."

"You didn't tell me that, either."

Her lip curls. "Didn't I? Must have slipped my mind."

Oh, that's magnificent. I've been well and truly outplayed. Apparently it's possible to be equally thrilled and appalled. "So, in your informed opinion, will they help us?"

She returns to stone-faced gruffness. "Only time will tell."

✳

"You will have my army on one condition."

From the head of the banquet table, the Eraz of Los Province, tall and lean with dark, wiry curls, doesn't deign to use honorifics. Given the circumstances, he knows he can get away with it.

The Emperor-elect doesn't let it ruffle his feathers. Or, he doesn't let any ruffling show. Nor does his mother. The two other members of the Council of Five present – Galen, the Regent's mother, and Daprul, the Losian former imperial wife, look on with practiced decorum.

Nisai gently puts down the three-pronged scoop the Losians favour for cutlery and finishes chewing the

319

mouthful of pulled dodfruit and blue-claw crab, before replying. "Name your price, Prusah."

"This." The Eraz gestures expansively to the feast – tender fish and mollusks glistening in their half shells, crustaceans and crisp-toasted kelp, savoury palm fruit stew and kuslai melon with its pale-green flesh crushed to a silky puree – and out to the vista beyond. The banquet has been laid out on the manses' viewing balcony, built to take in the best view Lostras has to offer – the tidefall, where the Aramtesh River plunges more than five-hundred feet over the Cliffs of Los to unite with the ocean below. So wide is the river and great the drop that a fine mist drifts back over the entire city, supporting its unique microclimate and the several rainbows that arc over the palm-thatched roofs from dawn until dusk.

In this evening's sunset, from where I'm sitting, the nearest rainbow hovers behind the Emperor-elect, so that he appears to wear a crown of coloured vapour. One can only hope it's not the closest he'll ever come to wearing a crown.

Nisai reaches for the bowl of lemon water to rinse his fingertips. "I'm not sure I fully comprehend your meaning."

Wise move, forcing the Eraz put all his game pieces on the table.

"Then let us be direct. You can have all of my province at your disposal if, when this business is all done, you reward such loyalty with the recognition we are due. If we win this war for you, Lostras will become the new capital of the Empire."

"What you ask," Nisai begins, "will fundamentally change the composition of Aramtesh and the Founding Accord."

"Exactly." The Eraz smiles, all teeth and no mirth. "We shall no longer be on the outer fringe, at best mocked, but more usually forgotten."

The Emperor-elect reaches for another helping of flaked white fish. Splendid to see this stand-off isn't affecting his appetite.

"It could very well work," he muses.

"It *will* work. If we draw this zealot's forces into our province, it's on our territory. Nobody knows Los or how to survive the Wastes like the Losians. It's the only strategy at your disposal that affords you a fighting chance if we end up at war against the larger force."

Nisai looks up and down the table. "May I remind you all that there have been several reports now that Zostar has found a way to control the powers of several Children of Doskai, that they will do his bidding. It may not be so, only tales born of fear. But if one Doskai-possessed man can level a city's walls, what do you think an army of them can do?"

Daprul, the former imperial wife from Los Province, leans forward. "Make Lostras the new capital and I shall grant you the information you need."

I almost drop the fresh-shucked oyster that was halfway to my mouth. She'd actually consider withholding at a juncture like this?

Everyone regards the Emperor-elect, but nobody objects or offers counsel. Not his mother or Galen, Iddo's mother. Not Kip. And certainly not I.

We all know there is no other choice.

CHAPTER 30

RAKEL

The last time I smelled the sea, that peculiar tang of salt and seaweed left to rot in the sun, was when Ash and I found ourselves in Lapis Lautus, the smuggler city off the east coast of Trel Province. Now, as we near the northern edge of Aphorai Province, it rushes up on the wind to greet me again. And once it does, it's everywhere, as if it wants to consume the land.

In Lautus, the calm, azure waters – protected by a cove and the marinas – seemed to welcome the city's visitors. Here, at the edge of the Empire, it roars a warning.

"How can it be so ... fierce?" I murmur.

"The cliffs plummet to open ocean from here at the border," Ami explains. "They get steeper along the north coast, and the waves crash against them, with such insistence that they erode the rock over the turns, altering the coastline so significantly in some places it needs to be updated on maps every few turns."

So it *is* trying to devour us.

We continue down the last of the slopes. In the distance, outlined in the light of the sunset, the last remains of the ancient temple site cowers against the coastal wind. A handful of columns of fluted stone still stand, like those at the top of the Aphorain temple. Three arches bear up alongside. The rest is jumbled piles of chiselled rock.

As we near, I discover something about the ruins I never expected – they stink. There's the brine and weed of the ocean, but something much more nose-wrinkling, too.

Scat.

Layer upon layer of white bird markings that must have built up over countless seasons. Where the birds are now is anyone's guess. Maybe out over the waves fishing for their supper. Or roosting somewhere that the seas are calmer.

Wherever they are, this place remembers them. Too strongly. I hope we can find what we're looking for and move on quickly.

I slide from Lil's back as Ami and Barden dismount from their camels, leaving them to rest with their feedbags – there's nothing in sight for them to eat.

We begin wandering through the ruins. I don't expect to be the person who spots what we need – my distant vision still isn't exactly eagle-eyed – but even the others don't find anything obvious. No carvings. No enclosed spaces. Just columns. Arches. A flat area. All covered in white bird scat.

I don't know what I was expecting. A sign?

Ancient weapon stored here.

Hardly.

"We'll wait until morning," Ami decides. "There could be something we're missing in the low light."

She's doing her best to sound optimistic. But her smile is pinched and close-lipped, not the gap-toothed grin she gives when at ease. She's worried.

So am I. What if we don't find anything? We would have wasted more time while Zostar gets closer and closer to realizing his own plans. The Empire will erupt into civil war. So many will die. And if Zostar wins, even those who survive might wish they hadn't. Even Ash. At least, that's what I tell myself: if he left because he didn't want to hurt us, then he can't begrudge us looking for a weapon to stop those who would deliberately cause harm on a massive scale.

We camp far enough away from the fallen columns that the air is bearable. With the sun gone for the day but the wind still blowing in from the sea, the cold begins to bite. We're all exhausted and don't talk much. But when I roll into my blanket, it takes me a while to nod off. I'm not sure if it will be the sea that will haunt my dreams, or wave after wave of Aphorain soldiers marching to their deaths against Zostar's forces.

The next thing I know, Barden is gently shaking my shoulder.

"Dawn's about to break," he says, handing me a palmful of rock figs. He's built a campfire, and the scent of honey-sweetened barley porridge beckons me.

"Thanks, Bar. Has she eaten?" I jut my chin towards Ami.

"You think I'd let her start work on an empty stomach?" He returns his attention to the copper pot over the fire and mumbles something under his breath.

"What was that?"

"Nothing."

"Don't be like that."

"Fine," he huffs. "I was just saying I hope Nisai is feeding himself, too. He always gets so absorbed in things he forgets to eat."

"Mother hen."

He shrugs, a goofy smile curling his lips.

"Guess it's as good a way to get promoted as any, eh? Become indispensable to the future Emperor."

His smile vanishes and I hold up my hands. "I'm joking. Really. We should seize whatever happiness we can." What I don't say is that with what's coming, who knows how much of it there'll be to go around. If any. "As soon as we're done here, it'll be straight on to Lostras. You can get back to happily mother-hen-ing all you want."

I scarf my food, roll away my blanket and join Ami in the Ruins of Stink. She seems unbothered by the smell, too intent on the task. "Look for patches of ground that seem unusual, parts of the temple that are buried, that sort of thing. We're looking for an underground repository, and the entrance may have been covered by the shifting sands."

I begin to pace the fallen columns but see nothing unusual. Maybe I don't have an eye for it. Or maybe my vision is still not what it was. I can't quite tell if the edges of distant objects are blurrier than they should be, or if they're further away than I ever saw sharply.

But Ami doesn't turn up anything either, and she's the expert.

Frustrated, I return to the camp.

Barden's scrubbed the dishes with sand and is packing them away. "We'll only have a day or so before we have to find a source of fresh water," he reports.

"I know," I snap. But it's not him I'm sore at. It's the whole situation. "Sorry, Bar, I—"

"I get it. Me, too."

We begin searching the ruins. Sometimes I think I see something, a symbol or letters carved in the weathered stone. But when I scrape away the layer of bird scat, there's nothing of note.

I spy another unusual looking stone. Again, nothing.

The morning passes in cycles – a whiff of hope, chased away by salt and brine and scat.

"Over here," Barden finally calls.

He's standing at the edge of the cliff, so close that when the wind gusts my heart lurches against my ribs like it's trying to drag me back to safety.

I used to be fine with heights. But that fearlessness is getting eaten away by caution. Images crash into my mind as the waves crash against the cliffs thousands of feet below. Climbing down into Belgith's Canyon after fleeing Aphorai City in the depth of night with Ash. Luz's sure grip as she pulled me back from the edge of the ice ravine when we journeyed to the Sanctuary. The last place I want to be is now on a cliff edge above churning water.

But Barden is Barden. He's always anchored wherever he goes. Teetering on the edge of the world is no exception.

I force myself to step tentatively closer.

"What is it?"

"Here." Barden drops to his knees and stretches on to his stomach. "You'll have to get close to see it."

I follow his lead, and crawl forward, flattening on my front as I near the edge. Flakes of limestone go skittering over the cliff and disappear into the ocean's raging waters.

"Down there. In the cliff. See that overhang?"

I swallow my fear and try to follow where Barden is pointing. "Got it."

"Now look what happens when the waves come in. Every now and then, when there's a bigger one. Wait for it…"

I watch, not sure exactly what I'm watching for. The waves swell towards us, one after the other like a never-ending military parade. Each one crashes against the cliff in turn, salt water spraying high and falling back down into a roil of blue-and-white froth.

"This one," Barden says, excitement in his voice.

The larger wave crashes much like the others, foam flying. I squint hard, gaining slightly better focus. Even though the wave has left the cliff behind, water continues to flow back out of the cliff like a temporary waterfall.

"There's something there," Barden says. "A cave. A tunnel. Maybe just a large depression in the rock. But there's something."

Whatever it is, it's going to be impossible to get to. Even if you could find enough hand-holds and ledges in the eroded cliff face, it'd only take the barest slip and it'll be all over. The ocean would claim you.

"Maybe it is something, maybe it isn't. Finding out would be a death wish. Nobody in their right mind would do it."

"I haven't lost my wits," Barden says defensively. "And I can climb."

It's true. He's been climbing trees and canyons and even the Aphorai City walls since we were kids. He's never once fallen. But this is different.

"No."

He gives me a sharp look.

"You'll have to have a rope. It's too risky not to." I look back to the plain stretching behind us, flat except for the tufts of camelthorn bush like the scraggliest of beards. Not a boulder or outcrop in sight. Nothing to use as an anchor but us.

I consider Ami's slender form. I suppose I could ask her to go. But why is her risk any less than mine? And the way she turned so pale she was almost green at the prospect of climbing down here pretty much rules out her being any use.

When I look back to Barden, he's narrowing his eyes, like he already knows what's coming next. He knows me too well.

"I'll go."

"Now hold on a—"

"Remember why I used to be the one to climb for the highest oranges back when we were kids? You're the heaviest, Bar. If you fall, who knows if we'll be able to hold you? Out of the two of us, I'm sure as stink I'd rather have you holding the rope than me trying to haul your deadweight back up here."

"We could use the animals," he says.

"I don't trust camels." My eyes go to where Lil is having the dust bath of her life, hooves kicking in the air as she joyfully rolls about. "And I doubt we'll have enough rope for it."

He stares down at the water. One wave crashes. Two. Three.

Finally, he gives me a grim nod.

We return to retrieve the rope Luz insisted we bring with us. I'm beginning to lose count of how many times she's saved our skins. Not that I'd let her know that, the result would be insufferable.

Barden unloops the rope's coils and dangles it over the cliff edge. I was more right than I wanted to be: it barely makes it halfway to the overhang.

"We'll have to use whatever we've got. Clothes. Lil's tack. Tie it all together, and we might just make it. But you'll have to be the anchor, not Lil," I say.

We set to work, turning out each of our packs, gathering anything that can be used to lengthen the rope's reach. I tie each section, test it and test it again, thanking Father for making sure I knew my knots from an early age.

Once we've done the best we can, I pull my satchel tight, tying a loop in the strap so it sits snug against my back. It's extra weight, but Barden can handle it, and there's no way I'm going down there empty-handed. If that cave goes back far, it'll be dark for one thing. And if it does tunnel in, who knows what I'll find down there. My knife comes, too.

"Keep your eyes peeled for anything that doesn't look like a natural occurrence. Strange symbols, carvings, a rock that doesn't look right," Ami says.

"I managed to find the Library of the Lost, I think I can figure this out." I sound snarkier than I mean to, but when I'm about to risk my life, the last thing I need is someone telling me the obvious.

The rope is at Barden's feet, several paces back from the cliff edge. I've tied myself to the other end, a pair of his leather trousers circling my waist. I refrain from making a quip about it being the closest we'll get to being in each other's pants again.

"I'll have you the whole time, remember that."

I smile at my best friend. "I know."

"But be—"

"—careful. I will."

He gives me a quick but fierce hug and picks up the rope.

I back over the edge of the cliff, my feet bracing against the rock. And just like that, I'm horizontal out over a hundred-foot drop to a watery grave. *Don't look down*, I chant to myself. *One foot after the other. Just don't look down.*

I look down.

My stomach flip-flops and I grip the rope harder; the slight but sudden shift in my weight sends my foot to sliding on the cliff's flakey stone. The rope goes even tauter as, out of sight atop the cliff, Barden and Ami counter my weight. I scrabble for a hold, managing to get my heels braced against the cliff again. For a few thunderous heartbeats, I don't move, just cling on, trying to get my breath under control, the wind clawing at my clothes and doing its best to blind me with my cheek-length hair.

"I'm fine," I call.

Inch after careful inch, I ease further down the cliff. Then I'm at the end of the rope. But I'm not where I need to be. Instead, I'm only level with the overhang jutting out from the cliff. The lip of rock beneath it, the floor of whatever the hole in the cliff is, must still be twice my height below me.

A drop like that is going to hurt, even if I manage not to twist an ankle or wrench a knee.

We have to know what's down there. If it's the weapons cache, it doesn't seem like there's any other way to access it. And the last thing I want to do is climb all the way back up the cliff to see if there's anything more to lengthen the rope with and then make the descent all over again.

I call up to Barden. "It's a cave. I can't tell how deep it goes from out here. Further than I can see at least. Can you lower me any further? Even a little?"

He shouts something down to me but though I can hear his voice, the wind and the waves steal the words.

"Lower me further!" I yell.

I'm eased down another arm length. It's still a sizeable drop. But it's not out of the question I won't be able to reach it again on my way back. I grip the rope above me, taking up the slack until I can pull myself free of the makeshift loop of a harness. I wait for the most recent wave to recede.

Then I bite my lip, tasting salt, and let go.

My feet hit the floor of the cave. I bend my knees to lessen the shock but the impact still jars my bones. I don't let myself pause to absorb the pain, instead moving quickly out of the next wave's reach, and peer into the gloom.

I can't smell anything but brine and wet stone and something vaguely rotten – a vegetable kind of rot. There's no cave monster in here, unless it's made of seaweed. Some kind of sea-moss lines the walls and the floor is slick with the spongy plant. The squelching noise as I pick up each foot would be comical at another time.

I rummage in my satchel for some yeb balm. There's nothing to make a torch with, no driftwood or anything but the rock worn smooth from a thousand tides. I dig a small, empty faience jar from my supplies. It's just translucent enough to serve as a makeshift lantern. I transfer a little of the paste in before lighting it. Sure enough, the flame glows through the faceted glass, enough to see a couple of paces ahead of me. I'll have to hurry. It'll get too hot to hold before long.

The cave starts out rough and worn unevenly, seemingly natural. But thirty or forty paces in – I didn't think to count – it becomes more obviously hewn by human tools – uniform and smooth. I'm reminded of the Library of the

Lost and a surge of hope warms my chest – if this is what we're looking for, it would have been built around the same time. Possibly even by some of the same people.

My jar lamp is heating in my fingers. I could take off my tunic and use it as a holder, but it's clammy enough in here, with the damp and the sea wind, that I'd be freezing. Instead, I set the jar down and retrieve another from my pack. It's almost empty, and carrot seed can be replaced cheaply at almost any market or city stall. I tip the contents out and make another yeb lamp in their place, leaving the already heated one on the ground to light my way back.

The floor of the cave begins to tilt upwards ever so gently. Soon I'm walking on dry stone, leaving the slimy weed behind. It feels good to be standing on solid rock again.

At the top, the air is still, the flame in my makeshift lamp doesn't waver. It smells different here, though. Beneath the distinct scent of the burning yeb balm, there's something both stale and sharp. It's a dead end.

There's got to be something here. I push onwards. There. Something small reflects back at me from the depth of the cavern. Then another. And more still, until there's a hundred flames gleaming darkly.

I cross to the nearest one and pick it up. It's a sherd of blue-black glass. Something tugs at my memory. The Library again. The spears I almost got myself skewered on racing across the trap-set flagstones. The ceiling inside the Library's main cavern, deep blue-black glass set with silver in a copy of the constellations of the star wheel. The polished surface of the Archivist's desk. And at the Sanctuary – the amphitheatre of the Conclave.

The blue-black glass has something to do with the weapon needed to stop Zostar and his shadow army? There must be more than sherds of it here.

But there isn't.

I move around the cavern, ignoring the growing heat in my jar of light.

Sherd. More sherds. Pieces in different sizes and shapes. And that's what they are. Pieces. Whatever this weapon is, someone has found it first. And they've left only the broken remnants behind. Or did the waves come all the way up here at some point? Have the water levels changed over the centuries? Was there a violent storm that surged into the cave and dashed whatever was here on the rock walls?

The thought makes me shudder. I need to find whatever I can and get out of here.

My gaze snags on a particular sherd. I pick it up, turning it this way and that in the low light. Something about it is strangely familiar. It's almost like ... the lip of an urn? Like the planters filled with rosemary at the door of Father's house in our village. Or like a much larger version of the faience jar in my hand. But then it's not quite as rounded. Almost as if it had a ... corner? Was all this glass once square vessels? Or at least some of it? And if it was, what did it contain? Spears? Swords? Arrowheads?

A shadow moves in the corner of my eye and I spin around.

There's nothing there.

Then another shadow moves.

Fear creeps up my throat but I force myself to calm, my only movement to stow the black glass sherd and so that I can draw my knife from my belt.

Another dark shape flits by. This time so close I feel it move the air next to me. The hairs on the backs of my arms stand straight up. I shouldn't feel shadows. Not normal shadows. Scents-be-damned, is it a trap? Some creation of the Lost God's? Something guarding against anyone finding the weapon to use against him?

But the smell in here isn't the tell-tale reek of a charnel house. Nothing that says death and decay, no rotting flesh like I smelled when I was healing Nisai of the last element of the poison – the dark decay of Doskai's powers.

Here the smell is something … living. Or something that's been here recently. The sharpness in the same family as the stink of a back-alley urinal.

A shadow slices past my cheek and I flinch, a thin line of pain in its wake. When I draw my fingertips away from my skin they're wet.

Then they're everywhere. Shadows. Dropping from the ceiling of the cavern, swarming around me, tearing at my skin and clothes. Fear finally wins and a shriek escapes my throat. My hand loses grip on the light jar and it smashes on the floor, the yeb balm leaking out in a last flare of fire.

The flame dies and I'm in the dark with a thousand flying creatures flapping and clawing and diving around me. I hold up my arms to shield my face, trying to retrace my steps towards the entrance.

The creatures follow, frenzied, tearing.

I break into a shambling run, the fastest I can move without risking knocking myself out if I slam into a rock wall. The floor slopes down. I'm going the right way. But before my feet find the weed of the outer cave floor, they find something else. Water.

I'm knee deep before I even realize. How has the water changed so much in so little time?

Tides, a distant voice in the back of my mind says. Unlike lakes and rivers, the sea has tides. And I guess this is what it means for the tide to come in quick.

A glance up and I see the last of the shadow creatures fleeing for the mouth of the cave. In the gloom they're much smaller than they seemed in the dark. Their tiny flapping wings frantic.

I suppose they don't want to get caught down here.

And nor do I.

I wade down to the outer cavern. My first glimpse of daylight reveals a huge wave swelling into the mouth of the cave, surging towards me. Instinct kicks in and I turn to flee back towards higher ground.

Then I'm shoved in the back by a wall of water. Salt fills my mouth and nose and eyes, stinging and blinding.

I kick out, but I can't figure which way is up, everything is roil and liquid rage. Barden and I used to swim in the oasis pool when we were kids, but that was water so calm you could see your reflection in it. It was nothing like this.

My lungs are desperate for me to cough out the water I've inhaled – it burns at the back of my throat and further down in my chest – but I clamp my mouth shut with all I've got. Another gulp down the wrong way could be my last.

Then my shoulder bumps rock. Hard. A cry of pain involuntarily escapes my lips.

The water rushes in.

Everything hurts.

I'm lying on my stomach on an outcrop of rock. Head, one shoulder and arm dangle over the churning rage of green-white waves. Something cuts into my stomach and chest. My satchel strap. It snagged on part of the outcrop and kept me here.

I scrape snakes of hair from my eyes, blinking away the saltwater sting. My tunic and trousers cling cold and sodden against my skin.

Cringing, I lift my head. I'm surrounded by sea on all sides. Where is this place? How long was I out? I crane my neck. There. Blurred, but unmistakable. The coastline. Maybe three or four hundred feet away.

In the opposite direction, the sky is all shades of grey, the clouds roiling as much as the waves with a coming storm, flashes of lightning coursing through it all like white fire.

I tear my eyes away and look back to the jagged rocks lining the shore. The thought of swimming that distance in the churn and swell should scare me, but somehow being battered and bruised and bone-tired leaves no room for emotion. I've only got the energy for one thought: I must get to shore. Soon. Before the storm hits.

I don't want to think about the odds of whether I have enough left in me. Doubt they're good. If I somehow do manage to make it, if the waves don't drag me to the depths, I know one thing: I'll never turn my back on the ocean again.

With a groan of effort, I unhook my satchel strap.

Sink or swim.

CHAPTER 31

ASH

A Ranger never gives up the hunt.

It's one of the things everyone knows about the elite imperial force. I never thought I'd experience it first-hand until Rakel and I were on the run trying to save Nisai. I definitely never thought I'd be mimicking them one day. But here I am, dressed in Ranger uniform, the stylized map of Aramtesh that acts as a badge of office hanging on a thin strip of leather around my neck. This one is bronze. Entry level. Still plausible that I won't be personally recognized by senior command.

I didn't ask Kip where she got it.

From what she told me of her past, I could guess.

And I wasn't going to push her any further – who knows where I'd be if she had decided not to turn away while I made a hasty exit?

I took pains to keep the Ranger garb hidden as I fled Aphorai City. The residents were chirping like baby birds whose nest had been disturbed. I couldn't blame them. The groundshake had wreaked destruction through several quarters, splitting the great walls as if Riker himself had descended from the sky and cleaved them with his axe. People gabbled in the street, frightened, some leaving, some deciding to wait for more news. No wonder, given the mixed messages that flew about the place.

The gods are punishing us! The enemy will soon fall upon us!

The Prince has left us to die!

Can't you smell the forest for the pines? He's saving us, they won't divert from the river now!

Protect your property, there will be looting, soon.

That last was probably the most accurate of them all. Without the full information, fear runs rampant, and civic responsibility goes up in smoke. With more luck than I deserve, I managed to get clear of the walls before it did.

It took considerably longer to make it to the river on foot. I followed it upstream, back towards Ekasya. At the first trader camp I made it to, the gossip was more pragmatic. Inside the main tent, merchants sat over cups of kormak fortified with spiced white spirit as they planned alternative routes for their caravans, and alternatives to the alternatives, just in case. Some, I was unsurprised and yet still horrified to find, were planning to divert their wares directly to Iddo and Zostar's forces. Armies have bottomless bellies, and delivering food to their marching path was likely to fetch as much coin as braving a marketplace on the brink of anarchy.

I took up a place near one of the traders. Average height, average build, average garb, the only unusual thing about him the missing little finger on his left hand. What was most noticeable about him was his kormak was just kormak, and he listened far more than he spoke. When he did add something to conversation, it was in quiet, reasonable tones, not the bluster of the other traders.

And he was going to the army. That was clear.

When I offered my services as an additional guard, he looked me up and down in a look that was more appraisal than arrogance.

"Remove your hood," is all he said.

"I'd prefer not to, if it's all the same."

"You want a job, my word goes."

"Then we are at an impasse, sir," I said, my voice still barely above a murmur as ours had both been during the exchange, and left the tent.

I decided it was best to do this alone. But one of his guards soon catches up to me. A tall woman. Lean. A spray of freckles across her nose and cheeks, sandy blonde hair hanging impractically loose to her waist. Though nothing about the curved sword at her hip or the bow slung across her back says impractical.

"Thought I'd made you when you came into camp," she says. "Not taking off your hood only sealed the deal." Her accent is thick, and it's not one I recognize.

"I'm not who you think I am." I turn my back and begin to walk away. I want to run, to put as much distance as I can between me and this trader's guard who thinks she has guessed my identity. But moving quickly is only going to attract more attention.

"Aw, stenches." Her voice drips with mock disappointment. "And here I was telling my boss you were someone like us. You'd fit right in like a bum in a bucket." Her tone may be playful, but the space between my shoulder blades goes cold, anticipating the pierce of an arrow.

"I have no idea what you're talking about."

"So you're not someone who'd as soon as stick a knife in this Iddo bloke as fight on his side?"

I stop mid-stride. What I would give for my old twin swords. Instead, my hand goes to the opposite wrist, where at least there's once again a dagger strapped to the leather cuff.

"Eh, you think I'm stupid enough to come out here, all alone, to *fight*? Anyone with half an eye open can see you don't carry yourself like an amateur. But anyone who's ever seen someone hells-bent on revenge can recognize it in you just as easy."

"I think I'd best be on my way."

"By your lonesome?" I hear her spit in the dust. "Gonna stand out like poop in a perfumery. Got much more chance of getting what you want if we travel together."

I slowly turn.

She grins, her chest rising like she's just won a hard-earned victory. Then she crosses to me in three long paces and proffers her hand. "Sal's the name."

I eye her sidelong. "Sal?"

"Half a name. The part I like. Last person who uttered the long version ended up short on hair."

"You decapitated them?"

"Stenches, no. You think I'm some kind of barbarian? I cut off their hair and sold it to a wig-maker." A gold coin appears in her hand. She flips it spinning into the air before it disappears again with a flick of her wrist. "You thought all those old rich folks kept their pretty scented locks when the rest of us go grey and bald because they eat their greens or something?"

Not what I was expecting.

"What's your quarrel with the army?" I tilt my head back towards the trader's tent. "Most in there seem unperturbed."

"Most of them didn't lose their home and livelihood when the Regent closed the borders."

Ah, so that's where her accent is from. The Seson Territories. The borderlands beyond the Empire. Rakel recounted how they'd passed through them on their journey to the Order's Sanctuary. How Iddo had ordered a wall to be built at the border, cutting off trade and those who sought refuge from the scarcity and lawlessness beyond.

Sal shrugs. "Not really the time and place for life stories though. You coming with, or what?"

I hesitate. "What are you selling?" I won't go along with someone who is supplying arms or the like. I have my scruples.

"Hope."

"Sorry?"

"Come see for yourself."

She leads me through the camp to a set of half a dozen camels with their legs folded neatly beneath them in the sand, dozing. Their handler is sitting with his back against the lead animal. He's short, stout, bald and couldn't be more than a turn or two older than me. He's also asleep. No wonder they need more guards.

"Who've you brought to visit, Sal-Sal?" he asks without opening his eyes.

Not so asleep after all.

"Bil, this is…"

I hold out my hand. "Ash."

"That short for something?"

341

"Yes. But the last person who used the long version lost an arm."

Sal leans back, head tilted to the sky with laughter. When she recovers, she gestures to the barrels. "Good barley ale. Better than drinking water on the trail – you never know if it's going to turn your guts liquid. And the rest? Bil, show him the other wares."

Bil reaches into the pack he'd been lounging against. He produces a prayer braid, and a leather envelope, opening it to reveal a full set of sacred oils in small vials.

"You're religious?"

"Nope. But people who think they're going to die will pay handsomely for their last prayers."

I scowl. "That's disgraceful."

"Is it? We sell high to the rich, and use the profit to subsidize cheaper prices for the poor. No point in trying to get blood from a stone, you see. And if the result is that we bring hope or comfort to the sorry last days of those who either want to fight for Iddo or have been forced to, is there really anything so wrong with that?"

It took three days to track down the army.

At first the only sign was a dust cloud stretching across the horizon. My lips pressed into a thin line at the sight.

"What's got bees in your britches?" Sal asks. "Can't be more than a day or so away now."

I thought it might take longer, that we'd have to travel back upriver to Ekasya some ways before finding them, given the bulk of the force would be infantry on foot. Instead, I only say, "It's bigger than I had imagined."

"Think the youngest ever Commander of the Imperial Rangers got to where he was just because of his daddy? I mean, that's part of it, sure. But he wasn't going to be taking any chance about this. Bet he didn't move until he knew he had the numbers."

That does sound exactly like Iddo. Strategy first, always strategy. The thought weighs on my heart, forcing me to admit that all this time I've been harbouring a last hope. A hope that this was Zostar's doing far more than Iddo's. Somewhere, somehow, I'd still carried the belief that if I could get to the elder Kaidon son, if I could talk to him face to face, he might still be swayed to the side of mercy. He'd see the horror of what Zostar is doing to Del, Mish and the others. He'd put a stop to it.

Was that always a fool's faith?

It didn't have to be this way, housecat.

The last time I saw him, in the dungeons, he was already set on the way he was going to handle the Empire. He never would have listened to the likes of me. Now, if he's caught wind of what's happened since, he'd be even less likely to. There's only one person I've ever known capable of changing Iddo's mind. And after the disaster in Aphorai City, I can only hope he is putting as much distance as possible between himself and the army below.

I shake my head, muttering a curse. "How did they even find so many willing to go to war?"

Sal tosses her coin in the air.

It's the only answer I need.

As we near the army, the dust thickens. The sounds of the force on the move – the pounding of several thousands of marching feet, the barked orders and morale-boosting songs, the rumble and squeak of hundreds of wagons carrying weapons and supplies – combine into a dull, continuous roar.

Sal and the other guards seem to know what they're doing as they angle towards the train trailing the infantry column, drawing level with several other wagons. There's a mix of merchants with accents hailing from all over the Empire. Plenty of nondescript leathers like Sal and our band wear but there's also no small number of Trelian hats, plumed and wide-brimmed. I even spot the antique style clothes of several Edurshain – no doubt antivenom is a valuable commodity for an army on foot.

The last sends my mind to Mish and the others. I need to stay focused on why I'm here – I have to work out a way to find them.

As night falls, Sal and I join several other wagoneers around their campfire, seeking information. Both she and Bil have made friends among the traders and smiths, cooks and camp followers. For the believers, there's Bil's prayer braids. For the rest, there's Sal's barley ale. As the evening goes on, she even passes around an enameled clay jar of spiced spirit.

I lean closer. "Gifts, Sal? You're getting soft."

"More like a down payment on information. If barley ale started them talking, spirit will have them singing like songbirds." She rises to her feet. "I'll go get another jar. Keep your ears open, eh?"

I nod. I'm just as interested in what they have to say as Sal is in a business opportunity.

When the first jar of spirit is empty, Sal still hasn't returned. Bill and I exchange a look.

"I'll go check on her," I say.

I weave back through the wagons and tents, to where we'd struck camp.

"Sal, did you hear? Tonight Zostar is giving some sort of demonstration."

I pull the tent flap aside and step through. It's pitch black, and I almost trip over something heavy on the floor. I pause, waiting for my eyes to adjust, and mutter a curse at Bil for letting the candles go out again.

"Sal?"

Something collides with the back of my skull and I crumple forward, pain lancing through my head.

The last of the light goes out.

CHAPTER 32

LUZ

The war machine of Los Province is well-oiled.

Preparations to depart for the Wastes take place with calm efficiency. It's in the midst of them that the trio of would-be shadow slayers arrives at the manse granted to Prince Nisai after his deal with the Losian Eraz. It takes more than a few minutes of fast talking to unruffle the gate guards' feathers — some of them had thought the note the newcomers bore from the Emperor-elect was a forgery, and no small wonder by their bedraggled appearance. Finally, with diplomatic relations smoothed, I signal for the gate to be closed on the bougainvillea-crowned walls of the inner courtyard.

We take up seating in the shadow of the palm-thatched roof. The manse seneschal looks as if she wants to rescue the cushions from the rattan furniture before the travel-stained arrivals flop down on them.

I raise an eyebrow in her direction.

She diverts her attention to organizing refreshments.

"You've been industrious," I say by way of greeting. They all seem relatively unscathed from their journey, except for

346

a patch of faded green-yellow blooming across the girl's cheek. The bruise must have been a sight to see when it was fresh.

"Who did you get into a scuffle with?"

"The ocean," she replies flatly.

I decide not to press the matter. Travelling here from the coast of Aphorai Province, rather than via the river, forces one to traverse some particularly rugged coastal terrain. That they were able to make such good time is thanks to Asmudtag's grace. "So, what do you have for us?"

The girl sets her bag on the table and flips it open. With a flourish that could only be described as sarcastic, she produces an object that's about the length of a kitchen knife – a jagged sherd of blue-black glasslike rock that seems a broken part of a larger whole.

I raise an eyebrow. Some who follow the Primordial would refer to it as Asmudtagian glass. There's something in that, a frustrating tease of a clue. If only I could comprehend exactly what sort of puzzle it hails from.

The girl removes another piece of the glossy stone. And another. Laying them out side by side along the mosaic outdoor dining table. The objects clearly originated from the same source, but they're irregularly shaped. If they did come from a larger whole, it's impossible to guess at first glance what that was. The one possible deduction to be made is that the planes are too precise to be natural. They were deliberately worked, and, at one time, polished.

"*This* is your weapon?" Kip scoffs. "I could do as much damage with my bare hands."

I'm certain she could.

"What, pray tell, is it?" I ask.

"We were hoping you could shed some light on that," Copperlocks admits. "I attempted a comparative analysis on the road but didn't have any particular insights."

"There was a lot more from where this came from but I couldn't make sniffer from sitter before I was forced to retreat," Rakel agrees.

Copperlocks holds up one of the sherds. "This was the only reason we knew we had even found the right place."

I take the piece she proffers. "Old Imperial? No, it's…"

"*Pre*-Imperial. Some of the etymology still lines up, though. So, if you were to make a deduction from the letters here—"

"Shadows."

"Indeed."

The Emperor-elect gingerly picks a sherd up and examines it from various angles. "Perhaps, when new, they make decent blades?" he offers. "Axes? Arrow heads?"

Rakel shrugs. "Do you think your mother will have a better idea? Or the Losian imperial wife? Or Yaita? Has she woken up yet?"

"She is here and in a stable condition," I assure her. "Though she still sleeps much of the day. And we won't tarry long. Zostar has diverted from his route to Aphorai City and marches for Lostras, no doubt having got wind of the new capital."

"So we're preparing to move out," the Emperor-elect says. "I will face my brother across the Wastes. The Losians have the advantage on home turf, and hopefully we'll be able to put on an equal show to convince my brother to engage in genuine parley."

"We may be able to hold out against the troops marching this way," I say, picking through the sherds of blue-black glass. "But if the reports of Zostar's shadow warriors hold even half-truths, we won't stand a chance. We must investigate the Losian weapons cache."

"Let us hope that it has been kept safer than its Aphorain counterpart," Nisai says.

"And," I add, "time is of the essence." I snap my fingers, and a servant steps forward. I take the map from them and spread it across the table. "The Losian cache is ever-so-conveniently located within Zostar's likely warpath. We must arrive ahead of his forces, or our only chance will be burned out quicker than cheap incense."

Copperlocks gnaws at one of her delicate fingernails, these days ragged to the quicks. "It's almost as if it were a divine plan. Doskai leading us into the path of destruction."

Destruction. A notion skirts around the fringes of my thoughts. By the Primordial's grace…

"Divine or otherwise, if we don't leave soon, we're all going to the sky. Your Highness, I'll set out with the others imminently. I'm sure the province army will have birds or some way for me to get word back to you."

"No need. I'll be coming with you. The Losians are set to depart in the morning."

"Large forces move slowly," I counter.

"Not this one. The Losian army hasn't needed to deploy since the Empire was founded. But that doesn't mean they haven't been ready."

Kip rarely smiles. But at Nisai's words, she practically beams.

We departed the river docks of Los in a flotilla of serpent boats.

The breeze angling in from the clifftops was light, warm and scented with salt and frangipani. Anyone could be forgiven for thinking we were off on a pleasure trip if it weren't for the fact that the passengers were soldiers and the cargo was weaponry and marching rations. Copperlocks passes the time with her scrolls, and this time Rakel joins her. It's a small joy in all the chaos to see her reading. Amber and Lostras engage in a delightful cultural exchange – swapping the crudest jokes from their respective provinces late into the night, some of them so brazen or debauched that even I found my cheeks warm.

Between the Losian Province Commander, the Eraz and the three former imperial wives, the decision was made to take the river to the Great Bend, the northern entrance to the Wastes. The Regent's outfit were predominantly on foot. If we could get into position first, they would be forced to march across the Wastes, hopefully tiring them further before a potential clash.

Our boat, only lightly loaded and faster than the others, sees us disembarking ahead of the main force. As we set out, I'm satisfied by the symmetry from when we first journeyed to the Sanctuary together, except for the replacement of the Prince with Copperlocks in our troupe of intrepid travelers. His Highness stayed with the main group – it's safer with an army surrounding him as he continues to strategize with the Province leaders for the coming stand-off between the forces.

Daprul, the Losian member of the Council of Five, was painstakingly accurate with map instructions to her Province's ancient temple site. I have no doubt that it is the boon of local knowledge that sees us directly to the sacred site on the edge of the Wastes.

But it's not what I had been expecting, given the reports from the others on the appearance of the Aphorain cache. Where I'd imagined an archaic temple, perhaps with a column or two toppled, a crumbling of the outer stone, it's nothing grander than several plinths covered in sand and scree.

"We're about to lose the sun," I observe. "We should decide on our camp for the night."

We climb an outcrop above the plains to find the Wastes laid out before us. Thankfully, the wind is blowing the right way to prevent the sulphur stench from overwhelming us. Even so, the girl rides with a cloth tied over her face, and I'm tempted to do the same now that we've paused. Lord Amber and the Losian Ranger grimace through it.

"I doubt we'll find a more suitable place to camp between here and there."

"Aye," Lostras agrees as she sets about gathering scant fuel for a fire.

I see to our mounts while the sunset deepens towards dusk. On the horizon, what must only be two or three days' ride along the southern edge of the Wastes, dots of orange light appear. Closer still, pinpricks glow in the night, no doubt from scouting parties. I stop, frozen in my tracks. The sheer size of the force out in the dark indicates Zostar and the Regent have been far more proficient at recruitment than even I'd anticipated. I'd venture half of those gathered around the fires are Rangers and Trelian mercenaries hired with funds from the imperial coffers. That doesn't change the fact that they outnumber the force we've brought here. By magnitudes.

I twist my silver ring around my finger. The Losians know this terrain, but even so, their chance of prevailing is slim. And that's before the reports that Zostar has bent a contingent of Children of Doskai to his will are factored into the odds.

It takes more time than I'd care to admit to shake off my brooding.

Our own fire is established by the time I return. The others are eating their trail rations in silence. I decline mine. The sight of the gathering army has murdered my appetite.

"A lot of your people down there, Lostras."

She perks up at that. "Losian banners? They've made good time, then."

"Rangers."

Her shoulders slump. "The Wastes will take care of at least some of them."

"How so?" Rakel asks.

"They confuse people. Turn them around."

"They get lost?"

"Something like that." Her eyes are wide, the whites shining in the firelight.

I raise an eyebrow. "Come now. It doesn't take a perfumer's nose to sniff out that you're not telling us something."

She tosses the dregs of her cup of kormak on to the coals. It hisses into steam that smells like charred cinnamon bark. When it's dissipated, she regards me, wild eyes flattening once again into her usual level stare.

"The Wastes are haunted."

I sputter my own kormak. Kip? Believe in ghosts? It's almost as ludicrous as the assertion itself.

She shakes her head and unsheathes her sword, taking a handheld whetstone to it with an intensity no doubt intended to shut me out. But she's not getting away with this that easily.

"Do explain."

"Tell us, Kip," Rakel chimes in.

"My father met a man who'd made it out once. A soldier. Not some kid who still reeks of his naming day incense, a veteran. He said the place itself was overpowering."

"Tell me something I don't know," I drawl. If jokes were people, there would be enough about the rotten-egg stench of the Waste's sulphur pools to populate a city.

"You want to hear this or not?"

I hold up my hands. "My apologies. Please, go on."

"The land itself is a maze, twisted rock and geysers and steam vents forcing you to detour and backtrack until you don't know your nose from your arse. And even if those don't get you, it's full of things that want to kill you. Flesh-eating insects. Tarantulas. *Snakes*."

She almost spits the last. Like their very existence is a personal insult.

I make a mental note to ask her about that one day.

"So, should we investigate this cache?"

"Now?" The wild look returns to the Losian's eyes. "In the dark? You should wait until morning."

I look pointedly to the southeast, where Zostar's army has made their own camp. "We can light torches. Surely time is of the essence, Lostras."

The Losian lifts her shoulders in an exaggerated shrug. "If you'd like to go searching for ancient weapons against the Lost God when his moon is about to rise over an allegedly haunted battlefield, be my guest."

"Only if you'd like to go and ask that army to spend tomorrow having picnics rather than bearing down on us and half the population of your Province with their magical doom soldiers," Rakel says as she assembles a light jar and ignites it with a burning stick from the fire.

Nobody else argues with that. Because there simply is no plausible denial.

We spread out and start searching the site.

"Over here," Copperlocks calls. "Help me with this slab."

Barden complies, levering his considerable bulk against the stone. It doesn't budge. "Kip, help us, would you?"

The Losian glares at him like he'd asked her to shove her hand into a fire.

"Please, Kip."

"We pledge to protect you against any pesky ghosts," I add.

She throws up her hands but moves alongside Barden. They heave in unison, and the slab starts to move aside with an ear-grating rumble.

We each look to the other in turn.

Finally, Rakel steps forward and shines the light jar into the maw of the temple's underground cavern. The light reveals a stone staircase descending into blackness. One wouldn't exactly call it the most inviting of entryways.

"Through," Rakel mutters, her foot already on the first step.

"Sorry, petal?"

"Nothing," she snaps, and follows Lord Amber's lead into the ground.

Copperlocks pauses at the entrance. Then Rakel's voice comes echoing to the surface: "It's safe … at least it seems that way."

"I'll stay on guard up here." Kip says.

I raise an eyebrow. "Not concerned for the dangers we may face down there?"

"She just said it was safe, didn't she? And you can look after yourself."

I let it drop and begin down the stone stairs. Great stone blocks line a tunnel that opens out into a low-ceilinged cavern. It's bright, and getting brighter as Rakel lights the sconces evenly spaced along the walls, laid with something combustible and so desiccated over the centuries that the flames leap high as soon as the burning yeb balm touches them.

The light dances across the stone and reflects back from dozens of long boxes lined up in rows on the cavern's floor. They're about three feet wide and tall and as long as a … tall person. It doesn't take a genius to work out what they are.

"Coffins," Rakel breathes.

Copperlocks runs a hand over one, blowing ancient dust from its surface. She coughs delicately. "Sarcophagi, technically. There's writing carved into the surface. Pre-imperial again."

"Looks like the same blue-black glass as the Aphorain cache," Rakel muses. "Guess we're in the right place, now we just need to find the weapons."

"There are other caverns," I observe. "If we spread out, we'll be able to cover more ground."

But there's nothing but rows and rows of the blue-black glass caskets.

Asmudtagian glass.

"I'm loath to be morbid," I begin. "But I expect we should look inside."

Copperlocks nods enthusiastically. "I've heard of places beyond the Empire where they bury their dead with weapons to help them battle their way to the afterlife."

It takes a group effort, but between Lord Amber, Rakel and me, we manage to shift the slab of Asmudtagian glass so the casket is halfway open.

Rakel wrinkles her nose. "I've smelled something like that once before. But it was from a flower. Vanilla."

Inside, a desiccated body, arms folded over its chest, stares hollowly up at us. Its skin is preserved but blackened and stretched over the skeleton, head bare of hair or adornment. On closer investigation, its robe seems to be encrusted with the last remains of crumbling feathers.

There's no doubt it's Asmudtagian. And I can only think of one reason why these bodies were not sent to the sky upon their death: those left behind didn't think they would be welcome there.

Which means…

By the Primordial's grace, could this get any worse?

A superior army bearing down upon us. Zostar's reported ability to bend Children of Doskai to his whims. And the only hope we had to combat such a threat turns out to be an ancient burial site of those who lost their lives the last time we faced such an enemy.

This. This is what happens when the Order declines over the generations. When we've been caught up in politics and our own dogmatic squabbling about how best to maintain balance, the world has been tilting around us.

It shouldn't have been like this. It should have been averted. I should have found a way to prevent this.

A cold, sickly feeling worms its insidious way into my core. I clamp my eyes shut and bow my head. But there's no way to swallow down the rising truth.

I've *failed*.

Sephine's voice pierces my heart. *We'll one day find our salvation in Asmudtagian destruction.*

I've failed, and now there's only one last thing to try to bring the world back into equilibrium. An extreme measure. One that only the audacious or hopeless would entertain.

There's no other choice.

While the others are still intent on seeking another cavern for their cache of ancient weapons, I retrace my path up the steps to the surface.

"Find anything?" the Losian former Ranger asks when I reach where she guards the tomb's entrance.

"Nothing of substance. Lostras, do me a favour? Give this to Rakel?" I hand her one of my camel's saddlebags. There's an array of ingredients in there, restorative and destructive. Who knows what she'll come up against when I'm gone, and I'm going to need supplies of an entirely different ilk. "And inform his Highness I've some pressing business "I'm not your errand girl," she huffs.

"Oh, go on, be a love, won't you? Just this once? And while I've got you, who captains the fastest of those serpent boats that got us here?"

"Iza," she says. "Captain Iza." She folds her arms over her chest. "Why do you want to know?"

"Just taking a precaution. You know me, ever vigilant. I'd dared to think that's what you liked about me."

"Never once said I liked you."

"Oh," I say, eyes wide and innocent. "My mistake."

"No. And yes. I almost thought I did like you for a while there. But now? Going gets tough and off you slink." She waves her hand for me to get out of her sight, her lip curled in derision. "Better get skulking then."

I allow myself a tired sigh. I wished I'd been able to get to know her better. I'd venture we'd be famously compatible under different circumstances.

Alas, this is how it must be.

CHAPTER 33

RAKEL

The one good thing about descending into a possibly haunted underground cavern in the middle of the night is that at least the rotten-egg smell of the Wastes is slightly less potent down here. Though that's possibly because of the dry-sweet scent of decay as much as anything. I try not to think about it too hard.

Ami kneels beside one of the blue-black glass coffins. She licks her thumb and rubs at a particularly stubborn section of dust. "Bring some light, would you?"

I do as she asks, hovering the flame above the casket. Where the dust has been cleared, the surface gleams, still keeping a fine polish after what Ami says could be close to a thousand turns. It's carved with flowers and a series of symbols I don't recognize. Guess that must be pre-Imperial.

"What's it say?"

"It's difficult to translate directly," Ami muses.

"In essence, then."

She trails a finger beneath the first line.

Here lies Masgib, sister to Kaiseth, first Keeper of Shadows.
Who gave her life in service of the Primordial's equilibrium

May her soul find sanctuary in Asmudtag's eternal embrace.

I frown. "So, this is literally just a tomb?"

She gnaws on a fingernail. "Perhaps 'weapon' somehow get misconstrued over the generations. We could be missing an etymology or translation detail. Perhaps the other sarcophagi reveal more?"

She stands and walks to the next casket, dusting it off with her palm before beginning to read:

Here lies Alodai, sister to Kaiseth, first Keeper of Shadows.
Who gave her life in service of the Primordial's equilibrium
May her soul find sanctuary in Asmudtag's eternal embrace.

She moves further down the line of coffins.

Here lies Yaznesh, sister to Kaiseth, first Keeper of Shadows.
Who gave her life in service of the Primordial's equilibrium
May her soul find sanctuary in Asmudtag's eternal embrace.

"How many sisters did this Kaiseth have?" I grumble.

Ami gives an almost-smile at that. "I don't expect it's meant literally. It's probably a recognition of lineage."

"Then why does it say that? Wasn't Kaiseth the first *Scent* Keeper? Isn't that a bit of a weird coincidence?"

She rocks back on to her heels. "That's what all the histories say. Perhaps there's something further in the Order's records that could shed light. Any insight, Luz?"

There's no answer. I peer into the dark behind us, but beyond where Barden holds another light jar aloft, there's nobody there. He shrugs. "She probably went to check in with Kip to make sure we still have time before Zostar's army close in."

Ami nods. "Let's investigate a few more of the sarcophagi, make sure the pattern holds."

We do. And it does.

Here lies Esis, sister to Kaiseth, first Keeper of Shadows.
Here lies Nurroth, sister to Kaiseth...
Here lies Praikai...

Ami shakes her head. "I can't deduce anything further from this. Time to see what Luz makes of it."

Up on the surface, Kip stands where we left her, her formidable frame silhouetted against the first rays of dawn.

"Where in the sixth hell is Luz?" I ask.

"Gone."

"Gone where?"

She spits in the dust. "Said something about wanting a fast boat."

I throw up my hands. A massive army topped up with magical doom warriors approaches. The so-called weapon to stop them turns out to be nothing but an ancient graveyard. And now this?

"Trust Luz to pull one of her disappearing acts just when we need her most," I mutter.

"Left this, though. Wanted you to have it." Kip nudges Luz's bag with the toe of her boot.

I open the pack and sort through the various vials and jars. The sight of sultis no longer makes me shudder – it has its uses. There's more highly flammable yeb balm among other things. And a jar labelled "last resort". That *does* send a chill snaking up my spine.

"She can't have gone far," Barden says, taking up the spyglass from Luz's pack.

"Any sign of her?" I ask.

Kip shields her eyes from the sun and scans in the other direction.

Barden swings around, following her gaze with the spyglass.

"No sign of Luz…"

"Why do I sense there's a 'but' coming?"

Barden grimaces. "Don't shoot the messenger but…"

"Spit it out."

"We have company. There's soldiers coming through the Wastes. Hundreds. Maybe more. And I don't think the Losians could have made it from the river in this time."

"Stink on a reekin' stick," I curse, kicking the ground.

"And they're not flying a standard."

Anyone who doesn't want to announce who they are can't be good.

Kip scowls. "If they outflank us on the other side, they'll have us surrounded. We have to warn the Prince."

"Wait." Barden holds up a hand.

"Waiting could get us killed," I say, but I do as he asks.

"There's something familiar about them."

I suck in a breath. "Rangers?"

"See for yourself."

I take the spyglass and scan the rugged terrain.

Barden was right. By the way the early morning light glints off metal, there's a lot of them. And then I see what he was talking about.

I choke back a sob.

CHAPTER 34

ASH

I have no inkling of what occurred between the blow I took to the head and regaining consciousness.

All I know is that I'm in a cage.

And it's moving.

The wagon beneath me is completely unforgiving as it bounces over rocks and into ruts, so that if I loosen my grip on the bars I'm likely to bash face or limb. My head pounds from the blow I took back in the tent, and I fight to retain consciousness, at times slumping against my mobile prison only to earn new bruises to mark the regret.

When I'm awake, I try to piece together the snatches of conversation around me. But all I can glean for certain is that we're heading towards the setting sun, deeper into Los Province.

If I had a coin for every time a bigot at the Ekasyan court drew great amusement from a joke about Losians carrying a foul odour wherever they go, I'd be able to put a down payment on a manse in one of the capital's finest boulevards. Yet I never met a Losian who smelled even slightly unpleasant.

It's not the same case for the land.

The marching army still hasn't reached the Wastes proper when the cloud of noxious sulphur and the gods-only-know what else reaches me. It sends my mind reeling back to the temple, to the ceremony Rakel had convinced me to undergo to see if she could rid me of this curse.

All I can do now is pray that she recovers. And that the gods keep her away from the thing that could harm her most – her desire to help me.

The stench is so overpowering it's a good thing Rakel isn't here. Even I'm struggling to keep my last meal – the dried meat and half a sabre-shaped yellow fruit my captors pass through the bars – from reacquainting itself with my mouth.

Twisted towers of red rock rise out of the plain, casting gnarled shadows. At irregular points between them, fetid pools belch and bubble. It's beneath a particularly huge formation that one of the guards calls a halt. I strain to see up ahead through the bars. Are they making camp already?

Keys rattle, and my guard swings my cage open. I've never seen him before my capture, but the stylized bronze map of Aramtesh hanging around his neck tells me all I need to know. Ranger. Somehow I've become Iddo's prisoner.

"Out," the guard grunts.

I'm not about to argue.

My feet on the ground, he cuts the binds around my hands and shoves my pack against my chest. "Go."

I frown. It could be a trick. And if it's an act of mercy, it's a misguided one. The Wastes are one of the most inhospitable places in the Empire. Leaving me here is tantamount to a death sentence. "But where?"

The guard shrugs. "Out there. Try to rejoin us, you'll wish you hadn't."

Death sentence it is.

Wheels creak in progress as the wagon resumes its trek, slowly pulling back to join the tail of the military column.

I figure there's only one way to approach this. Head deeper into these hostile lands, out of sight of the main column, and rejoin them from the other side. The forces are large enough and stretched out enough that if I execute this correctly, I stand a chance of not being recognized. Especially if I start with the stragglers.

The Waste's green-yellow pools boil before me. I stand still and observe the first group in my path, looking for patterns. I'll have to have a route planned if I'm going to avoid the intermittent jets of steam that shoot up, geysers of mud spewing high into the air.

It takes longer than I'd like, but eventually I work out a path. I hitch my pack and start towards the first pool.

The crust around the water is a multitude of yellows, greens and blues, shining almost like metal. I poke at it with the bleached length of dead tree branch I picked up some ways back. The entire shelf collapses into the bubbling mess. I keep moving, taking extra care not to step near the edges.

I'm almost through to the next patch of clear ground when the last pool – one I thought stagnant – erupts. It splashes near-boiling water and sludge mere inches from my face, the steam that roils with it stinging like vinegar in an open wound. I rub it away, only for my eyes to begin smarting, burning hotter with each passing heartbeat. Tears stream. They only seem to make it worse, as if it's spreading rather than diluting the residue from the noxious gas.

I force myself to get clear of the pools and fumble for my waterskin. It's low, but if I can't see, how am I going to get anywhere to find more? I tip my head and, as frugally as I can, splash liquid into my eyes, hoping it will do a better job than the tears. It provides small relief.

I kneel, blinking and crying for what seems like an hour, though my moons under Ekasya Mountain taught me how pain stretches time. Gradually, I will myself to calm, keeping my eyes closed for five breaths before letting the tears flow, hoping to flush out the last of the liquid. My fingers go to the prayer braid around my arm. They find nothing. I'd left the one I'd bought in Aphorai with Rakel. But I'd replaced that with one from Sal and Bil. Was I stripped of it when I was arrested?

For what it's worth, I send a silent plea to Kaismap to preserve my vision.

The burning begins to subside.

A coincidence? After everything that's happened, it would be fanciful to think my prayer had been heard. Wouldn't it?

I rise carefully to my feet. The last of the sun's rays seem harsher, the light reflecting off the muck-yellow pools an invasion. But I can see. That's the main thing.

Tilting my head up further, I make out a lone figure in the distance.

Who in their right mind would be wandering alone out here? Another prisoner left for dead?

Or perhaps my eyes, still stinging, are deceiving me?

Only one way to find out. The figure is in the direction I was heading. It's no slight to my plans to investigate.

As I near, I observe their clothes are plain workmen's gear, nothing announcing their allegiance. They could still be a scout, so I keep myself hidden as I approach, following the shadow of one of the mushroom-shaped rocks sprouting from the arid plain.

There's something slightly familiar about the figure. The breadth of his shoulders, the bulk of his arms. The kind of physique only certain trades acquire. Blacksmiths, even.

What would have drawn him to this gods-forsaken place?

My mind goes back to the Ekasyan slums not so long ago. The smithy had been boarded up. No sign of the man who had told me time and again that I was cursed. The man who locked me in the cellar when the Lost God's moon rose to block the light from the other. The man my mother fought against for me, before we fled on to the streets only to starve.

I take another look. He's got no supplies. He can't be travelling. He couldn't be; he'd not have made it this far on foot. Unless he's camped here? But who would camp here? And why? Is he with the imperial forces?

"Father?"

"Ashradinoran." His voice is flat, hollow. "Such a holy name."

It was the name of one of the Empire's earliest temple scholars. The very man credited with the aphorism I've lived my life by: *magic belongs with our shadows, behind us.*

"It was wasted on you," he says, as if he'd heard my thoughts. He's facing away from the sun, so that his features are shadowed. I can still see them twist into the cruel disdain that came before his temper erupted. "I should have known. You were supposed to be born in the month of Bozenai."

It's the month I'd always celebrated my name day, so none of our neighbours would know the truth. The month

Mother would let me choose which incense I wished to light. I used to ask for the fresh, clean citrus blend for Riker, the youthful god. The deity of adventures and the harvest festival and of song. I so loved to sing as a child.

I should have chosen Kaismap's foresight. Maybe then I would have lived a wiser life. I take a step back and rub my eyes again. What was in that muck? Or is my brain addled from the sun?

"But you came early," he intones. "An entire moon early. Such was your soul's determination to reach for evil." He shakes his head in disgust. "And who was left to pick up the pieces? Me. I was the one who had to lie about where your mother was. To hide your first cries from the neighbours. For what would they have thought if they knew you were born on the Days of Doskai? What would they have *done*?"

At the last of his words, his form wavers, darkens. His face contorts into a gruesome mask, blackening before my eyes as if burning without flame. He reaches for me, hands digging into the flesh of my upper arms. I look down, horror coursing through me. His fingers have turned to claws, puncturing the skin.

Tendrils of shadow are unfurling from the wounds.

I jerk back, pushing him from me. The threads of shadow stay tethered, tearing at my flesh as if they were barbed. It's agony. Like only one thing I've ever felt before.

The separation of the beast.

I hear a guttural moan and realize it came from my own mouth.

Somehow, I free one of my swords and bring it slashing down on the ropes of darkness yoking me to the abomination. They pass straight through with no effect. In desperation, I reach up with my bare hand and yank the shadow free from the opposite shoulder. The pain is red and blinding white, searing through my blood. I sway on my feet before righting myself. With an involuntary moan of agony, I free myself from the shadow ropes on the other side.

The next breath, I flee.

I run, skirting burning sulphur pools and weaving between the towering rocks. When my sides are heaving and sweat pours down my face I pause to catch my breath. It's an effort to force myself to turn around, to see if I've been pursued by … whatever that was.

"He won't be able to track you."

I swing back around only to come face to face with another shadowed figure. It wears a cloak despite the heat. I consider running again, but what would that do? Will another apparition appear? My hands clench at my sides. If this is anything like the last, my weapons will be useless.

The figure pushes back its hood.

It's like gazing in a silver mirror.

The same grey eyes – *my* eyes – stare back at me.

"Come, I'll guide you where you need to be."

I stumble back. "I'm not going anywhere with you. Not listening to anything you say. Not coming a step closer. Leave me be."

"I'll never simply let you be. You should know that by now."

This time, it's me who lashes out first.

The other me dances away, disappearing between two of the huge rock formations. I give chase, my legs pumping, feet pounding the ground until I round the boulder, skidding to a stop before a wall of shimmering heat. The shade, apparition, whatever it was, waves from the other side of a chasm, mocking me, then disappears. I reach out, then pull my hand back too late, rewarded with a scalding burn that immediately blisters.

The oven-hot air emanates from a huge vent in the earth that drops off like a cliff to depths so great that they're invisible. It must run a mile or more in length, blocking the way forward.

I retreat from the vent, slump down on to the nearest patch of dry ground that's not on fire or spouting acid.

What kind of existence is this? I may as well end things here and now. Throw myself to the mercy of the underground. Judging by the temperature spouting from the vent, it'd be over quickly.

And what would Rakel think of that?

I gingerly press the angry blister on my hand. *Honour can broil with shit and sulphur*, she'd said when I was considering falling on my sword after I thought we'd failed to heal Nisai.

Still, honour has always been a part of me. Joining Iddo's army was honourable in a way. It was to save others from me. But if I truly wanted to do that, to make people safe from my curse, wouldn't ending it here be the logical conclusion?

Or is honour wandering this place in endless purgatory? Facing down demon after demon in the Wastes? Weathering the pain?

My father's words come back again and again. The curse he made of a child. An otherwise innocent boy. There's one last honourable thing I can do. One last promise I can keep. The one I made to some children just like that small boy growing up in the Ekasyan slums.

If I'm going to be a danger to anyone, I'll be a danger to Zostar and those who have willingly joined his cause. Because I promised Del, Mish, Lark and the others I left behind beneath Ekasya Mountain. I left them in Zostar's hands to make them into the monsters they never asked or deserved to be.

I must save them from my own fate.

No matter what the Ranger who released me said, I'm going back. Zostar and his army were heading deeper into the Wastes along the banks of the river. Large forces are hard to hide. If I backtrack to the waterway, I'll find them easy enough.

I retreat to where I'd left my pack and waterskin.

Another sulphur pool geysers into the air, this time drenching me. I wait for the pain of the terrible scald, but it's cool.

Almost refreshing.

I wake in a cage.

It takes a few, blinking moments to realize I never left. I have no pack. No waterskin. Definitely no swords. But I still have a prayer braid.

The tepid water they used to rouse me from my latest hallucination stinks of soap and last night's stew. It's the wash bucket from the camp kitchen. I splutter and curse colourfully enough to make a slums fishwife proud.

"Now is that a way to greet a friend, eh?"

"Sal?"

"As I live and breathe."

"Can you get me out of here?"

She scratches her chin, brow mock-furrowed. "Why would I want to do that?"

My eyes narrow. The fog clears enough for me to remember the last time I was outside this cage. "Sal…"

"Look, it was too good a deal to pass up. There's a bounty on your head, set by the Regent himself."

"You sold me out." I thump the heel of my hands on the bars.

"Hey now, none of that. You said you wanted to have a little chit-chat with him." She produces her gold coin and flips it spinning. "This way we get what we both want."

"I could slice you from neck to navel, you know."

"Don't doubt it. But you'd have to get out of there first. Find yourself some sharp-sharps. Now shut your ale-slurper, we're about to be in well-to-do company."

I grip the bars and peer up ahead. The wagon bearing me and my prison is still moving, though it looks like most of the column has called a halt for the evening. I can't see either Iddo or Zostar, but there's a pavilion set up with pennants snapping in the wind. Rather than the Kaidon phoenix, they're stitched with the Trelian bull of Iddo's home province on imperial purple. I'd expect the leaders will be meeting with their highest ranked officers, processing news from scouts, assessing any threats, deciding on the strategy for tomorrow.

Outside the tent, there's something that snags more of my attention. A long line of figures wait in turn for the evening meal.

When I last saw them we were covered in the filth of the Ekasyan dungeons. The last time I saw them, I left them behind.

Del. Mish. Once so innocent. Now they wear sleeveless tunics edged in purple and black over leathers. As one reaches for a plate piled with food by a camp cook, I see a shadow at their wrist. A mark of the Blazers.

Did they take it on willingly? Have they been brainwashed? Or is this yet another in a long line of maltreatment and indignity?

I have to find out.

But first I have to get myself out of this cage.

CHAPTER 35

LUZ

The boat slices through the water. More accurately, it glides, buoyed by speed and the military discipline of its oarspeople. I used to find the idea of Losian boat races amusing. Renowned soldiers going for a paddle to secure bragging rights by being the first to cross an arbitrary line? It seemed a far cry from honing the necessary attributes for surviving in battle.

The reality is far from what I'd envisioned.

The Losians row in shifts, ensuring the oars are always moving. They're all incredible physical specimens: broad shoulders, tapered backs, arms sculpted from muscle. But even so, at the breakneck pace they're maintaining, each crew only lasts for a short session, before another moves up to take their place, slotting in behind their comrade and dipping the oars back to the river before the boat has lost a lick of speed.

The captain joins me in the prow. She mops her face with a cloth and reties her blonde braids away from her face – they were the shade of golden summer fields before she took her shift at the oars alongside her people, now

374

they're resin-dark with sweat. She smells of coconut oil, leather and the musk of physical exertion. One has to admit it's not unpleasant.

I attempt a smile, but I suspect the result is more wan than charming.

"If anyone can get you there in time, it's us," she insists.

Her accent twangs in a way that reminds me of Kip. My hands tighten on the rails as I wonder how she fares back at the battlefield. Truthfully, I wonder for all of them. The Emperor-elect. Yaita's girl. Copperlocks. Even Amber.

"Primordial willing," I tell the captain, forcing myself to relax. Nothing will be gained from wasting energy conjuring potentialities.

"Eh, the First One has nothing to do with it." She looks back towards the current shift of rowers, their shoulders stretching and bunching, skin gleaming deep brown to sun-weathered pink in the last light before dusk. "Want to know how we're the most decorated crew this side of the Wastes?"

"I adore information."

"We train on the same river, but unlike our competitors, we do most of our sessions on the north side of the city."

"North?" That gets an eyebrow raise out of me. "Who in their right mind would have anything to do with the river in such close proximity to the tidefall?"

"I said we're the most decorated, not the sanest. The tidefall pulls like a hundred aurochs yoked as one. The strongest bitch of a current you'll find in the Empire. Rowing against it is the best training ground Aramtesh can offer."

A lesser being would gape at her. "A current dragging you towards a five-hundred-foot drop."

375

"Exactly. We're no strangers to rowing for our lives." She grins, and it's the grin of a madwoman.

I find myself smiling, genuinely, back.

"Like I said, we'll get you there in time for whatever it is you're doing."

"I had hoped I'd made it clear I won't talk about that."

"Eh, what I don't know can't be tortured out of me."

"Does that mean you'll refuse to carry a letter back for me after you've dropped me off?"

"Never said that, did I?" She jerks a thumb towards the hatch leading to the lower deck. "But for now, I'm going to catch some hammock time before second moonrise. Got a tapped barrel of sugar spirit below. From the finest distillery in Lostras. You'll never again taste its like." It's her turn to raise an eyebrow. "Care to join me?"

There are worse things I could imagine doing on what could be one of my final days of breathing. Who wouldn't want a last gasp of the finer things in life before their potential end?

I follow her below.

✳

Dawn finds me back in the prow.

It's eerily quiet apart from the creak of the oars, the delicate splash as they enter and exit the water with precise efficiency. Mist rises from the river in silver tendrils. When the sun burns away the last trappings of night, the sight I've been chafing to see comes into view on the horizon, a solitary figure standing sentinel on the otherwise flat river plain.

Ekasya Mountain.

Sephine's words echo in my mind: *We'll one day find our salvation in Asmudtagian destruction.*

The political and religious centre of the Empire, crowned by the imperial complex, cloaked in a city where Aramteskans have fought and loved, celebrated and mourned, traded and created for centuries. And there, limned black against the early morning sky, the mountain where millions of prayers have been offered to the heavens, where generation after generation have worshipped. Unbeknownst to anyone who doesn't follow the ways of Asmudtag, deep below that peak is what brought it all into being.

The key to saving us all.

Until the last breath.

I made the Order that pledge back when I was too inexperienced to know that an open-ended promise is a fantasy. But then the Order stagnated, and now the balance has tipped too far. Our future cannot be left to be decided on a battlefield.

Until now, I'd thought promises were the very substance that made us. Instead, they're sticks of incense. Burning bright to begin with, their scent clear and strong, even as they consume themselves. But sift through the ashes of many an eternal vow, and the only thing you'll find is an unwitting lie.

Everything must end.

The Order.

Magic.

Even the gods themselves.

CHAPTER 36

RAKEL

Father wore his old uniform, the leather leg tied off below the remains of his own. He smelled of mint soap and rosemary beard oil and not even the faintest whiff of illness. His cheeks were full of colour. He rode straight-backed in the custom saddle he'd made for himself, and his hands were steady when he flipped the reins over his gelding's neck as we rode back from the Shadow Keeper tomb into camp.

So Yaita *did* smuggle him the cure.

A Losian soldier escorted us through the makeshift camp. Father explained he'd arrived with the Aphorain army. Once they were sure Zostar wasn't interested in sacking Aphorai City, they'd used the little known and less-travelled desert mountain passes to avoid the imperial army's blockade of the river, not flying a standard to give them extra cover.

A tent has been pitched on a rise in the middle of the forces. Inside, a table dominates the space, a map of the Wastes covering its top. Carved figurines have been placed on either side of an open area between the rock formations

378

and larger geysers on the map – the plain located below the camp. Each Province Commander and Eraz stands stiffly around the table.

Nisai is at the head, caught up in a strategy debate with the others. "I have to go myself," he insists. "My brother may very well not listen to anyone on this. But he's definitely not going to be swayed by a messenger. It has to be me, or this was all for nothing. There will be no true parley."

"The risk is too great, Your Highness. There's nothing to protect you if they dishonour the white flag, or on your return if negotiations fail. What if he sets those… If they can do the things your former Shield was capable of…"

Nisai pinches the bridge of his nose as the other commanders weigh in.

A little further away stands another figure.

Yaita.

I haven't yet seen her back on her feet, and I'm surprised at the strength of the relief that wells up inside me. I go to her and, for the first time, we embrace.

There's no similar display between her and Father. But before he joins the other commanders at the strategy table, there's a nod that seems … respectful. Like a door on the chance at affection has been closed, and any awkwardness is now behind it.

"Are you well?" I ask, guilt at the edges of my voice. She wouldn't have been unwell if it weren't for me.

"I still feel a little weak, but I'll be fine."

"I'm sorry, I—"

She cuts me off with a raised hand. "We've all made mistakes."

Part of me smarts at not being given the chance to explain, but the other part, the part that had been more worried than I'd care to admit that she wouldn't recover from saving me in the Aphorain temple, sags in relief.

"Walk with me?" she asks.

I nod agreement, and we exit the tent.

"Did you recover the weapon? Zostar reportedly has more Children of Doskai than we'd estimated."

I relay what we'd found in both the Aphorain and Losian caches, that they'd only turned out to be burial grounds.

"Buried, not sent to the sky," Yaita muses. "Ami's sure the name was Kaiseth? Do you trust her?"

"She's not responsible for Esarik's actions. And what reason would she have to lie?"

"And their being sealed in Asmudtagian glass would support the notion… It's believed to be protective."

"What notion?"

"It's too much of a coincidence. Kaiseth was the first of the Scent Keepers. In the legends, Asmudtag gave her the elixir to channel their will, so she could lead the resistance against Doskai's shadow armies."

"You mean…"

"Kaiseth was a Shadow Keeper as much as a Scent Keeper. It's where the Order began."

I look out over the soon-to-be battlefield, scrunch my eyes shut, open them again. The connection is finally clear and not in the way I'd hoped. "There is no weapon."

She smiles sadly. "Not quite."

"The weapon is *us*."

She nods.

"But there were dozens, maybe hundreds of bodies buried in the Losian cache. Maybe as many more again in the Aphorain cache before it was destroyed."

I don't need to say it. We both know what's on my mind. There's only a handful left of those who've survived the first imbibing of the Scent Keeper elixir and lived. And most of those are in the Sanctuary up in the mountains beyond the Empire.

I squint into the sun, down to the flat expanse of ground where we expect to meet Zostar's forces. It's dotted with pools of belching bile-coloured sludge. Even from up here, the stench is awful. Sulphur – just like one of the main ingredients in Sephine's shadow ceremony. An idea begins to seep into my mind.

I pat Luz's satchel. "There might be something that could hold them off."

I just hope there's enough yeb balm in here to get the job done.

It's a scramble to prepare in time for the parley, but somehow we make it.

"Ready?" Nisai enquires.

He's preparing to mount the horse my father gave him – speed will be key if anything goes wrong out there. Then he, Kip, and several of the Aphorai Province's best troops will ride out under a banner of truce to parley with the army that awaits us across the Wastes.

"If we end up needing it, you'll only have to give the signal," I assure him.

"Will you ride with us? In case something … goes wrong?"

I nod. If Nisai is willing to put his life on the line to try to head off a battle before there's any carnage, so am I. And if anything happens out there, the sulphur concoction I've got burning in a handheld censer will soon tell us if my idea is going to work or not.

"What if it doesn't work?" Barden asks. "Or it does work and the wind changes?"

The truth is, I don't know. It's not like I've ever done anything like this before. The ceremony with Ash in the Aphorain temple was similar, but in an enclosed space, and nowhere near this scale. But I'm not about to remind Barden of that. "Luz's satchel is a treasure trove of substances," I tell him. "These are things that will buy us some time if we need to flee." I give Lil's neck a rub. "Ready, girl?"

We ride out on to the plain. Barden bears the white flag of parley. It flaps in the wind above our heads, already smudged with yellow-green sulphur dust.

Far ahead, the leaders from the other side are there, waiting. It's hazy, but it looks like eight or so of them. Towards the centre, a figure sits tall and balanced in the saddle, his broad chest emblazoned with the Kaidon family crest. Iddo.

Next to him, a shorter figure, slight beneath his black robes, his tufts of white hair straggled by the wind. I've never laid eyes on him, but I don't need to have. The stories have been more than enough. Zostar.

Four guards flank them, two in imperial palace colours and two in red and black, no doubt bearing the sigil of the Brotherhood of the Blazing Sun. It's the last two figures that wrench at me. They're on foot. Slight frames dressed in too-big soldier leathers. They couldn't have seen more than thirteen or fourteen turns.

It feels like hours pass between leaving the ranks of our allies and meeting in the middle of the ancient battleground. But the sun has hardly moved when we come within earshot of each other.

"Greetings, brother," Nisai begins. "I'd say 'well met', but…" He makes a show of looking around us before shrugging, the movement slow and weary.

"Prince Iddo shall be addressed by his title as Regent," one of the palace guards growls.

Nisai doesn't let them get up his nose. He simply waits, holding his mount in check, maintaining a neutral expression.

Iddo removes his helmet. His expression is flat, but he looks older than when I last saw him, back in Ekasya after Nisai was healed. His features are now framed by lines that will only wear deeper with each passing turn. "I don't want to hurt you, little brother."

"Then don't," Nisai responds. "We can stop this. The wounds are deep, but they can be stitched. There does not need to be carnage simply because two sides have shown up at a battlefield. I do not even wish to seize power from you. I would happily co-rule. You've always had skills that I lacked."

He pauses, waiting for that to sink in.

"But know this, brother. I will never, ever abide the atrocities that have been committed by those in your company." He doesn't acknowledge Zostar; instead, he looks to the two young people, gaze brimming with empathy. "And I will do everything I can to prevent history repeating."

"You've spent too long with your precious scrolls, brother. Two provinces in rebellion. A false capital. A weakened border on one side of the Empire. A coast ruled by pirates and smugglers on the other, and larger threats beyond. The

Empire needs strength now, not words and compromise. If you will not step aside, then I have no choice but to end this here."

Iddo looks to Zostar.

Black Robes remains silent.

"By whatever means necessary," Iddo finishes.

Nisai regards his older sibling solemnly. "We always have a choice, brother. *Always.*"

A look passes between them. Guess this is a conversation they've had before.

The Regent's expression turns pained. "Ack, little brother. It's not that easy."

"Why, Iddo? Why is turning around, taking your army home, putting all this to rest, not easier than the bloodshed that will ensue if we continue on this collision course? You're a soldier. You've done a soldier's duty, trying to protect your own. But this isn't protection any more. This is conquering. I know you feel it's inevitable. That there's only one course. But there isn't."

Iddo barks a bitter laugh. "And what else would you suggest, little brother? I come serve you in your far-flung new capital? Keep you secure while you dream impossible dreams and neglect reality?"

"It's no secret I have ideas for what the Empire could be. But I would have your input as an equal voice at the table. Let us sit down and discuss this."

"Talk begets talk." They're the first words Zostar has spoken. "It's men of action who triumph. My Regent, we're done here. Let us rejoin our forces."

He nods to one of the Blazers, who yanks the white parley flag from the earth and throws it down.

"I don't want to go to war with you, brother," Nisai calls as Iddo and his escort retreat back towards their force's lines. "You of all people know I don't. But mark my words, I will. I will fight for hope. For everyone to feel they have a choice. Including you."

At that last, Iddo turns in his saddle. He watches Nisai for a long moment. Then he closes his eyes, bows his head, and faces forward again, disappearing into the dust haze.

We retrace our steps to our forces.

"How did it go?" Ami asks.

I drag my finger across my neck.

"That good then."

Nisai squints across the plain, shielding his eyes, then turns to me. "Once we light them, how long will those fires burn?"

"Until dusk, give or take? I'm not an expert, though, it's not like I've worked with this stuff before."

"Let's hope it's long enough for my brother to see reason."

CHAPTER 37

ASH

"Get him ready for the Regent," barks one of the senior officers.

The guards move the wagon carrying my cage closer to the command tent, dragging me out by the bindings around my wrists, and tether me to the rear of the wagon like a pack animal in a train. There's only thirty yards or so now separating me from Del, Mish and the others. I have to get them out of here. But first I have to get their attention without drawing the ire of the Rangers that watch them like hawks.

The air shimmers with the last heat of the day, so that the figures in the distance waver like they're made of water. As they return from what I now know is to become the battlefield, Iddo's chariot draws close to a black-robed figure riding a donkey. It can only be Zostar. They appear to be talking. Iddo points an accusatory arm, then pulls back the reins, wheeling the horses and his chariot around.

Did he speak to his brother, out there? Knowing Nisai, he would have parleyed. He'd want to exhaust every possibility to prevent bloodshed.

I crane my neck to follow the elder Kaidon son's path, straining against my bindings until the ropes cut into my flesh.

Iddo drives his chariot back towards the command tent, riding directly before the first lines of infantry that are now fully in place. The vanguard is made up of mercenaries and conscripts, grist that he can afford to be crushed. I'd expect the trained section of his army – the palace guards, Rangers, household contingents from the Trelian river lords that came to the so-called Regent's aid will attack from the side, outflanking and harrowing the opposing army even as they break through the first lines. Judging by the landscape up ahead, they're determined to push Nisai's forces up against the towers of rock and bubbling pools, using the terrain as an additional weapon.

Iddo shouts something to his officers, but he's too far away, I can't quite make out the words. And I can't delay just to hear them. I've got higher priorities.

Behind the vanguard ranks, Zostar raises his hand, and one of the smaller figures steps forward. I don't recognize them, but it's clear she's one of the young ones from beneath the Mountain, around Del's age. My fingers twitch, ready to reach for the twin swords that were once almost an extension of my body. But my hands are tied in all manner of the word. I no longer have anything to stop whatever is about to happen to the poor wretch.

For a few heartbeats, nothing happens.

Then I see it.

Shadow, emanating from the hands and arms of the girl. It's amorphous, like the blackest smoke. Coils seep into the air towards the frontline of soldiers. Searching. Seeking.

A chill snakes up by spine, lifting the hairs on my neck. This is no self-defense response. It's like the girl has control of the shadow. The chill I'd felt now seems like the back of my neck is being gripped by the hand of a dead man.

Then it's clear where they're destined.

My jaw clenches tight against the desire to cry out a warning. I can't draw attention to being tied here, if I want to find a moment to escape. And is a warning even deserved?

As if sensing the shadow's approach, Iddo's horse skitters to the side.

He shortens the reins, continuing to orate to his troops, unaware of what is roiling towards his back. Then the shadow has closed the gap, shrouding the figure of the Second Prince. Some of the soldiers must see it now, the way they jostle back into the line of their comrades behind them, trying to retreat.

Iddo's broad back stiffens. His mount rakes the ground with its hooves, straining at its traces. This time, he doesn't rein it in. Then the horse's scream echoes out across the battlefield. It rears. The Commander of the Imperial Rangers, now self-appointed Regent of the Empire, topples from his chariot.

I expect him to roll, to slowly haul himself to his feet. One, three, five heartbeats pass and the crumpled form on the ground doesn't move. I'd think I was hallucinating again. But deep down, viscerally, I know what I see is true.

Iddo Kaidon is dead.

And it seems to give nobody pause but me. Zostar reaches the ranks. The Blazers riding with him nod, one raising a signal.

Forward march.

The battle begins.

And even after all I've been through, all I've seen, I can't quite believe it has come to this.

My thoughts are interrupted by someone stepping up behind me. I'd drop into a stance ready to fight or flee, for all the use it would be given my bindings.

"That deal ended as well as a rusty nail through the tenders."

The voice is familiar. "Sal?"

"Here," she says, holding out a knife, motioning me to present my hands so she can cut through my bonds.

"But it was *you*." I accuse as she slices the ropes. "You were happy to sell me out."

"I was."

"What's changed?"

She glances towards the edge of the battlefield, where Iddo's lifeless form has been dragged unceremoniously in the dust so that it isn't trampled under the feet of his own soldiers. What an ending for an Imperial Prince. I still can't come to terms with that actually being his body.

Sal shrugs. "My buyer is dead. All deals are off."

"Here I was thinking you'd had a crisis of conscience."

"Not likely. Got something for you, though. A peace offering." She holds out a prayer braid. Judging by the five scents that waft towards me, it's been freshly infused. I let her tie it around my upper arm.

"I thought you didn't believe."

"I don't. But you do. And I'd bet more than the price of a prayer braid that whatever you're planning, you're going to need to back yourself fully."

I'm not sure if I should be thanking her or cursing her for selling me out in the first place. She doesn't wait for my response before slipping back through the wagons. It appears, when it comes down to it, that Sal doesn't have the stomach for war.

I want no part in it, either. I intend to do what I came to do, and get out of here.

Keeping the wagons between me and the frontline, I creep closer to where Zostar has lined up his charges.

"Del," I hiss.

He doesn't turn.

"Del!"

My only reward is a guard glancing warily in my direction. I'm still in cover, and my call among all the other murmuring isn't enough to have him stray from his post. Still, I'm not about to try that again.

I'm still trying to think of a strategy when Zostar returns. He speaks with the guards, but I can't grasp the words. Then he turns back to the front, his men herding Del and the others after him.

I follow.

CHAPTER 38

RAKEL

Nisai sits atop his horse, flanked by Kip and several Aphorain soldiers. He holds a spyglass pressed up to one eye, intently watching the other side of the parched plain.

"Do you think his brother would have listened?" I ask Barden.

He spreads his hands. "I'm not sure what he'll do. Though Nisai holds out hope."

"Can you see anything?" I try not to sound as frustrated as I am. I've got no chance of making out details at this distance. Everything that far away is still blurred.

"It looks like something's happening, but..."

"No," Nisai chokes.

Finally, I catch movement. A horse. Bolting across the plain towards us. Its distinct markings come into focus. There's no doubting it's the same one that had drawn Iddo's chariot.

I move out to meet it before Barden can stop me, steering Lil with my thighs, arms held wide. Directly in its path, I call out to the frightened animal. For a moment, I think it won't stop. That it will charge straight into us. But at the last chance it slows to a canter. Then a trot. A toss of its head.

I start Lil into a walk, so that when both horses meet we're not in a direct confrontation. Making soothing noises, I move in from the side and take hold of its bridle, gathering the reins in my fist and leading it back into the ranks.

I hand it off to one of the soldiers. "Take it out of harm's way."

If only we could do the same.

I thread Lil back to Barden. He looks at me sadly. It tells me all I need to know.

And across the battlefield, Zostar's forces have begun their march.

I give the signal.

Off to each side behind us, archers raise bows nocked with flaming arrows. They let fly, finding their targets. For a moment, nothing happens. And then there's a low *whoosh* as the first sulphur pools out towards the centre of the battleground – now laced with a yeb balm and cooking oil mix – ignite. A column of green-stained flame leaps from each pool to the sky, before settling back down to the surface, setting the pools to simmering.

Steam-smoke begins to rise as the leading line of Zostar's soldiers approach the first pools. Shouts of irritation ring out – no doubt the smoke stings eyes and lungs. But it's not the soldiers that we most need it to protect against.

When I'd found Sephine's recipe for the shadow ceremony back in the Aphorain temple, I hadn't realized what I'd truly discovered. Unlike the braziers during the ceremony where I tried to free Ash permanently from Doskai's influence, those pools don't have any Scent Keeper elixir in them to channel shadow. But here on the battlefield, I'm desperately hoping the sulphurous smoke will have a similar effect in the temple – dampening Doskai's reach – preventing the full devastation of his Children being released.

The weapon all this time was those who could wield scentlore.

Scent Keeper.

Shadow Keeper.

They are one and the same.

And all we have is me. And Yaita. Because the very Order who was supposed to stop this from happening would rather play their own power games in their safe little Sanctuary. Too out of touch to know or care about the here and now. About the people down there forced to risk their lives just to win safety.

For the first time in my life, I wish for nothing more than Sephine by my side.

Instead, I look to Yaita. She gives me what I expect is meant to be a reassuring smile, but it's too tight to work.

Below, out on the field, the armies engage. The clash of metal on metal rings out, hundreds of echoes bouncing back from the gnarled towers of red rock. With the spyglass to my eye, I try to see if the tide of battle is turning either way. But I can't make out outlines through the smoke, let alone pick out standards or allegiances. It's a small price to pay if the burning sulphur is what is truly holding off Zostar's shadow warriors. While it does, maybe we have a chance.

Each moment seems twice as slow and heavy as the one before.

I wince every time a scream pierces the air above the shouts of battle rage. And later, I struggle not to retch as the stench of blood and urine, of fear-sweat and spilled bowels, begins to swirl into the acrid sulphurous smoke. The perfume of pain and death.

Something Ash once said to me comes to mind: *Nobody wins a war. Some people survive it, that's all.*

I train the spyglass on the pools. The flames have all but died. They'll smoke for a while still.

But when they stop, when the air clears...

CHAPTER 39

LUZ

I may be Aphorain born and bred, but in all my days I have never experienced such heat as the heart of Ekasya Mountain. By the Primordial's grace, navigating the streets above was easy, given the capital was near-empty of ordinary citizens. Darzul's operation to help the refugees escape was executed admirably.

Now, sweat trickles down the back of my neck to soak my shirt. I stink to the sky. Yet how pretty one looks or smells matters little when one has a load of explosives strapped to their back.

I've thankfully long passed the last of the sewers, where the effluent of the imperial complex is piped into a single tunnel to flow out to the river. They may act like their feculence smells of roses but I have empirically observed that is a patent falsehood.

The descent through floor upon miserable floor of the dungeons wasn't much better. Witnessing the places where my kind were imprisoned and tortured was unpleasant enough. But when Zostar's men left this place with its skeleton guard – so few it was possible to pick them off one by one – they also left behind any of the prisoners who were not of worth. Their bodies are now in various stages of decay. Even if I had scruples about the deaths that will come from what I'm about to do, they would be paling against the urge to even the ledger.

But there's no time for petty revenge quests now. There's a greater balance needed, one bigger than I, or Zostar, or the Empire itself. An ancient asymmetry of human foibles in divine minds. It's that which keeps me moving one foot after the other, ever deeper into the Mountain.

The first vent is built beneath the palace as the conduit for the hot water the imperial family and their ilk enjoyed from the thermal springs. A myriad of tunnels tangle around each other at this level, so that it won't take much power to bring several down. Alas, only utmost precision will keep it all from caving in on my head.

With that splendid thought firmly in mind, I keep moving, ever deeper.

At the second duct, scorching air buffets me; the centre of the earth is a forge and the bellows are being worked by the Primordial themself. In mere moments, it makes my skin feel as if it has been sun-scorched from a day in the desert. I turn away from the heat and scrunch my eyes shut, dousing them with water from my canister.

Any further than this, and the pack I'm carrying is at risk. I set the haul of volatile material down ever so gently. It's only going to get worse from here, and the last thing I want is the heat to cause a reaction. Nobody enjoys a premature conclusion, least of all me.

Working with individual packs of explosive powder, I cover a generous area of ground, affixing them at measured points along the tunnel walls with sticky resin, checking and double-checking the fuses. Each is coated in highly flammable yeb balm to ensure that once it's lit, it doesn't sputter out partway to its destination. It also means that if there's one misstep, one tiny particle of flame pirouetting up the tunnel on the searing wind, it'll all be over before its purpose could be served. Steady hands and deft fingers – by Asmudtag's grace, please do not fail me now.

Eventually, finally, everything is in place.

I retreat as far as possible. With a prayer to the Primordial on my lips, I light the fuse, and sprint in the opposite direction.

The fuses detonate each of their targets with percussive roars that join forces, rushing up the tunnel to hit me in the back. Powdered rock and debris follows in a choking cloud. I cover my face with my sleeve until it subsides.

Satisfied there's no more rock to fall for the immediate future, I wipe the grime from my forehead and retrace my steps to check my handiwork.

Only part of the tunnel has collapsed. Some of the packets remain along one wall, intact.

It's not enough. It has to be completely sealed to generate the pressure required. Otherwise it could take days, moons, even turns until the blockages I've already created further down the line will take effect. I don't need a messenger scroll from the battlefield to know that's going to be too late for us all.

I hunker down over my pack to check my supplies. There's probably enough powder to do the trick if I use up the last of it here. But there's nowhere near the length of fuse to run back up the tunnel far enough to give me any hope of clearing this place before it comes down on my head.

I rock back on my heels. My mind doesn't attempt to find another avenue. It's clear there isn't one. This is it. I swore to serve Asmudtag, to work towards keeping the world in balance until my last breath.

I never fancied living long enough to descend into doddery frailty. And I'd venture there are far more tedious ways to depart this earthly realm. One could have a worse ending than instant cremation by Primordial inferno, my ashes joining the maelstrom destined to slay the gods themselves. Even a Scent Keeper doesn't live as long as a legend. And a legend I shall be.

So, if this be the end, I'm ready. At least I'll be going out with a bang.

I reset the explosives and prepare to light the last fuse.

CHAPTER 40

ASH

Once the battle begins, there's enough distraction for me to steal closer to the frontline where Zostar and his young prisoners have advanced.

"We can do this voluntarily or we can do it the other way," the old man barks, holding up a leather mask I remember from the testing – various scents would be funnelled through until we were breathing nothing else but his concoction of vile smoke.

Among the older ones, Mish pipes up. "This is not something we are resisting through fear or rebellion." She looks around, gestures to the green-yellow haze, coughing for emphasis. "I think it's the smoke."

Since I first smelled it, the sulphur-stink reminded me of the night at the temple when I made the mistake of letting Rakel try to remove my curse. There was something in the smoke that made things … not more controlled, but less powerful. A kind of dampening. Is this what's happening to the others?

My theories are interrupted by the world exploding.

Or at least that's what it sounds like. A roaring wall of noise that impacts my ears like it had solid substance.

A few heartbeats later, there's a tremor underfoot. I crouch lower behind the wagon I'd been keeping between me and Zostar. I'd think it a groundshake like the ones Aphorai is plagued with. But this is different. The ground vibrates in waves, as if it were ripples on a pond that someone had dropped a stone into miles away. If I were to wager, I'd say they were coming from the southwest, not from Aphorai.

Some of the rearguard soldiers, waiting for their turn to engage, have dropped to the ground, as if under attack. Others look around with wild eyes, seeking the source. More than one of the mercenaries flees, only for Zostar to order them cut down by Rangers.

Finally, everything stills again.

What in Kaismap's far-seeing name *was* that?

The green-yellow smoke still obscures most of the battleground, but the sounds of combat continue. The explosion clearly didn't come from the field of engagement. What could have caused it?

There's no time to investigate.

Because Zostar orders the nearest Blazers to roll another wagon forward.

"The other way, then," the white-haired physician grates.

One of his men throws a lit candle into the cart's bed. I have no idea what is in there, but it soon begins burning, sending up columns of black smoke.

And, as the dark, acrid cloud eddies upward, a hundred amorphous shadows rise to join it.

The children's faces are blank, eyes unblinking, mouths slack. The old man raises his arms. Again, like the conductor of the palace orchestra urges the players to stay with each other, the shadows seem to keep time.

I don't know how he's done it. But it's like he's in control of their curses. When I left them behind underneath Ekasya Mountain, I feared they would become like me.

This is much worse.

They are but a madman's instruments of destruction.

Then the guards roll the burning wagon further on to the battlefield. The children follow. For the first time, I dearly hope Nisai found his ancient weapon. Because otherwise, I have no idea what might bring them to heel.

Except, perhaps, me.

CHAPTER 41

RAKEL

I lived my entire life until recently in Aphorai – I know a groundshake when it happens. But the massive, distant explosion, followed by the waves of tremors, was no ordinary groundshake.

Yaita looks to the sky. "Salvation in Asmudtagian destruction," she murmurs.

Wasn't that what Luz had said back in Aphorai?

But there's no time to ponder.

The last of the pools have gone out. The sulphur smoke swirls with each gust of wind. The battlefield is still choked with it, but it's only a matter of time before it dissipates or spreads too thin to be effective.

Then another source of smoke joins it. Thick. Ink-black.

I swallow down the acid rising from my stomach.

I'd heard Luz's reciting of the legend of the Shadow Wars. I'd heard tales around the fire from my father's old army comrades. I remember Ash talking of them in reluctant snippets. Even after witnessing his power in the throne room in Ekasya, on the training ground or at the height of the temple in Aphorai, I wasn't prepared for this.

The sky turns black. The screams from the battlefield intensify. But I can't see anything except a dark cloud of terror and confusion.

"Do you have any yeb balm left?" my mother asks. She's keeping her voice light, but there's a determined, almost resigned expression on her face.

"A little."

"Give it to me, would you?"

I do as she says.

"Now, leave me. Go to your father."

"And then where?"

There's nowhere to go. The shadows on the battlefield writhe and contort. It's hard to tell the difference between them and the roiling black smoke. The only thing I'm sure of is that all of it is getting closer. To our reserve troops. To the Prince. Barden. My parents. Almost everyone in the world I care for.

One of the shadows breaks free from the main battle, angling towards where we stand. Yaita opens the jar I'd given her and drips dark liquid from a vial into it. The all-too-familiar sickly-sweet scent of overripe fruit reaches me. It's Scent Keeper elixir.

"Get back!" she shouts.

Before I can think to stop her, she lights the jar and tosses it to the ground. Flames burst over the sulphurous dust, licking into the air. The nearest shadow dips and weaves, lunging towards us. Yaita steps between it and me, so close to the burning path of earth I'm worried her robe will catch alight.

The shapeless shadow seethes towards her. Or maybe it

is drawn by the new source of smoke.

When it's close enough, she lunges for it, sinking her hands into it like it's something solid. I know that experience. I've done it before. But only with Nisai's poison – a bare fragment compared with this – and then with Ash – someone I knew and trusted. Never with something this big, and determined to do violence.

The shadow writhes, bunching darker. I cast about. Consider the contents of my satchel. Luz left me Scent Keeper elixir.

Yaita's feet almost leave the ground for a moment as it tries to wrench free of her grip. She holds fast. I should try to help her. How do I help her?

And then, like something snapped, the shadow turns back on her, going slack like it's giving up. It sinks into her skin. She collapses to the ground.

I scramble over to her still form, gently rolling her on to her side.

No.

She coughs, and black blood-bile dribbles from her lips.

Not again.

The awful sounds of the battle keep raging, but I can still somehow hear my heart pounding in my ears.

For a moment, I'm back in Aphorai, in the terraced gardens of the Eraz's estate, surrounded by smoke as Sephine lays dying. She's sacrificed herself for Nisai. She couldn't save him.

Could I save my mother? Do I have enough strength? Enough ability?

Asmudtag is all. Light and dark. I consider the vial of Scent Keeper elixir in my satchel. I've learned what channelling the will of Asmudtag means. Am I willing to sacrifice that much of my light? Even my own life?

My mother stares up at me, or is it the shadow-filled sky? I thought she'd despair at my hesitation. But there's no accusation in her eyes. "To sacrifice yourself for another is to betray yourself," she manages. "I would not have you do so for me. No parent should."

There are so many things I could retort. How can she call herself a parent when she wasn't there for all those turns I needed one? I know now why she did the things she did. It was a strange, cruel kind of mothering. But maybe it was the only way she knew how.

Maybe I would have done the same thing in her place.

I take her hand in mine. My throat tightens, a deep-seated part of me fighting tooth and nail not to give quarter. But I force the words through. "Go by the grace of Asmudtag, Mother."

The barest whisper of a smile curls her lip. "You've never called me that before."

I shrug.

Shrugging at a time like this? Say something meaningful. Something good. "I…"

"May the Primordial watch over you, daughter," she whispers.

Her chest stills. The life goes from her eyes.

For the second time in my life, my mother is dead.

The chaos of the battlefield intrudes again and I realize I've been sitting, staring and stung, focused only on the body of the woman who gave me life. A woman I barely knew.

I give myself a shake and drag my fingers gently over her

eyelids to close them.

Barden appears at my side, one of his large hands gently squeezing my shoulder. "We need to get out of here," he says, looking warily to where shadows writhe above us, blocking the sun one minute then diving into the Losian and Aphorain forces the next, cutting the soldiers down like a scythe to barley.

There's no way they can hold out much longer.

Then up on the bluff, I catch movement. A lone figure in a hooded cloak. It could be anyone, but for that familiar gait.

"What in the sixth hell…"

Barden rubs sulphur-reddened eyes.

I rummage for the spyglass. "Stenches, Bar. It's him. It's Ash."

"Last time you had anything to do with him, I almost lost you."

Ash is heading towards a dead end. Towards the cliff. He can't be running away. And I won't believe for a moment that he's going all the way up there just to choose his own end.

I gesture to the shadows above. "Nothing is stopping them, Bar. My mother is gone. Luz is gone. I'm out of tricks. Ash wouldn't be going up there for no reason. I have to believe that. And if he's got a plan, I have to try to help."

Barden stares at me, stone-faced. "You'll never make it up there through this. Leave him. He's made his choice. You don't owe him your life."

"I'm doing this for *me*. For us. For everyone."

His expression turns pained. Finally, it softens.

I look to my mother's still form. "Please. Take care of her?"

"I will," he says solemnly.

I give him a quick, fierce hug.

Then I shoulder my satchel, and run for Lil.

CHAPTER 42

ASH

When I reach the top of the rock formation, I notice a strange cloud on the south-western horizon. It's pale grey, but almost uniformly so, not the patchiness that comes with normal rain clouds. And it's nothing like Zostar's hurricane of darkness.

There's no time to contemplate why. Below, the battle rages. Zostar's command of Del, Mish and the others' shadows has them tearing through the ranks of the Losian and Aphorain contingents. If I don't do something now, there won't be anything left to save. Zostar will plunge the Empire back into a cycle of war until there's nobody left to stand in his way. In his god's way.

I never thought I would do this.

I'd tell myself there's nothing else I *can* do.

But since we were young, Nisai said we always have a choice.

Now, I make mine.

I search for the part of me I've always avoided. The part I've kept suppressed with drugs or discipline. Sometimes only with sheer, white-knuckled desperation. And now, I seek it willingly. Invite it to come out.

The pain is welcome.

The tearing free is catharsis.

For the first time, I see the winged lion for what it is: my darkness, my shadow, but also my loyalty and my love.

It isn't a formless curse. A Lost God's amorphous malevolence. It is me.

All of me.

The beast leaps from my shoulders, claws raking my flesh. Its great wings beat the air, buffeting me as it grows larger and drives higher.

My knees buckle and I crumple over. I half feel, half observe from above as my head lolls to the side, watching with something akin to fascination as crimson soaks into the sun-baked rock beneath my prone body.

My energy drains with my blood and the connection with my shadow begins to fade. I force myself to bring it back into focus. Below, Zostar is puppet master to those poor, wretched souls. He must be stopped.

I send my shadow up, up, high over the battleground, keen eyes scanning for its target. I feel a strange wonder course through me at a high, pale grey cloud drifting ever closer to the Wastes. And then ... there. The wagon belching smoke as thick as tar.

As if he felt me watching, Zostar looks up, so I'm looking through my lion's eyes and into his.

My shadow banks, wings beating silently, then gliding in a spiral lower and lower. I could dive upon him, but I want him to watch my approach. I want him to have the chance to recall, if only for a few heartbeats, what he and his men subjected me to. I want him to know me as his end.

Something hits me, the impact snatching my breath. Except my shadow self doesn't breathe – the attack hurt my prone body back on the rock.

Only then do I realize my mistake.

Zostar has recalled Del and the others from the battling mortals. The children I promised to save, and failed. Now they and their powers are Zostar's puppets. Their wraith forms are solid to my shadow where everything else passes through.

He's using them to protect him.

Darkness whips around me. My shadow tries to fly free but the others are circling into a vortex. Every time they touch me, my human body jerks with the infliction of another gash or bruise. I can't sustain much more of this on top of my own shadow's rending from my flesh.

I have to get to Zostar. And soon.

I angle straight towards him. A hawk in a dive. The children's shadows give chase, but they're smaller, slower, their forms not as solid as the winged lion.

My claws are outstretched. They puncture the zealot's torso as easily as fingernails sink into ripe fruit, then lift him up, for one, two, three wingbeats.

Until I let him go.

His black robes billow out for a heartbeat, almost as if he's going to float to safety. But he's falling, not flying. He lands with a sickening crack into the wagon carrying the giant brazier.

And begins to burn.

Black robes disappear in the column of foul, black smoke.

He's dead.

Or if he's not dead, he very soon will be.

But the shadow children are too far gone into their rage. They keep harrying me. I fly higher, ever higher. If I can just make it to the pale grey cloud, maybe I can lose them long enough to come back to my mortal body unpursued.

My shadow whirls in the air, wings pumping.

The others follow. Searing. Lashing out. The pain like nothing I've experienced since leaving Ekasya Mountain.

It's a fight to maintain consciousness. I must persevere. Higher. The cloud is close, now.

I vaguely register a lion's roar of frustration and pain. But the sensation that runs through my body on the ground is vastly different. Not like the torment of the other shadows. It's a kind of relief, like the lifting of a weight.

Somewhere in the final struggle of my rational mind it registers: the cloud. Wherever it's coming from, it's somehow antipathy to my power. I vaguely register the scent of sulphur. Water steaming on rock. Other minerals. The perfume of the world's core.

It will be the scent of my final breath.

Something gently brushes against my cheek.

In the middle of the arid Wastes of Los, of all places.

Snow.

And through the pale drifts rides a girl on a black horse.

Or perhaps that's only my weakened heart's last wish.

CHAPTER 43

RAKEL

Lil had never better lived up to her name to when she bore me through the battle like a demon from the stories.

We wove between skirmishes. Past horrors I'll never truly wipe from my mind. And, finally, we made it up to the bluff, where Ash lay. Helpless. His life ebbing from him. Lil knew what I wanted, folding down on to her knees so that I could somehow get Ash on to her back.

When we finally emerged on the Losian side of the battlefield, Barden was there to greet us. "You look like a trio of ghosts," he said.

And no wonder. The pale grey cloud now covered the sky as far as we could see, and with it came a steady fall of ash, covering the world and everyone in it in drifts, like ethereal snow, scented with the barest hint of sulphur. Soon, that was all I could smell. A strange mix of minerals and char and sun-heated rock before rainfall.

With both Iddo and Zostar dead, the larger army lost its focus. The discipline of the Aphorains and the home advantage of the Losians soon forced the others to retreat. Many surrendered in the name of the rightful heir.

It took days to gather our dead, but in the darkness beneath the ash, who could say where night ended and day began? Thanks to Asmudtag, Ash was not one of them. He would have been, if he'd been left any longer. And he almost still was, because all I could do was treat his wounds the traditional way, finally accepting that he wouldn't want me to sacrifice myself.

Now, a great row of funeral pyres is piled high with the ingredients for sacred smoke, carried overland from the Losian serpent boats. Cypress would be the strongest scented among them all, invoking Azered to guide the souls of the fallen to the sky. But for the life of me, I can't separate out a single note.

There's carefully shipped krilmair oil, too, making sure there's all the heat we need and the flames won't stutter halfway through the ceremony. With the ash cloud now spreading to every horizon, who knows if this is going to have an effect, but we do it anyway. Maybe back when this all started I wouldn't have cared. But now it seems important to at least try for those of the fallen who believed.

I nod at the others down the line, holding their torches. We bend and touch the flames to the pyres. They ignite in a wave that leaps to the sky with a roar. I hope for all our sakes that it's the last battle cry of our lives.

Soon, the larger logs begin to catch. The heat intensifies and I'm forced to retreat a few steps. Along the line, I see the others do the same once, twice, three times as the fire grows hotter and hotter.

After some time, the others along the line retreat and turn away, off to make whatever final preparations they need to leave this place.

Barden stays.

We stand, shoulder to shoulder. I look up to where the light of the flames gild my oldest friend's features.

"Do you think you'll go back?" I don't have to say where. We both know I'm talking about our village.

He glances back to camp. "You know what they say about home being where the heart is."

"Or where the heart can find a princely standard of living?"

He laughs, gently shoving me with an elbow. "I offer him something, too, you know."

I give him an appraising look. All those times I found him in quiet conversation with Nisai, I thought it was Barden's ambition-fuelled charm that had caught the Prince's ear. But then I think of how Barden always used to keep something aside for those who needed it most. He'd send his pay home to support his sister and her baby. Every time we'd ride into Aphorai City he'd take honeybread or dried rock figs for the poor children. When we filched oranges from Old Man Kelruk's, he'd only eat one, and share the rest around our village.

Barden has his faults, we all do. But he's always had two admirable qualities: loyalty and generosity.

"Will you go back?"

"No." I smile. "I've got somewhere much more me in mind."

Quiet footsteps approach from behind.

Ash still limps, and his side is bandaged. The wounds from the shadow tearing free have healed, but everything else is taking longer. It seems the cloud dampens everything about him that's more than human.

Barden excuses himself, passing Ash with a wary look. He may have turned the tide of battle, but that doesn't mean Barden will ever fully trust him.

"Did I hear you say you're leaving?" he asks.

"Soon, yes."

His expression might seem stoic, but I know him well enough to see the sadness beneath.

"You know I will face all kinds of dangers with you. We're a team." I take his hand. I hope it's not for the last time. "But there's only one person who can truly heal you. And I think we both know you need to focus on them for the time being, not on me."

"Who?"

"You."

CHAPTER 44

ASH

The pyres burn all night.

If merciful Azered still has any sway over the afterlife, may she guide the souls of the fallen to their final rest.

On the edge of camp, I greet the first dawn beneath the volcano's spreading cloud. For that's what we finally recognize it for: Ekasya Mountain has erupted. And if the strange letter that arrived with a rogue Losian serpent boat after the battle held any truth – it had a little help.

Seated cross-legged, I carefully infuse each braid of my prayer band with the essence favoured by each of the Younger Gods. Perhaps what Rakel thinks is true – prayers will no longer reach them through the ash cloud. I'm no longer sure they ever heeded my devotion. But neither thought is going to stop me from praying. Some actions you perform in the hopes of a subsequent outcome. Some acts are their own reward.

"I thought I'd find you here."

I don't turn. I don't need to. I know that voice better than my own. "A creature of habit."

Nisai lowers himself slowly beside me, grimacing as he sets his crutches down. "These cold mornings aren't going to get any easier."

A pang of guilt aches in my chest – only a turn ago I would have been at his tent to aid him at a heartbeat's notice.

"There's no easy way to articulate this," I begin.

"So just say what you need to say, Ash. I'm still me."

"I'm going to stay here with Del, Mish and the others. Until we know what the fallout of all this will be." I look up to the soot-clogged sky. "I think it's best they – we – stay in the one place in Aramtesh where we know we'll do no harm. I wondered if you'd authorize supplies to be left behind when the rest of the forces depart? It's never going to be a pretty home, but I'd like them to be comfortable. Nobody can rehabilitate under duress."

"That seems wise." Always so calm and measured. After everything he's been through.

I shake my head with a self-deprecating smile. "Possibly the first wise thing I've done in a long time. Maybe ever."

"You've always had a quiet wisdom, Ash. It's one of the reasons I love you." He looks at me, eyes shining as much with affection as melancholy.

I swallow the lump in my throat, but don't try to hide the emotion in my own expression.

"And Rakel?" Nisai asks.

"She's going to make a fresh start. Somewhere of her own choosing. I hope I'll be able to join her one day, but even if I can't, she deserves a good life."

His smile is genuinely pleased. "If anyone has earned it, she has. Though she shouldn't get too comfortable. I may have need of her yet."

"Ha! I'm glad I won't be around for that conversation," I say, recapping the last vial of prayer essence. "I wish I could return to Lostras with you. There's nothing more I'd like to see than the coronation."

"You can rest easy on that front. I meant what I told you back in Aphorai. There won't be a coronation. The rulers of antiquity tried to build a system that would not be vulnerable to corruption. Perhaps they succeeded in some ways. We had the art and literature and scholarship of the Great Bloom. We avoided war for centuries…"

He trails off, gazing out over what has become of the battleground. The residual sulphur tinging the mist gold in the otherwise steely light. "And then we almost lost it all again. On my father's watch, and with the helping hand of my brother, no less."

"You're not your father. Do you not realize that yet? You would be such a different Emperor than he was."

Nisai sighs. "Incrementally improving on my father's reign isn't enough for me."

My thoughts are stricken. He can't truly abdicate. He's the best of all of them; his brother did what he could with what he knew, but it was always misguided. Nisai would be different. Better than his father, than any of his siblings. "But after everything we've fought for…"

"I believe our very existence hinges on our unity. But an Emperor and a Council of the most privileged families in each province? I think our future lies elsewhere."

"What will you do?"

"The Council and I will report to a larger interim committee, of those we trust to have the people's best interest at heart. And then, as soon as we can ensure it will be a fairly and transparently staged exercise, we'll let

418

the people decide. Cast ballots on who they would like to represent them. An even amount from each province, each with an equal vote in laws."

"Sounds complicated."

"You know I thrive on a challenge."

I smile, relieved that his faith in his abilities is returning.

"But yes, I'll do whatever I can to make it possible for you to take care of your brethren. And then, I hope one day you'll be able to be with the one meant for you." For a moment his eyes are sad.

But it's the briefest of moments.

Because Kip is clearing her throat with as much politeness as she can muster. She's become so good at being unobtrusive that even I hadn't consciously registered her presence. I turn to see what she's alerting us to. Ah. Barden.

Without permission or preamble, he thuds down next to Nisai and wraps his arm around his waist. It's the most casual breach of so many palace protocols I'd lose count of them if I tried to make a list. When these two get back to Lostras, Barden's going to drive Nisai's valet to distraction.

Barden grins at Nisai. It's an open, honest smile. And I know in that moment, in all the Aphorain Guard's provincial disregard for court niceties, in the way he looks at Nisai like he's the light in the dark, that I need not worry. Between him – the partner I couldn't be for fear of compromising my duty – and Kip, the Shield whose loyal service won't be complicated by her feelings, Nisai has what he needs. Not safety: I've seen too much of the world to think Nisai will ever be safe as he sets about changing the Empire into a place for its people, a process that will make him so many enemies among the entitled. But I can rest knowing he'll be supported.

Cared for.

Loved.

Everything I'd ever want for him.

The realization is bittersweet. I'm truly not needed any more. It's a thought that brings liberation, and, immediately upon its heels, a first wave of nostalgia.

I tie off the final band in my prayer braid and roll to my feet. "Perhaps if it bears out that magic is truly behind us, and once things are stable in the new capital, you'll permit me to visit."

Nisai gives me his lopsided smile, the one that used to signal mischief and fun when we were young. It's a smile I'll miss dearly. For we both know his mission will take turns, not moons. But one day I'd like to think his promise of a new Aramtesh will come true.

"I'd like that," he says simply.

I step back, regarding the man I've dedicated the majority of my life to. Our eyes meet, and we hold each other's gaze until, finally, I will myself to thump my fist to my chest – a former Imperial Family Shield to the soon-to-be former First Prince of Aramtesh.

Nisai nods gravely.

We both know it's my final salute.

CHAPTER 45

RAKEL

Lapis Lautus.

City of thieves. Safe harbour to smugglers. Domain of the merchant princes. Built literally out to sea, the sparkling pink stone skyline rises beyond the Trelian Cape – not on Empire land, not liable for imperial taxes. Everyone says that in Lautus, you can buy anything, you can buy anyone. An honest kind of lawlessness.

From my first visit, I knew that if I had my way, I'd be back.

And here I am.

Only this time, things are very different.

Ever since Ekasya Mountain blew up, the whole world seems muted of colour. The ash cloud hangs there, turning the sky milky grey. It's never-ending, like it covers the whole world. Maybe it does just that.

I toss a purse of zigs to the gate guards. "Keep the change, neighbours."

It's half again as much as the toll but I want them to remember me as good for the silver if I ever need a favour.

Because if I'm going to make a life here under the volcano's ash cloud, it's going to be built on zigs and goodwill.

Making my way through the different sectors, Lautus and I begin to get to know each other. I skirt the fish markets with their marine reek – not that I can smell it. A pang of sadness hits me at that – if I'd regained any of my sense of smell since the Wastes, surely I'd notice it here. But there's nothing.

I wander the stalls of jewellery and curios in the antique district. Stroll up and down the fresh produce jetty where farmers and smugglers alike pull up their canoes and skiffs to display fruits and vegetables. Fresh or not-so-fresh, after so many able-bodied left the fields for the civil war, they're fast becoming a precious commodity that everyone wants in on. For a time, I linger among the spice sellers, but don't get a whiff of anything, and leave with a sigh.

I've a destination in mind.

Ah. There it is. Same place as last time – the dumpling stall. The ones that Ash insisted I try. Filled with cheese and dipped in a sweetly fragrant red sauce like nothing I'd ever tasted before. I order a dozen, my stomach rumbling in appreciation of the choice, and head back to the marina.

Perching on the edge of the wharf, dangling my legs over the water, I watch the gulls circling in hopeful loops above me. This is the place Ash and I sat when we first came to Lautus. The place where we were first brave enough to admit that something more than the need to clear our names and save a prince might have grown between us, like a flower manages to bloom in the gap between flagstones.

That day, the sea was an impossible blue, like liquid crystal. Today it's reflecting the drab grey above.

I bite into one of the dumplings. It's tasty, salty and savoury, but not the revelation it was last time. Maybe it's because I can't smell them. Maybe it's because food tastes better in good company.

I wonder if Ash and I will ever sit here together again, sharing food and stories, the distant smells of the market and the bustle of the city in the background. If we could, would he finally let himself wonder at the infinite possibility of what's on the other side of that sea? At what the future might bring?

I don't spend too much time dwelling on it. The unlikeliness of it is too raw. Better to keep busy.

With my supper finished, I gather up my satchel and make my way towards the next sector. It's posh here; I remember from last time that they burn a particular incense in the street. Rich and smooth. I make a note to ask the ingredients when I reach my destination. At least then I can try to reimagine what the scent was like.

There it is. Last time I was here, I relied on Ash to do the reading. This time, the sign with the beaker held by metal tongs above the apothecary's door is clear to me.

Proprietor: Kreb Atrolos.

The man with the pointed beard and the gems winking all the way up one ear was dead-set against hiring any assistants. And I doubt he'd warm to the idea of competition opening up nearby.

But he adores playing Death in Paradise – the Aphorain scent skill game of potentially deathly drinks.

And he never said anything about not wanting a business partner.

*

Moons later – not that we can even see the moons – the ash cloud still hasn't cleared.

The autumn winds didn't whisk it away, or if they did, they blew more of it in to take its place. The winter rains didn't wash it clean, instead staining Lautus's spires and towers with grey sludge, as if the pink stone was weeping tears of smoke.

Guess that's the price you pay for trying to kill the gods. I imagine Luz would be satisfied with a job done properly. A fanciful part of me wonders if she's up there somewhere, eyebrow raised in amusement as she watches us try to pick up the pieces and go about our lives.

It should be the beginning of spring. But the cherry trees lining the main avenues are yet to blossom. Word in the streets is that the farmers on the mainland are worried there won't be enough sun and warmth to bring the seeds up from the soil. Then there'll be food shortages. Even in a city that draws much of its bounty from the sea, things could get ugly.

The only plant that manages to keep normal cycles without fail is what the Lautians call melbon jasmine. It's a different sort of flower to the jasmine I'm used to: hundreds of blooms in tight sprays, the outer petals pink rather than white. It tumbles over fences and climbs walls in back alleys like it hasn't a care in the world.

It's the first thing I single out when my sense of smell returns.

One moment I'm noticing a surprise whiff of honey sweetness, the next I'm suddenly aware that it's perfuming the whole city.

Just like that. I can smell again.

I snap off a jasmine sprig on my way from the market back to the apothecary. I want to know what Atrolos makes of this.

The dented old bells above the door jangle as I enter.

"Found the first jasmine to open," I announce. "And get this… I can smell it!"

No reply from the back room.

"Atrolos?"

My hand goes to my knife. We've been protected from any trouble up until now. We pay our dues to the merchant princes, and we're well known to the highborn for providing the best stock, and to the lowborn for having the most generous hearts – Atrolos drives a hard bargain, but he's always been open to me doing work for the needy on the side. We make a tidy profit for us and then some. We can afford to be charitable, with enough to spare now that Rot cases have been mysteriously decreasing by the day, the ulcers of one patient after the other scabbing over and healing to pink, new scars. Even without dahkai.

I creep past the jumbled shelves. The skull on the desk watches me with hollow eye sockets. I want to ask him what he's seen. Is there an intruder?

There's definitely something different. I sniff the air, but I can't pick up any scents other than the jasmine. Until I notice it. Something familiar. But it's deep in my memory, struggling to be called back up.

It's … woody. Rich. And yet just a little bit sharp. Clean. Like forests. Tall trunks and a carpet of spiked leaves beneath, aromatic as they dry in the late afternoon sun angling beneath the boughs. The hinterland of Hagmir. An essence I used to carry with me to clear my head. And a good alternative to standard armour oil…

Cedar?

There's more, too. The memory getting stronger as I step closer to the doorway leading to the back room of the apothecary.

Sandalwood. Warmer. Richer. Softer.

And just a touch of something green … galbanum.

I edge towards the door.

It's him.

It's really him.

Ash rushes to me, wrapping me in his arms. My feet leave the floor and he's spinning me around and we're both laughing between kisses and I don't think I've ever been happier than in that moment. Finally, he sets me down. I take his hand and, almost shyly, lead him upstairs.

And, finally, he convinces me he's found his own freedom.

Later, much later, I lay with my head in the crook of his shoulder, my hand resting on the hard planes of his chest.

"It's completely gone, then? The shadow?"

"As far as I can tell, the only darkness that remains in me is human. No more or less than the next person."

"And the others? The children?"

"After a while, even when we sparred and I used every way possible to provoke them to rage, they no longer displayed any shadow signs. Those who still had homes have returned. The others went to Lostras, where Nisai has set up care for them. I finally dared to believe magic is where it belongs. Behind us. I think it's the volcano cloud. Nothing can get through it – prayers, curses."

So Luz was right: *Our salvation will be in Asmudtagian destruction.*

I hope, in the end, she found her peace.

A full turn since Ekasya Mountain erupted.

It should be warm, but it's icy. Off-shore gales whip the waters surrounding the city into a frenzy. The door to the apothecary swings open with a particularly strong gust that sends the candles on one side of the room guttering, and blows the rest clean out.

A figure steps in from the street. Clad in the nondescript studded leathers of a trader guard, the hood drawn up against a chill that has no place here in summer.

They push the door shut behind them with no small effort.

Ash takes up one of the still-lit candles in a pretense of relighting the others. It doesn't escape me that the move puts him between the stranger and me.

My eyes flick to the jar of powder Atrolos keeps behind the counter in case of any trouble either of us can't talk our way out of. "Can I help you, traveller?"

The figure slips around Ash and approaches with what can only be described as a saunter. Slowly, I slide my hand along the shelf towards the jar.

That's when the first waft of the stranger's perfume reaches me.

Violets.

I peer closer. Tall. Lithe.

It couldn't be…

The stranger pushes back their hood.

My jaw drops.

"Oh, do get yourself together, petal. I'm not a shade."

"You survived," Ash states the obvious. Guess he's stunned, too.

"It would appear so, wouldn't it?"

"When we didn't see you after the Mountain … your letter … we thought … How did you get here?"

Luz shrugs. "Barge. Litter. Camel. And, believe it or not, this fine pair of legs isn't painted on." She gives me a slow wink at the last. "But you'll have to excuse me for not regaling you with that epic. I have something rather more pressing to discuss." She produces a box.

My eyes go wide as she hands me the container, gleaming darkly in the candlelight. Smokey glass, but if my vision no longer deceives me, it's a slightly warmer shade than the blue-black version I've seen before. Almost as if there are purple undertones in its depths.

I open the lid.

Inside, a tiny flower nestles in a tinier copper pot. I've never seen its like before. Seven petals extended from a centre of heart-blood crimson. Each petal begins in a purple so deep it's almost black, then gradually pales until the edges curl delicately into lilac ruffles.

It doesn't seem to give off any perfume.

"It's very pretty," I offer.

"Burn it," Luz instructs.

I eye her warily. After all we've been through, after turning the world upside down, what is she up to?

"Burn it," she repeats. "But first, get both of yourselves a mask." She produces the same custom cut layered cloth she'd used when we passed through the sultis valley on the way to the Sanctuary and ties it over her face.

She's serious about this.

I do as she says, rummaging behind the counter for a clean personal-sized brazier and set it on a stand. I examine the flower more closely. "How much?" I ask. "A petal?"

"The whole thing."

"If you say so…"

"Masks first." Her tone leaves no room for argument.

It's standard equipment in the apothecary, and Ash and I comply.

Once my mask is securely in place, I take up a pair of stem cutters and snip the flower off clean, placing it in the brazier. Then I take a dried reed stick and light it from one of the vanilla candles that Atrolos still favours, before setting the flame to the purple bloom.

I watch closely, curious to see how a specimen I've never seen before will burn.

It doesn't.

More to the point, it stays alight, but doesn't get consumed by the flame.

"What in the sixth hell…"

"Don't hold back, petal. I said a few choice words myself, when I first found it. Well, that was until…" She gives herself a visible shake, as if spooked. "Listen carefully. I'm going to ask you to remove your mask for a single breath. Are we clear? One breath only. Then straight back on."

"Can't you just tell me what's going on?"

"I think it's best you experience for yourself. I promise you, I will not let you come to harm. Whatever my promise is worth in this new world. You, though." She gestures to Ash. "Your mask stays exactly where it is."

I stare at her for several long moments, then do as she says, removing my mask, taking a single sniff, and fixing the cloth back over my nose.

Luz looks expectant. "Well?"

"Well what?" I retort, irritation prickling my temper. I've barely had a chance to take in the wonder of the flower that doesn't burn. The flames only heighten the glory of its colour, the depth and mystery at the bloom's core.

"What do you think?"

"What do I *think*?" I gape at her, incredulous that she has to even ask. "You mean what do I *know*. We must do everything we can to preserve these. Have you found any seeds yet? Or is it a bulb?"

Somewhere in the back of my mind, I notice my voice is strangely high pitched. "Where did you find it? We need to make sure they're somewhere they can thrive. We should put guards on the plantation. Plant more as soon as get through the first growth cycle."

I'm talking much more rapidly than I usually would. But what else can I do? They need to understand how serious this is.

"Ah, Rakel?" Ash takes my hand.

"You'll help, yes? We should leave soon. Where are they growing, Luz? Where did you find it? You have to tell me. I can help. We'll make sure—"

"Rakel," Ash repeats, bringing my hand to his mouth, gently kissing the back of it. "Look at me, please."

But I can't tear my eyes away from the exquisite flower. It's the most beautiful thing in the world, and I will do anything to ensure its future. Anything.

I vaguely register Luz has opened the door and Ash is leading me outside. He gently removes my mask. I shake him off.

"What are you doing?" I snap. "We need to pack. Make a plan. If you're not going to help, I'll go alone." I'd have no chance of besting Ash physically, so if he won't help, I'll have to sedate him. How much does he weigh exactly? I'd need to get the dose just right. And I'll have to figure out a way to force Luz to tell me where she found the first specimen so that I—

"Do something for me first," Ash says. "Take a few deep breaths."

I tap my foot, impatient.

"In," he coaxes, like I'm some kind of child.

I do as he says. I suppose he could be some use in this, it would be better to take him than drug him. But if he starts to stray from the—

"Breathe out."

I shake my head. There was something I was supposed to be doing. What was I supposed to be doing?

"In," Ash repeats.

Luz moves closer, tilting my head back with long, cool fingers and peering, intent, at my eyes. "She's almost back to us,"

Back? Where did I go?

"How do you feel, petal? Any urges to go to the ends of the earth to spread the beauty of a particular floral specimen?"

"Ah ... say what now?"

Luz nods, satisfied. "It's passed." She proffers a small, ornate container. "Smelling salts?"

"Thank you." I've never been happier to breathe their stinging, smarting vapours.

"I inhaled so much it took me a good hour to get over it the first time," Luz says. "Lucky I had brought it back to the Sanctuary for testing. Payuz locked me in a cell until I came back to myself."

Ash glances warily towards the apothecary window. "I thought magic was finally where it belongs – with our shadows. Behind us."

Luz gives a one-shouldered shrug. "That was the plan, yes."

"Then," I begin, "how do you explain … whatever this is?"

"I was hoping you would help me figure that out on the way to Lostras. I've got a captain waiting at the marina. I daresay the voyage would only take a week or two, if this wind holds. Time to test our former Prince's new leadership group."

I glance above us, noticing something I haven't seen for an entire turn — a patch of blue in the volcanic ash-clogged sky. It's a small area, but true. And through it, rays of sunlight slant between the buildings, all the way to the ground.

"'The fingers of the gods', they used to call that," Ash murmurs.

I look from Luz, to Ash, and back to Luz again. Followers of Asmudtag believe that nothing can be destroyed. Only channelled. Absorbed. Changed.

"Can … can gods be reborn?"

Luz taps her nose. "You're still sharp, petal."

Inside, on the counter, the pristine flower continues to burn.

ACKNOWLEDGEMENTS

Wahey, duology achievement unlocked!

And yet it might have all been ashes if it weren't for...

My amazing agent, Josh Adams—I feel so fortunate to be a part of the Adams Literary family. Thank you for all that you do for me and my words. In the UK, my wonderful agent Caroline Walsh and the David Higham Associates team (special shout out to Christabel McKinley!). May your magic never wane.

At Scholastic UK: my editor, Linas Alsenas. Second books can be tricksy beasts, and only Kaismap knows how you guided this one into the world. Thank you for your editorial insight and keen nose for story, and most of all for your engagement and support every step of the way. Pete Matthews: your eagle eyes are ever appreciated. Gen Herr: thanks for shepherding this one over the line. Liam Drane: you've wrapped another magnificent cover around my words, thank you. My gratitude to the wonderful publicity and marketing teams for getting the word out, to the rights team for many fabulous adventures abroad, and to Lauren

Fortune for lighting the *Shadowscent* incense right back at the first chapter.

Thanks to my treasured early (and thereafter!) reader-cheerleaders: Lauren, Serena and Claire. Gratitude to fellow writers and readers (you know who you are) who gave feedback on various intersections of representation. To Sarah and the team at 4160Tuesdays: thank you for being s(c)entsational humans, for sharing your expertise and knowledge of the perfume industry, and for bringing the *Shadowscent* world to sniffable life in ours.

Mentors, champions and awesome writerly folk who made sure I didn't stray into the Wastes during my first year of the author road, especially: Amie, Samantha, Eliza, Lili, Jay, Nic, Ellie, Alwyn, Melinda, Tom, Laure, Patrice, Sophie, Kitty, Emi, Kat, Sim, Christina, Laura (x2), Amber, Sarah, Justin and the residents of the House of Progress.

Not-yet-mentioned friends and family (blood and found) who were the bestest backup team when I'd lost the plot (in all the ways!): Dida, Manu, Phil, David, Kirsty, Brendan, Pip, Andrew, Hattie, Katherine and Andreas.

To Roscoe: we made it. Thank you for your love, patience, and support, and for believing in me, especially during a year when I struggled to believe in myself.

And the finale: to the readers, booksellers, bloggers and bookstagrammers, festival programmers, librarians, educators, literacy advocates and organisations: thank you for all you've done to support me and the *Shadowscent* duology. It means so much, and I couldn't do this without you. I hope we'll get to share other stories in the future.

Until then, scents keep you…

ABOUT THE AUTHOR

P. M. Freestone hails from Melbourne, Australia and currently resides in Edinburgh. She is a Clarion Writers' Workshop (University of California) graduate and a Scottish Book Trust New Writers Award winner, and she has degrees in archaeology, religious history and a PhD in the sociology of infectious diseases. You can learn more about P. M. Freestone on her website:

www.pmfreestone.com

Follow Peta on Twitter (@PM_Freestone) and Instagram (p.m.freestone)